THE SHACKLES OF A NAME

A TALE FROM THE SPIRALS OF DANU

MARTIN ADIL-SMITH

The Accipiter Corporation

Published 2014 by The Accipiter Corporation

info@accipitercorp.com

ISBN: 978-0-9926964-3-6

Copyright © 2014 Martin Adil-Smith
All rights reserved.

The right of Martin Adil-Smith to be identified as the author of this work has been asserted by him in accordance with the Copyright, Designs and Patents Act 1988, and international law.

All rights reserved. No part of this publication may be reproduced, stored in or introduced into a retrieval system, or transmitted, in any form, or by any means (including but not limited to electronic, mechanical, photocopying, recording or otherwise) without the prior written permission of the publisher. Any person who does any unauthorized act in relation to this publication may be liable to criminal prosecution and civil claims for damages.

A CIP catalogue record of this book is available from the British Library.

This book is sold subject to the condition that it shall not, by way of trade or otherwise, be lent, re-sold, hired out, or otherwise circulated without the publisher's prior written consent in any form of binding or cover other than that in which it is published and without a similar condition including this condition being imposed on the subsequent purchaser.

Join "The Spirals of Danu" at the following social networks
www.facebook.com/spiralsofdanu
www.twitter.com/spiralsofdanu

Dedicated, with all humility and respect, to Soke Kevin Pell and the students of Ishin Ryu Ju Jitsu

Also by Martin Adil-Smith

The Demons of Emily Eldritch

A Gathering of Twine

The Beggar of Beliefs

The Call of The Black River

The Shackles of a Name

Forthcoming titles in The Spirals of Danu series:

The Blooms of July

Disciples of The Veil

PROLOGUE

February, 1333 – Izumo Bay
The half-light of the rising sun told those standing on the stony beach that the hour of the rabbit was approaching. The feeble rays of the winter dawn picked out the dark clusters of huddled men as they pretended not to notice the morning chill that seeped into their bones, making their joints ache. Although the conversation between the comrades was usually easy, today each man stood in tense silence, looking out across the choppy sea. Every clan lord felt not just the full weight of his battle armor upon him, but also the responsibility of history.

The advancing warmth of the lightening sky was beginning to burn off the sea mist that swirled around them, and the retreating murk revealed a multitude of advisors and retainers surrounding them. The smell of sea-salt and recently extinguished campfires hung in the air, mixing with a faint scent of distant cherry blossom. The less experienced counselors shivered and then regretted their displays of weakness.

The huddle of Lords saw every restless twitch, but did not take their eyes off the ocean before them. This was the time. This was *their* time.

Despite the throng, each man felt very alone and not even the occasional mutterings from their entourage could break through their wall of thoughts.

The sound of advancing footsteps echoed across the shoreline and the guards instantly raised their spears in the direction of the approaching silhouette.

"Lord Ashikaga," the messenger bent low, prostrating himself on the stones.

The General's reply was little more than a grunt through his ornate battle-helmet. "What news?"

"Honorable General, Lord Nawa's forces have landed on the island, although one ship has been lost. The battle has begun."

Ashikaga turned to Lord Nitta. "It is time. You have my command to attack the government."

For a moment, Nitta hesitated. "The battle for Oki is not yet won. If we attack the Bakufu without…"

"The battle *will* be won," Ashikaga interrupted.

Nitta bowed his head in submission. "My Lord, as you command," and then, turning to a retainer, he whispered a few words. The sound of hooves filled the misty morning air as messengers raced away to the secret garrisons that surrounded the parliament. In a few short hours, the battle for Kamakura would begin, and the rightful heir would be restored to The Chrysanthemum Throne.

Across the water, a single scream pierced the morning air, and the sound of clashing metal reverberated along the short stretch of coast.

Lord Soma stood with his arms crossed and laughed thickly.

Ashikaga remained impassive. "Lord Soma, you have an observation?"

Soma nodded. "The day is ours."

"How so?"

"I know my cousin, Lord Nawa, well. His soldiers too. They are the finest warriors. They do not scream in death, but go to it willingly. Those are the cries of cowards. They do not truly follow The Usurper. They simply follow power and flee like dogs when it leaves them."

More cries echoed across the water, followed by the battle call of charging soldiers. As the mist continued to recede, the Prison Island of Oki revealed itself, less than a mile from the shore. The dark volcanic rock contrasted against the morning light and, from the shoreline, Lord Soma could see the collection of squat buildings that made up the penal complex. Several were already on fire, billowing thick black columns of smoke towards the heavens.

Soma narrowed his eyes. There was something there. Something on the sea…

"General…" he began.

Ashikaga had already seen it. "Attend," he ordered

Footsteps pounded along the beach, followed by the sound of narrow wooden boats thrown into the water.

Nitta turned to the scouts on the small rise that marked the boundary between the beach and the expanse of wild grassland beyond. "Is it him? Can you see?"

The small boats met the approaching craft. Their crews rapidly lashed themselves to the smaller vessel, creating a stable platform, as more soldiers thrust long poles into the water, driving the raft to shore.

Ashikaga smiled thinly. "It is him. We shall see the Kenmu Era restored."

The raft hit the shoreline, driving hard into the pebbles, as the sun finally broke the horizon, bathing the land in a pale yellow glow.

On board the raft a slender cloaked figure rose, a cowl pulled down over his face, and began an unsteady walk to the prow.

The Lords knelt as one, followed by their clansmen.

Placing a foot gingerly onto the shoreline, the figure approached the Lords, and stood in front of Ashikaga.

"General," although male, the voice was light and musical. "The Chrysanthemum Throne thanks you and your men for your assistance."

His head bowed, Ashikaga replied. "The honor is all mine… Emperor Go-Daigo".

CHAPTER ONE

August 1356 – Fujigatani Village, Inzai Valley, Shimosa Province
Despite his youth, five-year-old Yoshimoto could sense something was out of place as he crossed the village square with his older brother, Tanemochi, and their governor, Watanabe.
War is coming.
Something about the way the trees moved. The taste of the air. The way the ravens cawed. The hour of the snake bade him welcome and whispered to him again.
War is coming.
Of course, this was nothing new. For all of Yoshimoto's short life, there had been violent conflict. Ever since The Great Traitor, Lord Ashikaga, had betrayed the Emperor Go-Daigo twenty years ago, and tried to install a puppet onto The Chrysanthemum Throne, the country had been in a perpetual state of civil war. Although Go-Daigo was now dead, his son, Go-Murakami, now ruled in his place and Yoshimoto's father, Lord Soma, bravely fought for the Loyalist cause against his one-time comrade.

In truth, Lord Soma had been gone so long that his youngest son barely remembered him. Instead, the boy relied on the tales told by his elder brother; how their father, an expert archer, had directed an army of twenty-thousand to hold off the advance of The Usurper's Hordes so that the Emperor and Lord Nitta might escape a siege. The Emperor survived. Lord Nitta had not.

And how Lord Soma had rescued the granddaughters of his cousin Lord Nawa when their castle fell. And how his army fended off twin attacks from both the Sea Pirates and The Great Traitor at Itsukushima. There were many other tales, but those were Yoshimoto's favorites.

Yes, the young boy knew the stories of war, but this morning they felt too close, as though they were pressing on the walls of his quiet home.

Yoshimoto stopped and looked across the village square, to the extensive bamboo grove that marked the boundary on two sides of his village. To the west and the north, they gave way to forests of pine and birch that lined the black slopes of Mount Akiro. To the east were the rice fields and the Tega Marshes, and to the south lay the main road that meandered around the base of the mountain range before joining the principal merchant routes to Yeddo and Kamakura. The morning's light breeze brought the scent of fresh sap, reminding Yoshimoto of the games of hide-and-seek he played in the forests when he and Tanemochi were supposed to be learning about which mushrooms were safe to eat, and which were not.

"Come on Yoshi," Tanemochi said, gently pulling at his younger brother's hand. "Stop daydreaming. We'll be late for our lessons."

Yoshimoto sighed loudly, pulled his hand away, and whined, "But I don't want to. You will become clan Lord after father, and I will be a farmer. Perhaps I will breed warhorses for you. Why do we need to write our family tree a thousand times?" The boy fell silent as Watanabe turned to fix his young ward with a steely stare.

The Governor, the loyal vassal of Lord Soma, had not long turned fifty and his gray hair was beginning to turn silver as the lines on his thin face were deepening into a morass of thoughtful crevices. Watanabe had fought by his lord's side countless times and Soma Tadashige could think of no-one better to entrust the education of his children to than his kindhearted liegeman.

"Why?" The Governor said softly. "You ask… why? How do you know what the stars have planned for you? Maybe your brother will need a mighty warrior by his side. Maybe he will need a loyal vassal to run the clan estate whilst he battles to keep the Scourge of The Chrysanthemum Throne from your door. These are honorable lessons for an honorable lord."

Yoshimoto said nothing but kicked at the ground, not meeting his governor's eye, and then bowed quickly, showing he understood his chastisement.

"Come on Yoshi," Tanemochi said after a few moments, and took his brother's hand again. "The girls will be waiting for us."

Watanabe tapped Tanemochi on the shoulder. "That is Lady Yumiko and Lady Minami."

It was Tanemochi's turn to look at the ground, and he grunted an acknowledgement before similarly bowing.

Watanabe knelt before the boy, took his chin in his liver-spotted hand, and forced his ward to look at him. The Governor's voice was deep and velvety, belying the years of war he had seen. "A Lord is respectful. Lady Yumiko and Lady Minami are honored guests of Lord Soma. You should treat them with the reverence that your father would for, in his absence, you are his representative and your actions reflect on him."

"I understand," Tanemochi said quietly. "I am sorry."

Yoshimoto understood his older brother's crass blunder. The Governor had scolded him many times for similar lapses of etiquette. Lord Soma had rescued Lady Yumiko and Lady Minami, the grandchildren of Lord Nawa, when his comrade's castle fell. Despite The Governor directing his charges to acknowledge the ladies as cousins, Yoshimoto had yet to understand what their relationship to the Soma Clan really was. He had studied, under duress, their family trees and although the Nawas and the Somas had once been related, it was many centuries ago.

Regardless of this, the two girls were close enough in age to Tanemochi and Yoshimoto that Lord Soma had instructed they were to receive the same tutoring as his sons. The hope was that, one day, the Imperial Court would accept Lady Yumiko and Lady Minami, leading to the granting of and further concessions to the Soma Clan through strategic marriages.

As the two boys climbed the steps of the wooden building that formed their teaching hall, Yoshimoto could see his cousins through the windows, already kneeling on the soft yellow tatami mats with their calligraphy brushes placed neatly in front of them. At nine years old, Lady Yumiko was the same age as Tanemochi, and Lady Minami was just a year older than Yoshimoto. Both sat absolutely still, a model of demure discipline.

Yoshimoto sighed at these paragons of obedience and looked up into the bright sky. Despite the morning's early hour, the sun was already beating down and the air was becoming hot and muggy.

It felt like it was going to be a long day.

*

The Plains of Yeddo
"ATTACK!" Lord Soma roared.

The front line of the cavalry surged forward, and the sound of a thousand horses thundered across the field.

"Archers!" Banners rose across the plain followed by long bows, to give the cavalry a covering volley.

"Fire!"

For a brief instant, the sky darkened as innumerable arrows flew across the face of the sun. A moment later the field echoed to the sound of screams and shrieks as the front line of the enemy infantry fell, allowing the cavalry to pierce through the tattered lines.

Lord Soma sat on his dappled mare, watching the battle unfold before him. "How does it look?" he asked his strategist.

Lord Mutsu, a distant relation of the Soma clan, addressed his lord. "We are still outnumbered. But I believe that, with your brother's help, we will win the day."

The plan was a good one. General Ashikaga's forces were at their weakest for many years, after an argument within his clan had seen several smaller families join the Loyalist cause. But those faithful to the true Emperor were still outnumbered, and The Great Traitor was threatening to retake the lands he had lost... and more, because now The Scourge of The Chrysanthemum Throne was within two days march of Fujigatani.

Although the odds were against the Loyalists, Lord Mutsu had devised a strategy that was beautiful in its simplicity. Bales of hay had been set alight, and the wind carried the smoke down the plains, obscuring Soma's depleted army. The cavalry that had charged the enemy, under cover of a volley of arrows, met Ashikaga's infantry briefly before beginning their return to the Soma line. The plan rested on the enemy infantry mistaking this retreat as a sign of victory and pursuing the cavalry into the thickening smoke where the forces of Lord Soma's younger brother, Lord Chikatane, who were hiding along the line of the pine forest, would flank them. In the confusion, Lord Soma's own infantry would then advance, catching Ashikaga's army in a pincer movement and then finish them.

At least, that was the plan.

*

Fujigatani Village

Lady Altera moved silently through the bamboo forest, the smell of dry wood and moss filling her nose. Her steps were almost cat-like, and her silence absolute. Her black hair was in the short bob style of a foreigner, but despite this and her gender, her men followed her without question.

Following her were more than a hundred archers and infantry, all wearing the parallel white bars on their shoulders that denoted the Ashikaga Shogunate. A similar number of cavalry was less than half a mile away, safely hidden from the view of any watchtower-guards who might be on duty. Approaching the edge of the forest, she signaled to the archers to string their longbows and light the braziers.

*

The Eastern Road to Keishi

The mounted warrior galloped along, his tired chestnut mare kicking up the dirt along the road. He did not like being on his own, especially during these troubled times, and he spurred his horse on, desperate to catch up with his comrades who could be no more than a few hours ahead.

He should, of course, have known better. As a Tianxian mercenary, he was only in this forsaken land for the spoils of war, but the girl last night... she had been intoxicating. The way she had tried to fight him off... the way she had spat in his face as he had held her down, and of course the cry from the pit of her soul as he had entered her.

Ahead he saw a figure dressed in the familiar weatherworn garb of the farmer caste.

"You there, peasant. How far to Keishi?"

The farmer made no reply, and did not even lift his head from under the traditional straw hat to show he had heard the mercenary.

Just my luck. A dumb mute. Inbreeds.

The peasant was much closer now. "Hey! Peasant!"

The figure stopped, but still did not raise its head.

"Hey! How far to Keishi?"

The peasant tilted his head to one side, as if listening to a distant nightingale. "How far?" he said slowly.

The mercenary narrowed his eyes, suddenly suspicious of the accent that was not local. His hand began to move towards his sword, and his horse trotted sideways to flank the stranger.

Still without raising his head, the stranger replied, "Too far for you!"

As the peasant brought out his sickle, the mercenary was shocked to see a metal ball and long chain attached to the hilt. In one fluid movement the peasant whirled the chain, let go, and as the ball wrapped around the mercenary's neck the peasant pulled back, simultaneously strangling him and dragging him from his horse.

The mare bolted and the peasant ran to the fallen form of the mercenary, who was now beginning to stand, and plunged the blade of his sickle repeatedly into the gaps in his armor in a rabid frenzy, oblivious that he was covering himself in thick dark blood.

The lone rider, gurgled, spluttered, and fell backwards as vital life essence poured through his armor.

The peasant looked at his gore-covered sickle in contemplation. "Who knew these things actually worked?" He shrugged and pulled the now lifeless body of the mercenary from the road to the shade of the forest.

Rummaging through the dead man's pockets, the peasant brought out an array of cloths and small sharpening stones. "Well, at least you knew how to look after your sword."

Finding a bundle of papers, the peasant held them up to the morning light, trying to read the finely written script. "Don't worry… Gui Kwon. Old Celus here will make sure that your name continues."

With that, Celus began to remove the mercenary's armor and put it on himself.

*

Mount Akiro

The frail form of the rag-covered figure clung desperately to the pitted volcanic rock, as the wind howled around the cave entrance, threatening to tear him from the mountain face and into oblivion. Despite being August, it was bitingly cold near the summit of Mount Akiro, and the sleet in the air suggested snow would come to the peaks soon.

Struggling against the gale, the hunched figure finally made its way into the cave mouth.

"Master Otsuno! Master Otsuno!" the young man gasped. "It's here. It has begun!"

Within the cave entrance, an old man sat completely still, his feet crossed, and his hands resting on his knees, palms upward. The harsh glare of the morning light reflected off his bald head, and in places seemed to almost bleach the mass of wrinkles into absolute smoothness. In front of the elderly monk, a small fire sputtered in the wind before popping back to life and a plain kettle and bowl sat beside it, unused.

"Master Otsuno!" The apprentice moved forward as if to stir his master.

"Not so fast, young Gasan," a voice said from the gloomy recesses of the cave, causing the apprentice to jump back in fright.

"Master?"

A young man stepped from the deep shadow. Although his face was unlined, and his robe was pure white, he bore a strong resemblance to the aged monk who sat cross-legged by the fire. "As you can see, my technique is improving. Now, what is causing you such distress my apprentice?"

Gasan panted. "It's here Master. The Eye of The Oni. It's here."

The young man's expression became stony and his tone took on a dangerous edge. "Are you sure?"

"I am Master. Come and see," Gasan replied, retreating to the cave entrance where the wind once again began to tear at his tattered robe.

The young man turned, melting back into the shadows until the darkness was once again absolute.

Master Otsuno's eyes snapped open and then squinted, adjusting to the harsh glare coming from the cave entrance. With the difficulty that came of such advanced age, the old monk took his stave and, leaning on it heavily, struggled to stand. Hobbling, and taking careful steps, Otsuno approached where Gasan stood waiting.

The sight that met him astounded him. High above the village of Fujigatani, the sky had darkened to a purple-black bruise. The clouds seemed to boil from within, and lightning balled and flashed across the menacing scene.

"She is here. She has arrived," the old Master said grimly. "Come Gasan. The time is now."

"But Master," the apprentice protested, "it will take us many hours to reach the village."

"Then we'd better get going," Otsuno replied, and stepped out into the gale.

*

Fujigatani Village

Yoshimoto and the other children were concentrating on their calligraphy so hard that they did not notice the sky darkening, or the lengthening of shadows in their teaching hall. However, the change in weather had not escaped the notice of Governor Watanabe and he moved across the floor to the window to look outside.

A storm is coming.

It was not unusual for this time of year. Typhoons battered the coast regularly, and one or two would come this far inland each season. Across the village square, the black imposing form of Fujigatani Castle stood, its high vaulted wooden roof providing an excellent view across the Inzai Valley. Any other Lord would have had his children educated within the castle walls but Lord Soma had decreed that his offspring should take their lessons in the village. His people should know and recognize their next ruler and not feel as though their Lord was some invisible power that only materialized to alternately tax and conscript them.

Lightning forked from the sky and a peal of thunder rumbled ominously, causing the children to jump and realize for the first time the darkness of the day.

Watanabe could hear the horses in their stables whinny and stamp their feet, but there seemed to be no reason to worry. The storm was still high up, and the rain had yet to begin. Maybe it would pass them by before it came much lower.

*

From the line of the trees, Lady Altera signaled to the archers to light their arrows. She raised an arm silently and placed her other hand on the black hilt of her sword, readying herself for battle.

In a single fluid movement, she silently dropped her arm, watched the first volley of flaming arrows arc high into the sky before beginning their descent on the unsuspecting villagers, and with a battle cry sprang forward, leading the infantry charge.

*

The Plains of Yeddo

The wind had unexpectedly turned, blowing the smoke back into the Loyalist army. Lord Soma spluttered and choked, and all around him was the noise of war. Metal clashed. Men screamed. Horses shrieked and bucked, throwing their riders. A messenger approached through the murk, relaying vital information to Lord Mutsu.

"What news?" Soma asked his strategist, desperately trying to control his skittish mare.

"My Lord," Mutsu began, "There is no sign of your brother's forces. I fear they have fallen before they could take their position. We should retreat unless we too want to suffer the same fate as Lord Chikatane."

For a moment, Soma felt the cold touch of indecision. If he stayed then there was every chance he would be killed and there would be nothing between Ashikaga and Fujigatani Village… and his sons. However, if he fled, the Emperor would most likely believe him to be inept or worse a coward, and strip him of his land and titles.

Reason won over. If he were alive then at least he would have a chance to redeem himself.

"RETREAT!" Soma turned his still skittish horse and began to gallop toward the edge of the plain, hearing his order repeated along the line as he went.

As he crested the rise, he pulled his horse up. There, along the boundary of the field, were at least a thousand infantrymen, their spears pointing directly at him. The Great Traitor was outmaneuvering him.

Soma pushed his mare to the side and still more troops poured out of the forest, all carrying the Ashikaga banner. Despite his years of training, he felt panic begin to set in.

Turning the horse around again, Soma desperately searched for an opening. There was none, and a sense of resignation weighed heavily on the Emperor's General as the acrid smoke began to envelop him.

Too late, he saw the archers draw their bows back.

A volley of arrows thudded into Lord Soma, throwing him from his mount, and landing him heavily on the ground and knocking the wind from him.

Soma did not look up. He did not need to. He could hear the enemy soldiers charging towards him.

Desperately, as the smoke rolled over him, he tried to reach for his sword, and unfasten his cuirass. They would never take him alive.

*

Fujigatani Village

Young Yoshimoto raised his head. Something was wrong. Something was…

The world grayed over, becoming a high contrast black and white. Something drew Yoshimoto's attention to his right, where Lady Yumiko sat. The dark haired young girl seemed to be unaware of a small dense black cloud directly behind her head. It was like a swarm of flies, but the noise they made… it was like the sharpening of a thousand knives.

The cloud moved as if to envelop Yumiko and, without thinking, Yoshimoto dived on her, throwing her to the floor.

The world returned to color, and Lady Yumiko looked up at Yoshimoto, stunned that he would dare touch her. A split second later, a flaming arrow crashed through the window, its dark metal head embedding itself deep into the spot where Yumiko had been. It was like nothing Yoshimoto had ever seen; a meter long, the shaft was thick bamboo, and the arrowhead was a ghastly array of cruel serrated edges.

Watanabe span around, his eyes wide with anger and fear.

The world grayed again, and Yoshimoto turned to look back at his brother. There was another cloud, this time behind Tanemochi. The older boy looked incredulous at what had just happened, and his eyes were wide in shock.

Yoshimoto tried to move, to get his brother away from the cloud, but he was too far from him.

Once again, the world returned to color, and Yoshimoto knew it was too late. Another flaming arrow came through window; its evil metal tip entering through Tanemochi's back and erupted through his abdomen, sending a splatter of entrails and gore over the boy's calligraphy papers. For a moment, Tanemochi looked from his brother to the still flaming arrow protruding from his stomach, and the back to his brother, before toppling over to one side. The flames sputtered in the growing pool of blood and died.

Watanabe realized what was happening. "MOVE!" he roared.

The three remaining children looked at him and stayed still, their bodies frozen in shock.

In a single move, Watanabe crossed the floor, picked up Yoshimoto under one arm and Yumiko under the other. He kicked Minami hard. "MOVE!" he roared again and exited the teaching hall as the little girl scampered after him.

Outside Watanabe froze. Everything seemed to be on fire and bodies lined the dirt road. Bodies of people he knew. Bodies of his friends. Loyal clansmen. The bell at the shrine began to ring frantically, sounding the alarm. Above him, Watanabe saw the storm cloud descending, balling and rolling as it did so. He recognized The Eye of The Oni only too well. Turning, Watanabe saw soldiers running into the village from the tree line, cutting down unarmed farmers in their wake. They were Ashikaga's dogs.

From his right came the sound of pounding hooves. A cavalry charge from the main road. Watanabe knew that they meant to cut off all the escape routes. His choices were to take the children on to the mountain road or into the Tega Marshes.

High overhead lightning forked across the sky, exploding into Fujigatani Castle and sending a shower of rubble down into the village and across the entrance to the mountain road. The ground seemed to buckle and rip as it tried to absorb the energy, and another arc exploded into the mountain peak.

Otsuno!

Although it had been many years since The Governor had seen his former master, he knew well enough the old monk watched over the Soma clan from his mountain retreat. But not anymore.

Watanabe put Yoshimoto and Yumiko down, and gathered Minami in. Kneeling down, he addressed them. "We have no time. We need to leave right now. Hold my hand, and run."

At a sprint, the line made up of the old man and three young children moved across the village square, past the burning stables and storehouses, and into the thick reeds of the Tega Marshes, leaving everything they knew far behind them.

*

The Plains of Yeddo

Through the smoke and murk, the mounted silhouette of The Scourge of The Chrysanthemum Throne came. The stupidity of his enemies never ceased to surprise him. How could they ever expect to win when Heaven itself shined on him? The portents had all been there… the three stars in the sky, guiding him for the previous week. All had fallen before him.

A man cannot deny his fate, he thought as he trotted on. Past the dead and the dying, past those screaming for mercy and past those resigned to their fate. He had only one target.

Pulling up his white steed, General Ashikaga dismounted, and, clutching his spear, he approached the prone form of Lord Soma.

"Ah, Tadashige," Ashikaga began, noting the lazy gash across his one-time comrade's belly. "Even in defeat you are a failure. Was seppuku too much for you?"

Soma's lips moved wordlessly and dark ichor frothed up, dribbling down his chin and cheeks, before the fallen lord broke into a toothy bloody smile.

"Never mind," Ashikaga said. "As usual, I have the stomach for what you do not." Raising his spear high above him, The General drove the shaft down, piercing Soma where his helmet? met his neck guard. The blade sliced through the fallen lord's throat and buried itself into the ground with an audible crunch of dirt and bone.

Soma gurgled briefly and although the light in his eyes faded, his smile remained.

Ashikaga brought his spear up and, with a deft flick, cast off the blood that had slaked his weapon's thirst. For a moment, he stood, wondering at Soma's smile, and then his eyes widened as he realized the reason for his enemy's mockery.

"Find the sword!" he roared. "Find his messengers!"

*

The Akiro Mountain path to Fujigatani

The blasted volcanic landscape was a maze of crisscrossing footpaths and, even though Gasan had made this journey thousands of times, he still occasionally lost his bearings and he was now checking his landmarks.

In contrast, Otsuno knew exactly where he was going, and although not as spritely as his young apprentice, he was a good deal more surefooted. Gasan was therefore surprised, when he turned around, to see that his Master had stopped completely.

"Master? Are you unwell?" Gasan asked, adjusting the small pack of provisions on his back.

Otsuno continued to stare, seemingly through his apprentice, focusing on some distant point that Gasan could neither see nor comprehend.

"Master?"

Otsuno slowly turned his head to look at Gasan. "A great man has just passed," the old monk whispered, and sat down heavily. "He was a student of mine. I knew him from when he was an infant. His father too."

"Master?" Gasan went to Otsuno's side, fiddling with the opening of his pack in order to provide the monk with some revitalizing herbs. "Are you sure?"

Otsuno nodded, tears welling up in his old hazel eyes, his voice beginning to crack. "Lord Soma is dead."

The two men sat in silence as the wind tore around them, buffeting them against the unforgiving rocks.

"Tanemochi will succeed him," Gasan said eventually. "He will have inherited his father's aptitude."

Otsuno looked sadly at his apprentice, but said nothing.

*

Fujigatani Village

Thick black smoke rolled off the wooden houses, spewing into the heavy sky as though some dormant serpent had awoken too soon from its ancient slumber.

Lady Altera looked about her as her men went from door to door, pulling what few survivors remained into the light before running them through with their spears. At her feet lay the charred remains of Tanemochi, curled in a fetal position. She kicked the body over to examine the features more closely.

Satisfied, she raised her head. "I want the body of every child brought to me," she called out. "There are three more of them out there. They *must* be found."

High above, the dark clouds rumbled and swirled, revealing for the briefest moment, the outline of some monstrous form in the sky.

Lady Altera looked skywards, and muttered "Yes Mother. I understand."

*

Yugyo Monastery, Sagami Province

As the wooden door slid open, the kneeling form of Taka kept her eyes low as the Monastery Council scrutinized her.

Abbot Sonkan's voice was gentle yet authoritative. "Please Mistress Taka, you may enter."

Still keeping her eyes low, Taka slid her sandals off and shuffled into the gloomy Council Chambers. The door slid closed behind her, shutting out the daylight, although the smell of burning incense from the shrine lingered on.

"You may approach," Sonkan said again.

Taka remained kneeling and once again shuffled forward, across the floor of straw mats, keeping her head bowed. From underneath her thin dark eyebrows she could see the cross-legged forms of the three men who made up the Monastery Council; Abbot Sonkan was the head of their order; Master Mifune was responsible for training the would-be monks that found their way to the monastery; and Master Kyuzo was responsible for the relationship between the monastery and the outside world.

Taka knew that her position was one of privilege. Comparatively few women ever entered into Orders, and none had ever served on The Council.

"We have considered your petition Mistress Taka," Sonkan began, "and The Council are disturbed by what you have brought before us."

Taka remained low, and made no reply.

Master Mifune spoke next. "Mistress Taka, how did you come by this… document?"

Raising her body slightly, but keeping her eyes to the floor, Taka's reply was humble and soft. "Master Mifune, it was my apprentice, Nikko who discovered the prophecy. She has been helping me catalogue the entire library since she joined our Order three years ago. She is a diligent worker, and possesses an exceptional memory. When we saw… the phenomenon in the night sky, she brought me the document and said it was one of the first that she read when she joined, which is why she remembered it."

Mifune nodded and looked to Sonkan. The change in the night sky had worried them all. The appearance of three stars was surely a portent of a coming change and, in a country that had been in a constant state of upheaval for nearly seventy years, more was not welcome.

Of all The Council, Sonkan seemed the least disturbed. "Do you have the original document Mistress Taka?" the old Abbot asked.

Taka bent low again. "I do Master Abbot. Nikko's document was a wider teaching that simply referenced the prophecy. But we have been able to locate the original."

Taka reached slowly inside her robe and brought out an old roll of cracked parchment that had faded into a deep yellow with age. Keeping her head bowed she shuffled forward and offered the parchment to the Abbot.

Sonkan unrolled the aged document with great care, lest it turn to dust in his hand, and slowly read the simple brushstrokes that was the script of his ancestors.

"Three stars turn,
The child will come,
To we faithful who do not sleep,
Our raptures burn,
With prayers begun,
So shall darkness fall from the deep."

Sonkan handed the parchment to Mifune who similarly considered the verse before passing it to Kyuzo.

"Mistress Taka," Sonkan began. "You are the head of our vast library. What do you think this means?"

Taka remained low. "Master Abbot, that prophecy is one of the oldest documents in our library… it was written at least a thousand years ago. I believe that it means that a hero is rising. I think that it refers to the darkness not only over our country, but also over all the monasteries within Ashikaga's lands."

"You think the fall it speaks of is that of Ashikaga?"

"Master Abbot, I do. Few would deny that Ashikaga has cast a shadow over both The Chrysanthemum Throne and the whole country."

Sonkan considered this and looked to his friend. "Master Mifune, what do you think?"

Mifune's voice was as coarse as Sonkan's was gentle. "There is great disorder in our land," he said slowly. "This prophecy… I will concede that it does relate to the three stars we have seen, but the rest of it is vague. Maybe a new power is rising. However, I would urge caution. There is much that is hidden from us in these dark times."

Sonkan turned to Kyuzo who simply nodded in agreement and the old Abbot returned to face the head librarian. "Mistress Taka, The Council thanks you for your diligence in this matter. I believe that Fate shall proceed as it will. No doubt, if this prophecy is accurate, the hero you believe in will find his way to us."

*

The road to Fujigatani Village

Although it was the next day, the acrid smell of smoke hung in the air like some preternatural mourning veil. The summer sun beat down over the marshes, and the atmosphere of the hour of the horse was thick and muggy, tinged with the tang of charred meat.

Despite the mid-day heat and his own exhaustion, Tatsuo trotted along the dirt road, desperately clinging to the rag bundle in his arms. He had cast off all of the insignia that marked him as belonging to the Soma Clan; sent his mare into the woods to divert his pursuers; and had removed his armor. After rolling on the forest floor, he looked like any other lowly peasant and prayed to Amaterasu that the Hordes of Ashikaga would pay him no attention.

His prayers were to go unanswered.

As Tatsuo rounded a bend, he saw yet another checkpoint. Quickly, Tatsuo tried to scamper into the cool shade of the forest but a shout and the sound of running feet told him it was too late.

"What do we have here?" the lead soldier sneered, jabbing his spear at Tatsuo. "Another Soma dog?"

One of his comrades laughed. "Does the dog sit? Does the dog beg?" He too began to jab his spear.

The third, the captain, remained stern. "Where are you going, Soma scum?"

"Please," Tatsuo began, bowing deeply to his tormentors. "I am just returning from Imayado. My father… he is very ill."

"And where does your father live?" the stern soldier continued.

"Please… he is in Fujigatani village," Tatsuo replied, still bowing.

The soldiers laughed at the joke. "Not anymore!" The first said. "There is no more Fujigatani. There is no more Soma."

Tatsuo's eyes widened. It was not possible that Fujigatani had fallen. It could not be…

"What do you have there?" the captain said, indicating with his spear at the bundle of rags under Tatsuo's arm.

"This? This is just my provisions. A little rice and…"

The captain's frown deepened; the bundle of rags was the wrong shape for provisions.

"Let me see," the captain said, reaching forward to take the bundle by force.

Behind the three soldiers came a polite cough and they span around, spears pushed forward menacingly.

Old Master Otsuno smiled toothily and leaned heavily on his staff, his wrinkled brow beading with sweat in the noon heat. "Greetings," he said looking at the soldiers. "Three against one does not seem to be very fair."

The three soldiers looked at each other, and then laughed.

"And what are you going to do about it old man?" the first snorted.

"Tell us a tale from the age of the gods? Bore us to death?" the second chimed in. Even the captain was smiling.

"Me?" Otsuno's smile was fading. "I thought we might even things up."

From the line of the forest, Gasan let his bowstring go, and watched as the arrow split the helmet? of the first soldier, sending his brains exploding into the dirt in an orgy of blood and bone.

The Captain, seeing he was under attack, charged Otsuno with his spear raised. The old monk stayed still until, at the last moment, he moved his staff slightly, deflecting the spear, and spun with a speed and grace that defied his years, connecting a well placed chop into the base of his attacker's neck. The Captain fell silently into the dirt, never to rise again.

The remaining soldier, now wide-eyed with terror, dropped his spear, and began to flee. Gasan, emerging onto the road, let another arrow go, and watched with satisfaction as it punched into the retreating soldier's back, through a lung and pinned him to the road where blood began to pool around him.

Tatsuo trembled in fear as his two saviors approached, unsure whether a lesser evil had given way to a greater.

Otsuno smiled. "Don't worry. You are safe now," he said, helping the shaking man up from the mud road.

Tatsuo, still in shock, looked down at the bodies of the fallen men, and then back to Otsuno. "Are you Soma?"

Otsuno laughed. "Yes. Let me guess, you are… Shimabuku?"

Tatsuo shook his head. "Shimabuku is my brother… how…?"

Otsuno's smile broadened. "You must be Tatsuo then. Yes. You have your mother's eyes. Come, help us get these bodies off the road."

Tatsuo was baffled. "But… who…?"

"Don't worry," said Gasan, walking past the confused man to help his master move the dead soldiers into the undergrowth. "You'll get used to it."

"But…" Tatsuo was struggling to understand everything that had just happened. "You killed them. They'll be missed."

Master Otsuno stood up from the body of the first soldier, still smiling. "What was I going to do? Tell them that you are not the messenger they were looking for? It had already gone past that, young Tatsuo. After all, you *are* the messenger they are looking for, aren't you?"

Tatsuo once again struggled for words and Otsuno sighed and hobbled towards the bewildered young man, leaving the bodies to Gasan.

"Come," said Otsuno softly, "sit." The two men sat on the grass bank between the forest and the road. "You have come from the battle on the plains, yes?"

Tatsuo nodded his head.

"You have come with a message," Otsuno continued. "Lord Soma is dead. His army defeated."

"Yes… but how…?"

Otsuno smiled sadly. "Lord Soma and I were once very close. I felt his passing."

"But… who *are* you?"

"Don't you recognize me young Tatsuo? You and your brother used to help me pick jasmine for my cha when you were a child…"

Tatsuo's eyes grew wide. "Master Otsuno? I thought you were dead. I mean no disrespect… but…"

Otsuno laughed. "...But I was already an old man when you were a child, and here we are thirty years on. Why, I must be over a hundred by now!"

"Yes... but..." Tatsuo's mind was reeling.

"How?" Otsuno said and then leaning in close he said in a whisper, "maybe there really is something in this Yamabushi crap, eh?"

Tatsuo felt himself instantly transported back to that night in his early teens, when he and his brother had talked until the morning sun began to creep across the horizon, about how the Yamabushi were just crazy monks on the mountain, pandered to by the local lords. They had no real power. The only power was in the might of one's army.

Tatsuo prostrated himself at Otsuno's feet. "Master. Please... I beg your forgiveness."

"There is nothing to forgive Tatsuo... please, sit up. We were all young and foolish. Even me. *Especially* me. Come. Tell me of our Lord's end."

Tatsuo recounted the battle as best he could. He had seen the winds change and the smoke blow into Soma's army. He had seen Ashikaga's men advance and break the Soma line, and had heard Lord Soma sound the retreat. Then he had seen his Lord cut down in a hail of arrows. By the time Tatsuo reached him, he had already attempted to end his own life before the enemy took him, and entrusted his retainer to take the message of his death to Fujigatani.

Otsuno sat in silence, weighing Tatsuo's words. "And what of Lord Chikatane? Where were his reinforcements?"

Tatsuo shook his head. "I did not see them. Lord Mutsu said that they must have been routed."

Otsuno contemplated the possible scenarios, until he spotted the bundle of rags by Tatsuo's side. "Is that what I think it is?"

Tatsuo nodded. "Lord Soma made me swear that I would deliver it safely to Lord Tanemochi..."

Otsuno said nothing, but shook his head.

"Is it true what those soldiers said?" Tatsuo whispered. "Is Fujigatani really gone?"

Otsuno's reply was grim. "Yes. Gasan and I saw it ourselves. Ashikaga's forces brought the Oni with them. The devils swept through the whole village, burning and killing everything."

Tatsuo's heart was pounding. This could not be. This could not be the end of the Soma clan. "What of young Yoshimoto?"

Otsuno's eyes narrowed. "What do you know of the boy? He would not have been born the last time you were in the village."

Tatsuo looked to the floor. "I only know what they say. That he has no interest in the clan. That he wants to be a farmer."

Otsuno's stare was piercing. "What else do *they* say?"

Tatsuo still did not meet the old monk's eye. "They say he is simple. That he would rather watch a mushroom grow than learn the clan history. They say he has inherited none of his father's ability with the bow, and his spear-work is clumsy. Some even say he is not even Lord Soma's son, but a foundling adopted by our Lord and…"

Otsuno held up a hand. "Yoshimoto *is* Lord Soma's son. That much I do know."

Tatsuo looked up from the floor. "Is he alive? If he is, we must find him… He must lead the clan and seek…"

Otsuno looked to the younger man, and Tatsuo instantly fell silent. "Young Yoshimoto," Otsuno began, "is, at the very least, something of an enigma. Let us say… he is beyond my sight. Always has been."

Tatsuo started forward. "So he could possibly still be alive?"

"Possibly? Anything is possible Tatsuo. However, is it probable? Possibly." Otsuno broke into a toothy grin. "Gasan," the old monk called out.

"Here Master," Gasan trotted over from across the road.

"Have you seen to our friends?"

"I have Master. I have taken the bodies into the woods. No one can see them from the road. They did not have many provisions on them, so their camp must be near."

"What do we do now?" Tatsuo asked.

Otsuno thought for a moment. "Ashikaga will probably be leaving the valley. Yeddo is loyal to him, so he will replenish his supplies and troops there before pushing on to Yoshino. His only goal is to defeat Emperor Go-Murakami and take the royal regalia. With that, he can legitimize his own pretender to the throne and the power of his Shogunate will be absolute. It will be worse than the reign of Fushimi - I fear for this land. Nevertheless, his thirst for power does give us an opportunity.

"If he does intend to move on to Yeddo, then his troops will only be in the valley a few days. Indeed, they may be withdrawing already. We should return to what remains of Fujigatani, collect whatever supplies we can, and then get to Yoshino ahead of Ashikaga and warn the Emperor. I know a shortcut across the mountains… Well, don't look at me like that. Help an old man up. We have work to do."

*

Fujigatani Village

Ashikaga's troops were not retreating from the valley. It was the hour of the rat and night had fallen, extinguishing the sun and plunging the valley into an inky darkness. Watanabe moved stealthily on his belly through the reeds towards the border where the village met the marshes, his robe smeared with mud. He could smell the thick smoke in the air and, from his concealed position he could see that fires were still burning, casting distorted shadows across the scene.

The village that The Governor knew was gone. All that was left of the wooden buildings was ash and a few charred timbers. The invaders, who seemed to work tirelessly, were now pulling down what few stone buildings there had been. A number of troops had begun to demolish the castle, no doubt to ensure no remnant of the Soma Clan's influence would remain.

Although Watanabe had never seen Altera's hordes, he knew these figures well. His old master had taught him of the demons who wear many masks; spirits who looked like men, but when they walked it was as though their joints had grown backwards, clicking like crickets in the nights.

The Oni.

Watanabe dreaded to think what other monstrosities Ashikaga had called up from the nightmare realms of Jigoku. The only light was from the pools of fire that pockmarked the now ravaged landscape, silhouetting Ashikaga's troops as they moved between the ruins of the village. They were searching for something. Bodies seemed to fill what had been the village square and, at the center, Watanabe could see the imposing figure of Lady Altera, directing the various groups.

This was the first time The Governor had laid eyes on this creature, although her reputation preceded her. The Oni Witch. She was one of Ashikaga's most feared lieutenants and some said that she was also his concubine, whilst others declared her a sorcerer of immense power. Others said that she was a foreigner, and had learned her formidable skills in the Tianxian Wars. Now that the Ming Empire was beginning its ascendancy, some said that her armies were no longer required and she had come across the sea to Oyashima in search of dark sacrifices.

Although armed with only his short sword, it took all of Watanabe's will to prevent himself from rushing at the vile creature and avenging the death of his clansmen.

A polite cough behind The Governor made him jump and Watanabe rolled over, bring himself into a crouching position, his blade in his hand ready to strike at any adversary. A young man stepped out from the reeds and presented himself to Watanabe with little more than a perfunctory nod. Dressed in a traditional plain white robe, the young man's features were smooth and his wide cheekbones and flattened nose marked him as being of Soma heritage, whilst his bald head suggested a monastic lifestyle.

"Oh Watanabe," the young man sighed, "what am I going to do with you?"

The Governor's voice was little more than a hiss. "Who are you? Identify yourself!"

The young man sighed again. "Whilst my powers have grown since we last met, I must say that I am disappointed that you do not recognize me."

Watanabe studied the young man's face and, in shocked realization, his eyes grew wide. "Master Otsuno?" his voice was barely a whisper.

The young man nodded. "Come on. I have some friends you need to meet," and he turned back into the long reeds.

"Master," Watanabe reached for the young man, who instantly recoiled.

Otsuno raised a finger. "Not for touching. Soon maybe, but not yet."

"Master, I apologize," Watanabe said bowing, "but I cannot leave. I have… survivors with me."

Otsuno narrowed his eyes. "Yoshimoto?"

Watanabe bowed again. "Yes Master. And Lady Yumiko and Lady Minami. I could not save Tanemochi," and his voice began to crack as he spoke his ward's name.

Otsuno's usually playful tone was gone, replaced by a stony seriousness. "Where are they?"

"Not far from here. Perhaps a few hundred meters. Certainly no more than a mile. However, they are in the marshes and I do not want to be away from them for too long. I came back here to try and collect whatever supplies I could, but you can see…" Watanabe gestured to the distant silhouettes of the Ashikaga's troops that moved back and forth across the remains of the village.

Otsuno seemed to consider this and nodded to himself, as if agreeing with some internal monologue. "Very well. We will collect the children and then return to my camp." The young man turned into the reeds.

"But Master? What is at your camp?" said Watanabe, moving noisily through the undergrowth after the retreating figure.

"Friends. And maybe hope for our country," came the disembodied voice.

*

The Eastern Road to Keishi

The horse trotted on, seemingly oblivious to the weight of the numerous satchels and bags lashed to its back, and the man that had taken Kwon's name walked next to the stolen mare. He was tired and his arms ached from his recent exertions.

Despite being the hour of the tiger there was already a faint glow on the eastern horizon, signaling that dawn was approaching, and there were movements in the surrounding fields that told of farmers beginning their daily duties. As he rounded a corner, Kwon saw the approaching form of a peasant carrying two buckets of water.

Raising his hand in salutation, Kwon addressed him. "Greetings."

The peasant could tell that Kwon was a Tianxian mercenary from the style of his armor. Although he had never met one himself until now, the countryside was full of rumors that Ashikaga was preparing to mount an attack on Go-Murakami and, as such, soldiers of fortune were becoming increasingly frequent.

Bowing low lest he offend the Tianxian, he replied, "Morning's blessing upon you Master."

Kwon clumsily tried to imitate the bow. "Yes… do you know how far it is to Kurama Temple?"

The peasant frowned. Mount Kurama and its temple had nothing to do with the Clan Wars. "Master, it is at least thirty days ride. Maybe more if your mount is carrying…" the peasant eyed the bulging bags on the steed, "a great deal of equipment. But Master, Mount Kurama is not for the likes of warriors such as you."

"And why is that?" The peasant did not appear to be a threat but that did not stop Kwon watching him closely.

"Master, they say the Tengu King has risen… that Sojobo himself stalks the slopes terrorizing any faithful that would make the pilgrimage to The Temple."

"Do they now?" Kwon replied. "Excellent," and with that the mercenary flipped a coin at the bowed form of the peasant and clicked his tongue for his horse to walk on.

"Master, thank you," the peasant called, scrabbling in the dusty road for the coin. Finding it, he held it up, but in the gloom was unable to discern any of the features other than that it was silver. Slipping the coin in to his robe, he sighed, picked up his two buckets, and continued his journey.

As the peasant came around the corner, he stopped dead, and in his shock dropped his buckets, spilling the water into the ground.

More than a dozen bodies littered the road. Severed arms lay not far from their owners. Heads seemed still to roll gently from side to side as if only recently removed from their bodies, and the earth was stained dark with warm blood.

The peasant could tell that these too were Tianxian mercenaries and their insignia matched that of the warrior he had spoken to not five minutes before. In his horror, the peasant turned to call to the soldier, but the night had already swallowed him.

Kwon looked down at his blood soaked armor. It was just as well it was dark. If the peasant had seen this gore covered apparition, he probably would have died of fright. With the rest of the Tianxian group dispatched, there was no one left to deny his new identity.

Kwon smiled to himself, and patted the hindquarters of his steed. A month was a long walk, but he had walked further in the past. *Much* further.

*

The Tega Marshes

Watanabe moved through the dense reeds keeping the bleary-eyed children close to him, followed by Master Otsuno. It had not taken him long to reach the small clearing, although to call it a camp was to exaggerate the effectiveness of the leaf blankets that covered the dozing youngsters, and Watanabe was still amazed that Otsuno was able to hold his projection. Although he had heard of such tricks, he had never seen them. Part of him now wished that he had continued his training with the monk, but he realized that, with the death of his own father, the call of the Clan was stronger.

For his part, Otsuno said nothing of this, but followed The Governor silently, and kept a close eye on the children.

Watanabe stopped and sniffed the air, detecting the faint of trace of smoke from the small fire.

"Straight on," Master Otsuno said, smiling broadly. In the half glow of the morning light, Watanabe could only see a disembodied toothy grin.

The marshes gave way to a short strip of grassland that formed the buffer between the wooded slopes of Mount Akiro and the Tega.

Watanabe turned to Otsuno. "Master, this is open land, and it is getting light. Ashikaga's men are still searching. Is it…?"

Otsuno closed his eyes and tilted his head slightly to one side as if listening to distant voices. Opening his eyes, the old monk spoke softly. "The devils are still in the village. It is safe to cross. But we must hurry."

The group jogged quickly across the open ground, not stopping until they were deep into the woods. Mount Akiro rose sharply before them, and Watanabe doubted that the children would be able to scramble up such a steep incline.

"Master…" Watanabe began.

"Don't worry," Otsuno said, kneeling down to address the children. "Now we're going to see some friends of mine, but they are up on that plateau," Otsuno pointed to a ridge that was at the top of a seemingly sheer wall. "I want you to place your feet where I place mine, yes?"

The children nodded in silent unison. All three of them had said very little since the attack. Lady Minami's eyes were red from crying and her older sister looked pale and drawn from two nights of restless sleep. However, Watanabe was most worried about Yoshimoto. The boy had barely said a word in the past forty-eight hours and seemed not to look just down at the ground, but through the very world itself.

"Very well then," Otsuno continued. "Follow me."

The young man set off and was careful to make sure that his pace was not too fast for the children. The three youngsters followed in single file, and Watanabe brought up the rear. Impossibly, the ground seemed to flatten and level before them, and The Governor was surprised how easy the climb to the ridge was.

At the top, Gasan and Tatsuo greeted them, helping them up and putting blankets out for the children. A kettle gently boiled on the embers of a small fire, and Gasan poured warm cha for them all.

Watanabe looked out across the dark valley and toward the lightening horizon, gasping as he did so.

"It was not just Fujigatani?" he asked incredulously.

Gasan shook his head solemnly, but said nothing. The Governor could see his village below, illuminated by the fires that still burned, casting the troops that moved down there into obscene and twisted shadows. Across the valley, other pockets of fire sputtered, like the pools of Jigoku themselves.

Watanabe knew each and every location. The grain stores. The farms. The orchards of cherry trees. The small hamlets that acted as outposts. Even the lesser temples of each community now smoldered; he knew that would have been a deliberate attempt to drive out the *kami* that watched over the land; guardian spirits that resided in everything from the rocks to the trees, even in the homes and sake bottles.

From his vantage point, The Governor could see that not even the settlement of the outcast butchers and tanners had escaped. Nothing was left of the Soma Clan.

Master Otsuno sat down on the moss-covered floor as Watanabe turned from the scene. "Do not look so down-hearted Watanabe. We are not beaten yet."

Watanabe looked at his one-time master, incredulous that the monk could be so flippant. Thousands had died... the Soma Clan all but extinguished.

Otsuno continued. "May I present Tatsuo. I am sure that you remember him."

Although the men had last met more than three years ago, Watanabe had instantly recognized Lord Soma's loyal retainer, and bowed to him. Tatsuo responded in kind, bowing deeper and acknowledging the older man's superior standing.

When Otsuno spoke again, his tone was heavy. "Tatsuo brings news from the Plains of Yeddo."

Tatsuo bowed again. "Honorable Governor, I regret to inform you," his voice began to break, "that Lord Soma has been killed in battle."

Although Watanabe had suspected such news, the reality of it was like one of Otsuno's punches, and The Governor staggered as though winded. Behind him, the two girls whimpered.

"What of Lord Chikatane?" he asked.

Tatsuo bowed again. "There was no sign of him or his army. It is believed that he was routed before he joined the battle."

With Lord Soma and his younger brother, Lord Chikatane, dead, the oldest surviving male child should inherit the estate, with a regent to govern in his stead until he came of age. Usually, this would be a relative, and looking at the drawn face of Yoshimoto, Watanabe addressed Tatsuo.

"What of Lord Mutsu? As Lord Soma's third-cousin, the strategist should be the boy's regent."

Tatsuo remained bowed. "As I left the field, I saw that he was surrounded by The Mongrel's forces."

Watanabe did not need it spelt out. The Great Traitor had targeted every member of the Soma Clan. Only this boy remained. His ward. The reluctant Yoshimoto. However, what was there to rule? A shattered and ruined valley. Ashikaga's soldiers would drive what few survivors there might be into the hills where bandits would pick them off. And who would recognize the boy as heir? The fires would have destroyed all of the family records. The titles and grants of estate… all gone. Even the Clan Seals. There was nothing to prove that Yoshimoto was the rightful heir except the word of an itinerant monk and a man who claimed to be the boy's governor. Watanabe felt the weight of reality bearing down on him and, seeing that his one-time apprentice had turned ashen, Otsuno directed Gasan to bring more cha.

"There is something else," Tatsuo said.

The Governor's voice was weak. "What is it?"

Tatsuo shifted nervously, looking to Master Otsuno and then back to Watanabe.

Otsuno stood. "Watanabe, it is for the boy."

The Governor frowned, but stood aside. Tatsuo approached Yoshimoto who looked too stunned to take in anything more. The retainer knelt, pressing his head into the dirt in front of the boy's feet.

"Lord," Tatsuo began, "by the command of your father, the Honorable Lord Soma, leader of the Soma Clan, master and ruler of the Inzai Valley, and loyal vassal of the one true Emperor, Go-Murakami, I present to you your father's sword, that you rule in his stead."

From within the rags that he had carried so closely, Tatsuo brought out the sword of Lord Soma, and laid it at Yoshimoto's feet.

Watanabe gasped and, his eyes wide, he too knelt in the dirt, motioning for Lady Yumiko and Minami to do likewise. Gasan followed him, but Otsuno remained where he was, a look of amusement on his face.

Yoshimoto said nothing but looked at his father's sword in shocked awe. *The Ishin Blade.* The sword of One-Heart-One-Mind. Legend said that the God Amaterasu presented it to the first Emperor, Jimmu, for winning his favor by uniting the country under one flag. In deference to his loyal generals, Emperor Jimmu had presented them each with a sword that bore the crests of their family and conferred upon them both title and lands. The first Lord Soma had gratefully received the Ishin Blade and many said that it was the most finely crafted of all the swords. With it, he drove out the barbarians that roamed his new lands, and brought peace and justice to the Inzai Valley.

"Well?" Otsuno said, leaning forward and smiling broadly. "Pick it up. Become Lord Soma. It is your birthright, young Yoshimoto."

The boy did not move and made no reply, but remained transfixed by the sword, its black polished sharkskin scabbard catching the first rays of light.

Otsuno's eyes narrowed and his tone became more insistent. "Pick it up Yoshimoto."

Watanabe turned, and waved at the monk to be silent.

"Oh don't be ridiculous Watanabe. The boy is wiser than you."

The Governor reddened at the slight but said nothing.

Otsuno crossed to where Yoshimoto stood, and sat cross-legged in front of the boy. "We have not met before tonight, but I knew your father well. I trained him for a time. And his father. And even his father before him. But you are not like them, are you Yoshimoto?"

For the first time, the chubby five-year-old boy looked up, and into the young face of the monk. Seeing the distortion and blurring around the eyes he frowned, but shook his head in answer to the question.

"No. You never dreamed of being a great warrior. That was for your brother. You wanted something else. I hear you wanted to work the land – to be a farmer, yes?"

Yoshimoto nodded.

"It would seem that Fate has a different plan for you. We may all end up in the same place, but the path we take is of our own choosing. Do you know what it is that you want, Yoshimoto?"

Tears began to well in the boy's eyes, and, when he spoke, his voice was little more than a whisper. "I want my father."

"Why?" Otsuno asked.

Yoshimoto frowned. "Because he is my father, and I love him."

Otsuno smiled. "I remember a story that my Master told me, many years ago. He came across a woman who was crying, and he said to her 'Why do grieve so?' The woman replied that her infant son had died and she was mourning her loss. My Master asked her 'Did you mourn your son before he was born?' The woman replied that she did not. 'Then why grieve now?' my Master said, 'for he has only returned to where he was before.'"

Watanabe started forward and said crossly, "Now is not the time for such lessons. There is much to do. Lord Soma must raise an army, and..."

Otsuno laughed. "Lord Soma? Watanabe, Lord Soma is dead. The boy has not yet accepted the title." Turning back to young Yoshimoto, the monk continued, "Do you understand the story?"

Yoshimoto nodded.

"So? What is it that you want?"

Yoshimoto thought and looked through the monk, past the prostrate Tatsuo, the angry form of his governor, and out across the dark and ravaged valley. The memory of his brother came to mind, his fallen form in an expanding pool of blood as arrows rained down. In his mind's eye, he could see the slaughter of his father's army as they tried to retreat. He turned to look at his cousins, and imagined how Lord Nawa had similarly died. Yoshimoto felt a coldness enter him, like a stone settling in his heart, walling off all other feelings except…

Turning from the vision of destruction to face Otsuno, Yoshimoto bent down and picked up his father's sword. The boy's voice took on a steely resolve, as he looked directly at the monk. "I want justice."

A shadow passed across the monk's face. "Be careful young Lord. Do not state such a desire lightly. Embarking on this path will bring inevitable consequences. Consider your position; right now, you could become anybody. Do anything. You are free from the shackles of your name. All paths lie before you."

Yoshimoto's reply came stronger than before. "My path is set. I want justice. I want to put to death those who killed my father. I want to restore the Soma Clan."

Otsuno sighed, and looked first to Gasan in resignation and then to Watanabe. "The Lord has spoken."

Although he did not show it, Watanabe was proud that Yoshimoto appeared to have learned something of family honor and heritage from his many months in the classroom.

"Don't get carried away Watanabe," Otsuno said, sensing the man's emotions. "This will take planning." Turning back to Yoshimoto he continued, "You understand that this may take many years. The burden you are picking up… it will change you. Change those around you. You may even pass it on to your sons?"

Yoshimoto nodded. "I want justice," he said again.

"Very well then," the monk replied. "Do you know how to use that?" he asked, looking to the sword in the child's hand.

Yoshimoto considered lying, but thought better of it, and shook his head. "No," and then looking at Watanabe, "but I will learn."

"Hmmm…" Otsuno thought aloud. "The facts are these. You have no military training. No leadership skills. And no army. You will need all three if you are to bring down the Shogun. Do you understand?"

Yoshimoto nodded.

Watanabe stepped forward. "What do you suggest?" he asked his former master.

Otsuno turned to him, and then to Gasan and Tatsuo as if considering the options. "Ashikaga will no doubt be looking for our young Lord, and the two Ladies. He will know that if a rightful heir of the Soma Clan claims the Ishin Blade, they will become a beacon for all those that oppose him. Our Lord needs instruction and training, but here is not the place. I have friends in Yugyo Monastery where our Lord can at least begin his lessons – the monastery is small and out of the way. Ashikaga's forces will not think to look there. However, we cannot simply arrive at their gate. A second must vouch for our Lord. I know of one who will do so – Master Shonin. However, he is in Yokohama – the heart of Ashikaga's Shogunate. It will be a dangerous journey."

Watanabe stepped forward. "You cannot think of taking our Lord through the lands around Yeddo. That is the only way to get to Yokohama, and it will be crawling with Ashikaga's men."

Otsuno sighed and shook his head at his one-time apprentice. "West would be the only way to get to Yokohama *by land*. If we go east, to Port Choshi, we can charter a boat to sail around the coast, avoiding The General's men."

Watanabe grunted, and bowed his head in acknowledgement. It was a good plan.

"Secondly, we must get a message to Emperor Go-Murakami in Yoshino, and tell him what has happened here. He will need to muster whatever forces he can gather to repel the next wave of Ashikaga's attack. Fortunately, the road to Yoshino goes near Ise and we should…"

"No!" Watanabe stepped forward boldly. "We shall not speak of that. Not here."

Otsuno shrugged. "Our Lord will have to be told at some point, Watanabe. When do you suggest?"

Yoshimoto frowned. "What is it?" he asked. "What do I need to know?"

Otsuno looked from Watanabe to the boy, and then back again to The Governor. "Well? Do you want to tell him, or shall…"

"It should be me," Watanabe said, suddenly looking weary. The Governor approached Yoshimoto and prostrated himself in front of his new lord. "Lord Soma, forgive me. There is much of your family history that you do not know."

"What is it Sensei?" The boy's voice sounded fragile and full of trepidation, reminding Watanabe of his ward's tender age.

"Lord. It was many years ago, during the time of your Great Grand-Father. Another lord threatened the Inzai Valley… Your Great Grand-Father relinquished his claim to the Valley, and bequeathed it to the Ise Shrine in Yamada. In turn, Ise granted your Great Grand-Father, and all heirs of Soma, the title of Protector. No lord would dare attack lands owned by a shrine. However, the fact that your family had to relinquish their claim to the land was… it was a matter of embarrassment to your father."

"Sensei, then my clan does not own Inzai?" Yoshimoto asked.

Watanabe shook his head. "My Lord, no."

To The Governor's surprise, his ward smiled. "But my clan is obliged to protect it?"

"My Lord, that is correct."

"Then my revenge will be doubly satisfying, for I shall restore the honor of my Father *and* the Ise Shrine by slaying the rebel dogs."

Otsuno spoke next. "My Lord, it is more than that. Not only is the new Lord Soma duty bound to restore honor to the Ise Shrine, but they may also be of some assistance. Every monastery and temple trains their own *Sohei* – the warrior monks. The sohei of Ise are renowned and the shrine lays to the South East of Keishi, but one would go past it if one went via the Irago Cape and took the ferry. I would suggest that Gasan and Tatsuo get word to Ise and then travel on to Yoshino and The Emperor. In the meantime, I will take you and the Ladies to Yokohama to meet with Master Shonin."

"Thank you Master Otsuno. That sounds acceptable," Yoshimoto said bowing, and too late the monk realized that the boy was reaching for his hands in a gesture of gratitude.

"No! Don't touch…"

*

The world seemed to flash and Yoshimoto found himself standing on a grassy plain, next to an aged monk.

"Oh Yoshimoto," the old man said. "Where have you brought us?"

Yoshimoto looked about him in wonder. They seemed to be standing on a rise by the coast and everything had taken on a purple hue. The wind gusted around them, chopping up the already stormy sea. The boy could see that, beneath the waves, huge dark forms swam close to the surface, their immense bulks sending up massive swells. The air felt hot and dense, as though it was trying to push into the pores of his skin, and the spray from ocean was thick and greasy. Turning to look behind them, Yoshimoto beheld a tree like none he had ever seen before.

It was so tall that it appeared to reach to the very heavens themselves and every branch looked as if it were alight with a benevolent flame that did not destroy the wood but rather made it glow with a divine light. High, at the top, a single gigantic eye looked down at the two small creatures that had arrived before it, filling Yoshimoto with a feeling of love and warmth as he lost himself in the blue iris. This was home… this was where he belonged…

Yoshimoto pulled on the old monk's sleeve, indicating that he should turn around and share in this marvel.

As Otsuno wheeled around, the tree seemed to morph. The high boughs merged together becoming arms whilst the lower became legs, and both the monk and the boy now beheld the vision of a giant beautifully pale-skinned lady in the full bloom of womanhood. Kneeling down, she extended her arms towards them, opening her hands to expose a white lotus blossom.

The petals began to part, revealing a bright light, and the lady gently blew, bathing both the old man and the boy in heavenly rays.

*

Old Otsuno's eyes snapped open. His projection was gone, and he was back in himself, feeling all the aches and pains that age brought with it. He leaned forward from the boulder that braced him and Gasan rushed to him.

"Master?" the apprentice cried. "Are you well?"

"Oh yes," Otsuno said, standing. He was feeling better than just well. He felt… invigorated. Energy seemed to course through his tired arms and dusty veins. He knew that it would not last long but he would enjoy it while it did so. "Our Lord?" the monk asked.

Watanabe turned to face the monk. Yoshimoto was in The Governor's arms, looking blearily at Otsuno as though he had just woken from a deep sleep.

The priest brought a single finger to his lips, indicating to the boy that discretion was required until they could speak privately.

"What happened?" Watanabe asked.

Otsuno shrugged. "Our Lord merely broke my concentration. I cannot hold my younger form indefinitely and the sensation of feeling broke the spell and probably gave our Lord a little jolt. My Lord, is this not so?"

Yoshimoto nodded, but said nothing.

The monk turned to Gasan. "There is much to do my apprentice. You and Tatsuo should first go to Ise, and then on to Yoshino. Once you are done, meet us at the Yugyo Monastery. Time is against you, so take the mountain path. Do you remember the way?"

"Yes Master," Gasan replied. The Yamabushi Monks were famed for their knowledge of the mountains and even with the two-day advantage that Ashikaga's forces had, Gasan knew he should still be able to beat them to Yoshino by several weeks, maybe even a month. The young apprentice looked to Tatsuo. "Are you ready?"

Tatsuo bowed deeply. "I am," and then turning to Yoshimoto he continued. "My Lord, with your leave?"

Yoshimoto nodded and watched the two men depart.

"Good," Otsuno said once Gasan and Tatsuo were out of sight. "Now for the hard part. My Lord, I am going to ask something of you. Something very difficult indeed. Ashikaga's forces will be looking for you. Probably your governor and your cousins too. We will need to travel incognito."

Yoshimoto looked blankly at the old man.

"My Lord," Watanabe said, bowing. "I believe that Master Otsuno is saying that, in order to succeed, no-one can know who we are. We must give up our names."

Yoshimoto's eyes flashed with fear and anger. "No! I will not… throw away my father's name!"

Otsuno approached. "My Lord, that is not what I mean. Think of it this way. You are taking your name deep into yourself, hiding it until the time is right for it to come again. Think of the lotus flower," the monk looked meaningfully at the boy, remembering the vision of only a few moments ago.

"The new lotus flower is tightly bound, shielding itself from the world. Then when it has had enough sun and rain, it bursts into life, showering its seeds around. My Lord, that is how you must be. You must hide your true self away from the world until the time is right to burst forth and reclaim your birthright."

Yoshimoto nodded, understanding what the old man was saying. "Very well. What do you suggest?"

Otsuno smiled, glad that the boy had heeded his advice. There was a great deal of untapped potential within this one. "Lady Yumiko shall be… 'Gozen'. Lady Minami shall be… 'Masako'. And you my Lord… let me think. Yes, I see it now. I have just the name for you."

CHAPTER TWO

September 1356 – Utsunomiya Castle, Shimotsuke Province

Lord Ashikaga snorted in frustration, his nostrils flaring, and his eyes bulging. "Unacceptable!"

The other lords in the meeting chamber remained kneeling and looked to the floor lest they meet The General's eye and incur his wrath.

"Do you know what this means?" Ashikaga continued, striding up and down the wooden dais at the front of the chamber. "If even *one* heir survives he will become a rallying point… a beacon for all the other Oppressors!"

The twelve lords who made up Ashikaga's immediate lieutenants muttered an acknowledgement, and again shifted nervously. The truth was that they had already spent too much time looking for what few survivors remained of The Great Eastern Purge. Over the course of a single week, any lord of the Eastern Provinces who refused Ashikaga's rule had felt the might of his iron fist. The General's forces took no hostages. By fire and blade, Ashikaga cleansed the land. Word had quickly spread westwards and those who had considered allying themselves with The Chrysanthemum Throne were now swearing allegiance to The Great General. However, this was not enough for Ashikaga. He knew what a few insurgents could do and he had demanded that every member of each noble line be accounted. There were a few missing and, whilst his lieutenants absently shrugged and asked "What can a few rebel dogs do?", Ashikaga was himself an example.

He had fought a guerrilla war in the early days and with his supply lines becoming longer, any disruption would have had serious effects. He had been fortunate to benefit from Go-Daigo's lazy generals, and he was determined that there would be no slatternly behavior in his own ranks.

Ashikaga recognized the silhouette that appeared at the door, and The General grunted his approval for the late arrival to enter. The door slid back, revealing to the chamber the kneeling form of Lady Altera.

Ashikaga grunted again and Altera, swathed in dark robes, shuffled into the room, keeping her head bowed.

Ashikaga's voice was gruff. "Sit up,"

Altera rose to a seated position, but kept her eyes to the ground.

"What news?" The General barked, his mood not improved by the late arrival of his favorite lieutenant.

Altera bowed her head slightly. "If it pleases My Lord, I bring news of the survivors from the Nitta Clan."

Ashikaga stopped his pacing and looked to the woman. "Well?"

Altera slowly moved her hand to the two small sacks on her hip. Instantly the other Lords went for their swords, believing this woman, who should not even be amongst them, was finally revealing herself, and attacking their general.

"Hold!" Ashikaga snapped. Altera had frozen, and The General strode towards her still submissive form. Seeing that Altera did not have her sword with her, he gave his approval to continue.

Altera presented two rough cloth sacks to the feet of Ashikaga and bowed deeply, her head touching the floor.

"What is this?" The General's eyes narrowed.

Without sitting up Altera replied, "The last of the Nitta line. A distant cousin and a great-grandchild."

"Sit up," Ashikaga commanded and kicked the bags to the nearest lord, indicating that he should open it.

Altera sat up whilst the bags were undone. As the lord loosened the last knot and opened the bag, he turned pale and nodded to Ashikaga.

Despite inwardly feeling proud of this latest victory, Ashikaga strode back to the raised platform and continued to berate his commanders. "That woman is worth more than all of you. How is it that she can hunt down our enemies with less than a battalion and you all just blunder in the forest?"

"Witch," a young lord muttered.

Without hesitation, Ashikaga strode to the kneeling figure of the lord who has spoken, drawing his sword and, with a single deft strike, removed the man's head. The body fell lifeless to the floor, steam rising from the pool of expanding blood like an onsen on a cold day.

Nobody moved and the atmosphere became tense and still.

With a flick, Ashikaga removed the vital life essence from his blade but did not sheath his weapon. He surveyed the room, sensing the renewal of his absolute authority. The General did not like wasting commanders, but a demonstration of how he would deal with those who would speak against him was occasionally required.

"Get out," Ashikaga said eventually. "All of you. Get out and find me the mongrels who would oppose me."

As the lords shuffled out, Altera remained kneeling, only standing up only when she heard the door close behind her.

Ashikaga stepped down from the raised platform, approached her, and whispered, "Are they listening?"

Altera tilted her head to one side and shook her head. Looking up into Ashikaga's face, her reply was soft, "My Lord, two of them are still near. They question our... agreement. They are worried what forces you have unleashed.... Now they are saying that you are too strong for anyone to mount a challenge. That even Go-Murakami must fall... They are walking away."

The General permitted himself a rare smile. "They are learning. Come, walk with me."

Altera obeyed the order, and easily fell into step with Ashikaga.

"How did they die?" he asked, nodding to the small sacks.

Altera's reply was cold. "Not well. We found them in a small fishing village on the south coast. One of the huts had a small hole dug into the floor and covered with a mat. That was where they hid the children."

Ashikaga looked to Altera impassively. "Did you explain to the headman that you were acting on my authority?"

"My Lord, I did."

"And?"

"My Lord, he said he had heard that remnants of the Nitta Clan had fled north."

"But you found the children anyway?"

Altera bowed her head in acknowledgement.

"And what of the village now?"

"My Lord, as you commanded, it was burned to the ground. There were no survivors."

"Very good," The General muttered.

For a moment, there was silence between the two as they exited the meeting chamber through a side door, and stepped into the gardens.

The cool dusk told them that it was the hour of the dog, and suggested that the summer was over. Soon the rains would be upon them and, if Ashikaga wanted to end the rule of Emperor Go-Murakami this season, he would have to move quickly before the roads became impassable.

His castle stronghold of Utsunomiya had been the military power base of his family for generations and now, with his grip on the government in Kamakura tightening, all manner of politicians and advisers had swollen the once small village almost to city status. The castle had grown since the war had begun twenty years ago. Ramparts had been raised, the donjon extended, and the capacity of the barracks increased, all to make Utsunomiya an impregnable fortress of gray stone and dark wood.

"My Lord," Altera began, "what news of the Bakufu? Has parliament agreed to your proposals?"

Ashikaga's smile was thin. "They have now. I have... replaced those advisers who did not see things my way. Our ability to make policy is complete. But that is not your concern. You have performed well for me, Lady Altera. Had the Nitta Clan been able to revive itself, it would have proved an unnecessary distraction for the Shogunate."

Altera bowed her head. "My Lord, thank you. I follow your bidding in… recognition of our agreement."

The General stopped and turned to look at the young woman. They had known each other for many years, since before The Great Oki Raid, and yet her face remained untouched by the passage of time. "Yes, our agreement," he said slowly. "I do not believe that all the terms of that have yet been met."

Altera's eyes widened and her cheeks flushed with anger. Struggling to control her temper she replied, "My Lord, you have your power. That was our agreement. The Great Mother… requests that you build the shrines."

Ashikaga smirked. "Our agreement was for *absolute* power Lady Altera. You will get your shrines when Emperor Go-Murakami lies dead, his supporters have been crushed, and I have the Imperial Regalia."

Altera choked back her rage. She could have snapped the older man in two in a heartbeat, but this was neither the time nor the place. Silence descended between them and, in a rare moment of insight, Ashikaga regretted snapping at his lieutenant. Despite being a mere woman, she had proved to be the most effective of his deputies and The General realized he would be wise to retain her loyalty.

"I do not dispute your prowess on the field of battle," Ashikaga began. "However a single victory does not win the war, you understand? That said I recognize your considerable achievements. I will permit… shall we say a further three of your shrines, in addition to those already built? Maybe one in the north. Perhaps another in the west, and let us say another in a place of your choosing?"

Altera knew too well this was not a negotiation. "My Lord is most gracious," she replied, bowing her head.

"Now, what of the Soma Clan?"

"My Lord, the search goes on for the last Soma child. I believe that he is dead, burned in one of the houses. Nevertheless, we cannot be certain because some of the bodies were… unrecognizable. I cannot sense the boy, but, as a precaution, my troops are sweeping the area as far as the eastern coast."

Ashikaga considered this. "Do not underestimate the Soma. They are a resourceful clan, and one of the oldest this country has known. What of the mountain monk?"

"My Lord, there is no sign of him."

"Hmmm... you should assign your best men to hunt him and his apprentice down. If he really is a Yamabushi then he may seek the boy out, or worse, have him already. You cannot let the Soma Clan take root again, Lady Altera."

Altera bowed her head again. "My Lord, I understand. If the old man is as you say he is, we may require... a more formidable tracker."

"What do you have in mind?"

Altera considered her position for a moment. "There is one that we could bring forth. A Hunter, if you will. However, it will require a blood sacrifice. Not a death, but certainly a bleeding."

Ashikaga was used to Altera's dark arts. "Why a bleeding?"

"My Lord, simply put, the stronger the warrior that I bleed, the stronger The Hunter."

Ashikaga nodded smartly. "Then you will bleed me."

*

The road to Port Choshi

Master Otsuno always amazed Watanabe. Despite the constant drizzle, the old man remained completely dry whilst The Governor watched the children's robes get darker as they absorbed the water from the air. It was the hour of the goat and the leaden skies showed no sign of permitting the afternoon sun to break through.

"If this keeps up we should seek shelter in the woods. The children will get cold again," Watanabe said.

Otsuno nodded. "Oh, it will be like this most of today and tomorrow" the old man replied as if it was the most obvious thing in the world. "There is a tavern with an onsen not too far from here. Maybe a few hours. They're friendly to our cause. We can rest there."

Watanabe was glad to hear this. For the last few weeks they had relied on the kindness of strangers. Peasants who were still loyal to what was left of the Soma Clan would recognize either Otsuno or himself, and take them in with no questions. In the mornings, they received clean robes and provisions for a day or two – whatever their host could spare. Lord Soma's popularity was never in doubt, but the genuine affection the people of the countryside held him in took The Governor by surprise. He suspected that they partly honored their Lord, but another part of their generosity was the fear of what Ashikaga's reign of war and taxation would bring.

At this stage Watanabe was just grateful for whatever support came their way. Since leaving the valley a few weeks ago, their journey had not been without its trials. The early days had seen them sleeping out in the open since Ashikaga's troops had burned every dwelling in the valley. Only Otsuno's skills at foraging ensured they did not starve. When they did find a farm that was untouched, the tales they heard had chilled them; Ashikaga was pushing west, consolidating his grip on the country. However, more than that, he was not taking hostages and any opposition resulted in death.

They had kept off the main road, opting for the lesser-used paths that scrawled their way across the countryside. Even here, they had seen soldiers at checkpoints set up by Ashikaga's dogs. More than once, they had to hurry into the woods and lie low while the banner of the Shogunate passed them by. The soldiers infested the country, like maggots crawling over a corpse, picking it clean.

For their part, the children appeared to have adapted well, although Watanabe was concerned that they were not eating enough. It was Gozen – formally the Lady Yumiko – who seemed to be doing the best. Several times in the night, Watanabe had heard her younger sister, now Masako, sobbing, and the older girl had gone to her to offer comfort.

The boy was an enigma. For the first few days, the girls had struggled with their new identities, often calling each other by their old names, and Watanabe had gently chastised them, reminding them of the danger they were still all in. However, the boy… he was something else. Even the way he walked was different now. It was as though they had left Yoshimoto on the mountain, and a new child – this Jion - had taken his place.

Otsuno smiled. "Your thoughts were always very loud, Watanabe. I had hoped you would have learned to calm them by now."

The Governor's reply was barely a grunt. "Master, there is much to be worried about in these times."

"You know what worry will achieve. And you know what action will achieve."

"Master, I do. Forgive me."

"You are concerned for the boy."

Watanabe nodded as they strode on. The children were opening a gap between them as they skipped along, playing whatever game they had invented that morning. "He has… adapted quicker than I expected," The Governor admitted.

"Is that not the sign of a good leader? One who adapts in order to overcome?" the old monk continued.

"Master, it is but… Yoshi… I mean Jion never showed any aptitude in his lessons. Teaching him was like… as you would say, trying to hold water to a tree."

Otsuno smiled. "We all become what we need to be. Jion has chosen his path and he knows what will be required of him. He seems to be determined to meet that. It is a credit to your training of him, Watanabe."

The Governor grunted again. "Master, I wish that I could take credit. No, there is something else… something from within himself that is rising to the surface. You can sense it, can't you?"

The old monk chuckled. "Can you?"

Watanabe shook his head. "No. I was never able to do that. After I left you I tried to continue my training, but the demands of the Clan... what do you sense?"

"Ah, finally a question worthy of my apprentice. I sense... nothing."

Watanabe shrugged. "Master, maybe I was wrong..."

"You did not hear my answer. I sense nothing."

Watanabe's eyes narrowed. "Nothing at all?"

Otsuno carried on smiling. "If I close my eyes, I know that you are there and the girls too. However, Jion... it is as if he does not exist. His presence is but the faintest whisper."

"But Master, how is that possible? Life flows around all things. Isn't that was you always taught me?"

"You never completed your training, Watanabe. It is said that there are some creatures that do not cause life to flow around them, but rather *through* them so that they cause no disturbance."

"Master, I have never heard of such things."

Otsuno shrugged. "As you said, you did not continue your training after you returned to the Clan. Some believe there are three types of beings. There are those of heaven; the gods themselves. Then there are those who are in equal part heaven and earth; man and the creatures of the Kingdoms. Finally, there are those rare few who are wholly of the earth. They have many names, but the Yamabushi simply refer to them as the Farravashi. Some say they are the champions of humanity. Others, that they are sentinels who impart great teaching and wisdom when the time is right. However, I have never met one, and I do not know anyone who has. They are the stuff of legend. Nothing more."

"Master, could it be that Yoshi... that Jion is one of these Farravashi? Could he be our champion?"

Otsuno slowed and looked at his former apprentice hard. "Be careful, Watanabe. The boy will follow his own path. Do not seek for him to follow the one that you would wish for."

"Master, I understand. But is it possible?"

"Anything is possible, Watanabe. You of all people should know that. The Council at the Yugyo Monastery will be able to make a determination. But in the meantime, why don't you tell me a little about our new Lord."

"Well he has never really taken to nobility. Where Tanemochi was diligent with his studies, Yoshi... Jion was more interested in how the land worked and..."

"You know that is not what I meant Watanabe," the old monk said sternly.

The Governor bowed his head, acknowledging the rebuke. "Master, you ask of Jion's mother?"

"I do."

"Lady Soma died not long after Tanemochi was born. In his grief, Lord Soma swore that he would never marry again. Jion's mother was Lord Soma's favorite concubine. They say that she died in childbirth… but there was no funeral. No pyre."

"I see. Was she one of these new cultists that have been springing up? Was she buried? Oh, what are they called?"

"Master, The Kirisuto? I do not think so. The Kirisuto are confined to the northern tip of Ezochi, although sometimes their textile merchants come as far south as The Valley selling silks. Master, I was guardian to Jion's mother. She appeared to be completely normal except for…"

Otsuno sensed his companion's hesitation. "Yes?"

"Master, it was her pregnancy."

"What about it?"

"It only lasted three months."

Otsuno frowned. "And Jion was born completely normal? Fully grown as you expected?"

"Master, yes. I was not there for the labor but, when I saw the infant after… yes, he was completely normal."

The old monk considered this. "A normal boy from a normal mother… was Jion her first child?"

"Master, I am not certain. She came from outside of the valley. She did not talk much, but I understand she had lived in Yeddo for a while. That is where she and Lord Soma met."

"I see," replied Otsuno. "Is it possible that she was pregnant by another and hid it? Before she came to The Valley?"

Watanabe shook his head. "No, Master. She was resident in Fujigatani Castle for more than a year. She had no family and there were no male visitors."

Otsuno's smile returned. "None that you know of, Watanabe."

The Governor accepted the point and bowed his head in recognition. "Lord Soma believed that Tanemochi needed a companion, and so he recognized Jion as his son and gave him his name. The two boys were inseparable."

"Very noble of our Lord, although I hope that the weight of that name does not drown us all."

"Master?"

"It is nothing. Is Jion aware of his parentage?"

"Yes Master."

Otsuno considered what he had learned from Watanabe. He had yet to spend any time alone with the boy although he was keen to discuss the vision they had shared on the mountain. "I sense that there is much more to this story," he said finally, "but we are unlikely to ever know for certain the circumstances of his birth. We should catch up with the children and press on to the tavern."

Further ahead, Jion walked with Gozen and Masako, playing a game they had invented that morning called 'Shades', the objective of which was to walk a set distance whilst counting the number of shades of an agreed color. They had exhausted green several hours ago, and were now comparing the autumnal yellow that was creeping through the forest like a spreading mold.

"You did not count twenty-three," scolded the younger girl.

Gozen smiled knowing that she was teasing her sister. "Masako, I did. Jion, you agree with me don't you?"

The boy looked up. Despite only having been on the road for a few weeks, the fat around his arms and jowl was gradually wearing away, leaving a pointed chin and high cheekbones that clearly marked him as being of high Soma heritage and his short dark hair had grown past his ears. "Huh?"

"I thought you were playing with us?" Gozen said.

"Sorry. Master Otsuno gave me a scroll of battle tactics last night and I was thinking about it."

"There will be plenty of time for that when we get to Yugyo," Masako chided.

Jion nodded and looked back at the forest floor. "I guess."

"Were you up late reading the scroll?" Gozen asked. "Are you tired now?"

"Not reading the scroll, no..."

Masako interjected, "What *were* you doing? I hear you moving around. I know that you are up to something."

Jion shrugged. "I have bad dreams. I guess I toss and turn a lot."

When she spoke, Gozen's voice was quiet. "Do you dream of your brother? Of that day?"

"No. Not really. Well, sometimes. That all feels like a thousand years ago. Like it happened to someone else."

Masako spoke up again. "Then what *do* you dream about?"

"I'm not sure," Jion replied. "Purple skies. A woman in white with a lotus flower. Sometimes there is a black mountain and blue lightning. And on all the trees there is this sign..."

"What sign?" Gozen asked.

Jion reached into the fold of his robe and pulled out a wooden pendant on a leather cord. "Like this." On the wood were etched two concentric circles, joined by nine zigzagging lines that reminded Gozen of lightning.

"Did you make this?" Gozen asked.

Jion nodded. "I make lots of things. Here," the boy offered the leather cord to the older girl who bowed her milky white neck and allowed him to fasten the ends.

"Thank you," she said, thumbing the pendant before slipping it inside her robe. "Do you know what it means?"

Jion replied, "No. It is just something I made."

"Hey," demanded Masako. "Why does *she* get one? I want one too."

"I'll make you one tonight," Jion said. "I promise."

Watanabe and Otsuno had watched the children's play unfold before them without interfering.

Otsuno spoke first, keeping his voice low. "It seems that our new Lord is aware of what is needed to secure his future."

Watanabe agreed. "Master, Gozen is the elder, and the Nawa Clan was powerful once. They are too young to be formally betrothed, but maybe in a few years time."

"And what plans for Masako?"

Watanabe saw the trap. "That will be for our Lord to decide."

Otsuno laughed. "You never stop learning, do you, Watanabe?"

"I hope not, Master."

"Very well then. What would you *suggest* to our new Lord?"

"Master, the younger girl's best hope would be in a strategic marriage. The Nitta Clan has several children close to her age who might be suitable. They are already loyal to the Soma's, but by combining them with a Nawa alliance… I would view such a unified house as being very strong indeed."

"That may be, Watanabe," Otsuno said, "but no doubt our enemies will view it in the same way. Tread with caution."

*

Utsunomiya Forest, Shimotsuke Province

It was the hour of the pig and night had fallen across the land. Through the black shapes of the trees, Ashikaga could see the darker forms of Lady Altera's soldiers surrounding them. He was kneeling on the ground in front of a large cedar tree and a deep fire-pit encircled him. The ferocity contained within the earth warmed the surroundings and The General marveled at his lieutenant's knowledge of the land.

Altera knelt in front of him, the flames from the fire pit casting deep shadows across her face. "You must not be afraid. Do I as I tell you and no harm will come to you, understand?"

Ashikaga bowed in his head in acknowledgement, noting that Altera was no longer formally recognizing his rank or superiority. However, this was her domain and he would abide by her rules… as long as it suited him.

"Very well. Remove your cuirass."

Ashikaga loosened the knots that bound his chest armor together and laid it on the ground beside him. Around him, Altera's men took up a slow beat by drumming on the ground with the end of their spears.

"Now," Altera continued, "remove your top".

For a second Ashikaga paused. It was not seemly for a general to be seen… in such a state of undress. His ambition overruled his pride and he tugged his loose top over his head.

Altera shuffled on her knees until she was almost touching him, bringing a bucket of water with her. Dipping a ladle in and then slowly pouring water over his left arm she said, "By this water The Mother cleanses your heart."

Pouring another ladle of water over his right arm, she continued, "By this water The Mother cleanses your deeds."

Finally, Altera poured a third ladle over Ashikaga's head. "By this water the Mother cleanses your mind."

The flames in the fire sputtered and briefly turned blue before deepening to an ominous purple. Smoke began to pour from the ground around them, and Ashikaga began to panic that they would all suffocate.

Altera seemed unaffected and continued the incantation. "So is The Sacrifice cleansed and becomes worthy to be received."

The drumming began to quicken and Altera drew three small dark metal spikes from her robe. "Give me your left hand."

Ashikaga opened his palm to her.

"Like the eagle, so shall He dream of being awake." Altera brought the first spike sharply across The General's outstretched hand, drawing blood.

"Give me your right hand."

Ashikaga knew what was coming and presented his palm.

"Like the doe, so shall He speak of the flow of the corrupted lands." Altera drew the second spike across, again bringing blood to the surface.

"Sit back," she said to Ashikaga, "and bear me your breast."

The General sat back on his haunches, dropped his arms to his side, and waited for the inevitable.

"Like the salmon, so shall He know of the deep waters that collide." Altera slashed at Ashikaga's chest and the old general winced as blood began to drip down him.

Standing, Altera said, "Stay there," and crossed to the cedar tree.

The smoke had become so thick that it obscured the sky, but it was not acrid and did not burn Ashikaga's throat. Again, the rhythm of the beating spears increased and The General could feel the heat from the demonic fire radiating out.

"In the name of The Mother," Altera began, "I command the eagle," and she plunged the first spike in to the tree. "I command the doe," the second went in next to the first. "And I command the salmon."

From where he knelt, Ashikaga could see the tree physically darken, becoming as black as ash. Altera was holding her hands out to the sap that was now flowing freely from the cedar's wounds, but this too seemed changed into some numinous ichor.

Cupping her hands, Altera made her way to the fire-pit. Around him, The General heard the soldiers begin to chant, but the words were foreign to him, and he did not understand them. The air had become thicker, like a dense fog, and he felt his heartbeat quicken.

Altera stood at the edge of the pit and began to open her hands, pouring the corrupted sap in.

"By The Mother, by The Mother, by The Mother…" The words echoed and reverberated around the circle as the soldiers took up the chant.

"We seek," Altera began as the purple flames licked hungrily at the sap in her hands, "what does not want to be found. We seek that which walks outside of the circles. We seek that which knows The Twilight Ash…"

For a moment, the flames flared a blinding white, forcing Ashikaga to avert his gaze. When he turned back, the fire was out and the smoke was gone. High above him the stars screamed down as though the light of heavens would tear apart the pinpricks in the inky canopy.

Altera approached The General. "My Lord, it is done."

Ashikaga noted the return of the formal language. "Your hunter has arrived?" he asked, standing and putting his top and cuirass back on.

"He will be here by the morning."

"Very good, Lady Altera. I will see that he receives equipment and provisions."

Altera tried to suppress a smile. "My Lord, the equipment will be gratefully received. But the provisions… will be unnecessary."

*

The road to Port Choshi

It was the hour of the rat, near midnight, and the drizzle had increased to a full rain. Watanabe was glad to see the tavern as they rounded the bend in the forest path. Warm light spilled from the windows and just the thought of the hot waters of the onsen was enough to begin to relax him.

"Jion! Jion!" Up ahead, Gozen was shaking the boy.

Sensing the panic in the older girl's voice, The Governor and Otsuno broke into a jog and, as they reached the children, they could see the source of Gozen's concern. The little boy stood, seemingly transfixed, his eyes rolled back in his skull and his jaw was slack.

"What happened?" Watanabe demanded, taking hold of his ward.

"I… I… I don't know." Gozen's eyes were moist with tears that were ready to overflow.

"He just touched the door," Masako whined, fearful of any blame.

Otsuno's tone was reassuring. "It's alright little one. Show me where he touched."

Masako pointed to side of the door. "Just there."

"On the knot in the wood?" Otsuno queried.

The two girls nodded and the old monk examined the door before turning back to the boy and his governor.

"Has he ever done this before?" Otsuno asked.

They could all hear the strain in Watanabe's voice when he answered. "No."

"His brother?"

"No."

"The mother?"

"No. Why do you ask such things?"

Otsuno tapped Jion's head. "Because I do not believe the boy is in there," he said, getting no reaction from the child.

For Jion, the voices around him sounded as though they were underwater. The world had taken on a lilac tinge as he moved around the tavern at will. The reek of the cheap shochu almost drowned the aroma of cooking coming from the kitchen at the back.

Upstairs, Jion could hear the maids putting out the bedrolls, from outside horses snorted, and stamped in anticipation of the stable boy coming with their feed. However, despite all of this, there was a darkness; a shadow of some threat that he could not define. As he climbed the stairs, a noise reached him – a scraping like stone on metal, and he realized he could hear all the sounds of the rooms.

Soldiers!

There were soldiers here. Ashikaga's dogs, laughing about whatever village or farm they had taken the previous day. Jion turned. He had to tell Sensei Watanabe. He had to warn…

Jion's eyes fluttered open as he fell backwards into the arms of his governor and the cool of the night air slapped him into full consciousness.

"There My Lord," Watanabe said, inadvertently slipping into his old habits. "I have you."

Jion shook his head, his throat parched. "Soldiers," he croaked, pointing to the tavern.

Otsuno frowned. "Are you sure?"

They could all hear the sound of movement from within the tavern, presumably responding to the girl's cries from moments before.

"What is going on out here?" A large man had come to the door, and Otsuno recognized him as the innkeeper.

"We are on a pilgrimage," Otsuno said quickly. "We are seeking shelter for the night."

As the innkeeper surveyed the men and the children, more noises came from inside and a soldier stepped out onto the porch. "Who is making all this noise?"

From the sway of the soldier, Watanabe could tell he was intoxicated; the *kami* of the bottle had taken him.

"We are very sorry," Otsuno bowed low, motioning to the girls to follow suit. "One of our party is unwell and…"

"We'll not have any disease here," the solider barked too loudly, and Otsuno realized that the drunken man was in danger of turning violent.

"My Lord, we are very sorry for the intrusion," Otsuno said, and began to back away. "We will sleep in the forest. We sincerely…"

"Wait!" The solider snapped, and the party froze. "How much for the girl?" He approached Gozen. "She is nearly of age, right? Come here."

Otsuno moved in between them, and keeping his head bowed he said, "My apologies My Lord. She is but a humble pilgrim and…"

"Nonsense. My men will return her to you after…" the soldier went to push past the old monk. As he did so, Otsuno caught his arm and stepped behind him. His free arm came across the soldier's throat whilst the other hand came up and, with an audible crunch, severed the spinal column.

With a final wheeze, the soldier crumbled into the mud.

Otsuno turned to motion the girls to be quiet but, too late, Masako let out a piercing single scream.

The innkeeper's eyes were wide with horror. "What have you done? You have brought death to us all."

From inside the tavern came the sound of more feet pounding to the doorway.

Watanabe hissed to Otsuno, "We need to leave right now."

Otsuno shook his head as two more soldiers burst on to the porch. "I think it is a little late for that."

Seeing their fallen comrade, two soldiers drew their swords and ran at the old monk. With a deft flick, Otsuno parried the first slash with his staff and, with a speed that defied his years, he followed the momentum of his body, smashing the other end into the back of the second soldier's skull. Otsuno continued the motion and brought the other end of his staff into the throat of the soldier who had slashed at him.

Both men collapsed into the mud almost simultaneously, and the innkeeper and the two girls stood in stunned silence.

Watanabe was unimpressed. "You still put too much weight on your back leg. You need to shift forward if you need to move into a forward lunge."

Otsuno bowed to his one-time apprentice, acknowledging the truth of the observation, and then addressed the innkeeper. "Are there any more in there?"

The innkeeper made no reply, but shook his head.

Otsuno continued. "Do they have horses?"

The innkeeper nodded.

"In the stables?"

"Please," Otsuno said bowing his head, "get them ready for us. We need to leave."

The innkeeper, still shocked by what he had just seen, nodded and fled into the tavern where he began shouting orders.

Otsuno looked down at the three bodies and shook his head. "I regret having to do that."

Watanabe, still cradling Jion, looked up. "Master, it was what was needed in the moment."

"I know. But it never gets any easier," the old monk sighed, and then looked to the two girls. "Are you both unharmed?"

Gozen and Masako nodded but said nothing. They had never seen anyone, let alone an old man, move with such grace and speed. Moments later the stable boy brought the horses around and wordlessly handed the reins to Otsuno before scampering back to the rear of the building.

The innkeeper came back on to the porch. "Go now," he said angrily. "We will take care of... these," he gestured to the bodies.

Otsuno bowed deeply. "Thank you. We apologize for... the inconvenience we have caused you." Turning to Watanabe, he continued. "Can the girls ride?"

"Gozen can. Masako has only had a few lessons."

"Very well," the old monk said. "You take the boy. I will take Masako. And Gozen, these are for you," he handed the older girl a set of reins.

Watanabe put Jion on to the back of the horse. "Which way?"

Despite recent events, Otsuno found himself smiling. "Still east. The forest thickens not far from here. Maybe an hour's ride. I know of a glade where we can make camp."

Watanabe grunted, not happy with the prospect of sleeping outside again but knowing that there were no other options.

"And Watanabe," Otsuno continued. "You will need to let me have some time with the boy. He is more than what he seems."

*

The Forest of Irago

It was the hour of the ox and Gasan and Tatsuo lay flat on their bellies as yet another patrol of mounted soldiers rode past them.

"We cannot carry on like this," Gasan hissed.

Tatsuo grunted an acknowledgement. He had found the apprentice monk's self-righteous manner wearing over the last few weeks, but had to admit the younger man's knowledge of the paths was superior to his own. Compared to this, the first days over the mountain had been easy. Here they were in the heart of Ashikaga's domain and soldiers teemed through the countryside by night as well as by day until the two men found themselves pushed off even the lightest of trails and deep into the forest.

"Do you have a suggestion?" Tatsuo asked, once the patrol had disappeared from view.

Gasan's reply had a haughty tone. He disliked Lord Soma's retainer as much he disliked him. "Actually I do. We enlist."

Tatsuo's expression was one of incredulity. "What?"

"It's simple. Ashikaga is calling on all the local lords for men to fight The Emperor. We present ourselves at the nearest barracks and once we have equipment and provisions we take a couple of horses and get to Ise."

Tatsuo had to admit that it was not a bad plan. "What about papers? We have nothing to formally present ourselves with."

Gasan conceded the point. "Could we forge something?"

"It would be worthless without a clan seal."

The young monk shivered in the cool of the early morning. Despite his years of training on the mountain, he longed for the warmth of a good tavern. "Any ideas?"

"Not really," Tatsuo admitted. "We need to push on if we are to beat Ashikaga's advance, but with all these patrols…" his voice tailed off as he heard the approach of yet more horses.

The two men quickly ran into the cover of the forest and once again lay flat as the patrol cantered along the narrow path.

"This is ridiculous," Gasan huffed. "I have never known so many movements at such an unholy hour."

Tatsuo agreed. "Ashikaga must be flooding the area with soldiers. I'll bet he is looking for something. Either us or Lord Soma or other survivors… anyone who could challenge his authority. This number of patrols is far from normal, especially in the dark."

"Well, well, well," a voice said behind them, and the two men rolled over to feel a sword pressing on each of their throats. "What do we have here?"

*

The road to Port Choshi

The dawn was cool and the small fire that Watanabe had lit warmed Jion. The growl of his stomach reminded the boy that it had been many hours since he had eaten. Hunger came with life on the road and Jion told himself that he would have to get used to it.

Otsuno had found a clearing for them deep in the forest, and none of them could even see the path from their camp. Watanabe sat cross-legged on the carpet of pine needles a little distance from Jion, half watching the sleeping forms of the girls and at the same time desperately trying to catch snippets of conversation between the boy and the old monk.

Otsuno handed Jion a small bowl of jasmine cha. "My Lord, we have much to talk about."

Jion nodded and said nothing, instead staring into his bowl.

"There is nothing to be ashamed of," the old monk continued. "Why don't we start with what happened at the tavern?"

Jion shrugged. "I saw the soldiers and tried to warn Sensei Watanabe…"

Otsuno took the boy's chin and lifted his face so that their eyes met. Watanabe growled loudly, but made no move towards them.

"The soldiers were inside, My Lord. You were outside. How did you know they were there?"

"I saw them. Sort of. I'm not sure."

"Very well," Otsuno said reassuringly. "Tell me what you remember."

"I was playing with Gozen and Masako. We saw the light from the tavern and ran ahead. I was first onto the porch and I put my hand on the door… I don't know. It was like a dream. But it wasn't. I felt warm and I went inside. When the innkeeper didn't answer, I went upstairs to find the lady of the tavern and that was when I heard the soldiers."

Otsuno stroked the boy's hair, trying to keep him relaxed. "Did you know that you were outside the whole time?"

"I guess."

"But you were inside too. Do you remember being outside?"

"No. I only remember being inside."

"What about what passed between us on the mountain. Do you remember that?"

Jion shook his head. "Not really. I know that *something* happened, but I cannot remember."

Otsuno nodded his head. "What about your dreams? I hear you talking in your sleep sometimes."

"I can remember them sometimes. There is a woman who is very pale and sometimes she is very big. Not fat, but tall. Like a troll. But she is very beautiful. Like a princess. And sometimes we are in a forest and sometimes we are on a mountain, and all the trees have this sign on them…"

Jion drew the two concentric circles in the carpet of pine needles, and linked them with nine zigzagging lines.

Otsuno tried to contain his shock, and pointed to the sketch in the dirt. "Do you know what this is?"

"No," Jion replied.

"It is an old sign. Some say that it dates to when Amaterasu first created Man. This is a symbol of great power. It represents both the womb and tomb."

"What's a womb?" the five-year-old boy asked.

Otsuno smiled gently. "It's a place in your mother's belly where babies grow. This sign… it is a reminder that all birth must end in death. It is a holy symbol."

"Oh," Jion replied. "Is that why it is on my father's sword?"

Otsuno's eyes narrowed. "What do you mean?"

"It's on the hilt of my father's sword. I thought that was why I dreamed about it."

"Can you show me?" the old monk asked.

Jion carefully brought the Ishin blade out from the rags that covered it, and presented it to Otsuno. "Here," he said pointing to the pommel. "It is just underneath the wrapping."

Carefully Otsuno adjusted the entwined silk ribbon that covered the shaft of the hilt. There, where the cap met the sword, was a tiny stamp, the same as the one Jion had drawn in the dirt. Otsuno sat back on his haunches, taking in what he had learned.

Eventually he looked to the boy. "How long have you known about this?"

Jion shrugged. "I don't know. Since we left Fujigatani. Masako and I were looking at it together..."

"Does Gozen know too?"

Jion nodded. "Yes. We showed her, but she wasn't very interested."

"I see. Jion, this sword is not a toy."

"I know," the boy muttered, resenting the chastisement.

"It is the soul of a warrior; the very spirit of a clan. You should not be playing with it. For a Clan Lord to show his sword to a woman... it could send an inappropriate message."

"It's alright," said Jion. "Masako is not a woman. She's a girl. Gozen said so."

Otsuno tried hard not to smile. "That maybe the case, young lord, but both will reach womanhood soon enough. Maybe too soon. You will be expected to protect them."

Jion nodded again, not really understanding.

Otsuno could see the boy's confusion and decided that the conversation about womanhood could wait until another day. "Watanabe tells me you saved Gozen's life. What can you tell me about that?"

Jion shrugged again. "I was trying my calligraphy and then everything went black and white and I saw this small cloud behind Gozen. It sounded like lots of insects... but they were metallic. And it looked like it was going to jump on her, so I pushed her out of the way."

"I see. When you were in the tavern, was that in black and white too?"

"No. That was in a funny purple."

"What about in your dreams? When you see the pale woman?"

"No. That's just normal. Master Otsuno, do you know who the woman is? She seems familiar."

Otsuno hesitated for a moment. "I am not sure. She bears a resemblance to a god who..."

"A god. Which one?"

Otsuno noted the boy was learning quickly which questions to ask. "The most likely one is Marishiten. Do you know who she is?"

Jion shook his head.

"Many different people give her many different names. Here in the Eight Isles, she is a very old god. More than five hundred years ago, they say she came to the warriors of the land – the Bujin – and became their protector. But the Bujin forgot about her as they prospered and so she lies, dead but dreaming, waiting for the day when a true warrior will rise and spread her teachings."

"But why am *I* seeing her?"

"I do not know," Otsuno replied. "Maybe she sees something in you. Maybe you are destined to be a great warrior."

"Master Otsuno, do *you* see something in me?"

The boy was becoming *very* good with his questions *very* quickly, and Otsuno shifted uncomfortably. "Maybe. I cannot be sure. I have friends at the Yugyo Monastery who will be able to say for certain. However, maybe we can… play a few special games in the meantime. Just you and I."

"What sort of games?"

"My Lord, *if* you have a gift… it is like a muscle. The more you work it, the stronger it becomes. Our game could work that muscle."

Jion nodded. He remembered the blacksmith in Fujigatani and his muscles. He had been very strong. "How do we play the game?"

"My Lord, it is about concentration. Life flows all around us. Like a stream. It swirls and it eddies. Sometimes, if you know where to look, you can put your finger into the stream, and the flow will change."

"Can you show me?" the boy asked.

Otsuno picked up one of the dead pine needles on the floor. "Hold this," he said, offering it to Jion.

The boy accepted it and studied it intently.

"Do you feel anything?"

"No. Do you Master?"

"When I touch it, I can see everything that needle remembers. The wind through the boughs of the tree. The warmth of the rising sun. The harsh cry of the heron."

The boy's eyes were wide. "From just this one needle?"

Otsuno smiled. "Yes. From just this one needle. Here, let me show you. Hold it in your hand… not too tightly. Now close your eyes and focus on the needle," the old monk said warmly. "Imagine it is glowing warmly in your hand. And the brighter it glows the more the world fades away until it is only just you and the needle that exist. And it glows brighter still, and now you do not exist. There is only the needle. You are the needle. The needle is you. It knows everything you know. You know everything it knows. Do you feel it?"

Jion looked up at the old monk, his eyes moist with tears. "No."

"It does not matter," Otsuno said, hiding his disappointment. "These things take time to learn. Maybe it will come."

"What if it doesn't?"

"Then we will discover other strengths and work those."

"Like marrying Gozen and making a strong clan?"

Otsuno paused. "Where did you hear that?"

"I heard you and Sensei Watanabe talking."

Otsuno knew this was impossible. Both men had kept their voices low and in any case, they were too far from the children to have been overheard. "When did you hear this?"

"Earlier. Before we reached the tavern."

"I see. Do you hear everything we say?"

"No. I only listen when I know you are talking about me. Have I been bad Master Otsuno?"

Otsuno tried to smile. "No. No, not at all. How is it you can hear us over such a distance?"

Jion shrugged and avoided the old monk's eye. "The Lady told me how to do it."

"What lady?"

"I told you. The one in my dreams. You called her Marishiten."

Otsuno could feel his pulse quickening. "Does she have another name? Has she told it to you?"

"No."

"What did she tell you to do?"

"It's difficult to explain. She doesn't use words. She just showed me that land has a voice, and if I take my shoes off I can listen to it and it will tell me things I want to know."

Otsuno was silent, taking in everything the boy had just said. He could sense the child was being honest, but the monk had never heard of such a thing. "Wait here a moment, Jion," and Otsuno crossed to where Watanabe sat, still watching them, and whispered in his ear before returning to the child.

"Jion," Otsuno began. "Sensei Watanabe has his hand behind his back. How many fingers is he holding up?"

Jion shook his head. "I told you, it only works when I take my shoes off."

Otsuno bowed his head. "My apologies. Please, remove your shoes. Now, how many…"

"Three… he just changed it to two. Three again… he's wiggling his thumb."

Otsuno was stunned, but nodded to Watanabe to stop. "Jion, when you have your shoes off, what else does the land tell you? Can you hear thoughts?"

The boy shook his head. "Not really. Only if they are very loud. And it is more of an impression."

Otsuno bowed his head again and went to Watanabe where he whispered in his ear before returning. "Jion, can you tell me what Sensei is thinking?"

Jion's brow creased in concentration. "Ummm... a stream. No, a river. It is flowing very quickly. There is a boy who is playing too close to it. He's fallen in and..."

Otsuno placed a hand on Jion's shoulder. "That's enough. Well done. How far can you... listen? Do you know the range?"

"Not far. Maybe a little further than Sensei Watanabe."

"Could you sense if soldiers were nearby?"

Jion shrugged again. "I don't know. I guess."

"Can you show me your feet?" Otsuno asked, leaning forward.

Jion put his foot out for the old monk, and Otsuno took it gently before examining it. "Your skin is soft," he said. "If you walk barefoot for too long you may hurt yourself. Maybe a few hours each day. And in the meantime, let's see if I cannot teach you a few more tricks."

*

Utsunomiya Castle, Shimotsuke Province

The pale light of the autumn morning began to creep through the town, as though the sun itself was trying one last time to breathe life back into summer.

Ashikaga looked out from the castle at the soldiers in the courtyard below. They were already practicing drills, and the sight of his well-oiled war machine made The General inwardly smile. Every day, the provincial lords sent more men. Some out of fealty, others through fear, having seen the destruction wrought on their uncooperative neighbors. Such small minds were unable to grasp the magnitude of his plan.

Many believed that the only thing The General wanted was war; a way to control the powerful Bujin class. Others thought that he wanted Emperor Go-Murakami dead; revenge for the way his father had treated the younger Ashikaga after so many years of loyal service. Neither was the case. War could never last indefinitely and Go-Murakami was simply an inconvenience. All Ashikaga really wanted was the Royal Regalia; the tools by which an emperor could be enthroned.

Go-Murakami had hidden them well and until Ashikaga had them his candidate for The Chrysanthemum Throne, Kogon, would never be universally recognized. Of course, there were those who whispered that Ashikaga himself would one day challenge for the throne. The General scoffed at such ideas for they were those of children. Only the Bujin Class was able to raise taxes, and Ashikaga had no intention of groveling and scraping to the provincial lords for a stipend. No, it was far better to leave the Imperial Line of Amaterasu as it was and rule Oyashima from behind the throne.

Because that was the real goal. By uniting the whole country under one Emperor, so the Shogunate could bring peace to all the provinces. With peace came prosperity and power, and they were vital if Oyashima was to face the threat from across the water in Tianxia. With rumors spreading that a new dynasty was in its ascendancy, it would be Ashikaga's power that ensured a united Oyashima would never again be threatened by its larger and more powerful neighbor.

Lady Altera's silent house drew Ashikaga's attention, despite the sharp barks of the drill-sergeants. His favorite lieutenant was a source of permanent consternation to the other lords, but as long she continued to deliver results, he would abide her. Altera's veranda was unusually quiet. At this time of morning, he would have expected to see her and her retinue preparing for either a patrol or raid.

"My Lord," a voice said softly behind him, and Ashikaga turned to the prostrated form of his *Hatamoto* – the Shogun's personal retainer. "Lady Altera begs an audience," Mizuno said.

So that is where she is. Ashikaga grunted an acknowledgement and Mizuno retreated to the sliding door. Through the paper windows, The General could see the silhouette of Lady Altera giving her swords to his retainer. Of course, such a gesture was merely for show. There were enough guards secreted in cubbyholes of this room to ensure that no would-be assassin would have time to draw his sword, much less get within striking distance.

Still, Ashikaga was glad to note the lack of weaponry when Lady Altera entered the room and knelt before him. There was something about the woman that unnerved him, and it was more than the fact that she was so proficient in the world of Men.

"What is it?" Ashikaga grunted, turning back to survey the various drills in the courtyard below.

"My Lord," Altera began, keeping her voice low. "Our… new gardener has brought us some information."

Ashikaga knew that she was choosing her words carefully, mindful of the innumerable ears that were listening to their conversation. Spies were everywhere, and it never did to be anything other than careful. The General nodded his head, indicating that Altera should come closer so that they could have a more private conversation.

"What does he say?" Ashikaga asked, feeling the unbandaged wounds on his hand as he repeatedly clenched and relaxed his fists.

"My Lord… the knot-weed has sunk a tuber in the east of your garden."

Ashikaga was not surprised. His lieutenants had been sloppy after the victory on the Yeddo Plains. Too much celebration and not enough attention to detail. "How many tubers?" he asked gruffly.

"My Lord, not many. No more than one or two. Does My Lord wish this… infestation to be removed?"

Ashikaga was tempted to say no. Whilst a possible survivor would be an inconvenience, it might be used to The General's advantage by flushing out any disloyal lords who may offer sanctuary.

"Yes," Ashikaga said eventually. "You have my permission to leave the castle and... remove this weed."

"At once, My Lord," Altera replied, bowing low, and retreating to the door.

She retrieved her weapons from Mizuno and returned to her house, where two of her commanders waited patiently. They stood around a third man, who was kneeling on the floor as an older woman oiled the stranger's hair at the back and the sides and then, gathering it together and doubling it over the crown, before tying it neatly. From a distance, dressed in a rough dark kimono, The Hunter would look like a native.

"We have our papers," Altera said, brandishing the documents of passage, which bore the Shogun's seal. "Is he prepared?"

"My Lady, he is," replied Ullar, bowing his head. He had learned the local customs well.

Altera returned the bow and turned to Birag. "Has he been able to provide any more details?"

Birag bowed his head before replying. "No. He just continues to stare into the bowl of water."

Altera looked at The Hunter. Outwardly, he appeared completely normal and it was only the obvious discomfort of the two commanders that hinted at the darkness that lay within. Altera knelt down opposite The Hunter, examining her work. His skin was pale to the point of being translucent, and whilst his shoulders were perhaps a fraction broad, his dark hair and smooth narrow face were well proportioned. Overall, Altera was pleased the way this one had turned out.

"What do you see?" she asked.

The Hunter did not look up from the bowl of water that lay in between them, but spoke in a low monotone voice. "The three stars have turned and she has come. In the East, beyond the fire, a corrupted saviour seeks sanctuary whilst his flock flies blind."

Altera nodded, satisfied with the response. "He will become more lucid the closer we get."

"What are our orders?" Ullar asked.

"Lord Ashikaga has decreed that any survivors are to be executed," Altera replied.

"What if it is a Twine?" Birag said. "What if it could be turned?"

Altera shook her head. "No," she said. "If it was a Twine... our mission in this barbaric land would be very different. This is something... else. But we can use our search for whatever it is to provide a cover for our hunt for the source of The Skylord metal – that is of paramount importance to The Great Mother."

"But still," Birag continued, "what if we could use it ourselves against…" The older man paused and cocked his head to one side as if listening to a distant voice. "We are not alone," he said.

Altera and Ullar instantly drew their short swords whilst the woman on the floor carried on attending to The Hunter, seemingly unfazed by the sudden commotion.

Altera motioned to Ullar and Birag to exit through the front and sweep around the rear whilst she went through the back door. The two men moved quickly and soundlessly, and Altera stepped stealthily across the matted floor. Now that Birag had brought it to her attention, she too could hear the faint breathing of an intruder. She cursed herself for not noticing it sooner and was conscious of the myriad of stratagems she was currently managing.

As she slid open the back door and rushed out, Ullar and Birag rounded the corner. Nothing. The breathing persisted.

Altera sighed and rolled her eyes, knelt down and reached under the wooden struts that slightly raised the building. She found the collar of the would-be spy and, using one arm, dragged him out.

Ullar and Birag flanked her, now drawing their long swords and bringing them to the man's throat. Altera gently pushed their blades down, realizing who the stranger was.

"Lord Yoshiakira," she said sweetly, "this is an unexpected honor."

The young man smiled weakly. "The honor is all mine," the son of Ashikaga said.

"I trust that my home provided… adequate comfort," Altera replied, looking back to the crawlspace. Although Yoshiakira was in his mid twenties, his was a slim build and he had clearly been able to slide in with ease.

Ashikaga's son bowed his head and smiled. "Very comfortable thank you, Lady Altera."

Altera nodded to Ulla and Birag to leave. She had nothing to fear from this boy. "Is there something that I can help you with today My Lord?" she asked, adopting the informal terminology. Ashikaga was her master, not this child. Not yet.

"There are… many rumors," Yoshiakira began as they walked toward the end of the garden where it would be more difficult for them to be overheard. "Some are uncomfortable with your… relationship with my father."

"I see. Is it unseemly for a woman to fight for her Lord?"

"Oh no no no. You misunderstand. These people who gossip… they say you and my father have… how do you foreigners say? A pact? A deal?"

Altera was wary and did not reply.

"The rumors say," continued Yoshiakira, "that you are not receiving your end of the bargain. Yes?"

Altera's patience was exhausted. "What is it you want?"

Ashikaga's eldest son smiled benevolently. "The same thing we all want. Peace and order. Lady Altera, your presence... it upsets some of the Lords. They say that Go-Murakami would never allow a woman into such a position such as the one you enjoy. They say Go-Murakami would preserve our traditions. They say maybe they should fight for Go-Murakami."

"So?"

"So maybe if you received your end of the bargain you would not need to be so... high profile. You would be able to retreat to one of these... shrines that you want built."

Altera's smile was thin and dangerous. "I am sure that your father will honor our arrangement in his own time."

"Maybe I would honor it sooner." Yoshiakira bowed his head. "Good day Lady Altera."

*

The Forest of Irago

It was the hour of the snake and in the pale light of the morning Gasan and Tatsuo half-walked and were half-dragged along through the winding forest path. Their hands had been tightly bound with rope, and tied to the war saddle used by the bujin class on their mounts.

Both men had considered fighting back against the bandits that had captured them, but they were outnumbered five-to-two and even if a few could have been dispatched, they would have exposed their flanks to the others. It was far better to bide their time and wait for an opportunity to escape. They would be no use to their lord if they were dead.

As the ground began to warm under the rays of the sun, mist began to rise, giving the forest a sense of the ethereal, as though the world of the night was passing into that of the day. Presently the trees began to thin, revealing a low makeshift stockade within a small clearing.

"Halt," a voice called out and the raiding party stopped, aware that several archers had now trained their weapons on them. "Identify yourself," the voice called again.

"It's me, Tamazaki," the lead bandit shouted back.

"Tamazaki is dead," the voice called back.

The lead bandit chuckled at the game they always had to play. "And I've returned for your worthless hide, Umezaki!"

"What is the password?"

"There is no password!"

The gates of the stockade swung open and Tamazaki dug his heels into his horse's flank, urging the beast forward. Gasan and Tatsuo stumbled behind the party, taking in the sight before them. The stockade walls had shielded their view of the camp that lay within; a ramshackle collection of flimsy buildings and tents that were arranged in a haphazard layout. All around bandits milled as though this lack of civilization was the most ordinary thing in all of Oyashima. Whilst some trained, others were visibly intoxicated, and in one corner, Gasan could see a full brawl. From the other end of the camp came the sound of a smithy, although the smell of charcoal did little to mask the prevailing miasma of piss and vomit.

Tamazaki brought his horse to halt outside a large rundown shack that seemed to form the center of the camp, and dismounted. Turning to Gasan and Tatsuo he said, "You will wait here. Nagamasa is our chief and he will decide what to do with you. If you try to escape, my men will kill you. Do you understand?"

Gasan and Tatsuo bowed low, indicating their submission, and Tamazaki disappeared inside the building allowing the two men the opportunity to survey their surroundings. The rest of the bandit patrol stood a little way off, eyeing them both with suspicion.

Gasan wrinkled his nose. "Have you ever seen such a place? They live like barbarians."

"It is becoming too common now," Tatsuo muttered in reply. "The clan wars are creating more and more *ronin*."

"What's that?" Gasan asked, mindful that his isolated upbringing with Otsuno had left him a little naïve of the wider world.

"Masterless bujin," Tatsuo replied. "When a lord is killed his warriors are expected to join him… to commit seppuku. But not all do. Some lack honor and run away. They try to find other employment, but either their cowardice becomes known or they lack the proper papers… eventually they turn to banditry and some find their way to places like these. Do you see over there?" Tatsuo nodded to his right.

"What is it?" Gasan asked, squinting at the collection of dilapidated buildings.

"You can smell it. They let the *eta* live there. That stench? That's the tanners. I saw some amputees on the way in too. They all live as one."

Gasan's face was one of disgust. "Urgh. The filthy animals. Why do they tolerate such abominations?"

Tatsuo shrugged. "There is no civilisation in places like these. It is just a melting pot of degeneration."

Gasan could feel the bile rising up in his throat. He could not believe that people could live like this, and he viewed them as little more than savages.

Presently Tamazaki returned. "Chief Nagamasa wants to see you immediately. Remember your manners or you will lose your heads."

The two men bowed again and knelt as the entrance door was slid back to reveal a gloomy interior. A grunt from the shadows of the dark chamber indicated that they were to enter. Gasan and Tatsuo shuffled into the room and prostrated themselves on the hard matted floor.

A figure stepped forward. Nagamasa – the bandit chief – was unusually tall for his people, and his broad torso filled his armor. Against the conventions of the day, he wore an open-faced helmet at all times, because one such as he was always on guard against assassination attempts.

Nagamasa considered the small bag of possessions that Tamazaki had claimed the two men had been carrying; a long staff, a sword, and some rice and cold vegetables. This was hardly what he would consider a successful haul from a night of raiding.

"You," the Chief barked, indicating to Gasan who raised himself slightly. "You're a monk?"

"Yes My Lord," Gasan replied, careful to use the formal term.

"You're a Sohei?" Nagamasa was eyeing the long staff.

"No My Lord, I'm a…"

Tamazaki savagely kicked out at the prone man. "You were not asked what you were. Just answer the question you are asked. Nothing more."

Gasan acknowledged the man, bowing low again, and muttering an apology. It did not feel as if his ribs had been broken, but they would certainly be bruised.

Nagamasa was smiling. He turned to Tatsuo and said, "You are not a monk."

"No My Lord."

"You are Bujin. What clan did you belong to?"

"My Lord, I am Soma."

Nagamasa narrowed his eyes. A few stragglers from the Battle of Yeddo Plain had made it this far. They had not made it any further. "Why are you with this monk?"

"My Lord, we are on a mission for Lord Soma."

Nagamasa eyes widened with shock. "Tadashige is alive?"

"No My Lord…" Tatsuo replied. He wanted to say more but remembered Gasan's punishment for answering questions he had not been asked.

"Hmmm…" Nagamasa mused. "Then his son survives. What errand has he sent you on with this monk?"

"My Lord, we are on our way to Ise."

"To report the attack on the Inzai Valley, no doubt. Do you seek their support?"

"Yes My Lord."

Nagamasa considered this for a moment before turning to Tamazaki and whispering to him. The junior man muttered something in return, and the Bandit Chief turned back to the two prone men.

"Very well. You may pass through our territory. Tamazaki and his men will escort you to the ferry at Irago where you will be given provisions. If we can, we will arrange safe passage for you on the other side. Maybe horses too. You will leave immediately."

*

Utsunomiya Castle
Ashikaga watched the mounted warriors leave through the main gate, Altera leading the battalion, and turned to his son. "Well? Did she take the bait?"

Yoshiakira bowed low. "Honorable father, I believe that Lady Altera supports you and your position."

Ashikaga frowned. This was unexpected. "Hmmm… nevertheless, I want our spies to report her every movement. We are close to our goal, my son. I do not want any…unforeseen factors to sway us from our destiny."

*

Kurama Temple
Kwon sighed loudly and rolled his eyes. How did he always attract this sort of trouble?

More than a hundred Sohei – the warrior guardians of The Temple – surrounded the foreigner, and each was equipped with a razor sharp spear. More importantly, they appeared to be very, *very* angry.

Kwon tried again. "I am here for Sojobo."

As one, the crowd of warriors cried out and jabbed their spears towards him menacingly.

A voice rang out. "Peace my Brethren." The circle of Sohei opened slightly, allowing a tall upright old man to pass through and address the foreigner. "My Lord," the elderly man said, nodding his head imperceptibly. "You have come at a time of great trouble. What is your business here?"

Kwon scratched his head. "It's a little complicated…"

"Your thoughts betray you My Lord. Most things are very simple when they are unraveled. I ask again, what is your business here?"

Kwon shrugged. "I seek to join you. I seek sanctuary from the world."

The old man smiled. "But there is more to it than that. You must know it is forbidden for us to admit foreigners."

"I do. I had a dream that the mountain was a center of power and peace…" Kwon replied.

"My Lord," the old man interrupted. "Please do not seek to deceive us. Your… untruths are quite transparent."

Kwon sighed. "Very well. The truth? I have traveled far… across more kingdoms that you know exist. There was a sign – the three stars? You saw them?"

The old man inclined his head. "We did."

"Then understand this. I am not like you. Any of you. Those stars… I am unable to see them. But in the land I come from my… comrades told me of their appearance and I was guided here. I believe that something very powerful will come here. Not soon, you understand. But in the years to come. And I must be here, to prepare for when it arrives… to help mold it into what it must become."

"That is quite a story Foreigner. However, I sense that you believe it. Still, as I have said, it is forbidden…"

"Master," Kwon said, addressing the man formally. "I know the rules. I know your laws. Do they not say that you admit worthy men and worthy men alone?"

Abbot Shimada inclined his head again. "That is our law. But you must know that we do not consider foreigners to be worthy. You are all barbarians who would pollute such a place like this."

"Then let me prove it to you," Kwon replied. "Let me show you my worth."

Shimada was satisfied to play the foreigner's game. "What trial would you suggest?"

"As I was trying to explain to your… acolytes here. Let me slay Sojobo. I will find The Tengu King and I will bring you his head."

"Even if such a thing could be accomplished, what would this prove?" Shimada smiled, knowing the impossibility of the foreigner's proposal. No mortal man could best The Tengu King.

"It would prove that I have skills to offer The Temple. I could teach your Sohei… if they are willing."

Shimada narrowed his eyes. Despite the foreigner's swagger, the abbot sensed that he at least believed in what he was saying. "My Lord, you have no spear or polearm. What skills do you believe you possess?"

Kwon reached to his side and presented his sheathed sword. "Fencing," he said. "Like none you have ever seen."

Shimada's heart sank at the man's delusion. "My Lord, such weapons are the preserve of Bujin. I agree that they have their place in single combat. However, you must understand that the trials we face are on the battlefield, with many soldiers about us. And against Sojobo? You have no chance."

"Very well, let me show you. Select your five best warriors and let them attack me. They may make kill moves. My sword will remain sheathed at all times."

Shimada had heard such arrogant boasts before, and they had all ended the same way. However, if this foreigner invited death, then who was he to deny a madman his final wish? The Abbot nodded to a number of the Sohei that surrounded Kwon.

Five men stepped forward and moved in a circle, surrounding the foreigner. With well practiced movements they began their attack. The first brought his spear down, cutting from above, whilst the second jabbed at the figure in the center. Kwon deftly parried each stroke with his sheathed sword, but made no offensive move, instead letting the report of hardened sharkskin against wood echo across the stone courtyard.

The two men began again; their strikes delivered quicker and with more force while a third joined them. Again, Kwon deftly deflected their strokes, this time side-stepping neatly and catching the shin of one of his attackers with his foot sending him stumbling forward.

The fourth jabbed in and using the hand-guard of his sword, Kwon similarly unbalanced him and sent him careening into the first.

"Enough," Abbot Shimada said loudly, clapping his hands together and then approached Kwon. "Who are you?" he asked.

"Kwon," the mercenary replied, bowing his head.

"That is a Tianxian name. Yet you are neither Tianxian nor of this land."

"I spent... some time in Tianxia. I take a name that people are comfortable with."

"I see," Shimada responded. "You have considerable skill with the sword. What style is it that you practice?"

"It is a hybrid... an amalgamation. I have been fortunate to have had many teachers over the years and have adapted the most favorable techniques of each into my own."

"In Oyashima, we do not consider this to be something to proud of. A student should pledge fidelity to one master, and one master alone. It is unseemly to spend a little time with each like some common courtesan."

"My path has been long," Kwon replied, no longer bowing but meeting the older man's eye. "It has not always been possible to remain in one place long enough to learn all of a master's secrets."

"I see. You have an interesting story Tianxian-who-is-not-of-Tianxia. Maybe I will hear more of it. Could you teach my Sohei what you have learned?"

Kwon nodded. "I could. With your permission, of course."

"Of course," Shimada smiled. "Then I give you leave to find The Tengu King. If you return with Sojobo's head, I will petition The High Council to admit you and if you meet our requirements, you will be granted the rank of Master. Is this agreeable?"

Kwon put his sword back into his belt. "It is. Now, which way to this goblin of yours?"

*

Utsunomiya Castle

Masijiro, Hatamoto to Lord Yoshiakira, crossed the courtyard, and presented himself to his lord's house.

"Enter," the Shogun's son said.

The door slid open and Masijiro shuffled in and prostrated himself on the soft matted floor, hearing the door slide closed behind him.

"Masijiro, my father has commanded that Lady Altera is to be observed during her expedition to the east. You will dispatch one of our agents in compliance with this order."

"My Lord, very good," Masijiro replied without raising himself.

"There is more. Our agent will always report that Lady Altera is a loyal servant and vassal of the Shogun, regardless of her actions. Is that understood?"

"My Lord, as you command," Masijiro replied again.

*

The road to Port Choshi

Watanabe sat in silence with Otsuno. It had been several weeks since the incident at the tavern and the old monk had still to give The Governor a satisfactory explanation of what had really happened on the road. The two men sat in the onsen, letting the warm spring waters soothe away the aches of their travels.

They had found this small village almost by chance and Otsuno seemed not to recognize it. To Watanabe this meant either it was relatively new, or that they were getting further and further from the regions that the monk was familiar with. The Governor suspected the latter and, whilst Port Choshi could only be another two weeks away, it placed them all in greater danger. If Otsuno was in an unfamiliar area and did not know the secret paths, then it meant they would have to use the main road, and that would increase the risk of running into Ashikaga's men.

"Your mind is very loud today," said Otsuno, his eyes still closed as he inhaled the steam.

"Master, we have all been through much. I was simply… reflecting. Jion will be six tomorrow."

"He had mentioned it to me," the monk replied. "But he does not wish the occasion to be marked. He says that was his old life and the circumstances of his new one do not merit such an extravagance."

"Master, your bond with the boy grows." Watanabe tried and failed to keep the note of jealousy from his voice.

The old monk smiled and opened his eyes. "It is simply the relationship between master and student. You should know that."

Watanabe remembered well. He saw the way Otsuno had taken the boy under his wing and had begun what rudimentary training their travels allowed, and it reminded him of the relationship he too had once had with his former teacher.

The Governor tried to change the subject. "Master, Jion's training is coming along. He seems to have many skills."

Otsuno made no reply but eyed Watanabe carefully, the smile fading from his face.

"Master," Watanabe continued. "Do you think that Jion can really restore the Clan? Unite the Provinces against Ashikaga?"

"Be careful Watanabe. He will become what he will become, not what you wish he would. Remember your training; a man's fate is a man's fate…"

"… and life is but an illusion." Watanabe finished the recitation. "I remember, Master. Perhaps it is better that we return to matters closer to hand. I know that the young Lord does not wish his birthday to be marked, but maybe we can do something when get to Port Choshi. He is too young for a Willow House, but maybe…"

"Ah Watanabe. It will be many months before we are in the port."

The Governor's eyes widened. "Master?"

"Can't you smell it? The change in the air?"

Watanabe shook his head and said nothing.

"The snows are coming. They are early this year. And they will be severe. The back roads will be impassable within two days. The main road within a week."

"Should we leave now? Get as close to Choshi as we can?"

Otsuno shook his head. "No. The port will be crowded. Too many people asking too many questions. I have already spoken to the inn-keeper here; the boy can work in the kitchens and the girls can help serve. The locals are sympathetic to our cause."

"Master," Watanabe bowed his head, acknowledging the wisdom of the older man's action but secretly furious that he had not been consulted about such an important decision. "What about me? What shall I do?"

Otsuno shrugged. "As you will. The local farms have brought their harvests in, but there will be plenty of work no doubt. Maintenance…"

Watanabe's nostrils flared in indignation. "You wish me to be a craftsman? But Master, such a thing is below my station."

The old monk continued to smile. "As the boy said, that was in your old life."

In the room above the two men, Jion sat cross-legged with his eyes closed, listening to the conversation below.

Masako whispered, "What can you hear?"

Jion shook his head. "They are just talking about wintering here. I am to work in the kitchen and you two are to help serve. We could be here several months. Master Otsuno says the snow will be severe."

"I'll not serve common peasants," Masako retorted too loudly. "I am a Lady of Nawa and…"

"Sshhh," Gozen chided. "We are not ladies any more. Not until our clans are restored." Turning to Jion she continued, "What else are they saying?"

"That's it," the boy replied. "It's gone quiet."

Masako sulked. "Maybe Sensei killed the old monk for his impudence… hey!"

Gozen had pinched her young sister. "Master Otsuno is just trying to look after us."

Masako crossed her arms and stuck out her bottom lip, her eyebrows knitting together in a frown.

Gozen returned to Jion. "What about in the village? Can you hear anything out there?"

Both of the girls had become aware of Jion's growing abilities when they had seen him take his sandals off for the first time on the road. Gozen had asked Otsuno to train her as well, and although she possessed none of Jion's talents, she could feel her mind becoming quieter and more controlled. Masako refused to join her older sister, saying that such things were beneath a lady and she would stick to praying to her kami the way her parents had done.

Jion leaned forward, and placed both hands on the wooden floor, listening to the sounds of the village. "There is not much going on. There's a couple of foxes on the edge of the wood. The monk at the shrine is wishing that his apprentice could make better cha. The blacksmith is complaining to the Headman about the tanners who serve the village. He says that an amputee has joined them and this bodes ill for..."

The door swung open, Otsuno entered the room, and begun to light the evening lanterns, noting that the children had still not tidied away their bedrolls from the morning.

"Ah," the monk said. "I see you are no longer listening to *our* conversation young Jion."

The boy reddened but said nothing.

"Very well then. We have the time it takes to burn this incense stick before it is mealtime. I would suggest some training. Gozen, will you join us?"

The older girl bowed her head in acceptance, her long black hair falling forward as she did so.

She's becoming a woman, Otsuno thought. *Maybe it is time to ensure she was dressed as such.* The old man decided that at the very least a lesson in hairdressing was required and made a mental note to speak to the innkeeper's wife.

"And what about you Masako? Will you join us?"

The younger girl shook her head.

"I understand. I believe that Sensei Watanabe is downstairs. Perhaps you could go and help him." Otsuno knew he could nothing with those who did not want to receive instruction. Masako left the room without the customary bow, and the monk made another note to speak to her governor about the young girl's etiquette.

Gozen brought one of the lanterns that Otsuno had lit to the center of the room and took the stick of incense from the old monk and lit that too before quickly blowing out the flame so that the fragranced smoke might filter throughout the room.

"Now," Otsuno began as the children sat cross-legged and closed their eyes. "Clear your mind. Let your thoughts be like the waters of a still pool on a summer day. Imagine that you are walking down a set of stairs deep into yourself. The further down you go, the further away the world is, until there is no world beyond the walls of this room. Deeper… deeper…"

Otsuno could sense Jion's mind becoming still, until it was almost imperceptible even to those experienced in such practices. Gozen's was following suit, although the girl displayed none of the raw ability of the monk's new apprentice. Still, the way in which both children had grasped the concepts of meditation and discipline was quite remarkable. Both were learning in weeks what had taken him months, and sometimes even years, to grasp.

"Deeper… until there is no world beyond yourself," Otsuno continued. "Deeper… until there is no you. And now there is simply nothing. Let yourself go… become unbound in the void."

Otsuno could sense that the girl was struggling with this final part; fighting against the final act of rejecting the concept of 'self' to become one with all. In contrast, Jion had completely relinquished himself. It was as though the boy was both land and air, and yet neither. His young face was serene, somewhere between a deep sleep and death. What little of Jion's essence that could be sensed was fast dissipating, like smoke on a soft breeze. The boy was both everywhere and nowhere.

"Now," Otsuno intoned, "reach out. Flow through the world. Do not sense the mountain. Be the mountain. Do not notice the stream. Be the flowing water. Do not…"

"Master!" Jion cried, breaking his master's reverie.

Otsuno's eyes snapped open. The boy seemed to be floating, just an inch or two from the ground, and his head had lolled backwards so that only the whites of his eyes showed and his short black hair seemed suspended.

The monk has never seen such a thing and tried to keep a note of panic out of his voice. "There is no master. There is only the life of the world for we are all one with…"

"Master!" Jion cried again. "A great darkness is coming!"

CHAPTER THREE

February 1357 – Irago Cape

Gasan felt relief flow through his body as he watched the figure of the bandit Tamazaki returning to the tavern where he and Tatsuo were staying. When the winter had arrived, it was the most severe in living memory. Blizzards had seen all of the roads become impassable and gales had whipped the seas into a frenzy, forcing the cancelation of all the ferries. Worse, the unexpected cold snap had caught out the rice farmers with many being unable to harvest their crops and, with the fisherman unable to put to sea because of the storms, food was becoming scarce.

Over the course of the winter, Gasan and Tatsuo had become as friendly with Tamazaki and his men as was possible under the circumstances. All were former bujin and, whilst none of them particularly enjoyed their new life of banditry, each viewed it as being necessary to survive. Such concepts were incomprehensible to Tatsuo, who had always been brought up to throw himself on to his sword should his lord command it, regardless of reason. However, the vassal of Lord Soma had seen the sense of holding his tongue.

Despite the cold of the preceding months, the first week of February had been unseasonably warm, and hope had sprung that their journey could resume. Every day Tamazaki had gone to the port to see if the ferry was running and every day he had returned with disappointing news. Today was to be different.

"Pack your things," Tamazaki grunted. "The ferry leaves in one hour."

Gasan beamed and ran into the house to pack what few belongings he had, but Tatsuo did not move.

"I believe that the time has arrived," Lord Soma's retainer said to the bandit.

"It has," Tamazaki replied, and entered the tavern before kneeling on the uncomfortable matted floor. "Sit and I will say my piece. You will reaffirm your promise?" The atmosphere had become still and tense.

"I promise," Tatsuo began, "that regardless of what you tell me, I will still make my way to Ise, and shall seek harm neither to you nor your men."

The reason for Nagamasa's unexpected benevolence had been a source of constant speculation between Gasan and Tatsuo throughout the whole winter. By rights, they should have been put to death, but whenever Tamazaki had been asked about it he had smiled and not replied. In frustration, Tatsuo had finally made the man swear to reveal his secret the day they were to depart Irago, and Tamazaki had agreed on the provision that neither Gasan nor Tatsuo sought retribution.

"Very well. Nagamasa believes that, if a Lord of Soma is still alive, then he will act as a rallying point for all the other lords who oppose Ashikaga."

Tatsuo's browed knitted together. "That's it?"

"That's it."

"Nagamasa seeks Ashikaga's death? Why?"

Tamazaki smiled. "Nagamasa does not seek Ashikaga's death."

Violence rose in Tatsuo's voice. "Do not mock me, bandit."

"You would be wise to control yourself in a place where you have… few friends."

"Then tell me – what is Nagamasa's plan?"

"There is no plan. Nagamasa merely seeks for there to be an opposition to Ashikaga."

"What? Why? Speak plainly before I cut it out of you."

Tamazaki had seen Tatsuo's hand go to his sword. With the benefit of hindsight, it might have been a mistake returning it to him, but the bandit remembered his days as a bujin and what his sword had meant to him. "Nagamasa seeks conflict. Not to engage in it himself you understand – the risk of injury is too great. But to have two forces constantly warring… it suits him. The more war there is, then the more ronin there are. In the last five years alone, Nagamasa's forces have increased ten-fold and his treasury a hundred. War is profitable."

Tatsuo was shocked at what he was hearing. "Is that all that is important to you? Profit?"

"What else is there? To die an honorable bujin death? Let me tell you something Soma, I have seen death and it doesn't matter if you die well or not. You are still dead."

When he spoke, Tatsuo's voice was low. "May the Buddha forgive you."

Tamazaki threw his head back and brayed loudly. "The Buddha? Ha! Did our masters not teach us that salvation comes through ourselves? Our lives are what we make of them."

Tatsuo slowly shook his head in disgust. "So what will happen when Lord Soma defeats Ashikaga?"

"*If* Ashikaga is defeated then Nagamasa will back the next agitator. If Ashikaga wins then Nagamasa will find some other dispossessed son who seeks revenge and similarly back him. Don't you see? It's not about Ashikaga or Soma or even The Chrysanthemum Throne…"

"It's about chaos," Tatsuo interrupted. "That's what Nagamasa really wants. He's been a bandit for so long that he can only exist through other people's suffering."

"Maybe. But every day he recruits more warriors. Every time a village is sacked, more tradesmen and farmers find their way to him. If you live long enough to see our camp again it will be transformed. You know, it started out as just a few tents. Then there were a few huts. The day we left, stonemasons were bringing in the first shipments from the quarries. Nagamasa will make a very fine life for all who join him."

"You don't really believe that, do you?"

Tamazaki paused before replying. "I do," he said. "I really do. Now, pack your things and let's get you to Ise. See if we can't prolong this war just a little longer."

*

The road to Port Choshi

Lady Altera was seething. The sudden snowfall had caught her out, and seemingly every other patrol too. They had been forced to winter in some blasted hovel of a village as their horses went lame and then died. This had further enraged Altera, as the beasts-of-burden in her own land would never have been so weak and useless. Now the snows had melted they had continued their journey eastwards and were now less than three days from Port Choshi. In all that time, their prey had remained elusive.

"My Lady," Ullar said bowing his head. "I bring news."

Altera ground her teeth and said, "What is it?"

"My Lady, our patrols have returned from their sweep of nearby villages."

"And?"

"There is no sign of our quarry, but the locals confirmed that the last of the snows have melted and the roads to the coast are now clear. We have also been able to secure more horses. They are being saddled as we speak."

Altera looked to the corner where The Hunter sat cross-legged, seeming to look through the flimsy walls of the house and out across the country. She was amazed at his resilience – it was unheard of for one of his kind to last this long - but he had seemed to accept the situation and weather it well. "Hunter!" Altera barked. "What is the position of that which we seek?"

The Hunter's response was near monotone. "East by North-East. And in ascension."

Altera looked to Ullar in confusion and then back to The Hunter. This was new. "What do you mean 'in ascension'?"

"The spark is now a fire. Soon this world will burn."

*

Port Choshi

Otsuno sat cross-legged watching the sleeping form of Jion and the two girls, as the dying embers of the sun cast their final glow across the sky. Outside, the life of the day was packing itself away in preparation for the coming darkness, whilst those that inhabited the night had begun to prowl the lengthening shadows. Prostitutes called to potential customers, the beggars moved off to be replaced by peddlers, and footpads skulked in the shadows of alleys as they observed ripe targets entering the taverns.

The old monk was amazed at how peacefully the children slept, knowing that danger was not far behind them. Jion seemed to show no trauma after his last episode. For nearly three weeks, the boy had been unconscious, seeming to float between two worlds, and they had only been able to sustain him by bringing a little fish soup to his parched lips. As predicted, the snowfall had been sudden and severe, closing all the roads, but when the boy had eventually opened his eyes, he appeared to be accepting the situation. Otsuno had probed him on what he remembered, but the boy claimed amnesia. However, when the old monk pretended to sleep, he had heard Jion whispering to Masako about another place; a land of purple skies, great creatures, and, more importantly, his communion with The Goddess Marishiten.

The snows had lasted longer than even Otsuno had expected and they had been forced to sell the horses to cover their keep at the tavern. However when the melt finally came, they had made good time to Port Choshi. It had been many years since the old monk had last been here and the village was now a bustling town full of noise and commerce.

Huge cauldrons boiled and bubbled, by turns rendering the blubber from the occasional whale that had been caught, and turning fish carcasses into glue. The whole town reeked of the sea and death. Yet it was not this that bothered Otsuno as much as it was the way of the people.

Merchants were everywhere. Buying. Trading. Selling. All for their little profit. Otsuno remembered a time before, when men were servants of the lords who acted as protectors over them. Now… the old monk saw something else in the eyes of the townsmen; a hunger in their souls that they tried to sate by buying lavish robes, ornate belts and shiny trinkets. The local lord was hardly seen and his vassals would only make an appearance to collect the taxes.

Otsuno was not surprised when he heard that there were fewer and fewer visitors to the nearby temple. People seemed to have replaced the *kami* of the town with glittering baubles. He had, of course, made his way to The Temple, but this too was transformed since his last visit. Now it was a place of worship to Ashikaga's Pure Land Sect. It was a gesture by The Scourge of The Chrysanthemum Throne to assuage the wrath of the countless warriors who had, over the years, fallen because of his imagined pride and honor. The bloody vengeance of the *Onryo* – the angry spirits of dead bujin – was legendary, and no Lord would dare tempt their wrath unless he was sure of his own kami.

Such temples were becoming more common, and whilst Otsuno did not object to their particular interpretation of the teachings of the Buddha, there were whispers in the countryside that there... there was something else. There was gossip of dark shrines within The Temples, hidden from view, which twisted the minds of all who worshipped there. Some even said the kami themselves were of the night, and that the endless cycle of light and dark was becoming unbalanced. At the moment, these were simply rumors, but the old monk sensed that there was more to Ashikaga's temples than met the eye.

The town should have been preparing for the *Hanami* Festival – the viewing of the cherry blossoms whose buds were swollen on the otherwise bare trees that lined the streets. However, there was no preparation. Instead, all the talk Otsuno heard was of trade and merchants and profit.

The door of the room slid open, and Watanabe bowed his head before entering.

"Master," The Governor said. "I believe that I have found us a captain."

"Very good," Otsuno replied, trying to disguise his obvious relief. He was ill at ease in this town, and would be glad to leave. "Where is he?"

"Master, he is downstairs in the tavern, waiting to speak to you." Watanabe's tone was curt.

A distance had grown between the two men over the winter. Despite Watanabe's protestations, Jion had continued his training once he had recovered from his experience, and had been joined by Masako who appeared to realize the benefits it brought her older sister. For his part, The Governor had done as his former master had instructed, and had undertaken maintenance for the local farmers over the winter, much to the consternation of his pride. What time he had been able to spend with the children was committed to continuing their lessons, and this too had been unsatisfying. Whilst Gozen and Masako showed exceptional skills in calligraphy and memorizing their family histories, other talents began to manifest. Both girls showed great potential in archery, and Masako was becoming quite the expert with the spear. Gozen had nearly mastered the tea ceremony, and her poetry and dance were as beautiful and accomplished as a woman twice her age.

Jion remained a disappointment. His footwork was clumsy, his artistry lackluster, and his mind seemed to fail to absorb even the most basic principles that Watanabe tried to teach. Several times The Governor had wondered if the wrong brother had died, but then he would catch Otsuno's eye and hurriedly try to quieten his thoughts.

The boy's only redeeming quality was his sword-work, which was better than average but was not worthy of note. Still, Watanabe was relieved to see Jion was becoming aware of the significance of the *Ishin Blade*, and had even taken to sleeping with it clutched in his small hands.

"The children will be safe here," said Otsuno, standing and stretching. "Let's go and meet this captain." The old monk closed the door behind them, and two men padded as quietly as possible down the stairs to the tavern below.

There were a few patrons sitting on the straw mats, but Otsuno was able to identify immediately the skipper as they entered the room. He was younger than the old monk had expected, perhaps in his late twenties, with short dark hair and a thin weathered face that suggested that he had lived more of his life at sea than on land.

Standing, the captain bowed his head, but sat back down before the old monk could return the pleasantry.

"Master," Watanabe began, "this is Captain Kagetaka of The Sophia."

"The Sophia?" Otsuno said. "That is not a name of Oyashima."

Kagetaka smiled. "No. She was designed by a foreigner."

"A barbarian?" Otsuno said. "We hear so many tales of them these days, but we have never seen one."

Kagetaka shrugged. "This one was washed up in the north of Yamato. My father was fishing and rescued him. In gratitude, he pledged his life to my family, and we discovered that he was a great ship builder. All his people are. He helped my father design many fishing boats for our village. But when the taxes became too much… he helped build my ship so that we could find other sources of income."

Otsuno knew well enough what the captain meant. Piracy. There were tales – mostly of smuggling contraband between Oyashima and Tianxia, but occasionally there were stories of fishing fleets being sunk and remote coastal hamlets being raided and looted.

"How fast is she?" Otsuno asked.

"What's your cargo?"

"Just my apprentice and myself, and three children."

"Your apprentice tells me you want to get to Yokohama."

"That's right."

"That's not going to be easy. Ashikaga has built his own fleet. It put to sea last year and since then my… usual routes have become harder to navigate without being intercepted. I'm guessing that you're not going to want us to be boarded. Am I right, old man?"

Otsuno did not react to the slight. He was used to the ways of corsairs and their dogs. "We do not."

Kagetaka nodded. "Very well. The voyage will take a week. Maybe less."

"That's fast."

"She's a good ship - none like her on the seas. But it will cost you."

"How much?"

"I'm not taking any *koku* here old man. Rice is worthless in a place like this."

Otsuno was not surprised. The town had become twisted, valuing what could not be eaten over what could. "You'll want the Tianxian coins. The Ming?"

Kagetaka nodded. "It's the only thing that is worth a damn these days."

Otsuno tried not to smile. "Very well. I have a few here…" The old monk began to grasp for the small bag on his belt.

"A few?" Kagetaka said, stopping Otsuno in mid reach. "It's going to cost you a thousand!"

Watanabe eyes widened in shock and indignation. "A thousand? Master, this is outrageous!"

"It does seem very high," Otsuno said in a more conciliatory tone.

Kagetaka smirked. "You'll find no other ship to take you, and if a captain says that he can outrun Ashikaga's fleet then he's a liar."

Otsuno paused, and then spoke again. "Very well. Give us a few days."

"Contact me when you are ready." Kagetaka stood, bowed, and left whilst the two men returned to the bottom of the stairs that led to their room.

"Master," Watanabe hissed. "Such a sum… it is impossible."

Otsuno brought his finger to his lips, and rolled his eyes towards the ceiling, indicating that Jion was listening. Gently, the old monk slid the door to their room and entered, followed by Watanabe. For a moment, both men sat in silence, contemplating recent events.

"Jion," Otsuno said warmly. "You do not have to pretend to be asleep."

The boy turned over, looked at his master, but said nothing. Although it took all his concentration, Otsuno had honed his own skills so that he could now just about sense the boy. Although the range was short, it had proved useful in locating the children when they first arrived in Port Choshi and they had insisted on exploring.

"Did you listen to our conversation downstairs?"

The boy nodded, but again remained silent.

"What do you think?"

Watanabe was stunned that his master should ask the boy's counsel, but held his tongue.

Jion sat up, crossing his legs. "The Captain believes what he is saying; The Sophia is the only ship that can outrun Ashikaga's fleet."

Otsuno nodded. "Do you sense any other captain who would be willing to take us?"

Jion shook his head. "No, Master. Sensei Watanabe has… drawn attention to us by seeking passage to Yokohama. The other captains talk amongst themselves. They do not know our true identities but some suspect that we are fugitives."

"I see," Otsuno replied, and then looked to Watanabe. "It was a calculated risk. But if one of the other pirate captains thinks that he can claim a bounty by informing on us… we should tread carefully." Turning back to Jion, the old monk continued. "How much do you think Kagetaka would accept? Can we negotiate with him?"

"No," Jion replied. "I don't think that he is even that bothered about the money."

"Then what does he want?"

The boy was silent and looked to the floor.

"Jion," Watanabe said. "Your master asked you a question."

The young Lord Soma looked up. "He has seen Gozen… walking outside, through the town. He… desires her."

"Hmmm…" Otsuno mulled this development. "Maybe we can use this to our advantage."

"Master!" Watanabe said in shock. "You cannot be serious. The girl has only just turned ten. That is far too young to…"

Otsuno held up a hand to silence his apprentice. "I did not say that we should give her to him. Just that we could use his desire to our advantage."

"How?" Jion asked.

"I don't know," Otsuno replied, half distracted by his own thoughts. "If we did find the money The Captain seeks, would he honor the deal?"

Jion nodded. "I believe so."

"And do you have any idea how we might raise such fortune?"

The boy was silent for a moment, and then answered. "Yes Master. I believe I do."

Otsuno narrowed his eyes, sensing something stirring within the boy. It was bad enough that he was bent on revenge, although the old monk was using all his skills to ensure his ward sought a better path, but now… he sensed that Jion was learning the ways of Men too quickly, without understanding what they really meant. "Let me hear it," he said eventually.

"Master, there is a house, at the other end of the city, where men place wagers."

Watanabe tensed, knowing the establishment – The Coming Dawn. Gambling was frowned upon and generally discouraged in Oyashima. Where such premises did exist they were tolerated, and in recent years The Governor had heard many tales of debauchery and vice; debts not being honored, Women of The Willow being forced into servitude, and even assassination. Such a den was no place for a child.

Otsuno replied, "You seek to place a wager?"

Jion shrugged. "Yes Master. They play *Igo* there. I could best any man. I know I could."

The game of Igo was centuries old and played by everyone from children to The Emperor himself. Generally accepted to be of Tianxian origin, players placed stones on a small grid, encircling each other until one side could no longer move. It was said that grandmasters could foresee the end of the game merely by the positioning of their opponents first stone. In towns such as Choshi, there were grand tournaments where fortunes were made and lost.

Otsuno smiled. "You think you could win an Igo Tournament?"

"Master, I do," Jion replied. "They are holding them every night. But late, when the players are already intoxicated."

Otsuno looked to Watanabe. "How good is the boy?"

Watanabe looked to his ward and then back to his master. "I must speak plainly. It has been many months since our Lord played and even then…" his voice trailed off for fear of causing offense.

The old monk understood well enough. "I see. Still, much has changed about our Lord since then. Perhaps you would play a few rounds with me first of all?"

Jion bowed his head in acceptance and Watanabe moved to the door where he called for the maid to bring them a board and a set of stones. She returned a few minutes later, presenting the set to The Governor before bowing low and leaving.

Otsuno set the board between himself and Jion, and offered the boy a set of polished pebbles. Jion took the white set, allowing his master to go first with the black stones. The monk smiled and placed his first stone.

Thirty minutes later, Otsuno frowned. That was the third game he had lost. During the first, he had been deliberately timid, allowing the boy to win in order to build his confidence. During the second, he had made things harder for Jion, but made enough deliberate errors to let the boy find a way to victory. The third game had been for real, and Otsuno was surprised to find himself defeated in under sixty moves.

"Did you teach him?" the monk asked Watanabe, as he reset the board

The Governor shook his in wonderment. "No. He never had an aptitude for it."

The next game lasted barely fifty moves, and Otsuno was flummoxed. The boy seemed to not only read his every move, but also anticipate every variable and permutation. The sound of stones on the board had woken Gozen and Masako, and although they remained on their bedrolls each had turned to watch the unfolding scene.

Otsuno reset the board again. Jion quickly won the game and Otsuno sat back in bewilderment, scratching his stubbly chin and eyeing Jion cautiously.

"Master," Watanabe said. "With your permission, may I…?"

"By all means," the monk replied, and moved across, allowing The Governor to take his place at the board.

Watanabe fared no better, and reset the board only to be defeated even more quickly.

The Governor looked to Otsuno and shrugged. "Master, he has… improved."

The old monk shuffled around to Jion, and spoke gently to the boy. "Lord, can you tell me how you… are able to win so easily."

The child shrugged and looked to the floor, fearing that he had caused offense.

"It is alright," Otsuno said soothingly. "I am simply trying to… understand."

"Master, it's like an echo," Jion said. "You place a stone and the board echoes back to you, telling you where the next piece will go."

"And you hear this echo?"

Jion shook his head. "No Master. I see it. Like a wave on the ocean. I can see where it will break on the shore and what sand it will drag out with it."

Otsuno thought he understood. He picked up a stone, put his hands behind his back, and then brought his clenched fists out again. "What hand is the stone in?"

"Master, it is your left."

The monk opened his hand revealing the stone. "Again," he said, putting his hands behind his back again.

"Master, it is in your left again."

Otsuno smiled and opened his hand to show the boy was right again. Turning to Watanabe, he said, "Please. Follow me."

Both men exited the room and slid the door shut.

"Now," the monk's voice came. "Where is the stone?"

Jion did not hesitate. "Sensei Watanabe has placed it on his head."

There was a pause from beyond the closed door. "And now?" said Otsuno.

"Master, it is under your right armpit."

"And now?"

"Master, you have placed it into your belt."

The door slid back and the two men entered the room. "It would seem that your skills are increasing," Otsuno said. "Look about the tavern. Tell me what else this echoing flow tells you."

Jion was silent as he cast his eyes around the room. "There are very few patrons downstairs. The innkeeper is worried that a nearby establishment is taking all his business and is considering whether he can afford to bribe their cook to start a fire and burn it down… He will go through with it, but the cook will report him to his master. The two men will fight and the innkeeper will be stabbed and die by the end of the week. One of the maids is worried about her father's debt. She will attempt to enter The Willow World, but will incorrectly apply the suppository and bear a child by the end of the year. It will be a boy who will die within three months. The maid's father will disown her. The stable boy is not concentrating on mucking out, but is thinking about a girl. He is too close to a horse that does not like him. It is going to step on his…"

A yelp from the rear of the building told them that the horse had indeed trodden on the stable boy's foot.

"And you can tell all this from… this flow."

Jion nodded, sensing that he was pleasing his master. "Yes Master. It sort of… it bounces from one thing to the other, causing an effect each time."

"And you can see where it will bounce to and what the effect will be?"

"Yes Master. But also where it has been."

Otsuno's eyes widened. "You can see into the past?"

Jion shook his head. "No Master. Not really. Well sort of." The boy took the Igo board and picked up a stone. "It's like this," he continued and flicked the stone, letting it bounce off the side of the board. "If I flick the stone like this, it will always land there," he said. "It doesn't matter how many times I do it. If I flick like this," he flicked the stone again, "it will always land there. So if you know that I have flicked the stone, and it is there, then you can tell how I flicked."

Otsuno looked to Watanabe in awe.

The Governor leaned forward. "So you are saying that you cannot see the past or the future, but you can deduce it? From where things are now?"

Jion shrugged. "Yes Sensei. I guess."

Otsuno realized the Watanabe had yet to grasp the magnitude of what the child was saying, and looked back to the boy. "Lord, how far can you… deduce?"

"Master, not far. The future is harder. It's like if I throw a rock into a pond; I know where the first ripples will appear, but it becomes harder to tell the further they spread out."

"I see," said Otsuno. "Lord, what do you see for our party?"

"We will make it to the Yugyo Monastery. After that, I cannot tell."

The monk pressed him. "And how will we get there?"

"On Captain Kagetaka's ship. We will be able to afford it from my winnings from the Igo game tomorrow night."

Watanabe and Otsuno exchanged a look, and the monk continued, "Lord, the game will no doubt require a significant stake if you are to win such a vast sum of money. Where we will get this stake from?"

Jion looked to Gozen and then back to Otsuno. "Captain Kagetaka desires Gozen. If you ask him to stake me he will accept Gozen as collateral."

The older girl gasped. "Jion! No!"

"It will be alright," the boy said. "I will win."

"But you said that you cannot be certain. The further out you look the less certain things are."

"Yes, but these are weeks and months, not days," Jion replied calmly.

Masako placed a reassuring hand on Gozen's arm. "It will be fine. It is the only way. Have faith in our Lord."

*

Utsunomiya Castle

Ashikaga stood on the castle balcony, watching the last trickle of people enter the castle before the gates were shut and barred for the night-time curfew. They would be the hostages he had been expecting. Word had spread of The August Massacres. Now, in the spring, those Clan Lords in the east that had not previously sworn allegiance now did so willingly, offering their children to be 'guests' of the Shogun as proof of their lasting fidelity. Those in the west… they were proving to be more stubborn. But they would come around to his way of thinking soon enough.

The General turned, stepped back into the room, and grunted, indicating to Mizuno that he could let Lord Yoshiakira enter.

"Father," Yoshiakira knelt low, prostrating himself.

"Rise," Ashikaga muttered. He had been in a bad mood all winter, but now the snows were melting, his army could resume their outdoor training. Once the rainy season was over, he would be able to continue his campaigns in the west, and finally crush Go-Murakami. "What news do you bring?"

"Father, I have a further report on Lady Altera," his son replied, rising to a kneeling position.

"What does it say?"

"That the Lady remains a loyal servant. She is approaching the east coast, presumably closing in our quarry."

"Has she sent any messages?"

"No Father."

"Have any foreigners met with her?"

"No Father."

"Hmmm…" Ashikaga considered the information. Despite the favorable reports of Lady Altera's movements over the winter, The General remained deeply suspicious of her. "Has she visited any temples? Any shrines?"

"No Father. The report states that she had remained dedicated to her mission at all times. Indeed, she appears to be going out of her way not to interact with any villages or temples. Further, her men are impeccably behaved. Not one of them dares defy her orders."

"I see," The General replied. "Can we trust our informant?"

"Oh yes Father. I selected him myself."

*

Irago Cape

The ferry was little more than a large barge, and Gasan was relieved when it docked. He often felt nervous when a skiff took him across a river, and the choppy waters of the Irago Cape had made him feel sick.

For his part, Tatsuo seemed at ease with the three hour crossing, although tension remained between him and Tamazaki.

As they stepped off the boat and on to land, Gasan turned to the bandit leader. "Will you give us horses to continue our journey?"

Tamazaki's response was curt. "Our orders were explicit. We are to see you to the gates of Ise."

Gasan eyes widened. "You're coming with us all the way?" He was worried that the disagreement between him and Tatsuo would erupt into violence.

"It will only be two days. Three at the most. We wouldn't want you to be waylaid by bandits."

*

The road to Port Choshi

Lady Altera's battalion galloped on through the night, The Hunter leading the way. They were less than a day from Port Choshi, and with each passing mile, The Hunter became more and more certain of their prey's position.

Altera signaled to Birag who brought his horse alongside. "We're heading for the coast," she said. "Make sure the men are ready. Have the bows brought out and every man is to have a full quiver. There is no rest now until we find our target."

"My Lady, very good. We shall be within the city walls by midnight if we do not stop."

"I know. And tell Ashikaga's spy to hang back once we reach the port. We don't want any unnecessary casualties once the battle begins."

"My Lady, you think our quarry has... acquired support?"

Altera's voice was like sharpened steel. "If it was me, I would have brokered any deal necessary."

*

Port Choshi

Watanabe had to admit he was surprised at how easily things had come together. Kagetaka had seemed quite willing to provide Jion's stake in the Igo Tournament in return for Gozen, even though the girl was not worth a fraction of it. It made him uneasy to think what the captain would do with her if the boy lost, but The Governor tried to put such things from his mind.

"Now Jion," Otsuno said as the party walked down the street towards the gambling den, the evening closing in around them. "Remember what I have taught you. Concentrate. Focus. Do not be distracted. Let events flow through you.

"Yes Master. I understand," the boy replied. All around he felt the flow of the town's daytime life yawning and stretching, and the things that only come out in the dark readying themselves for the night.

Watanabe walked behind them, with the two girls by his side. The strain was showing on Gozen's face, whereas her younger sister seemed to be more relaxed with the entire venture

"This is an unnecessary risk," Gozen said. "You are putting our Lord in danger."

"How so?" Watanabe asked, knowing that what the older girl really meant was that *she* was being put in danger.

"What happens if the gamblers are drunk?"

"I think we are relying on that," The Governor replied.

"What if they refuse to pay?" Gozen persisted.

"No man refuses his debt. Besides, there will be guards there to enforce things. No establishment such as this would want to be known as a place of welchers. It would be bad for business."

As the group walked up the three steps to the gambling house, two guards moved from their position to the porchway entrance, blocking their way.

"No monks," the first said to Otsuno. "And no children either. What do you think this place is?"

Otsuno smiled gently, allowing his face to crumple into a mass of friendly wrinkles. "Please," he said. "It is the boy's birthday. He has come to play Igo."

The guard's voice was gruff. "This is not a nursery old man. Take your pennies somewhere else."

Otsuno remained smiling. "These pennies?" he showed the bulging bag of coins to the guards and felt relief as their eyes widened.

"Wait here," the first guard replied, and disappeared inside. A few moments later, he reappeared with a short fat man.

"Greetings," the chubby proprietor said, bowing slightly to the group. "I am Mura, master of this establishment."

The group returned the bow, and Jion noted the film of greasy sweat on the man's head. He was balding and his skin was sallow. The boy thought he could smell something underneath the perspiration. A smell of ammonia as though the man was constantly urinating. Jion quickly recognized the stench from his master's teachings; the fat man was unable to digest sugar, but was probably unaware.

"I understand your son wishes to play Igo?" Mura said to Watanabe, making immediate assumptions.

Watanabe nodded. "That is right. The monk here is the boy's tutor. The girls wish to see how their brother performs."

"Yes, yes," Mura said looking at each of them in turn. "And you have coin?"

Otsuno showed the pouch and was disappointed that the gambling master did not react in the way his guards had done.

"Hmmm... well," Mura replied. "I suppose we can make an exception to our usual house rules. But you," he looked to Watanabe and Jion, "will have to remove your swords."

"No!" Jion retorted and looked at Mura with defiance. "A sword is a bujin's soul!"

"And is the little master a bujin yet?" Mura said chuckling.

Watanabe leaned forward, whispered into Jion's ear, and then turned to Mura. "Forgive my son. He has yet to learn... diplomacy. We will of course present our swords to you."

"Very good," Mura replied, bowing, and slid the door open for the group to pass through.

Inside, the gambling den was hot and the air was filled with incense. The room was square and more ornate than the exterior suggested. Although not crowded, it was busier than Watanabe had anticipated and he could see many groups playing versions of Shogi, Daifugo and his personal favorite, Cho-Han. The Women of The Willow were also present, fawning over winners and plying others with alcohol. Watanabe could tell these were of the lowest rank. They would be neither clean nor well practiced in the art, but so quick and rough that they could quickly move on to the next client. The Governor was beginning to regret bringing the girls to this place, but maybe it was better that they see how the world really was.

"Please," Mura said, "this way."

The fat man led the party towards the back where they knelt in a semi-circle. Mura clapped his hands for drinks to be brought for the new guests, and Otsuno made eye contact with each of them in turn, silently reminding them of their promise not to accept any hospitality. There was no telling what would be in the bowls of a place like this.

Watanabe had noticed the quieting of chatter as they had moved through the room. They were not the usual party to be seen in a place like this, and they were drawing unwanted attention.

Behind them the entrance door slid open, and then closed again. The Governor half-turned and was not surprised to see the figure of Kagetaka approaching them.

"Ah my friends," The Captain said in informal tones that immediately rankled with the children. "I had hoped I would find you before the tournament began."

Otsuno bowed his head, but Watanabe looked at the man hard. "What are you doing here?" he asked.

"Me? Why I am just here to support my new friends… and keep an eye on my investment. Thank you Mura," Kagetaka said, accepting a bowl of rice wine and eyeing Gozen.

Jion could smell the over-powering alcoholic vapors from where he was seated, but said nothing as the corsair drained the bowl in a single gulp and smiled broadly at the stony faced group about him.

"This is Zukimoto," Mura said, introducing a short thin man who appeared to be in his mid thirties, his hair flecked gray at the temples. "He will be your challenger tonight."

Jion bowed low on the mat, and Zukimoto followed suit, each demonstrating respect for the other. A maid brought an Igo board, and they drew straws from Mura to see who would go first. Jion held the longest straw and opted for the white stone.

"The best of three rounds?" Mura asked.

Watanabe bowed his head. "Yes."

"Very good," Mura replied. "And your stake?"

"We shall put it here," Watanabe said, taking the pouch of money from Otsuno and placed it to the side of the Igo board.

"Good, good. Well good luck…" Mura turned to leave.

"Master Mura," Watanabe said darkly, causing the fat man to stop and turn.

"Yes my friend?"

Watanabe did not react to the slight of the informal tone. If this had been Fujigatani he would have removed the man's head for such impudence. "The house's wager? Against ours?"

"Of course," Mura said clapping his hand together. "How forgetful of me," and he motioned to the maid to bring the house stake. The girl returned with a pouch and placed it next to Watanabe's purse.

"I'd count it if I were you," Kagetaka muttered to The Governor.

To everyone's surprise, Jion reached over and picked up both bags, weighing each in his small hands before placing them back down.

"Your stake," Jion said to Mura, "is short by one hundred and twenty two coins."

Mura laughed but his eyes were cold. "Such a boy you have there," he said to Watanabe.

The Governor remained impassive. "Do we need to count it?" Watanabe knew that Mura held the balance of power with his armed guards, but if word ever got out of deliberate dishonesty, the fat man would be ruined.

"Let me," Mura said hurriedly and took the bag, counting the coins quickly. "I am so sorry," he said eventually, bowing low. "I will punish the girl immediately. Come here…" he said angrily to the maid.

"No need," Watanabe said. "I am sure it was an honest mistake. But you will see the difference made up, yes?"

"Of course. My apologies. I am so sorry. This has never happened before…"

Watanabe watched as the extra coins were added to the purse, then turned to Jion and whispered, "Are you ready?"

Jion nodded, turned to the board, and placed the first stone.

Less than five minutes later Mura was muttering harshly into Zukimoto's ear. The boy had not just won, but had routed the grandmaster with a bewildering array of tactics and feints.

"Please," Mura said to the group, "a five minute recess." He took Zukimoto firmly by the arm, leading him into an adjoining room.

"That was very good Jion," Otsuno said.

"Master, thank you," replied the boy, bowing low.

"I'm impressed," Kagetaka said nonchalantly, taking another sip of rice wine from his bowl. Despite this being his third serving, he seemed unaffected by the alcohol. "Where did you learn to play like that?"

"My Master… taught me well," Jion said, bowing his head and indicating towards Otsuno.

"I'll say. Maybe when you're older I can take you out in Naniwa or Yeddo. We could make a fortune."

"Maybe," Jion said noncommittally. To have refused the corsair would have been rude. "Master," the boy said turning to Otsuno, "may we speak? In private?"

Otsuno looked to Watanabe who nodded, and the monk took the boy's hand and led him to an alcove. "Are you alright?" he asked.

"I'm not sure," Jion said.

"What is wrong?"

"The Echo… it is distorting. I cannot read it as I did before."

"What do you mean?" the monk asked, worried by this sudden turn.

"It is like when we were back at the tavern… before the snows came."

"When you passed out?"

"Yes. I was listening to the echo of the flow… and then it broke apart and overwhelmed me."

"I see," Otsuno said, trying to put the pieces of the puzzle together. The boy was an increasing mystery to him. "Can you explain?"

"Not really. It is like I can listen so far, and then I find something that warps the echo and…" his voice trailed off, and for the first time Otsuno saw strain and worry on the boy's face.

We have put so much on his young shoulders, Otsuno thought, realizing how fragile his new apprentice really was. "It will be alright, Jion. Do not let your mind wander. Keep your focus just on the game. Do not let the echoes from beyond the town distract you."

"Yes Master. But I think the… distortion is coming closer," the boy was pale and the old monk could see in the half-light of the candles that he was sweating.

"Very well. You only need to win the next game and we can pay the captain and leave this place. Can you do that?"

Jion nodded, and turned back to the board as Mura led Zukimoto back in. The boy felt sorry for the man. He could tell that he only worked for Mura to pay a debt, and if he lost this game it would not only cost him his life, but that of his wife and child too.

Jion tried to put the thought away. He was already feeling sick from the distortions and did not need anything else to distract him. Watanabe muttered something to Otsuno.

"He is fine," the monk replied, and then turned to Mura. "The next game?"

"Of course, of course," Mura said smiling, although not as broadly as before. "Let us begin."

Zukimoto made the first move, and Jion followed him. The second game was longer this time. The boy had begun to sweat profusely and paled as the evening drew on. Despite this, it was Zukimoto that the group noticed; the man was visibly shaking, and when Jion put down the last stone that sealed his fate he cried out loud in anguish and swept the board away.

Masako turned to Gozen and spoke softly to her older sister. "I told you to have faith."

*

Yugyo Monastery, Sagami Province

Nikko hurried through the cold night towards her mistress's chambers, the sound of her wooden sandals echoing on the flagstones. Whilst it was not unusual to be summoned at such an hour, to be called in such a manner suggested an admonishment.

Kneeling on the hard straw mat, she prostrated herself. "Mistress Taka," she said.

Taka turned to observe the younger girl but did not give her permission to rise. The older woman noted that, despite all the years her apprentice had been at the monastery, she seemed to have barely aged, and Taka put it down to the clean air and simple living. This was the first time she was going to rebuke her novice, which itself was a reflection on how well she had trained her.

"I understand you have made others aware of the prophecy you discovered?" Taka said.

Nikko tensed, but did not rise from her prostrated position. "Yes Mistress."

"Against my explicit instructions?"

"Yes Mistress."

Taka paused. It was good that her apprentice had immediately admitted the offense, but a transgression has been committed. "Can you explain yourself?"

"Mistress, Nobuo overheard The Council discussing the matter and he came to me with some of the other Sohei to ask if it was true. I only told them what I had discovered and…"

"Enough. Some say that you are preaching the prophecy as truth now…"

"Oh no Mistress, I would never…"

"SILENCE!" Tension filled the night air. It was one thing to disobey a direct order, it was quite another to interrupt one as senior as Mistress Taka.

Taka relented and relaxed. "Nikko, sit up. The prophecy… it is an ancient text. It could have many meanings. That is why The Council needs to debate these matters and consider each possible interpretation before it acts. *If* it acts. Such… idle chatter is not becoming of a novice and distracts The Council. Do you understand?"

"Yes Mistress," her eyes were glassy and rimmed with tears from the rebuke.

"Very good. You will fast for three days as penance."

"Yes Mistress."

*

Port Choshi

"No," Mura said flatly, and jabbed a fat finger at Watanabe. "You cheated. You did not tell me that the boy was… was… a genius. He used a trick… he hypnotized my man…"

Watanabe was conscious that the guards had slowly encircled them all, their hands drifting towards their swords. The other patrons had stopped playing their respective games and silence had descended on the gambling den.

"Come on Mura," Kagetaka said cheerily, stepping forward as he did so. "A bet is a bet. Sometimes you win. Sometimes you lose. Tonight you lost. Your luck had to run out some time."

"No," Mura said stubbornly. "It was not fair. They should play again… the boy should be blindfolded so that he does not fool my…" the words died in his throat as he realized how ridiculous he sounded.

"Come now," replied Kagetaka, still smiling. "You'll win it back in a week. We both know it…" the captain leaned forward and whispered something into Mura's ear.

The den master looked back at him and harrumphed loudly. "Take your stinking money," he said pushing both coin bags into Watanabe's chest. "And don't ever come back."

As the group turned to leave, Otsuno felt Jion's sweaty hand begin to slip from his. The boy was becoming faint, and even in the low candle light, everyone could now plainly see he was unwell.

"Don't forget your swords," the monk said to Watanabe as they moved towards the exit. The Governor nodded and retrieved their weapons from the guard at the door who eyed him impassively.

As they stepped out into the night, Otsuno hoped that the cool air would invigorate his young ward, but the boy only seemed to lean on him more heavily as they exited the building.

Kagetaka turned to Watanabe. "I believe these are for me," he said, taking the pouches of money from The Governor, and then eyeing Gozen he muttered, "Shame."

From the hill behind the port came the sound of galloping hooves, filling the air like thunder, followed by the cries of those caught in their path, and the party turned to the source of the commotion. A stream of black horses was coming down the hill, nearly invisible against the black of the night.

"Master..." Jion began to swoon and leaned heavily on Otsuno.

Watanabe saw the approaching charge. "That's not good," and turning to Kagetaka he said, "We need to leave. Right now."

The corsair nodded and ushered the party towards the docks. Whilst he tried never to carry cargo that attracted this sort of trouble, he had his own scores to settle with the Ashikaga Shogunate, and any opportunity to put The General's nose out was welcome.

*

Altera's brigade sped on, descending the hillside track towards the town below. "What's our bearing Hunter?" she called over the wind.

"Mistress, dead ahead." The creature's skin had become luminescent, seeming to shine with an inner glow. It was close to completing its mission. It was about to realize its reason for being.

*

Kagetaka hurried the party down the small wooden jetty to his ship.

"What is this?" Watanabe said astounded. "It's nothing but a heap of rubbish."

"This heap of rubbish made the Tianxian Run in less than three weeks, now get on. Kiyomori! Igurashi!" The corsair called to his first mate and pilot. "Get the crew ready. We're leaving. Now."

"Aye Captain!" the two figures chorused and began barking orders at the dozing crew.

"It's going to be close," Otsuno said as he hurried the children on board.

Watanabe was helping untie the ropes from the dock and looked up. "We'll make it."

They could all hear the pounding of hooves echoing through the streets, closing in on their position. Igurashi had taken his position on the con, and Kiyomori was snapping at the oarsmen.

"Pull you sons of motherless dogs! Pull!" The drummer began to pound the large Taiko drum, setting a rhythm for the oarsmen

The ship begun to move away from the dock and Watanabe and two other men who had been untying the ropes were forced to quickly scramble up the retreating gangplank.

"We're safe," Kagetaka said as he saw the ship cast off from the dock.

"Don't count on it," Otsuno said darkly. He too could now sense the darkness that Jion had so feared. He could feel that whatever was approaching was disrupting the flow of life all about them, spreading death and fear.

By the half-moon, Otsuno could now plainly see the details of the vessel, and understood Watanabe's previous outburst. The Sophia appeared to be a heavily modified version of a Tianxian Junker. The hull was some thirty meters long, with a modified deck underneath the main sail where ninety men manned the oars – three to each one. The sails were silk, and there appeared to be two main masts instead of the customary one, with each sail at an angle to maximize not only the power of air currents, but also provide additional stability. There were smaller sails too, and these would be unfurled once they were out of the bay. Further, there appeared to be two rudders; one at the front and another at the back, with five men on each. The old monk could only guess at their size if it took so many men to manage them and deduced that Kagetaka must have detailed maps if he was able to navigate the shallows of the south coast.

"You worry too much old man," Kagetaka said smiling broadly, noticing the anxious look on Otsuno's face. The dock was now nearly fifty meters behind them, and The Sophia was about to enter open waters.

The sea air had helped Jion recover and he turned to look back at the port, seeing the swarm of black clad warriors descend on the dock where they had been only minutes before.

*

Altera's forces had stopped on the dock, but were not retreating to the town, as the boy would have expected.

"Prepare!" Altera barked as she watched the retreating ship. She would have her quarry. There could be no escape. "FIRE!"

The mounted archers loosed a volley of arrows high into the night sky.

*

Jion knew what was coming and even as the arrows whistled through the darkness, he prepared himself.

The world turned to black and white and Jion looked about him for the cloud of chattering insects. He knew the men on the deck were expendable and as he twisted around, he saw that Otsuno had gathered Gozen and Masako into him, and they cowered against the side of the ship – they were safe.

And then he saw it, behind Kagetaka. With impossible speed, the boy ran into the corsair, shoving him with all his strength. Turning again, he saw another cloud forming behind Watanabe. Jion ran towards his sensei and…

The world returned to its nighttime hues as Jion connected with his governor. The arrow struck the upper part of Watanabe's arm, passing straight through. Despite his years of training, Jion's governor cried out shrilly, only to be drowned out by the shrieks of the dying from the main deck.

Kagetaka looked at the boy in shock and wonder, and then down at the outsized black arrow that had punctured through the deck where he had been standing a split second before.

Otsuno moved to his one-time apprentice, ripping the cloth of his own robes to tie into a knot above the wound. Gozen was sobbing at the gore and death about her and her younger sister, seemingly less traumatized by what she had just witnessed, put her arm around her in comfort.

Kagetaka continued to stare at Jion and finally knelt, bowing low. "I owe you my life Little Master."

*

From the dock, Altera could only watch at the retreating ship. "Did we get them?" she said to The Hunter.

"No Mistress."

When it came, Altera's voice was icy cold. "Raze the town," she said. "Burn everything."

*

Kurama Temple

Kwon knelt by the pool in the courtyard, acutely aware of the stench that clung to him. The koi carp should have been asleep, but had been disturbed as the Tianxian washed the gore and muck from his armor, and now came to the surface to nibble at his fingers.

Kwon let them. Their muscular bodies felt soothing against the back of his hands, and the little nips reminded him he was still alive. Dawn was coming, and the faint light on the horizon cast everything about him into a dark pastel tone.

He looked over his shoulder at the Sohei guards that surrounded him, spears pointed at him. There seemed to be more than last time, but maybe he was just imagining it.

From the other side of the pond, a large wooden door opened and the familiar figure of Abbot Shimada glided out to greet him.

"Ah," Shimada said. "The foreigner has returned. You were gone for so many months… we feared that we would not see you again."

"I have completed my task," Kwon said, trying to stand and bow at the same time. Every part of him ached and mud packs covered his multitude of wounds. "The head of Sojobo…" fatigue overtook the master swordsman and he sunk back down to the side of the pond, just nodding to the bulging bloody satchel on flagstones.

"You were successful?"

Kwon did not reply but nodded, and held his right side where he could feel his stitches beginning to come loose. He did not feel much like retelling his story; the months lost in the mountains; the final confrontation with the demon from the deep; or that he probably would have lost both feet and a hand to frostbite had it not been for a kindly peasant who had brought him back to within sight of the temple grounds. Kwon had no money and carried nothing of value, and had only been able to reward the man by gifting him his prize dagger – one of the few weapons to have survived the epic battle.

"I see," Shimada said, "and where did you find the Tengu King?"

Kwon leaned heavily against the side of the pool. The smell of his sweat mixed with the gore of the goblin was becoming overpowering even to his foreign nose, and he knew that those surrounding him must be equally repulsed, for this was a nation that prided itself on cleanliness. "Three peaks over. With the snowfall… it took me several months to get there."

"And yet you had such few provisions with you," the Abbot replied now noticing Kwon's emaciated form.

"Let's just say my masters have taught me to fast. They taught me *very* well," Kwon winced again. It felt as if he still had a piece of the goblin's shattered spearhead in his side.

"Yes," Shimada said cautiously, "very well indeed. And what of Sojobo's dwelling?"

"It was a cave. I burned everything inside."

"Everything?"

Kwon nodded.

"It was said the Tengu King held a vast library; many ancient teachings, not just of our Lord Buddha, but of Masters of the East and even further. Did you see such a thing?"

Kwon nodded again.

"And you burned that too?" Shimada's eyes were widening with the shock of what the foreigner was admitting to.

"Yes," Kwon said weakly.

"But… such knowledge… it would have been invaluable."

"Believe me Master Abbot, you would want no part of such dark teachings anywhere near your temple. I have seen before what such power does to the heart of a man. It twists and corrupts until brother fights brother, and fathers slay sons. Now, I will happily discuss the finer points of your goblin menace with you, but first I beg a favor."

"What is that?" Shimada enquired

Kwon wrinkled his nose. "Can I please get a bath?"

*

The Southern Sea

The Sophia cut through the waves like a sword through a bamboo shoot, the wind billowing in her sails as the sun beat down, warming her through. Under such conditions, the oarsmen were unnecessary and were taking a well-deserved rest.

In their cramped quarters, Jion sat with Gozen and Otsuno while Masako enjoyed a tour of the deck with Watanabe. It had been three days since they had left Port Choshi, and for two of those they had been able to see the pall of smoke that had hung in high in the air over the town, like a widow's veil. No one had said anything, each knowing the fate of the citizens who had dwelt there. The boy had been crying and held his legs into his chest, back against the wooden hull

"There there," Gozen said soothingly. "You have nothing to be ashamed about."

"But I do," Jion said, another sob wracking his small chest. "I could not save my father, I could not save my brother, and even Sensei is injured because I was not quick enough."

"Jion," Otsuno said soothingly. "A man cannot carry the world. He must simply carry one rock at a time."

"You are still young," Gozen continued, not understanding the old monk's point. "As you get older your strength will increase. You must not be so hard on yourself."

"And besides," continued the monk, "more than forty days have passed since the untimely demise of your father and brother. By now, they either will have entered nirvana, or have been reborn. Whichever is the case, you should rejoice."

At that moment, the door burst open and Kagetaka entered the small room. "I am sorry to interrupt, but we have got trouble."

Otsuno gathered the children to him and they followed the corsair up on to the deck.

"What is it?" Watanabe asked as he joined them.

"There's something out there," Kagetaka replied. "The lookout in the crow's nest said he can see a blockade."

"I don't see anything," Watanabe replied, looking at the horizon.

"Be my guest," Kagetaka said, offering the rigging to The Governor. "Go up and look for yourself."

Watanabe looked at the height of the mast and thought better of it. The bujin were ill at ease on the sea and panic set in when the shoreline disappeared from view, letting them know they were truly in The Deeps. "I believe you," he said.

"Good. Every soul on this ship is loyal to me. No-one here wants anything other than to get you safely to your destination." The corsair turned to Jion. "I owe you my life, Little Lord. You can trust us."

"How big is the blockade?" Otsuno asked.

"Bigger than we expected. A score of ships. Maybe more. Ashikaga has been busy over the winter."

"What are our options?" Watanabe said.

"We could turn back," replied Kagetaka.

"No," Otsuno interjected. "We *must* get to Yokohama."

Kagetaka shrugged. "Then we run the blockade."

"Can we?" Gozen asked.

"There's not a ship that can outrun The Sophia," the corsair replied. "But it is another matter if we can lose them before we make Yokohama Bay."

"Captain!" the man in the crow's nest called. "You're going to want to see this."

Kagetaka frowned at the unusual request and hurriedly climbed the rigging. When he came back down a few moments later his jovial attitude had evaporated, replaced by a stony demeanor which both Otsuno and Jion found more difficult to read.

"Do you know who it was that was pursuing you?" the corsair asked.

"Not by name," the monk replied. "We guessed it was Ashikaga's forces."

"What does he want with you?"

No one replied.

"I don't suppose you are going to tell me who you really are either, are you?"

Watanabe avoided the question. "What is the matter? What does your man see?"

Kagetaka turned to The Governor. "Ashikaga has more than a score of ships out there."

"How many in total?" Watanabe asked. "Thirty? Forty? Surely not fifty?"

The corsair remained impassive. "At least a hundred. Probably more."

The party collectively gasped.

"But," Masako began, "the Clans fight on land. Everyone knows that."

"It seems that someone forget to tell Ashikaga," Kagetaka said. "This could get... bumpy."

Otsuno frowned. "What do you mean? What are you thinking?"

"We'll take The Sophia out into The Deeps. If we're lucky they either won't have spotted us, or they won't have the nerve to come after us," the corsair replied.

"And if they do?" the monk asked.

"We should be able to outrun anything they have once we are past them, but..."

"But?" Watanabe said.

"They're big ships. Biggest I've ever seen. It means they'll be hard to maneuver and they'll wallow in the swells. But if they intercept us before we're clear of their parallel... I'll wager they'll have grapples. Big ones too. If we're caught... we don't have the manpower to repel them."

"Then we go down fighting... like bujin!" said Masako, stamping her foot.

The sight of the child's stubbornness made the older men laugh, but Gozen felt uneasy.

Kagetaka looked to Otsuno and then to Watanabe. "Last chance. Turn back or try your luck again?"

Otsuno made the decision. "We *have* to get to Yokohama. The boy is everything."

Kagetaka brayed loudly and slapped the old man on the back. "I hope we meet in the next life old man. You'd make an excellent corsair." Turning to his first mate he called out, "Hoist the main sails... hoist everything! Igurashi... Anjin! Take her into The Deeps."

"Aye Captain," the voices from the deck chorused.

The ship seemed to come alive as bodies ran the length of the hull, pulling ropes and manning the rudders. A myriad of sails unfurled, joining those on main masts that were already billowing like cushions.

"Looks like your lucky kami is with you today," Kagetaka said. "The winds are in our favor."

"Captain!" It was the man at the top of the crow's nest again. "They're turning!"

"Damn," the corsair muttered. "They've seen us."

Jion, who had remained silent up to now, pulled gently on Otsuno's hand. "Master?"

"Yes?" the old monk replied.

"This water... the sea... The Goddess is here."

Otsuno narrowed his eyes. "What do you mean?" he whispered. "Does she speak to you?"

Jion shook his head, his hair catching in the wind. "No. Not like that. But she moves here. She moves through all things. But here... she is more... free."

The monk believed in the boy's exceptional abilities, but could not understand what he was being told. "Can you talk to her? Give us an advantage?"

Again Jion shook his head. "No," he whined. "It's not like that. I cannot tell Her to do something. I can... direct it. But I need your help."

Otsuno finally understood. "Very well. Let us go below deck."

Nodding to Watanabe to keep a watch on the girls, the monk took the boy back to their cramped quarters.

First lighting a candle, and then a stick of incense, Otsuno sat and crossed his legs. Closing his eyes, he heard Jion sit opposite him. At this range, the monk could easily sense his ward, and he felt both passion and worry bubbling inside the child, threatening to boil over.

"Calm yourself Jion," Otsuno said gently. "Close your eyes. Still yourself. Imagine a trapdoor in the hull floor. You can open it, and walk down into the water. You can breathe easily. The further down you walk, the darker it becomes. Down. Down. Further still, down. You can no longer see the ship. There is no ship. There is no land. There is no you. There is only the water. You are the sea. Infinite. Limitless. Boundless. You flow around all things."

Jion could feel himself floating. He was the ocean. He could sense strange and distant lands where men never bathed and others where they wore thick coats of animal skin all the time. He ebbed and flowed, forgetting himself, becoming both the rock of the craggy seabed and the air above. He could smell the sea salt, and the smoke of faraway fires. But he was always the water. Always flowing. Faster. Faster.

"... you are the water Jion," Otsuno continued. "See the boat. See yourself. Let the water push the boat. Guide us out of harm's way."

The hull creaked as a swell from the deep rose up and gently kissed the stern.

"... from behind Jion. Push the boat from behind. Let your spray join with the air. Become the wind."

The ship lurched forward as a sudden squall filled the sails dragging The Sophia forward.

"...guide us on..."

The wind began to increase in intensity, and the hull creaked loudly as another swell came, lurching the ship forward.

"... you are the wind..."

What had been a breeze was quickly becoming a gale, and a stronger swell buffeted against the hull, causing the ship to list momentarily at a sickening angle.

In Jion's mind, the face of his brother rose unbidden, blood-stained and contorted in pain. The stone in the boy's heart glowed, and then began to smoke. The men who had done this, who had taken his family and denied him his fate, were out there. The figure of Tanemochi turned over, revealing the pus-filled gash where the arrow had entered.

The stone in Jion's heart burst into flames, and with his mind the boy reached out across the waves. There was Ashikaga's fleet. Like toy ships in an onsen. Like the little Tianxian paper boats he had played with in the moat of Fujigatani Castle with his brother only two summers ago.

Jion was the sea. Jion was the air. He could see the enemy fleet clearly, and, from the deep, he sent a swell straight up. One of the ships lurched up, and then came crashing down in the trough of the wave, breaking her main mast. In his mind, the boy could hear men screaming. How small they seemed. How insignificant. Jion smiled.

The gale around the Shogun's fleet turned suddenly and a great wave swept over the starboard sides of three of the enemy vessels, capsizing them and throwing their crews into the sea. Jion knew well the creatures of the deep and told them of the great feast to be had at the surface…

The door burst open revealing a soaked Kagetaka, his hair now limp and dripping. "By the Buddha, I don't know what you two sorcerers are doing, but you're going to tear the ship apart!"

Otsuno's eyes snapped open, realizing for the first time the sounds of distress coming from the ship, and the monk was shocked to see Jion's face contorted into a cruel sneer.

"Jion … Jion!" Otsuno shook the boy but his ward did not open his eyes. Turning to the corsair he said, "Drop the sails!"

"Are you mad?" Kagetaka snapped back. "We'll be caught for sure!"

"I very much doubt it. Just do it! I… I need to reach him."

Kagetaka snorted and stomped loudly out of the room and back to the deck. Otsuno cradled the boy in his arms and tenderly stroked his brow.

"Jion… Jion," he whispered. "Come back child. Come back to us."

From the darkest depths of the waters, the malevolent force that Jion had become heard his master's soothing voice, like a balm on a wound. He knew he could carry on the assault on the fleet. But these men were not responsible for the deaths of either his father or his brother. They were simply the tools of Ashikaga. It was like blaming the bees for a poor harvest when the farmer had starved them all year.

From the ocean floor, Jion reached up. Up and up until he struck the surface in a spray of foam and sand. Becoming the wind, he moved across the land, tearing up trees and blowing down homes.

Ashikaga… where are you?

As he blew north he saw the mounted horses riding away from the charred remains of Port Choshi. To his surprise, they collectively looked up… at him. Against his will he felt himself being drawn down. Down and down as he scrambled through the clouds. Down into their mouths. Down into their very…

"JION!" Otsuno slapped him again, as hard he could this time.

The boy's eyes flickered open, and he felt the weight of his physical self. The wind had settled, the seas calmed, and the hull no longer creaked like an old cart. Around him stood the corsair captain, Watanabe, and the two girls. Otsuno held his head in his lap, caressing his temples.

"Now," barked the clearly furious Kagetaka, "would someone like to tell me what in the name of bloody Jigoku is going on?"

*

The Ise Grand Shrine, Ise Province

Tamazaki brought his steed to a stop, and then wheeled around to face the rest of the contingent. "This is it," he said to Gasan and Tatsuo. "The Ise Shrine."

"Thank you," Gasan said as he and Tatsuo dismounted, and began pulling the satchels full of provisions from the horses back.

Tatsuo said nothing, but continued to stare at Tamazaki. The two had not spoken since the ferry had docked and the tension made Gasan nervous.

"It was our honor," Tamazaki said to Gasan, digging his heels into the horses flank, prompting it to trot forward. As he passed Tatsuo he said, "Maybe we'll meet again."

Tatsuo made no reply, but turned to watch the retreating bandits. "I hope we do," he finally muttered.

Gasan hoisted the satchels on to his back and approached the bujin. "Ready?"

Tatsuo eyed him, not understanding how a man could let such an insult pass without action. Tamazaki did not support them or Lord Soma. Quite the contrary – he would actively seek their deaths if they were successful in their mission. Had Lord Soma still been alive Tatsuo would have taken the bandit's head and never thought of him again.

"Let it go," Gasan said gently, following Tatsuo's line of sight. "You bujin are all in love with death. You cannot serve our Lord from The Great Void."

"At least death is honorable," Tatsuo replied, and turned to face the steep stone stairs that led up to the Ise Shrine. The forest here was mainly bamboo, dense and letting little light through. Leaves were beginning to bud, and after the rainy season had provided them with water, no doubt the summer would see a glorious canopy.

"Come on," Gasan said. "We need to find The Saio."

"The Saio?"

"It is like an abbot. But with more power. The Saio is politically astute and liaises with Clan Lords and merchants alike. They are all very diplomatic and have brokered many agreements over the centuries."

"Do you know him? This Saio?"

"It is not a he, but a *her*. And no, not personally. Only by reputation. The Yamabushi seldom come this far west. The east and the north are our territories. Good mountains," Gasan smiled. "We don't like the flats so much."

"Her? The Saio is a woman?"

"You did not know?" Gasan asked, surprised at the bujin's ignorance.

Tatsuo shook his head. "No. I thought all shrine elders were men."

"It depends on the sect. Most are, but here… Ise has long been patronised by The Chrysanthemum Throne, and it has always been a member of the Imperial Family who has held the position of Saio."

"Who is the current Saio?" Tatsuo asked.

"Princess Sachiko."

Tatsuo's eyes widened. "The Emperor's sister?"

"The very same."

As they climbed the steps and passed through the Torii Gate, Tatsuo felt the hairs on his neck prickle and his hand instinctively moved to his sword.

"You must not draw that here," Gasan hissed. "This is holy ground… one of the most sacred sites in all Oyashima."

"I know," Tatsuo replied grimly, looking about him. The shrine was in the middle of the forest, and now the bujin could see the leaden sky, dark and heavy with expectant rain. "But where is everybody? Where are the Sohei? Where are The Council Elders? And why is it so quiet?"

"They are probably preparing for the *Hanami*. You saw the cherry trees on the way in. They will be in blossom soon."

"No," Gasan replied. "There is something wrong here…"

From behind them came the sound of a footstep, and Tatsuo wheeled around drawing his sword several inches out of its scabbard.

"Peace be upon you," the figure said and bowed low.

Tatsuo could see the man was unarmed and sheathed his sword. The figure was short and thin, but stood perfectly erect. Clothed in the customary white robes of the monastic class, the bujin was surprised that the man's head was not completely shaved, as was the custom of those who had taken orders, but instead the hair was cropped into a bob reminiscent of the foreigners.

"Blessings of the Buddha," Gasan replied, bowing lower. "Please forgive our intrusion. We bring a message for The Saio."

"The Saio?" the monk replied. "Who should I say the message is from?"

"Please, it is from Lord Soma and very urgent."

"Lord *Soma* you say?" The monk was clearly surprised.

"Yes, Lord Soma. The Protector of The Inzai Valley."

"Of course. Please wait here." The monk moved off, hurrying up the short flight of steps and into the main hall.

Tatsuo could see the building was dark. It was the custom to rebuild the shrine every twenty years, and it looked like this incarnation was due to be torn down any day. The base of the wooden walls betrayed signs of damp and moss whilst the roof had dark patches caused by water penetration.

The bujin felt twitchy. Something was wrong, although he could not put his finger on it. It was more than the silence. It was the lack of incense. It was the sight of the wells used for cleansing and purification, overgrown with weeds and brambles. It was that when the monk had entered the main hall, he had neither removed his shoes nor bowed as he entered.

Tatsuo knew that monks all over Oyashima were strange. There were so many sects — literally hundreds if not thousands — constantly coming together under one treaty and then falling out the next day. And their myriad of customs and practices defied his understanding. Maybe this was just the way things were done in Ise. But he still could not shake the feeling that…

The doors to the main hall slid open and the monk that had greeted them hurried out, again without bowing. "Thank you for waiting," he said quickly. "The Saio will see you now."

"Now?" Gasan said surprised. "But we have been so long on the road… Maybe we can bathe and change our clothes?"

"So sorry," the monk said, bowing this time. "The Saio is very busy. She must see you now."

Tatsuo looked to Gasan. "Come on. Let's get this done," he said.

The two men, weary from their long journey, followed the monk across the courtyard flagstones and into the main hall, bowing as they did so.

To their surprise, the main hall was full of monks, all silently sitting and facing the dais at the front where a woman sat cross-legged on a cushion of deep purple, eyes closed. Tatsuo had difficult guessing her age because of her white makeup, but her black hair was similarly cut in the bobbed tradition of the foreigners, framing her oval face and accentuating her narrow nose. The door slid closed behind them, and the bujin felt the muscles in his stomach tighten.

"Who comes before The Saio?" the woman asked, not opening her eyes.

Gasan knelt and prostrated himself, motioning Tatsuo to follow suit. "Honorable Saio, we are humble messengers sent by Lord Soma, the Protector of The Inzai Valley, and your…"

"We believed Lord Soma to be dead," The Saio interrupted. "In whose name do you come?"

Gasan did not raise himself from the floor. "We come in the name of his surviving heir, Yoshi…"

Tatsuo elbowed him in the ribs, and Gasan raised himself, his face flushing with embarrassment at his companion's rudeness.

The bujin was sitting up, staring at the stage where The Saio sat. "I don't think we should be giving any details…" he muttered to Gasan.

The Saio opened her eyes, and where there should have been the whites of her sclera, there was only an inky blackness. As Gasan peered harder, he could see that whatever corruption had taken the woman's eyes had spread along her veins creating a fine network that resembled a dark spider's web.

"The sons of Soma do not represent Ise in The Inzai Valley or anywhere else," The Saio said. "That honor was given to another…"

"I think we need to get out of here," Tatsuo whispered under his breath, standing and dragging Gasan up by his armpit.

"…For the sons of Soma are corrupt in their faith, denying the breath of Namlu and the words of The Great Mother…"

"Yes… yes…" stammered Gasan, unsure what he was seeing or hearing, but knowing that this was not the reception he had hoped for.

All about them the monks and Sohei remained seated, their eyes closed in some secret rapture as they listened to the mad Saio's voice reaching a crescendo as Gasan and Tatsuo reached the door.

"…We are the Hope Against The Tyrants," The Saio chanted.

"We are the Hope Against The Tyrants," the hall echoed back.

Gasan and Tatsuo opened the door, turned, and froze.

Outside, in the cool light, the previously empty courtyard was now filled with armed bujin. Spears caught the light, reflecting the gloom of sky towards the men.

A tall armor-clad figure raced up the stairs to address them.

"Ah, Tatsuo! So good to see you again," said Lord Mutsu, one-time strategist to Lord Soma, bowing his head slightly. "As you can see… circumstances are what they are…"

Gasan heard the assembly in the hall behind them stand and take their staffs. The two men were completely surrounded.

"… there is a new order," Mutsu continued. "Won't you join us?"

Tatsuo's jaw clenched in rage, and his knuckles were white from the grip on his sword.

"Murderous cur," the bujin snarled. "What have you done?" and with that Tatsuo unsheathed his sword and ran at the traitor, followed by Gasan, his staff held high and screaming for revenge.

*

Yokohama Bay

The battered form of The Sophia limped into the port town of Yokohama. Listing to one side, it had taken all the expertise of the crew to repair the masts and keep the sea from filling the hull. For their part, Otsuno, Watanabe and the children had been confined to their quarters and a guard posted outside the door at all times.

Kagetaka had not been to see them in the five days since the surprise storm had swept away Ashikaga's fleet. In all his years on the water, the corsair had never seen anything like it. It was as though the very kami of the ocean had risen up, boiling underneath the hulls of the enemy, tossing them into the air as if they were a child's plaything. And the wind… by the Buddha, the wind. It seemed to carry the screams of the damned from Jigoku itself.

Kagetaka knew that the boy and the old monk were somehow behind it. The child was special and the captain recognised that he owed him a blood debt for saving his life, whether he liked it or not. The corsair had to admit that, on balance, he really did not like it at all. He had lost several men to the arrow attack as they had left Choshi, and many more had been swept overboard in the storm. In total he had lost a third of his crew, but men were easy to come by in these times, and a reduced complement meant for greater riches all round.

But still, his cargo of passengers unsettled the captain, and he barely said a word to them as they were called up from below deck to see the city of Yokohama as it came into view. The sun beat down on all of them, and the two girls tried to retreat into what limited shade the starboard side offered, complaining that they would turn brown like a commoner.

"We made it," Watanabe said. "Do you know where we will find Shonin?"

Otsuno was smiling, in part because they had survived this far and in part because Jion had come to him the previous night to confess his rage and bloodlust and that he would seek to control himself in future. The old monk felt that his teachings were finally reaching the boy. Now all he had to do was talk him out of this mad quest for revenge. That would probably be more difficult but at least he was on the right path.

"We'll find him in The Fat Heron. It's a tavern just to the north. He's *always* there. He claims it serves the best shochu anywhere in the Eight Isles." Otsuno said.

"We'll see about that," Kagetaka said on reflex, and then immediately regretted his jovial remark remembering he wanted as little interaction with his passengers as possible.

The group stood on the stone wharf, taking in the bustling town. Although more commercial than he remembered it, Otsuno sensed that the people were not as hardened as those in Port Choshi, and the old man was glad that city had retained its soul, at least for now. Watanabe turned to the corsair and gently pulled him to one side.

"I understand if you are angry with us," The Governor muttered. "You lost a lot of good men on account of... whatever it is that the boy can do."

"Men aren't the problem. I can get more men from anywhere," Kagetaka replied, "it's the ship. Look at her. She's one of a kind. She'll be here for several weeks undergoing repairs. I doubt I'll make any profit on this trip." The corsair knew that was a lie, but wanted to see how worldly Watanabe really was.

The Governor knew the cost too well, but allowed the corsair his folly. "That's as maybe, but remember the boy saved your life."

"Saved my..." Kagetaka bridled. "He was the one who put it in danger in the first place."

"Regardless," Watanabe continued, "You owe him a blood debt. Jion knows it and I know it. If you have any kind of honor, you'll acknowledge that."

The corsair looked about him and shook his head in wonder, and then looked back to The Governor. "Alright," he muttered, "what is it you want?"

"At the moment? Nothing." Watanabe replied. "But when the time comes, he will need to call on you. And he will expect you to pay that debt."

Kagetaka nodded, understanding the man's meaning. "Very well. There is a merchant – a silk dealer – by the name of Shiro. He trades out of the main market. He knows how to find me. In the front of his shop is a robe with an oak leaf embroidered into the back, and it will have a 'sold' label on it. You say to him 'Is the willow not mightier than this oak?' and he will ask why. You reply 'In the winter, the snow breaks the oak's boughs, but the willow shakes it off.' He will get word to me."

Watanabe did not reply but bowed his head to the corsair in a show of respect, and turned to the party on the dock. As he did so, The Governor saw Otsuno crumple against Gozen, pulling the girl down with him, and Masako shrieked loudly clutching her face in shock. Watanabe raced to the old man's side and Jion was kneeling next to him, cradling his head.

For a moment, the monk's eyes fluttered open and he whispered, "Gasan…" before slipping under the black wave of unconsciousness.

CHAPTER FOUR

April 1357 - Yugyo Monastery, Sagami Province

Even though it had been a long six weeks, Jion sensed that it was more than their journey that had aged his master so. The maze-like lines on Otsuno's face had deepened and he now walked with a stoop, relying heavily on his staff.

The group had found Master Shonin with ease, and, for three weeks, he had tended to his friend. Otsuno had been feverish and had shouted incomprehensibly as he thrashed about. Shonin had spoken gently to the semi-conscious monk, placed a cooling flannel on his brow, and brought warm miso soup to his dry lips, never leaving the older monk's side until he was sufficiently recovered.

Despite the worry of his master's condition, Jion was secretly glad there would be no more training, at least for a while. Whatever power he had called upon at sea, it had exhausted his abilities and now his hearing was no better than either Gozen's or Masako's. In a bid to prevent the children disturbing Otsuno, Watanabe had resumed their education although none of them took to it with any enthusiasm.

It had been mid-March when Otsuno had finally regained consciousness. Although he was too weak to walk, he spent several days talking in private with Shonin and Watanabe.

"What happened?" Watanabe asked. "On the wharf? What brought about this episode?"

Otsuno looked into his lap and then up at The Governor. "The more time a master and apprentice spend together, the stronger they become. You were my apprentice for five years. Lord Soma was something similar. Gasan and I... it was nearly thirty years. Even when he was not with me, I was with him. You understand?"

Watanabe nodded his head but made no reply.

"Something has happened at Ise," Otsuno continued, his voice was frail and began to crack with emotion. "Gasan… has passed over… into The Great Void." The old monk's eyes were glassy.

"Could it have been a disease… or an accident?" Watanabe asked.

Otsuno shook his head. "No. It was sudden. And very, *very* violent."

"What about this other man?" Shonin asked, speaking for the first time. "His companion? Tatsuo?"

"I cannot tell," Otsuno replied. "I only knew him a while, and even then as a boy. I do know that he was with Gasan at the time. The land still echoes with their battle cry, but…" he broke off and looked back down into his lap, ashamed that he should mourn a loss when all his teachings told him to celebrate such a passing.

Watanabe's expression was grim. "But Ise are allies of the Soma Clan… of the Emperor himself. How could such an attack be possible?"

The monks said nothing but looked at each other meaningfully.

Shonin eventually spoke. "For many years, Ashikaga has sponsored The Pure Land Sect… temples and monasteries have been built in their name. All in a bid to assuage the wrath of the fallen bujin and the kami of the land."

"So?" Watanabe asked.

"Some now say that these temples are… turning, becoming dark places. In the last three years, there have been rumors… of shrines being erected within a temple grounds that twist a man… make him strong but make him crazed too. Capable of terrible things."

"It was like that at Choshi," Otsuno said to The Governor. "I didn't realize it at the time, and the dark shrine cannot have been there long, but the people… they were becoming hard. You saw it too."

"But where are they coming from?" Watanabe asked. "Ashikaga is not a holy man. What would he know of such things?"

Again, the monks looked to each other and Shonin answered. "The rumors speak of a lieutenant… a woman…"

"I have seen her," Watanabe interrupted. "She was directing the forces at Fujigatani."

Shonin nodded. "She is powerful. Some say that she is a sorcerer, others that she is Ashikaga's concubine. But all say that this… this darkness is her doing. That she brings with her black arts from the east."

"But there is only the sea out there. We all know that," The Governor replied.

"At this moment, it does not matter," Otsuno said hoarsely. "If Gasan has truly fallen at Ise, and this witch is spreading her poison… then things are far worse than we imagined."

"Master, what do you mean?"

"The High Priestess at Ise is the Emperor's sister, and it would have been she who personally held the land deeds to The Inzai Valley. Ashikaga is no fool; he may believe he can defeat Go-Murakami and seize the royal regalia, but he knows that it is quite another thing to defile a temple's estate. It is something that had bothered me for some months, and with the fall of Gasan, I can now only presume that the guardians of Ise not only knew about the attack on The Inzai Valley... but they must have sanctioned it. And that means that a member of the Imperial House has been turned."

Watanabe said nothing. The old monk's words had confirmed his worst suspicions. If his master's theory was true, then they were all in far greater danger than they could have possibly imagined.

It had been the first week in April when Otsuno had brought Jion forward for Shonin to assess the boy. The Yugyo Monastery, although small, was renowned for the quality of Sohei it produced, and several generals had been trained by its stable of masters over the years. However, admission was not easy, requiring the nomination of two Masters and then a test by The Monastery Council. For his part, Jion had recovered some of his talents, but when he tried to reach out with his mind, it felt tender and bruised.

"Rage and revenge will do that to you," Shonin said, sensing the boy's discomfort.

"You believe that it is a great source of power, but it is caustic... burning you. If you let it flow through you, it will make you its servant, transforming you into the very thing you hate."

For a day and a night, Jion and Shonin had sat opposite each other, cross-legged in silent meditation as the monk tried to sense the mysteries and secrets within the child.

It was the following morning when Shonin finally opened his eyes and looked first to Otsuno and then to Jion.

"You have... potential," he said slowly. "But you are troubled. I saw through your eyes what happened on the ocean. You nearly lost yourself. Chaos will always try to find a way in. It is not enough for you to *know* the Gentle Way of the Yamabushi. You must *become* it."

"Will you be his Seconder?" Otsuno asked.

Shonin thought for a moment and then spoke softly. "Child, within you is the power to either save The Eight Isles from the Scourge of The Chrysanthemum Throne, or to crush it under your boot as you become far worse than Ashikaga could ever be. *If* I second you, I am placing not just millions of lives into your safekeeping, but also the fate of all Oyashima in to your hands. Do you understand?"

"Master Shonin, I do," Jion replied soberly, bowing low as he did so.

"Very well then," Shonin said. "I shall take that as your most solemn vow, forever to be held inviolate. I will second you."

So it was that the group set off on the three-day walk that would deliver them to Yugyo Monastery. The Sohei were in the courtyard, training as part of their routine when the party arrived, and whispers quickly filled the halls and dormitories. No sooner had Otsuno presented himself to the gate guard than the door to the main hall burst open and a small troupe of men, all dressed in the customary white monastic robes, made their way across to them.

"By The Buddha," Abbot Sonkan exclaimed. "Can it really be? Otsuno? Is that you? I thought I sensed your approach, but I did not really believe it…"

Otsuno bowed low, encouraging the rest of this party to do likewise. "Master Sonkan. I humbly request admittance to your most honorable…"

"Otsuno!" the Abbot chided. "Don't be silly. You are always welcome here. There is no need to stand on ceremony. Come, come. You must be exhausted. Master Mifune? Will you do the honors?"

Mifune began barking orders to the assembled Sohei. "Nobuo; go and tell the cook to prepare some food and cha. Nikko, fetch Mistress Taka."

*

The sun had begun to set when Watanabe slid open the door to his room to be greeted by Master Shonin. The Governor's bath and massage had been particularly relaxing, and he had not realized the knots that had built up in his muscles during their time on the road.

Shonin bowed deeply to Watanabe and shuffled into the room.

"How is Master Otsuno?" Watanabe asked.

"I cannot be sure," Shonin replied. "He claims to be fine, but… well, you can see for yourself."

"Maybe a period within The Temple will restore him?"

Shonin shook his head. "I think it is more serious than that, Sensei. I was only a boy when I took orders within this monastery… younger than your ward is now. Although Master Otsuno never taught me, I remember him well and he was an old man even then. That was seventy years ago. Not long after the Mongols attempted to invade for a second time."

"You think that Master Otsuno may be preparing for the Great Void?" Watanabe asked, visibly upset.

"It may be, but there is something else."

"What is it? Is it Jion?"

"No. Well, maybe. Perhaps in part. Sensei, all of the Masters… they know the Flow of Life. They embrace it, and in turn it nourishes them, allowing them to go about their work for far longer than an ordinary man would expect."

"So?" asked Watanabe. The Governor had heard of such practices, but only The Monastery Council and the most senior adepts knew the skills.

"Sensei… I do not know how to say this… It has been many months since I was last here. Yokohama is my preaching ground… but when I returned with you… Sensei, *all* of The Monastery Council looks as if they are afflicted with the same malady that has struck at Master Otsuno. That is what I have come to tell you."

Watanabe's eyes narrowed. "I do not understand. The Monastery Council must have deputies appointed, ready to take over when a Master passes over?"

Shonin shook his head. It was clear that The Governor did not grasp what he was hearing. "Sensei, you misunderstand. The Masters are losing their grip on the Flow of Life. It is slipping from their grasp. From all of us."

Watanabe's eyes widened with shock. "You mean that the teachings are failing us?"

"Maybe. But it is more likely that something is… taking the flow from us."

"Ashikaga," Watanabe muttered, shaking his head. "It will be his Oni and their cursed demon magic."

"Perhaps," Shonin replied. "But it does mean we should tread with care whilst we are here."

"What do you mean?"

"If The Monastery Council is losing their sense of the flow… they will only see what they see, and not the way things really are. It maybe that their judgment becomes clouded…"

"You think they will not accept Jion? That they will not train him?"

Shonin raised a hand to calm the rising note of indignation in Watanabe's voice. "It is difficult to say. He is older than one who would normally be admitted, but his abilities… may prove of value. I will make representation to The Council, but after that I must return to Yokohama. There is always rumor and gossip in a port and it may be that I can discern what Ashikaga's Oni are really up to."

*

Abbot Sonkan was weary but, despite the ache in his back, he sat bolt upright on the large silk cushion. For nearly a whole day they had interviewed Otsuno, Shonin, and then finally the boy.

The story had seemed incredible. Assassination and the loss of an inheritance were common-place in such times, but the rise of the Oni and the corruption of hallowed land… these were dark seasons indeed.

Sonkan turned to his right to address Mifune, and bowed his head slightly. "What is your opinion, Master Mifune?"

The Council Elder was silent for a moment as he weighed the arguments. "Let us consider the facts," he said eventually. "There can be little doubt that the boy has been deprived of his heritage. He does have a proposer and a seconder. We should put aside for one moment his talents, and focus on the matter that disturbs me most; this quest for revenge. Such a path… it is not our way. It can only lead to death and madness."

Sonkan turned to his left and said to Kyuzo. "Master. Your opinion?"

Kyuzo bowed his head in return. "I agree with Master Mifune. However, I am mindful of Master Otsuno's claim that the child can be turned from such a destructive path. If this were the case then the boy would be a valuable asset."

"And what do you both perceive the risks to be?" Sonkan asked.

"These talents that Master Otsuno speaks of may be nothing more than a mirage… perhaps a series of coincidences," Mifune said.

"We should also consider that Ashikaga's forces will continue to seek the child. That may put all of us at risk." Kyuzo added.

Sonkan nodded in agreement. "Does The Council consider the risks to be worth the rewards?"

Mifune spoke first again. "It is dependent on two things. Firstly, does he really possess any abilities? And secondly, can Master Otsuno and his Sensei control him?"

"I would also ask The Council to consider his age," Kyuzo said. "It is rare for one as old as he to be admitted into our order. Three or four years old is the recommended limit. The boy is already six. Whilst I acknowledge the impeccable work his Sensei has carried out with the two girls, Master Otsuno himself admits that Jion has been difficult to teach. He must *want* to learn. At the moment his hate blinds him to all else and I cannot sense whether or not he would accept our instruction."

Sonkan addressed Mistress Taka, who was kneeling on the floor in front of the three elders. "Mistress Taka, is there anything in our creed that dictates an upper limit on age?"

"No Master," Taka said, bowing low. "However, our tradition had always been to admit younger novices rather than older."

"What was the age of the oldest novice we have admitted?" the Abbot asked.

Taka consulted the scroll in front of her that was the Yugyo Creed, and tried to suppress a smile. "Master Abbot, the oldest novice we have admitted was twelve years old."

The Council collectively inhaled. *"Twelve?"* Mifune asked, incredulous. "I have never heard of such a thing. Who was it?"

"Master Otsuno," Taka replied.

Sonkan permitted himself the smile that Taka had denied herself. "So there is proof it can be done. No-one here would doubt Master Otsuno's wisdom, and there can be no finer example of a Yamabushi."

"Master Abbot," Kyuzo said, "perhaps Master Otsuno is the exception that proves the rule. Although he is by far the oldest and wisest of us, let us not forget that it has been many years since he dwelt within our walls. He rejects the monastery for his itinerant way of life and his precious mountains."

"That may be the case," the Abbot said, "but if Ashikaga's Pure Land Sect continues to grow, and brings these dark shrines with them, then the boy maybe our only defense against them. Perhaps we should invite him to… demonstrate these abilities. It may give us all a better understanding of what we are dealing with."

"Master Abbot," Mifune replied bowing his head. "I do not agree. If the boy really does possess these abilities then he will be all the more dangerous to us as Ashikaga hunts him."

Sonkan conceded the point and turned to Kyuzo. "Master Kyuzo, what is your opinion?"

Kyuzo looked to his two friends and fellow monks and considered the arguments before replying.

*

Utsunomiya Castle, Shimotsuke Province

Yoshiakira stood on the small rise that looked over his father's castle, his left arm out straight, as the falcon wheeled, cried out, and returned to perch on his master's leather glove. Ashikaga's son placed the hood over its head, and gently stroked its neck, calming the creature and admiring its predatory beauty.

The sound of approaching horses caused him to turn and the familiar form of Lady Altera rode into view. Yoshiakira dismissed his bodyguards with a nod of the head – this was to be a private conversation.

Altera pulled up her steed, dismounted, and bowed deeply to Yoshiakira.

"My Lord," she said.

"My Lady." Yoshiakira's bow was noticeably shallower than the foreigner's. "We are glad that you have returned."

"My Lord, I wish that all held your view." Altera's rebuking by Ashikaga for failing in her mission was common knowledge, increasing her pariah status amongst the other lieutenants.

"I am sure that in time everyone will come to… appreciate your commitment."

"Thank you, My Lord. I hope so too."

"What does your Hunter have to say about the missing child?"

"Little. He was greatly weakened by… whatever it was that attacked us."

"Ah yes. The typhoon that so reduced my father's fleet…"

"My Lord, I mean no disrespect by interrupting, but that was no typhoon. I have seen such things before – many times in Tianxia. This… it was something else. Something targeted."

Yoshiakira suppressed his surprise. "You mean a Divine Wind?" The last time anyone had claimed such a direct celestial intervention was when the fleets of Mongol Hordes had been destroyed at sea more than seventy years ago.

"No, My Lord. This was something more… earthly. I believe that the child is being taught *Mikkyo* – the magic of your land."

Yoshiakira snorted loudly in derision. "Come now My Lady. Such practices have been extinct for nearly five hundred years. And besides, your… talents are surely a match." The General's son had seen much of Altera's abilities in the last few weeks and was coming to believe that she would be the key to unlocking not only Tianxia but also the kingdoms of Baekje and Silla. Once Oyashima was subdued, the armies of the Ashikaga Shogunate would push west, taking back what was rightfully theirs.

"Maybe My Lord," Altera replied. "But the child grows stronger. Even now my Hunter is losing his… scent."

Yoshiakira was surprised. "Really? It would be a shame if such a creature was no longer… useful."

"My Lord, he has narrowed his search to the southern coast. But wherever the child is… his exact location is being masked. Would My Lord condescend to releasing the Prisoner? He may lead us to his master."

Ashikaga's son nodded. "Very well. I will have the documents prepared."

"Thank you My Lord. And what of… the other matters. Our agreement?"

"What does my father say?"

"My Lord, his temples continue to expand, but he has prohibited any of them to install the shrines I seek."

Yoshiakira paused. "A pity," he said eventually. "I would have hoped that the Shogun could have understood their potential. But now is not the time to act. The summer campaigns are about to start and these will provide you with ample opportunity to win back my father's favor. If there is no improvement after… let us say twelve months, we will revisit the situation."

"Thank you My Lord." Altera bowed low again and retreated.

*

Yugyo Monastery

Jion knelt outside the main hall, trying to listen to the discussions that were taking place inside. Nikko knelt alongside him. For the last three days she had been his constant companion; introducing him to the library and educating him in the myriad rules and regulations that made up the monastery's substantial Book of Law.

"Don't worry," she said soothingly. "The Monastery Council always takes their time. They are very thorough."

"I wish they would hurry up," Jion said, shifting uncomfortably on the hard floor.

Nikko permitted herself a smile. "From time to time, we all do. But you must learn patience."

Jion was not content to let the matter lie. "If all they do is talk, when do they act?"

"Shhh," Nikko said gently, understanding the boy's frustration. "It is not seemly to talk about The Council like that."

When Jion next spoke, his voice was much lower. "Do they always behave like this?"

Nikko sighed. "Unfortunately... yes, most of the time. The Council are great thinkers."

"If *I* were in charge, I would make a decision and act. I would not sit around talking all the time."

Nikko smiled again. "I'm sure you would. But you are not in charge. Still, you must be patient. There is great potential within you. We all sense it. If you are admitted to our order, I will watch you with great interest, young Jion."

The door slid back and Otsuno appeared. "Young Lord, The Council requires your presence."

Jion bowed deeply to Nikko and shuffled through the doorway, bowing again to the Abbot and other members of The Council.

"Please Jion," Sonkan said, "be seated. We thank you for your patience. Yours is an... unusual case. We wish to discuss with you the episode at sea."

"Yes Master Abbot," Jion replied, bowing deeply and then kneeling.

"After you became one with the ocean, you say that you then became... the air itself?"

"Yes Master Abbot."

"And you came upon those who had pursued you to Port Choshi?"

"Yes Master Abbot."

"You have previously told this Council that the approach of this group made you feel sick and faint. How is it that you came upon them without ill effect?"

"I do not know, Master Abbot. It something that Master Otsuno and Master Shonin have discussed with me at length. It may be that whatever power they wield can only affect my physical self. But I cannot say for certain."

"I see," Sonkan replied. "And what happened when you came upon this group?"

"I was in a rage Master Abbot. I had... lost control. But when I discovered them I intended to smash them... but I could not. There was something amongst them... it dragged me down. In to them. As if to devour me."

Sonkan looked to Taka who was flicking through an array of parchments, before finding the one she was looking for and approaching the Abbot. Whispering in his ear, she handed over the parchment and returned to her previous position.

"Master Otsuno," Sonkan said. "You are perhaps the longest serving of the Yamabushi Order. Did you spend much time in our library during your training?"

Otsuno bowed low. "I regret Master Abbot that I did not. I was not as disciplined as I wish I had been and spent more time adventuring in the forests than I did studying."

The Council collectively chuckled. Otsuno's games in the forest at the expense of his tutors had become the stuff of legend and had inspired successive generations to practice their skills more openly than the Monastery had wished they would.

"I'm sure we all wish we had spent more time in the library," Sonkan said, smiling. "Nevertheless, we are fortunate that Mistress Taka knows our records better than any other."

Taka flushed with pride and embarrassment, and bowed deeply to The Council. "Thank you Master Abbot. But it is really nothing. I could not have cataloged so many records without the help of Nikko."

"That's as the case maybe," Sonkan replied, "but we are grateful for your diligence. You see Master Otsuno, Mistress Taka, and Nikko, have uncovered some previously forgotten teachings."

"Really?" Otsuno replied. "May I be so impertinent as to ask what these are?"

"You may Master Otsuno. You will no doubt have been made aware of the discovery of a 'prophecy' linked to the omens in the sky last year?"

"The three stars?" Otsuno asked. "Your novices talk about little else."

"Such is the way of young minds to be easily distracted," Sonkan smiled, remembering the follies of his own youth. "But alongside the prophecy were other documents... perhaps more pertinent to our current situation. We were all taught of three types of beings; the gods; those who are both heaven and earth – man; and those uncommon few who are simply the earth – the Farravashi. However, it would appear that many centuries ago, our forbearers were taught of a fourth type."

"Master Abbot," Otsuno bowed deeply. "I have never heard of such a thing."

"Neither had The Council, Master Otsuno. It was only the boy's description during our first interview that alerted Mistress Taka who remembered the other documents with the prophecy."

"I should congratulate Mistress Taka on her diligence," said Otsuno, bowing to the librarian.

"Thank you Master Otsuno," Taka returned the bow, "but it was only my duty."

Otsuno looked to Sonkan. "Master Abbot, may I ask what is taught about these beings? The fourth type?"

"You may Master Otsuno. It is of great interest to all of us. It is said that there are beings forged from The Great Void itself, and given life within the womb of the world. Life flows from the gods. It flows around Man. It flows *through* the Farravashi. But in the case of this nameless fourth... they devour life, Master Otsuno. To know them is to know absolute annihilation."

Otsuno frowned. "Annihilation, Master Abbot? No rebirth?"

"That is right, Master Otsuno," Sonkan said. "It would appear that, if what your apprentice says is true, he had a very lucky escape."

Jion felt himself bridle. "You dare you insult me? Of course what I say is true."

"Jion!" Otsuno snapped, and turned back to The Council. "Please Master Abbot, I beg forgiveness of my apprentice. He is young with so much to learn."

Sonkan had been as shocked as the other Council members at the boy's outburst. "Yes," he said cautiously. "Perhaps that brings us on to our next order of business."

"Master Abbot?" Otsuno asked.

"The Council has deliberated whether your apprentice should be formally admitted to our order and trained," Sonkan replied. "You understand that it would be unusual for one of his years to gain entry, but equally The Council are mindful not only of your history Master Otsuno, but also your considerable skills."

"Thank you Master Abbot," Otsuno bowed low again.

"With that in mind," Sonkan continued, "we have devised a test."

"Master Abbot, of course. We shall submit immediately."

Sonkan motioned to Taka who placed another cushion on the floor, and from a pouch on her belt, produced a small black stone. It was nearly a perfect sphere, flecked white and had the smooth feel of eons spent in a current.

"Jion," Sonkan said. "Please tell me what you can about this stone."

Otsuno shuffled to the edge of the cushion and instructed his apprentice to do likewise.

"Now Jion," the old monk said. "Close your eyes... as before. Reach out with your mind. Feel the..."

"Yes Master," Jion replied, feeling himself dissolving into the air and then encircling the stone, probing its surface. It bore the faint smell of salt and Jion began to see the journey it had made back through the door, into the Abbot's quarters.

"Master Abbot has had it in his possession for many years," Jion said, seeing the stone on a shelf. "It was a gift from... the previous Abbot... and the Abbot before. It has always been passed on... to symbolize the impermanence of ourselves. An Abbot must surrender to the Great Void, but the land is eternal..." Jion was drifting back through the years, seeing the stone passed from one hand to another. "... it was found on a shore, not far from here... before Yokohama had a name. A monk was sitting on the shore meditating. He was so deep in his trance that he did not notice the tide coming in, and the first wave delivered this stone on to his lap. He took it and worked it into a sphere, marveling at its perfection…"

Jion's voice had become a monotone and the air in the main hall had become still as The Council listened intently to the boy's words.

"… it rested at the bottom of the sea. Sand covered it for generations. More than generations. Forever. It longed for the fires of its birth. For so long it was beneath the waves. It was there when the oceans were solid. It remembers how they melted. And the sun before the deep snow… it saw the fires in the sky. Silver serpents… rising up. Leaving before the ice came. Lords of the sky. Not all escaped. Some were left behind. They could not ride the serpents. One crashed. There was fire…. The stone saw the fall and the rise…"

Otsuno's voice was cautious. "Jion… come back child."

"Master?" The boy opened his eyes and looked to his Master and then The Council. Their eyes were wide and their jaws hung slack as they stared at Jion and the stone. The boy turned to look at the stone, seeing the source of their shock.

The stone hung in mid air, a few inches from the cushion, and was slowly rotating. Energy seemed to ripple and flash across its surface in a storm-like dance and then dissolve before reappearing again. Abruptly the stone dropped back on to the cushion.

Jion looked back to The Council. "Did I pass?"

*

Kurama Temple
Kwon sat cross-legged and in silence, watching the dawn of the day spread across the courtyard, warming the flagstones. The doors of his training hall were open, but no-one came. No-one ever came.

Outside other Sohei began their drills, practicing with spears and bows as their masters barked orders at them, correcting their posture and balance. Kwon was alone, but he did not mind.

It had been this way ever since he had been admitted into the order. Even though his head was now shaved and he wore the robes of a monk, he was not accepted. Kwon heard the whispers.

"A foreigner in our midst?"

"He is a devil."

"What was the Master Abbot thinking?"

Shimada had been as good as his word. When The Temple Council had seen the evidence – the head of the Tengu King, Sojobo – they had honored their part of the agreement, and had admitted Kwon. For months, he had studied their philosophy and their culture, becoming quite eloquent in the spirited debates.

As time had progressed, he had sought students to teach the way of the sword, but only encountered reticence and occasionally outright hostility. It was that he was a foreigner, and the few before him that had made their way to Oyashima had behaved badly, plundering and breaking the laws of the strict caste system.

Kwon sighed and stood. It did not matter. He was not here for the Sohei. He was here for The Prophecy Child. He had spent years in Sumerland hunting down the most obscure and rare texts, dodging The Second Born and their Raven Flocks. There were always tantalizing clues, but never the knowledge he sought. And when he had found it – the near indecipherable inscriptions in a buried cavern which must have dated to the dawn of time… it had led him first to The Great Queen of Murkwood, and then to here. It was only a matter of time until The Child appeared.

Unsheathing his sword, Kwon began his first kata. He could not let his skills rust.

*

Yugyo Monastery
It was Mifune who spoke first. "Master Abbot, the child is dangerous."

Kyuzo shook his head in disagreement. "Master Abbot, I do not agree. The child *could* be dangerous. Under our tutelage, he could be tamed, even honed and directed. If we reject him then we also reject Master Otsuno. They would have to go back out into the world where who knows how the child would develop. It is safer for all if he was with us."

Sonkan considered the arguments, and addressed Kyuzo first. "Do you believe he could counter whatever creature of The Great Void that Ashikaga has summoned?"

"No Master Abbot, I do not. He is a child, and he admitted how the Darkness nearly devoured him. But as his skills grow… it is possible."

"What say you Master Mifune?"

"If this Darkness you speak of is really hunting the child, then it will come here sooner rather than later. You cannot guarantee the boy will be able to defend us. You risk us all."

Sonkan sat back in his cushion and then turned to the Librarian who was busy taking notes. "Mistress Taka, please admit Jion."

Taka shuffled to the door and slid it open. Jion and Otsuno appeared at the entrance, bowed together, and stepped into the hall.

"Master Otsuno. Jion. The Council has reached a decision."

*

June 1357 - The Ise Province

There were voices in the darkness. Cries of disgust. Horror. Revulsion. The sound of people running away. Silence. Feet cautiously approaching. A gasp and another cry.

"*Eta! Eta!*" The defiled.

Someone fled, but someone else remained, cradling his head, talking softly. But he could not understand.

Tatsuo felt nothing as pedestrian as pain. The sense of violation went far deeper than that. He had been dishonored. Shamed. Humiliated.

Images flashed before his mind's eye. He had charged at the traitor Mutsu. Someone's spear had parried the killing blow, and he had spun into the courtyard where he was surrounded by legions of black-eyed Sohei. Gasan had followed him, his staff spinning and striking at the knees and elbows of their adversaries.

Victory was impossible. There were hundreds of Sohei. Maybe even thousands, and those behind them in The Temple, with the thing that called itself Saio, had spilled out. The best that could be hoped for was to avenge Lord Soma and die quickly and honorably themselves.

It had been a battle worthy of Amaterasu himself.

Tatsuo's blade had flashed, hacking at arms and necks, vital life essence flung into the air until it was raining blood. Gasan had joined him and the two men had fought back-to-back, parrying and counter-attacking whilst Lord Mutsu had looked on from the steps of the Grand Hall.

The inevitable came too quickly. A spear had been hurled and Gasan missed it. It had punctured the monk's knee, splitting it and pinning him to the flagstone. Even as he sank, his staff continued to spin, saving Tatsuo from another kill shot.

Tatsuo had begun to turn to defend his fallen comrade, but it was already too late. Lord Soma's loyal retainer saw a spear-blade slice across Gasan's neck, the head detaching in an orgy of blood and gore.

The bujin had fought on. Spears parried and a sword thrust through a throat, turning into a spin to take an arm and another. A high kick into a chest driving the fiends back.

Yes, he had thought, *this will be a good death*.

It was not to be. From behind came a dull punch, dizzying him. He had stumbled and turned, disorientated, and another had come from the side.

They were using the butt of their spears.

They want me as a hostage he thought. *NO!*

Sensing the end, Tatsuo had tried to loosen his cuirass, to drive his blade into his own stomach in the final act of seppuku...

He was not quick enough. The shaft of a spear had smashed against his face sending him sprawling to the ground, and into the inky oblivion of unconsciousness.

Tatsuo could not clearly remember what had happened next. It was as though he was in a dream. He remembered waking to find himself tied to some sort of table.

Mutsu had leered down at him. *Recant Soma. Join usss...*

Tatsuo had refused. They took his sword arm at the elbow.

He had tried not to scream. *By all the kami they will not get the satisfaction...*

Recant... recant... recant. We will make you whole. Join usss...

There were beatings. Next they had taken an eye and both ears, laughing and jeering as they did so. More beatings. Then they had broken the fingers of his left hand. Still more beatings, this time pouring salty vile smelling fluid over him. Then both his ankles were broken with a large iron hammer.

In between these sessions he was cast into a pit. It stunk of urine and feces, and in the darkness he could hear rats scurrying about. Time lost all meaning.

Finally they had taken a hot poker to his anus. This time he had screamed and then darkness.

Yesss.... Join usss... We are the Hope Against The Tyrants. The voices had come from far away.

And now there was the cool of day on his scarred face.

Someone was talking. "By the Buddha... I think he's alive. Get help."

He felt himself lifted. Carried along. Set down again. A bowl was pressed to his parched lips. Tatsuo gulped the water, but as soon as it hit his stomach he retched, vomiting it back up.

More voices. Some more cries of revulsion. But others more soothing. They were asking him something.

Tatsuo tried to respond but it felt like his tongue was stuck to the roof of his mouth and all that came out was a bestial cry and grunt.

A deeper voice now. Authoritative. Maybe a Headman. Someone lit an incense stick, and then he was carried again. Tatsuo felt his clothes being removed. A gasp at the scars on his body. Then water. Hot water gently lapping at him. Soothing the fire of pain and indignity.

Then being dried. A massage. The smell of hot sake and smoked fish. And then sleep. Darkness. Peace.

*

October 1357 - Yugyo Monastery, Sagami Province

The smell of autumnal rains hung in the air and Jion looked out from the library, across the canopy of the forest. He marveled how the turning colors so mirrored the fires that had ravaged the land during the summer. A messenger had brought news that Ashikaga's forces had been brought to a standstill as the smoke from the wildfires engulfed them on their marches.

Nikko smiled at the young boy who had marked his seventh birthday only the week before by spending the whole day studying.

"You seem... more content," she said. "Do you remember how you were when you came to us?"

Jion nodded. His head had been shaved in the monks' style, and he no longer had hair to fall across his eyes. "I do Mistress Nikko," he smiled. "Things were different for me then. I wonder if I was someone else. I missed my father and brother. I was always cold and hungry on the road. We were constantly afraid. I did not understand that such things are unimportant."

Nikko's smile widened. "You have learned so much in such a short space of time. Nevertheless, you must understand that this is just the beginning. It will take you many years to become a Master. And even then you will continue to discover new things when you take on an apprentice yourself. Abbot Sonkan tells us the relationship between apprentice and Master is two-way. Each learns from the other."

"I understand, Mistress Nikko," Jion replied. "The river flows ever on. So it is with us."

"Very good," Nikko said, bowing her head slightly. "But it is not enough to repeat the words of our forebears. You must live them."

"I will endeavor to do so Mistress Nikko," Jion responded. Down in the courtyard, he could see Gozen practicing with her bow and Masako with her spear. Both had embraced the monastic life and had similarly had their heads shaved. From the side, Otsuno was coaxing Masako whilst Watanabe corrected Gozen's posture. Tomorrow he would continue to his weapon training and the day after would be military strategy. The next day would be philosophy and after that would come the private sessions with Abbot Sonkan and Master Otsuno, where both monks helped him explore his abilities and become stronger.

Jion could feel his power growing all the time, and allowed himself a moment of pride.

Nikko's head snapped up from her parchment, sensing the change in the boy's demeanor, and looked straight at him. "Be careful young one. You may have come far, but you have infinitely further to go."

Jion bowed his head solemnly. "Yes Mistress Nikko."

*

April 1358 - Utsunomiya Castle

Altera did not need to ask who was at the door. She had sensed The General's son approaching. His step was heavy, as a man burdened. The previous summer campaign had been a disaster and there was even talk of Emperor Go-Murakami retaking Keishi. The mild winter had brought no better fortune, with mosquitoes spreading disease amongst Ashikaga's troops and allies. Some now muttered whether the Shogun had what it took to unify the country and face down the growing Tianxian threat.

"Come in Lord Yoshiakira," she said sweetly.

The door slid open and Yoshiakira shuffled in. "Lady Altera, how good of you to invite me to share your cha."

"The honor is mine My Lord. You can hear the nightingales in full song from here. I thought it would please My Lord."

Yoshiakira did not acknowledge the code word. "In full song Lady Altera?"

"Yes My Lord. Every last nightingale sings out."

The lieutenants and clan lords will support you when you become Shogun. And I will get my shrines.

*

May 1358 - Yugyo Monastery

The arrow hit the wall, well wide of the straw target and Otsuno shook his head. "Jion, you know better than this. How many times do I have to tell you? Breathe as you release…"

The boy was not listening to his Master, but had turned to the Torii gate at monastery entrance, his eyes searching.

Otsuno stood. "Jion? Are you listening to me?"

The boy's mind reached out, following the contours of the land; down the narrow forest track; over the swollen river; through the outlying villages.

"Something is coming," he said, his voice taking on the now familiar monotone quality. "Someone…"

Otsuno tensed and signaled to Watanabe to come over. "Who is it? Ashikaga's men?"

"What is the matter?" The Governor asked, standing.

"The boy senses someone approaching," the monk replied.

"No," Jion's brow furrowed in concentration. "A friend…" his mind's eye sped on. Through grassland, over hills and long forgotten holy sites, before finally alighting on…

"Buddha preserve us," the child whispered turning pale.

"Jion? Who is it?" Watanabe demanded.

"Child, what can you see?" Otsuno knelt in front of the boy, holding his arms. He had seen this reaction several times before in recent months, when Sonkan and he had pushed Jion too far in training his special abilities.

Sweat beaded on the boy's forehead and his eyes had become glassy with a faraway look. "What have they done to him?" his voice was barely a murmur.

"Watanabe," Otsuno said, looking up at The Governor. "Please get the infirmary ready. He's going to…"

Jion's eyes rolled back and he slumped into the old monk's arms.

For three days and two nights, the son of Lord Soma lay in a feverish sleep. His mind alternately straining to find the man who now approached, and then recoiling in horror and fear when it did so. Watanabe remained by his bedside the entire time, whilst Gozen, Masako, and other novices frequently came to see how Jion was progressing. Each time The Governor shook his head grimly.

It was on the third evening that the boy opened his eyes and turned to Watanabe. "Sensei?" he asked, confused by his state of undress and that he was lying in an infirmary cot.

"Jion! Thank the Buddha…"

"Sensei, why am I here?"

"You fainted…"

"No no no," the boy interrupted. "This is not for me. No. We must get ready." He threw off the blanket that was covering him, and unsteadily tried to stand.

"Lord! No," Watanabe rushed to him, taking his weight. "Please Jion. You are very weak. You must…"

"No!" Jion's voice had taken on a commanding tone that instantly reminded the old governor of the boy's father when he was addressing the troops. "We must get to the gate. Take me there. Now."

Without hesitation Watanabe grabbed a robe and dressed the child and began to lead him across the courtyard.

Otsuno came out of his room. "I heard shouting. What is going… Jion?"

"He says that we *must* get to the gate," Watanabe said, taking nearly all of the boy's weight.

The sound of distant hooves advancing slowly on the stony path reached them, and as one they turned to the entrance.

"Jion!" Otsuno ordered, unsure whether to prepare for an attack. "Who is it?"

The boy's eyebrows knitted together in concentration, allowing his mind to first settle and then focus on the approaching mounted figure.

Finally Jion said, "It's Tatsuo."

*

The Sohei swarmed across the courtyard as Otsuno's word reached them. Tatsuo – the lost hero of the Soma Clan now miraculously returned to them. They streamed down the hillside path to greet the figure, lighting the torches on the way. The sun was beginning to set, and the fires cast deep shadows into the surrounding forest as the smell of wood smoke filled the air.

A shout went up. And then another.

Tatsuo allowed himself to be pulled from his horse, embraced, and then carried to the monastery. The two farmers who had accompanied him were treated equally well, and were ushered into the finest bedroom chamber, reserved only for visiting dignitaries.

It would take many days of recuperation before Tatsuo could be brought before The Monastery Council where Jion, Watanabe and Otsuno had been invited to join the interview.

"... I can only imagine why they abandoned me," Tatsuo finished. "Maybe they believed I would never join them. Or perhaps they believed me already dead. I cannot say for certain."

Sonkan leaned forward, inspecting the battered figure before him. "Your injuries are indeed grievous. What else can you tell us of your captivity?"

Tatsuo bowed low and replied, "Master Abbot, I thank you for your kindness and hospitality. With your permission, I wish to relay the remainder of my story directly to Lord Soma and Sensei Watanabe."

Sonkan knew that the man intended no slight, and motioned Tatsuo to proceed.

The battered bujin turned and bowed low, first to Jion and then Watanabe. "Lord. I should declare that I have failed in my mission to rally the support of the Ise Shrine. I seek your permission to commit seppuku for my disgrace."

Jion shook his head. "Your death is unnecessary, Tatsuo. You have failed no one. You were not to know of Lord Mutsu's treachery. You are a hero of the Soma Clan."

Tatsuo bowed low again. "Thank you My Lord. However, Lord Mutsu is not the only traitor."

Watanabe frowned and felt his stomach tighten. "What do you mean Tatsuo?"

"My Lord. Sensei." Tatsuo continued bowing. "During my... interrogation the Dog Mutsu tried to bribe me. He offered me the position of Headman of Fujigatani... he claimed that the village had been restored..."

"The cur!" Watanabe snarled.

"... under a new Lord and vassal of Ashikaga."

Jion tried to ignore Watanabe's muttering and outraged pride. "Who is it?"

"My Lord, Mutsu claimed it to be Lord Chikatane... your father's brother. He too betrayed your clan at the Battle of the Yeddo Plains. His forces were never routed. They were wearing Ashikaga's uniform."

*

June 1358- Utsunomiya Castle

Lady Altera sat in her bedchamber as the candles burned low, casting distorted shadows through the screens. She paid them no attention, instead listening intently to the orders being barked from the barracks. Troops were mobilizing. Soon it would be time.

A silhouette passed in front of her door, followed by a second smaller shadow. The larger figure rapped the flimsy door, and Altera bade the two figures to enter. She had no reason to fear. Her own martial skills would be enough to end the life of both men, and Ullar and Birag were secreted in the alcoves should more men try to enter.

Ashikaga's Hatamoto entered the room, followed by Yoshiakira.

Mizuno quickly bowed to the seated woman and produced a scroll that he read from:

"Honorable Lady Altera. It is with great sadness that I report the passing of *O-gosho* – The Great Shogun, Commander-in-chief of the Defense of the North, Lord Ashikaga, from an previously undiagnosed tumor.

"His son, Lord Yoshiakira has been appointed Clan Lord by this court, and the Emperor Kogon has honored him with the title of Shogun. All of the lieutenants and clan lords have pledged fidelity to him. Will do you likewise?"

Mizuno folded the scroll away and moved his hand to his sword lest the foreigner should seek to usurp the new Shogun.

Altera bowed low, prostrating herself on the floor, and pretended not to notice Mizuno preparing to cut her down if she did not swear unconditional loyalty. The man was a fool if he thought he could outdraw her.

"My Lord Shogun. I am so deeply saddened to hear of the unnatural passing of your father… such a tragedy, and still so young. But my heart is gladdened by your accession, that you might carry on his great work. I pledge myself and my men to you, without reservation, hesitation or equivocation of any kind. May we swiftly crush the Dogs of the West and restore peace to this great land."

Yoshiakira stood, basking in Altera's words. It had all come to pass as she had promised. He bowed his head slightly. "My Lady, your vow is well received and no doubt we shall put your considerable skills to good use in the days and weeks ahead. I thank you for your loyalty and promise to serve our Emperor faithfully." Turning to Mizuno he said, "You may leave us. The Lady and I have… private matters to discuss."

Mizuno bowed deeply. "Yes My Lord," he said and left, sliding the door closed behind him.

Once he was sure that his Hatamoto was out of ear shot, Yoshiakira crossed the floor quickly to where Altera sat.

"I do not have much time," he whispered. "I am expected to meet the other lieutenants tonight to confirm our intention to continue the war. Everything has gone according to plan… just as you promised. All have sworn loyalty to the Emperor and to me. Some will deliver family members as hostages and we will arrange marriages with my relatives to seal the unions. What news do you bring?"

Altera bowed slightly. "My Lord, the prisoner has… found his way. Even now my Hunter is divining his exact location. We will have our quarry."

Yoshiakira leaned forward and kissed Altera gently on the lips. "Soon my love, we will have everything we ever dreamed of."

CHAPTER FIVE

September 1358 - Yugyo Monastery, Sagami Province

Mifune was fuming. "This is intolerable, Master Abbot. Something must be done. Such behavior... it is unheard of."

Sonkan raised a hand to calm his old friend, although in truth he had similar feelings. Once again Jion had escaped the confines of the monastery during the night and had no doubt taken to the hills.

"Master Otsuno," the Abbot said. "You were the boy's proposer. You know our rules."

Otsuno bowed low before The Council. "Master Abbot, I humbly beg The Council's forgiveness, and ask for their forbearance. Jion... he has not yet learned to control his emotions, and the news of his uncle's treachery... it has greatly disturbed him."

"Disturbed is not the word *I* would use," Mifune retorted. "We all sense it. He is angry. And we all know that will only lead to hate and suffering... for all of us if we are not careful."

Otsuno bowed low again. "Thank you for reminding us, Master Mifune. However, are we not also taught patience? The boy needs time to adjust."

Mifune snorted "Adjust? How long will that take? Master Otsuno, you more than anyone know of the risks that we have taken by harboring that child here. If the new Shogun chooses to pursue his father's policies and locates the boy... I do not know if we could repel such an attack."

Sonkan intervened. "Masters, please. Let us consider the balance here. Master Otsuno, you must acknowledge that the boy's behavior is not only disruptive to the other students but also contrary to our creed. He must be tamed otherwise he is a danger not only to himself but to all of us. Master Mifune, you yourself have witnessed the child's abilities. He has much to offer. Perhaps some flexibility might be considered?"

*

Nikko was sitting next to Jion's bedroll when he came through the monastery window, and he sighed when he saw her silhouette in the dark.

"You heard me leave?" he asked.

She shook her head. "They check on you every few hours. You know this. You will get yourself expelled. Why do you do it?"

Jion shrugged. "I have to do something. I cannot sit and wait here until Death comes for me."

"What do you do out there?"

"Nothing. Pick mushrooms. Climb trees."

Nikko's laugh was empty. "Come now."

"It's true." Jion knew that his voice betrayed the lie, and he slid under the blankets of his bedroll to avoid further questions.

"You know that there are whispers," Nikko said. "Some say that a *kami* of death stalks the streets of Keishi and Utsunomiya, seeking revenge for all the bujin the Shogun has killed."

Knowing he was being baited, the boy replied sullenly, "Keishi and Utsunomiya are many miles from here."

"Maybe an ordinary man would not be able to get there and back in a night. But you are not ordinary are you Jion… turn over and look at me."

The boy rolled over to look at his instructor, but said nothing.

"It is not the way of this monastery to kill. Life is sacred."

Despite himself, he had grown to trust Nikko and did not believe she would betray his confidence. "Says who?"

"You know who. The Buddha."

"And what of those who do not follow the Buddha's path?"

Nikko was silent for a moment, and then whispered, "You speak of the Goddess?"

Jion knew he should speak with care. Watanabe warned him that spies were likely to be everywhere. "What do you know of such things?"

Nikko moved closer to the boy so that even those who might be listening would not hear her. "The Goddess is rising again. We… her followers rise with her."

The heir of Soma sensed he was being tested. He had communed often with his Goddess and she had spoken secret words into his heart.

Nikko grew uncomfortable in the silence. "She knows," she said. "She knows that war is coming, and she seeks to be embraced once again by the bujin."

Jion nodded in the dark, satisfied with the response. "Marishiten knows war. She knows who is sacred and who is unjust."

The young woman sighed, relieved that the boy had revealed himself to her, but also worried because their situation remained precarious. "Maybe she does. But now is not the time for you to be making such... excursions. It is dangerous for you out there. For all of us. People will start to talk."

"They do already. They think I cannot hear them, but I can."

"What do they say?" Nikko asked.

"Some are scared of me... of my abilities. Others hope I will abandon my quest for revenge. Watanabe understands though. He knows what must be done and that my training here is simply a stepping stone..."

"Sshh," Nikko said. "You must not say that."

"But it is true..."

"It does not matter. If any of the Masters heard what you have just said... The Council would expel you immediately, before your training is complete. And that would affect more than just you. Think of Gozen and Masako as well. They are tied to you through blood and loyalty."

Jion was quiet for a moment. "I'm going to have to marry Gozen, aren't I?"

"You are too young to think of such things."

"I'm nearly eight," the boy retorted. "Plenty of my boys my age are betrothed in my..." he wanted to say 'village', but he caught himself. If Lord Chikatane had rebuilt Fujigatani, his people would populate it, not the Soma Clan. Jion realized that his home was truly gone.

Nikko conceded the point. "Maybe. But it will be many years before anything has to be done about it. And much can change."

"Nikko, do a husband and wife always have to pillow?" By dawn's early light, he could see his instructor flush a little, and feared he had caused offense.

"Where did you hear that word?"

"Sensei Watanabe told me. He said that when a husband and wife lay together it is called pillowing. Do they have to? Always?"

"No, not always."

"Have you pillowed?"

Nikko did not flush this time, but her eyes became rheumy as though filled with a distant memory. "Yes. It was a long long time ago."

"Was it nice?"

She paused and then said, "Yes. Very much. You should go to sleep. Your chores will begin in a few hours."

*

After breakfast, Watanabe called Jion to his chamber. He wanted to admonish the boy for yet *another* breach of the rules.

"Do you know why you are here?" he asked.

"Yes Sensei."

"What do you have to say for yourself?"

The boy remained bowed, prostrating himself on the floor. "I did as you asked."

Watanabe shuffled on his knees to the child so the two could whisper to each other. "And?"

"I sent myself over Ise. It was as Tatsuo said. There is something… I don't know. When something dies, I can see that the flow of life is broken. But… Ise is not broken. It is like everything is twisted. The monks… they walk like men, but they have the eyes of a *kami*."

"What else?"

"They believe Tatsuo is dead. But I saw the Oni Woman there. The Foreigner. She is following the new Shogun's orders; anyone who is a threat… who could be a rallying figure for the lords still loyal to the Emperor, is to be hunted and exterminated."

"Does she know where you are?" The Governor asked.

"No. The power of the monastery… it is like a parasol in the sun. It shields me from most of their efforts. But they can tell the general area I am in."

"Hmm… if they know the region then it will not take them long to deduce an exact location. When will they move against us?"

"Not until the spring. Yoshiakira is still trying to cement an alliance with the Northern Lords. Once he has their troops under his command he will resume his push west. He believes that he can bring peace to Oyashima, and only a unified land can face the Tianxian threat."

Watanabe shook his head. "How little the dog knows. Truly, he is his father's son. What size force do they have stationed at Ise?"

"It varies. There is a lot of movement. Between three and five hundred."

"Hmm… small then," Watanabe was lost in thought. "How well trained are they? Could we win if we took a contingent against them?"

*

December 1358

Abbot Sonkan had seen and heard many things in his life. Some had been both amazing and uplifting. Others had been horrifying. But now even the outspoken Mifune had been silenced by what Watanabe and Otsuno had just told The Council.

Unusually, it was Kyuzo who spoke first. "Master Otsuno, Sensei Watanabe. The Council does not doubt that you have achieved fine results with the boy in the last few months, although he remains some way behind his peer group… but this information you bring us… First we must say that we do not approve of how it was gathered. This monastery has strict rules and if your ward sought dispensation you should have approached The Council. However, nothing can be done about that now. So that leaves us with the question: how reliable is this information?"

"Master Kyuzo," Otsuno replied bowing, "the boy has many abilities and it is the general opinion of all his instructors that most lie inert at the moment, and probably will do so until at least puberty or until he is placed in great danger, which would force them to the surface. However, his gift of hearing continues to become ever more acute and he has the ability of… some kind of far sight or remote sensing. His previous skill of either controlling or manifesting the elements has not returned, but this seems to have been replaced, at least temporarily, with great dexterity. The boy is becoming increasingly diligent in his studies and has always been honest."

Sonkan spoke next. "Master Otsuno, do you really believe that the Shogun will discover the boy's location?"

"It can only be a matter of time," the old monk replied. "The Oni Woman appears to know Jion's approximate location. Yoshiakira has sealed his alliance with the Northern Lords, and all our spies report the buildup of forces in the border towns. They must be preparing for a push westwards as soon as the snows melt. If so, the Witch will be able utilize her own troops and…"

"Yes yes yes," Mifune interrupted, finally finding his voice. "We all know how dangerous Yoshiakira and his Oni are, and we all know the value of the boy. But could we not protect the boy further? Shield him completely…?"

Sonkan laid a calming hand on his old friend's arm. "Could we, Master Mifune? Look at us. All of us. We all suspect, though few of us speak of it. Our connection with the land is weakening. We no longer have the strength we once did."

"Master Abbot," Watanabe said stepping forward and bowing. "Jion believes that he may know the reason for The Council's… diminishment."

"Really?" Sonkan replied.

"Yes Master Abbot. The boy has described how the spirit of the monks at Ise has become twisted. They have not been replaced by Oni, but rather have become corrupted. Jion has identified what he describes as a dark shrine, and I believe that Master Otsuno saw one in Port Choshi too, although he did not know what it was at the time."

"Ashikaga and his Pure Land Sect!" Mifune muttered.

"No, Master Mifune," Otsuno said. "The Pure Land Sect is not in opposition to any of the beliefs held in Oyashima. Instead, it would seem that the Oni Woman is using these dark shrines within The Temple grounds to subvert the adherents."

"For what end?" Sonkan asked.

Otsuno spoke softly. "Who knows the way of the Oni, Master Abbot? But it may be that these shrines are twisting the power of the land from our grasp and were they destroyed, it would return to us."

"Your argument is convincing Master Otsuno," Kyuzo said. "This… pre-emptive strike you have planned… Would you take the boy with you?"

*

The Ise Grand Shrine, Ise Province

Lady Altera stood in the dark of the night watching the training of the Ise Sohei. The warmth from the braziers barely cut through the cold winter breeze that whipped around her, causing a flurry of snow here and there like a miniature typhoon. If she was cold, she did not show it, unlike her companions.

Lord Chikatane and Lord Mutsu shivered, their teeth chattering together.

"How many troops do we have now?" the brother of Lord Soma asked.

"Nearly tenthousand My Lord," Altera replied. "We train them in batches of a few hundred and then rotate them through the cities of the middle provinces. That way if there are any spies about, all they will see is a small contingent. We will overwhelm any attack."

As Chikatane and Mutsu huddled together, Altera cast her eye skyward, searching for Jion's presence. She had felt it every night for nearly twelve weeks.

Yes, she thought, *come. Come and meet your fate, boy.*

*

January 1359 – Yugyo Monastery

"How are you feeling?" Jion asked absently.

Tatsuo looked up from the board. "Very well, thank you My Lord." It was the hour of the monkey and a watery winter sun played on the snowdrifts outside, casting a cool light into the room.

"You should be wary of calling me that. Sensei Watanabe has told me that I need to maintain secrecy," Jion said, considering his next move.

"And Sensei is quite correct. But we are safe here… and I miss saying it."

"Why?" Jion asked, moving a piece on the board.

"I have been in the service of your clan all my life," Tatsuo said, rubbing gently at the stump of his arm. "Duty is all I know. Not to acknowledge you is to fail in doing my duty. I must be what I must be."

"A servant of Soma?"

"It is more than that My Lord. I *am* Soma. I simply serve the clan name, much like you."

Jion frowned. "How do you mean?"

"Sensei Watanabe told me about the little keepsake you carved for Gozen. That was very clever of you, My Lord. You served the clan well, as you do every day."

Jion still did not understand. "It was just a little pendant."

"Oh no My Lord, it was much more than that. It is a symbol… it binds her to you… always reminds her. Your father was like that. He knew not just the importance of strategic marriage… but he knew how to play the game. You look very much like him."

Jion smiled at the man's candor. "Did you know my father well?"

Tatsuo nodded. "Yes My Lord. I was one of his personal retainers and I served him for many years."

"What was he like?"

"He was a great man and a brilliant general. I know that he would be very proud of you," Tatsuo said softly, remembering the lord that had become his friend.

"I think he would be proud of you too, Tatsuo," Jion replied, sensing that under his vassal's composed exterior, emotions were bubbling.

"How so My Lord?"

"Because you have never wavered. Not once. You have used your sense of responsibility to overcome any… inertia. To always push you on… to fulfill your purpose. I thank you for that." Jion moved a final piece on the board, winning the game.

Tatsuo smiled. "Thank you My Lord. But really it is nothing. It is my duty to you. I would follow you anywhere."

*

February 1359 - The Ise Grand Shrine, Ise Province

The snowdrift was deeper than Watanabe expected, and he sank past his knee as he tried to move forward. Grunting, he shifted his weight and tried to move his other leg forward, battling against the mass of the snow and his own balance.

Behind him, under the cloak of the night, a thousand Yugyo Sohei followed him. These were the elite and, ever since Otsuno's report to The Council, they had been in a state of constant readiness.

As Watanabe crested the rise, he turned, helping Otsuno forward. It was against The Governor's better judgment that the old monk had joined the mission, although in truth there was something about his presence that put him at ease.

In the far distance, at the ferry port that Gasan and Tatsuo had used two years earlier, Watanabe could just make out the lights of The Sophia. The Governor had not expected Kagetaka to honor his promise but was pleasantly surprised that, after sending word via the merchant, the corsair had appeared at the monastery.

Kagetaka had reluctantly accepted the mission, and even as the Sohei had boarded for the ten-day journey, the corsair had complained that he was not being paid enough.

Watanabe smiled to himself. He did not like Kagetaka at all, and the fact that the corsair felt bound to Jion by a blood debt made The Governor happy. Ahead, he could see the outline of The Ise Shrine, just as Jion had described.

The Sohei began to fan out through the woods, waiting for Watanabe's order to attack.

*

Yugyo Monastery, Sagami Province

"It's not *fair*!" Jion raged. "*I* did all the work. *I* got all the information for them. I *should* have been allowed on the mission."

"But Jion," Gozen said, trying to calm him. "It is not that they could not use you. You heard what Master Otsuno said; you are just too important to risk."

"He's just jealous!" Jion continued to stomp around the bedchamber. "He knows that I will become a far greater Yamabushi than he ever was…"

Gozen saw Tatsuo raise an eyebrow – the hero of the Soma Clan had been made the children's personal guard – and tried to make Jion see reason. "But what could you do?" she said. "You are still not strong enough. You must be patient. We all must. Our time will come."

Jion almost screamed. "Patient? The men who betrayed and murdered my father are out there! And I will not be there for our victory. I dishonor my father and my clan by not taking their heads personally."

*

The Ise Grand Shrine, Ise Province

Lady Altera narrowed her eyes against the increasing winter wind, her brow furrowing. Something was wrong. She could sense the enemy moving through the forest… they would be at the shrine in only a few minutes. But the boy was not with them. He was still hidden.

"Go to the backup plan," she snapped in frustration to Ullar, who began to wave a banner against the bright coals of the brazier.

"There is the backup plan?" Chikatane asked in confusion. "We were not told of any alternate."

"You were not told because you did not need to know," Altera said icily as she watched the main body of her troops retreat from the courtyard leaving only a small contingent behind.

"But… but…" Mutsu stammered in the cold. "There are not nearly enough troops to protect The Saio."

Altera turned to him and looked hard at the older man. "We are not here to protect The Saio."

*

Otsuno's imitation of a deer bark was nearly perfect and having been given the sign, the Yugyo Sohei surged forward. Arrows filled the night sky as the archers laid covering fire for the infantry.

Watanabe led the charge, his sword held high and then cutting and hacking at the few Ise troops as they tried to repel the advance. Otsuno was beside him, parrying and defending shots with his staff. The Governor was surprised at the old monk's energy, thinking he would have sat on the sidelines, directing the attack.

The Yugyo troops broke against the line of Ise soldiers like a wave, and then engulfed them.

*

From the rise, Altera gave the command and her archers rained death down on the Sohei below. Maybe she would not achieve what she had wanted today, but she would give her attackers a bloody nose.

*

Watanabe instantly realized their mistake. They were caught out in the open courtyard with no cover. Men fell everywhere, screaming and twisting as the cruelly barbed arrowheads punctured through their light armor.

The Governor barked a command, and his troops that were still standing ran for the doorways of the buildings around the Main Hall.

"You should tell them to fire the shrine," Otsuno said.

"What? That is madness!" Watanabe replied, dodging another arrow as it slammed into the doorframe.

"No. Listen to me," Otsuno's voice was urgent. "The archers are up on the line of that rise… barely a hundred paces. Fire the buildings and the smoke will give you enough cover to send the spearmen against them."

Watanabe saw the sense of the old monk's counsel. "Fire the buildings!"

*

Altera saw the smoke begin to roll across the courtyard in thick billows, blanketing the attacking Sohei under a dark pall. It did not matter. The enemy had revealed themselves – that was what was important.

"Tell the archers to fall back," she said to Ullar.

"But My Lady," Chikatane bowed his head. "There are still Sohei in the buildings… and The Saio too."

Without looking at him, she replied, "The Saio is expendable. They are all expendable."

She turned from the view of the battle, hearing Chikatane and Mutsu gasp in shock. "And a man's fate is a man's fate," she muttered to herself.

The Hunter stood before her, gaunt and tall in the moonlight. "And death is but an illusion," he finished, smiling.

"Do you understand your mission?" Altera asked him.

"I do."

"Good. I do not care if it takes months or years, but you are to locate the boy. Once you have found him you will not engage but send word to me. You cannot take them on your own. Yoshiakira is sending me to the west for the next phase of the campaigns. Be patient."

*

The buildings around the Main Hall were ablaze, casting smoke and cinders high into the cold night air.

"Did you destroy the dark shrine?" Otsuno asked, panting so that his breath was visible.

"My men did. I saw to it personally," Watanabe replied. "Do you... feel any different?"

The old monk shook his head. "No. It may take time for its influence to dissipate. It is like the rain, no? It is still wet after a downpour. We must wait for the sun... for the land to heal itself."

Behind the sealed door of the Main Hall, both men heard a movement and turned in expectation

"This will be the last of them. I will gather the men. Today has brought us a great victory," Watanabe said.

The Yugyo Sohei that had survived the onslaught of the arrows now assembled, preparing themselves for the final rush of Ise troops that would no doubt pour through the doorway once it was unbarred.

As the big double doors swung open, they braced themselves for the inevitable wave. They were not prepared for what happened next.

Darkness. Nothing but darkness. No troops rushed out. No battle cry. No death.

"Be careful," Otsuno said, putting a hand on Watanabe's shoulder and leaning on it, his previous burst of energy now spent. "They are luring us in."

"The building is stone," The Governor replied. "We cannot fire it."

Otsuno nodded. "Maybe we could..."

A volley of arrows flew from the open door like dark bringers of death. Otsuno parried one meant for Watanabe, deflected a second, before a third beat him...

"Master!" Watanabe cradled his one-time mentor's head, as the dying men around him called out. Others charged in before a second volley could be released.

Otsuno tried to smile. "It hurts more than I imagined," he said, looking down at the arrow protruding from his stomach.

"We can get you back to Yokohama. There'll be a healer there..."

The old monk shook his head. "No. Thank you, but no. It is time. A man's fate is a man's fate, no?"

"And life is but an illusion," Watanabe finished, stroking his Master's brow. The old man looked so frail now and felt like a doll in his arms.

"One last request," Otsuno whispered. "Make it an honorable death."

Watanabe said nothing but nodded, and brought the monk up into a kneeling position. Standing behind his master, The Governor brought his sword high above him, a cold lump forming in his throat as Otsuno finished murmuring his prayers.

The sword sung through the air and, in the distance, a raven cawed at the approaching dawn.

*

With a heavy heart and arms of lead, Watanabe placed Otsuno's body on the hastily assembled pyre, and muttered a few words. Bowing his head, he then turned to what remained of the Yugyo Sohei. Barely a third had survived.

A commander stepped forward, dragging a limp body with him. "General Watanabe," he said.

"This is The Saio?" The Governor's voice sounded distant, even to himself.

"It is."

"Cut her to pieces. Then throw the parts in the fires. Nothing should remain of such a foul being. Then we go home."

Watanabe watched the Sohei hack the body apart with their swords, and then each man took a piece before moving across the Shrine grounds, casting The Saio's limbs into the fires, leaving The Governor alone with his thoughts.

He did not hear the step behind him and was startled when a voice addressed him.

"Watanabe..."

The Governor spun around, drawing his sword as he did so, ready to bear down on any assailant who would...

"It would seem there has been... an unforeseen development."

Watanabe's eyes widened at the familiar young man before him. Although his head was shaved like a monk, his youthful face was smooth and did not hint at the rigorous training the Sohei endured.

"Master Otsuno?"

The monk bowed deeply. "It would seem that life really is an illu..." Otsuno broke off, looking through Watanabe and his eyes widening in horror. "Oh by the Buddha, no..."

The apparition faded, its words hanging in the air like dew before the morning sun.

"Master?" Watanabe stepped forward, his eyes desperately searching and called out louder. "Master, are you there?"

One of the nearby Sohei turned to his comrade. "The poor fool has gone mad in his grief," he muttered.

*

July 1359 - Yugyo Monastery, Sagami Province

Jion sat cross-legged on the hard floor, his eyes closed in deep contemplation. Outside, the hot summer sun beat down and the air inside the monastery was a mix of sweat and incense. Crickets occasionally chirped from the long grass that surrounded the outer walls, and Gozen and Masako sat close by, listening intently to their instructor as he took them for their meditation.

From beyond the open door, Watanabe watched his young wards. He had feared what the loss of Master Otsuno would do to the boy and, though there had been tears, there had not been the violent tantrums he had expected. Perhaps the boy was finally growing up.

Hearing the soft sound of sandals on the courtyard flagstones The Governor turned and saw the figure of Abbot Sonkan approaching.

"Master Abbot," he said bowing his head.

"Sensei," Sonkan replied, also bowing. "How are the lessons progressing?"

"Well. I think we all recognize that Master Otsuno was an exceptional instructor…"

"You think the boy is not making the progress that he would have under Master Otsuno?"

"I did not say that Master Abbot…"

"No," Sonkan smiled. "But you thought it. If you stay with us, you will have much to learn about quieting that noisy mind of yours. Come, walk with me."

Watanabe followed the Abbot as he set off. "*If* I stay with you… I don't understand. Surely there is no question?"

"There are no questions Sensei. Only actions. And every action is really a reaction. Even if it is a decision not to react."

The Governor narrowed his eyes against the glare of the day as they stepped out of the shadows of the monastery outbuildings. "Master Abbot, please be plain with me," he replied.

"Very well. The Council has taken the decision to… curtail the boy's training. Specifically the instruction focussing on his abilities."

"What?" Watanabe was shocked. "Why? He has done so well… there have been no incidents…"

Sonkan gently placed a hand on The Governor's shoulder to calm him. "That is exactly the point. The Council senses… the boy has become cold. Not indifferent you understand, but something inside him has… has hardened. He applies himself to his training but we sense… an unnatural focus in the child."

"Master Abbot, I do not understand. Please… the strength of Jion's abilities will determine his future…"

"Very well. After Master Otsuno died, The Council expected to sense great confusion within the boy. Indeed, we were braced for it. The girls… we are not so worried about. Gozen will become a great diplomat and arbitrator. You can see that for yourself. Masako is… more of a blunt instrument. But she will do well. But Jion… we expected him to be torn between the revenge that he had sworn of his father's killers, and entering the priesthood. But there has been no internal conflict. He is simply using the training here to achieve his goal. The boy is ruthless, Sensei, and if he is allowed to succeed he will be a danger to all of us."

"I understand, Master Abbot," Watanabe tried not to show his disappointment that his plan had been discovered so quickly. "But if you deny the boy training in this one area, then surely he will just find another source to learn from. It would be better if he got this training from the monastery, that he could better be monitored."

Sonkan looked to The Governor, surprised that he was being so transparent. "We intend to fill his day with the customary instruction a boy his age would expect to receive. Watanabe, this is not a decision that we have reached lightly. The Council cannot guarantee Jion's actions. It may be that, in time, we reinstate the development of his abilities. But for now… we must safeguard our Order. And besides, more… customary instruction may help him catch up with his peer group. His special training has resulted in him lagging behind his contemporaries somewhat."

Watanabe sighed inwardly, knowing the decision was already made. "Have you told him?"

Sonkan chuckled. "With his hearing, I don't think we need to."

*

Jion looked out through the window, to the full moon that hung low and fat in the sky. Watanabe had told him of The Council's decision before meal time, and as instructed he had not reacted.

It did not matter whether The Council chose to train his abilities or not, he was growing a little stronger with each passing day. It might take years, but he would succeed.

Closing his eyes, he reached out with his mind until the moon filled him. She was there. All around him. Marishiten.

Feeling his consciousness dissolve and then reassemble, Jion looked up at the giant tree that sat in silhouette on the side of the hill. He felt the love of his Goddess fill him, healing his wounds, as She transformed herself into the milky white figure he had come to know and love.

The giant lady reached down to him and once again presented him with a lotus that slowly opened, its pollen seeds floating on the light breeze before settling on his skin and dissolving in to him. Every time he saw Her, he noticed something new. The curve of Her buttocks. The way Her hair fell across her chest. Her breath like incense.

Something moved to his right and he turned, seeing a small half-form in the shadow of the hill.

Jion's eyes snapped open. He was back in his bedroom chamber and he quickly got up and padded his way across the floor to where Masako lay on her bedroll. Her eyes were open and she was looking at him in fear.

"Was that you?" he whispered.

Masako nodded.

"How?"

The young girl sat up and beckoned him to come and sit next to her. "I know when you… go. I've always known," she said, keeping her voice low. "It's like you leave a wake… like a ship in the water. I just follow you."

"Does anyone else know?"

Masako shook her head. "No. I'd never tell. I promise. I don't think you can trust The Council here. They mustn't find out. They fear that they cannot control you."

Jion looked at the girl, wondering whether he could trust her. "What about Gozen? Have you told her?"

Masako looked to the sleeping form of her older sister. "No."

"Good." Jion thought for a moment. "How many times have you done it? Followed me I mean?"

"Not many," Masako was feeling fearful of the steely determination that had entered Jion's eyes. "This was the third time. I swear it."

In the corner, Watanabe turned over on his bedroll, muttering in his sleep, and the two children held their breath.

"What do you see?" Jion asked after a few minutes, sure that everyone was asleep.

"The hill. The tree becoming a woman. And then the lotus flower opening."

"Do you hear anything?"

Masako shook her head.

"Do you know who the woman is?"

"I heard Master Otsuno and Sensei talking… maybe a year ago. They said that she was Marishiten… the Goddess of War and that she was rising again to lead the Emperor's bujin against the Scourge of The Chrysanthemum Throne. Is that really who she is? Is it true that the Gods are on our side?"

Jion grunted an acknowledgment, but said nothing whilst he considered the situation. Finally, he held out his arm and took Masako's hand in his and gently squeezed it to reassure the girl. "Come. I'll introduce you properly to the Goddess."

*

August 1359 – Utsunomiya Castle, Shimotsuke Province

The afternoon sun beat down mercilessly on the castle, like a taiko drummer reaching a crescendo, and the whole city sweltered, taking on a lazy drone in the energy sapping heat.

Lady Altera was uncomfortable as she walked down the long corridor to Lord Yoshiakira's chamber, flanked by a contingent of his guards. Such escorts were common for the other lieutenants of the Shogun's army, but this was the first time she had been accompanied this way. She tried not to bridle at the insult; it was the custom of this land and she knew that she could diminish her position of influence if her reaction was viewed unfavorably.

The door slid open and Altera knelt and bowed, feeling her sweat-stained black robe cling to her back.

"Ah Lady Altera," Yoshiakira said jovially, fanning himself. "Please come in."

Altera shuffled forward on her knees and bowed again.

"Please, come and sit next to me. Would you like some cha?"

"Yes please My Lord," she replied. "Thank you."

Yoshiakira barked at a maid and then dismissed the guards. "I apologize for your guards. They were... a necessity."

"My Lord?"

"Holding the alliance together is becoming increasingly difficult. You will have heard that Go-Murakami has battled our forces to a standstill in the west. There is stalemate for the time being. Our allies are... dissatisfied by this and put forward ever more ludicrous plans."

Altera had heard the rumors. "My Lord is wise not to bow to such pressure. An army that is slaughtered to gain little is but a waste."

"My Lady, I appreciate that you are still learning our customs, but the way of the bujin is death. They actively seek it."

"Even if it does not serve their liege lord?"

Yoshiakira conceded the point. "Maybe you know more about our customs than you let on My Lady?"

"Only through your gracious instruction," she replied, bowing her head.

"That as the case may be, there is dissension and some openly question your position... and why you are privileged when they are not."

Altera ground her teeth and made a mental note that her spies should find those who talked so openly against her. "My Lord is prudent to order the guards to accompany me to give the appearance of equal favor."

"Maybe. In the fullness of time, we shall see. Now, what of your missions? What can you tell me?"

"As My Lord requested we have scouted in the far west, along the coast. The Clan Lords claim to be loyal to Go-Murakami. A few may be persuaded to join your cause in exchange for absorbing their neighbors' fiefs into their own, but unless they are supported they will be overwhelmed. The people seem loyal too. Merchants are merchants, and are the same as all the others in the Eight Isles. I believe that our biggest challenge will be Tsukushi."

Yoshiakira was not surprised. Oyashima's most westerly isle had always been problematic for his family. "Please Lady Altera, go on."

"Although Go-Murakami's court is in Yoshino, Tsukushi is his real power base. My spies inform me that he is seeking to establish an embassy in Tianxia and broker a deal with the new dynasty that is rising in that land."

"The Ming? Yes, I had heard similar. I would not worry. I have my own representatives who are offering this new dynasty an alternative."

"But My Lord, if Go-Murakami is successful… it will open a new source of mercenaries and weapons for him."

You would know, Yoshiakira thought and smiled. "As I said My Lady, it is something that I would not worry about. Now, what else? What about the children who escaped my father's Great Purge?"

Altera had hoped to avoid this conversation. "My Lord will be aware that the child did not join the battle at Ise. He remains shielded from us."

"That *is* disappointing."

Altera bowed her head. "My Lord, we inflicted a grievous injury to the rebels. Two thirds of their troops were slaughtered and one of their most important generals killed. The Hunter tracked the retreating force to the coast, but we were unprepared for their having assistance. It would seem that My Lord, and his father, were wise to consider the threat. The child is indeed gathering support."

Yoshiakira's face was grim. "A further disappointment. Where is your Hunter now?"

"Tracking the child is now his only mission. He saw the direction the ship sailed in, and moves along the coast gathering information. He *will* find the child… but it may take many months. The land is unfamiliar to him and we are unused to your weather."

"A pity," Yoshiakira sighed. "I had expected so much more, and you have disappointed me Lady Altera. You remember what our agreement was? More shrines in return for your success. I have upheld my part of the bargain…"

Altera knew how to play this game and smiled. "Oh but My Lord," she said softly, "our agreement was for far more than that. Was it not for everything that your father was entitled to?" She slid a hand across his leg and moved in closer, whispering into Yoshiakira's ear, "Your father had so many… privileges."

*

October 1359 - Yugyo Monastery, Sagami Province

Watanabe watched Jion exercising with the rest of his class in the courtyard, and sighed. Despite it being the boy's ninth birthday, Jion had insisted on training as usual, and whilst such devotion to his training was admirable, his spear-work was clumsy and he easily lost focus. Watanabe heard the instructor bark a correction at Jion, and turned back into the room, closing the door behind him.

"You have seen these things yourself?" Watanabe asked.

Tatsuo bowed. "I have Sensei. Jion and Masako have become unacceptably close. They eat together. Spend whatever free time they have together. They even meditate together. There is open talk of their… relationship."

"They are young. I don't suppose they have pillowed?"

"Not to my knowledge Sensei. But as you say, they may be too young."

"Does Gozen know? She would be within her rights to call off the betrothal and then we will all be in a fine mess."

"If she does, she has not said anything. She publicly states that it is her duty to marry the boy and unite their clans."

"And what about in private?" Watanabe asked. "What does she say when only her closest friends are with her?"

"Nothing Sensei. She is as prudent in private as she is in public."

"Hmmm… Sonkan was right. That girl will make a fine diplomat. Curses. Why can Jion not see what he is doing?"

Tatsuo knew the question was rhetorical and did not answer.

"We could split them up," Watanabe continued. "Increasing their training and make sure they do not share any classes. What do you think?"

"Sensei, I never had children and so I cannot say. However, having seen my comrade's children over the years… they are friends one month and the next… well who can say?"

"You think that they will fall out?"

"Nothing is guaranteed Sensei. But my sister-in-law used to say that her daughter always needed two groups of friends; one to play with whilst she was getting over an argument with the other."

Watanabe nodded. "Your sister-in-law was a wise woman Tatsuo."

"Thank you Sensei."

"And what about you?" The Governor continued, putting Jion from his mind temporarily. "Are your wounds healed?"

"Yes Sensei. Thank you for asking."

"One of the instructors mentioned that you are spending a good deal of time in the library. It is wise that you are studying the ways of our hosts."

Tatsuo flushed. "Actually Sensei… there is more to it than that."

"Really? You have an interest is Mistress Taka? She is a little older than you but…"

"Oh no Sensei. I spend my time with Nikko…"

"The assistant? She is quite young. Still I suppose…"

"Please Sensei. You misunderstand. She is teaching me… well we teach each other."

Watanabe's brow furrowed. "What do you mean?"

"I am… relearning the art of the sword, Sensei."

Watanabe looked to the stump that was the retainer's right arm. "But your sword arm… how can you learn?"

"Sensei, Nikko is teaching me from the texts of the sword… but with my left hand."

The Governor was both shocked and surprised. "A left-handed bujin? I have never heard of such a thing. Is it even possible?"

"We do not know Sensei. Nikko can find no mention in any of the texts of there ever having been a left-handed swordsman, but I am determined still to be of use to our Lord."

"How has the training progressed?"

"Slowly Sensei. But I have learned two forms with my left hand."

Watanabe was intrigued. "Please Tatsuo, may I see?"

"Of course Sensei." With that, the loyal retainer opened the door and stepped out in to the courtyard, drew his sword and began the elegant dance of the kata.

*

December 1359

Abbot Sonkan sat in his bedchamber, considering the deep snow that lay in drifts against the monastery walls. Despite the freezing cold, he found the scene both beautiful and peaceful.

"It is perfection, is it not?" Sonkan said to Watanabe.

The Governor shifted awkwardly, revealing his inner discomfort. "Yes Master Abbot." He had been summoned this morning having spent much of the previous evening nursing a tearful Jion.

"You have heard of the… incident during mealtime yesterday evening?"

"I have Master Abbot, and I have spoken at length with the boy about his conduct."

"It is a great shame. The Council believed that he had turned a corner. What account did the child give you?"

"Nobuo was teasing him until Jion lashed out." Watanabe did not mention the nature of the teasing; the questioning of the boy's parentage; the mocking of his skills; or his relationship with Masako.

"I understand that Nobuo was injured?" Sonkan continued, his voice low and even as he looked out across the frozen desert outside.

"Yes Master Abbot," The Governor replied, trying to avoid details.

"Are his wounds serious?"

"Master Abbot, Jion drew his short sword. We are fortunate that he has neither the strength nor skill to wield it properly. Nobuo will live, although he will be scarred. I understand it took several other novices to pull them apart."

"Have you counseled the boy on his behavior?"

"I have, Master Abbot."

"And?" Sonkan finally turned from the winter scene to look at Watanabe.

"Master Abbot," The Governor bowed his head. "I would beg for The Council's forbearance. Jion… he is a child caught between worlds. He was brought up in the ways of bujin, but now he is training in the ways of the sohei. By the warriors code he acted completely properly…"

"Ah," the abbot interrupted. "But we are not bujin here. We are Yamabushi. We seek to master our feelings and not to react until the time is right. Such rashness… it is deeply troubling."

"Yes Master Abbot," Watanabe bowed his head again.

"I have had a number of Jion's instructors speak to me over the last few months," Sonkan said.

The Governor's heart began to sink. Sensing what was coming he tried to remain composed. "Really Master Abbot?"

"Yes. There is great concern for your ward. He embraces the art of war, and yet despite his application his results are… at best average. Moreover he does not seek to balance his teachings by applying himself to the ways of meditation, which is arguably where he is strongest. Sensei Watanabe, I shall be blunt with you: were it not for the considerable talents of Gozen and her sister, your party would have been asked to leave. We understand that you have special circumstances, and the Yamabushi have always been loyal to the Soma Clan. However, it has now been more than four years since Lord Chikatane stole his brother's land, and in all that time he has done nothing but consolidate his position. Jion on the other hand… the only ally he has made is a third rate pirate; he has set about alienating all those who seek to help him, and he abused his abilities until he is almost impotent of them."

"Yes Master Abbot," Watanabe replied.

"Sensei, I am sorry but the role of The Council is to consider the well-being of *all* the novices in the monastery. Jion is becoming not only too great a disturbance, but also an increasing liability."

"Yes Master Abbot. I most humbly apologize for the disruption to the harmony of the monastery."

"That may be Sensei. But it is the decision of The Council that this is to be a final warning. If you wish to remain here, you will need to see that the boy adheres to our rules and improves in all his classes. Regardless of how highly we value Gozen and Masako, if there is any further infraction of our creed, or his grades continue to fall, you will all be asked to leave."

*

February 1360 – Yugyo Monastery

"You must learn to let your feelings flow," Nikko said, making the boy jump.

Jion had taken himself into the woods outside of the monastery to practice his archery skills in private, and had not heard the woman approaching.

The boy lowered his bow. It had not been a productive morning, and most of the arrows he had fired had been wide of the tree he had been using as target practice.

"It is not just enough to breathe," Nikko continued. "See the arrow in your mind's eye. See it connect with your target."

"Master Otsuno always said that I should keep my focus in the present... that it would shape the future," Jion said, whispering his master's name.

Nikko smiled and walked towards the child. "Master Otsuno is not here Jion. Let me show you." She took the bow from him, feathered an arrow, and in one fluid movement drew the string back and let go.

The arrow slammed into a tree a hundred meters away and Jion's jaw dropped.

"How...?" his voice trailed off.

Nikko shrugged and handed the bow back to the boy, saying nothing.

"No Librarian could do that," Jion persisted. "What were you before you joined the Yamabushi?"

Nikko smiled. "Does it matter? I am what I am now. The previous things... they are just labels. Farmer. Peasant. Bujin... even Lord, they are all just names. They have no weight... no substance. Do not hold on to a name when it serves no purpose Jion. We both know those who are honorable and those who are not... yet many share a title. A name has no worth. It is the way that you act that defines you."

Jion was not discouraged. "Few masters could have made that shot," he said pointing to the tree. "At least tell me how..."

Nikko knelt down beside him. "You know, I was not always treated well. It was a long time ago, before I came here... there were men who... hurt me. In my mind's eye that tree becomes them, and my aim never wavers."

Jion looked to the leafy forest floor. "I am always being told to let go of my past."

"You should... if it holds you back. If it stops you from achieving your goals."

"But you don't," Jion looked up into the young woman's face.

"If you hold onto anger, it will fog your mind... cloud your senses. If you just let it go then there is no motivation to your goals. But if you direct your feelings... focus them on a point, you can achieve anything."

Jion took up his bow, pulled the string back, and imagined the tree to be the face of the Shogun.

The arrow slammed into the bark, splitting the damp wood and burying the head deep into the trunk.

Nikko stood and smiled. "Good," she said. "Use your feelings."

*

April 1360 – Utsunomiya Castle, Shimotsuke Province

Lady Altera strode past the barracks and out to the main gate, the fine drizzle settling on her robes. The melt had come early this year, but the rainy season had seemed to last forever, and such wet conditions only brought disease.

The messenger had only just come through the heavy portcullis, but as soon he saw her he quickly dismounted from his dappled steed and knelt before his mistress.

"What news do you bring?" Altera barked. The interminable delays and false leads over the winter had required her to become ever closer to Yoshiakira until the Shogun had moved her bedchamber next to his.

"My Lady," the messenger offered up a scroll which Altera snatched from him.

It was still under seal and when Altera broke it she saw that it was in the agreed cipher.

"The dogs and cats play as one pack although some have become separated. The fury of the stars is unnecessary for the perfume of jasmine lingers in the woods. Our mother's kiss will be most welcome."

I have made way through many villages. Some peasants had to be dispatched and now others talk more freely. Do not send The Eleven because I believe I am getting very close to discovering the child's location. Stand by with your troops.

*

July 1360 - Yugyo Monastery, Sagami Province

Mifune was adamant. "Surely you must see the boy is a detriment to our order."

"But we have a duty not only to him," Kyuzo replied, "but also to his Clan. And besides there has been no serious infraction of our rules."

Sonkan mediated. "Master Kyuzo, whilst you are correct, the boy's grades have not improved. He is too caught up with the younger sister. He does not see the effect this friendship is having on either him or those around him."

"Master Abbot, you are of course correct," Kyuzo said. "But surely we should embrace him... show him his error."

Mifune flushed with frustration. "How many times should we embrace him? Once? Twice? Three times? On the other hand, maybe only when the roof is falling down about us will you realize that you cannot teach someone who does not wish to learn. Come now..."

The sound of a commotion outside The Council Hall interrupted their discussion. As the three elders hurriedly crossed the floor to see the cause of the latest disturbance, they heard the sound of running feet and then more cries.

Throwing the door open they saw the senior instructors running towards the far end of the training yard, where the novices practiced their sword skills.

"What is happening?" Mifune asked one of them.

"I don't know. But I heard Jion's name being shouted."

Mifune rolled his eyes and looked meaningfully to Sonkan and Kyuzo before turning back to the instructor. "Send for Watanabe. This is the last straw."

"Now now," Sonkan said as they hurried towards the gathering throng. "We should at least see the situation before we judge it."

At the far end of the yard, the three council elders could see Nikko clutching at Jion, shielding him with her body. Tatsuo was closer, screaming at the gathering throng who seemed to be equally shielding someone else; the bodyguard's sword was unsheathed and held high, his eyes bulging in rage. Blood was pooling around him, and one foot seemed to be on a body. Behind them came the familiar step of Watanabe hurrying to the scene.

As Sonkan approached, he could see that Tatsuo was indeed standing on a body, and the Abbot recognized it as Nobuo.

"Give them to me!" Tatsuo screamed at the crowd. "Cowards! Cowards all of you!"

"What is happening?" Watanabe said breathlessly, arriving at the same time as The Council Elders.

The crowd shied from the enraged one-armed swordsman, but still held two figures within their ranks.

Sonkan raised a hand. "Peace. Brethren peace. Tatsuo… please. Put down your weapon."

Seeing the arrival of Watanabe and the elders Tatsuo lowered his sword, deftly flicked it, casting off the sheen of blood, and sheathed it. Bowing his head slightly he said, "Elders, Watanabe. I apologize. I meant no disrespect to you or the monastery. But there was an assassination attempt on our young Lord."

Kyuzo was incredulous. "An assassination attempt? What happened?"

"Nikko and I were showing Jion some sword techniques… when these three," Tatsuo motioned to the body at his feet and the two still held within the crowd, "fired on us. I killed the first one, but the other two tried to flee…"

Sonkan's brow furrowed with concern. "Who are the other two? You can release them. Come forward. Choisai? Ienao? What happened here?"

Two young teenagers were pushed out of the protective throng to address the abbot.

"P… P… Please Master Abbot…" stammered the first. "It was not our idea. It… it was Nobuo. He had sworn revenge on Jion… after the fight last year. He… he made us swear to help him."

Sonkan's expression was dark and his voice was grave. "To help him do what?"

"We… we weren't going to kill him," the boy pleaded. "Nobuo just wanted to scar him… like he'd been scarred…"

"Scar him? With arrows?" Sonkan wrestled with his anger, bringing it under control. Kyuzo whispered to the Abbot who turned, looked back to Nikko and Jion and then returned to the boys in front of him. "Master Tatsuo? What is your account?"

Tatsuo was silent, and looked back to his ward. "Master Abbot, they were reloading their bows when I reached them. They intended to do far more than merely scar My Lord."

"Yes," Sonkan replied. "That may be the case. But Tatsuo, *where* are the arrows they fired?"

The one-armed swordsman shifted his weight uncomfortably before answering. "Master Abbot, I swear that what I am about to say is the truth. I saw it with my own eyes."

"Yes. Go on."

"Master Abbot, Jion cut the arrows down."

A ripple passed through the crowd, and there were a few mutterings of protest and denial.

"The boy cut the arrows from the air… with the sword? Before they reached him?"

"Yes Master Abbot."

*

The training yard was deserted and the blood had been washed from the flagstones. Sonkan stood in silence with the other Council Elders and looked to Watanabe, Nikko, and Jion. Tatsuo had been banished to the bedroom chamber under the pretext of watching over the girls, although everyone knew he would mostly likely be expelled for the sacrilege of killing on hallowed land. Choisai and Ienao were under guard whilst their fates were considered.

"Jion?" Kyuzo called out. "Prepare yourself."

The boy bowed deeply and drew his sword. "Yes Master Kyuzo."

"Watanabe? When you are ready," said Kyuzo.

The Governor bowed his head, feathered an arrow on to his long bow, and drew back. The small group collectively held their breath and even the nightingales seemed quieter.

And then the arrow was released, flying straight and true towards its target. They all heard rather than saw it; the hiss of the Ishin Blade through the air, and the arrow fell in two parts on to the gray flagstones.

Mifune harrumphed loudly. "That was not full power. Anyone could have made that strike."

Watanabe looked in protest to Sonkan and saw that any appeal would be denied. There had been much talk that afternoon about what had really happened. Whilst it did seem that there had been a genuine attempt on Jion's life, the cutting down of the arrows seemed improbable, especially against such a noted archer as Nobuo. If one aspect of the story was false then others may be too. In the end, The Council had called for a demonstration.

"Master Abbot," Mifune continued, "with your permission?"

Sonkan nodded, and Mifune took the bow from Watanabe and feathered an arrow.

Nikko called out, desperation in her voice. "Remember your training Jion."

The arrow sped through the air and again the Ishin Blade jumped, slicing down the deadly shaft.

Sonkan remained grim. "Again. Full power."

Jion seemed to barely move as the arrow pieces fell to the floor.

"Two," Sonkan said nodding to Kyuzo who picked up his own bow.

Watanabe pleaded. "Please. Master Abbot…"

Sonkan did not look at him. "Your man claims the boy cut down three arrows this afternoon. Two should be no problem for him."

The shafts left their bows simultaneously, only to fall to the floor with the barest of whispers at Jion's feet.

The Abbot nodded. "That is enough for today. Nikko, you will accompany me please."

*

Sonkan smiled. "Did I not say Master Mifune, patience?"

"You did Master Abbot. You are most wise."

Kyuzo closed the door to The Council chamber and listened to the retreating footsteps of Nikko to make sure that the woman was not secretly listening to their conversation. "I cannot agree," he said, returning to his cushion. "The boy did nothing wrong."

Sonkan accepted the small bowl of cha from the maid and, as was customary, offered first to Mifune and then to Kyuzo, who both politely declined and insisted the Abbot should drink first. "You are of course correct Master Kyuzo, but this does present the opportunity we had hoped for."

"How so Master Abbot?"

Sonkan emptied his bowl and placed it gently on the mat in front of him. "Are we agreed that the child is… at least difficult?"

Mifune nodded enthusiastically whilst Kyuzo was more reserved.

"He is only interested in what he is interested in and he is difficult to teach. Compounded with his disruption of the monastery's harmony and that he may bring the Shogun's forces to our door… perhaps it would be better for all if he found, let us say an alternative place of teaching."

"Where do you have in mind?" Kyuzo asked.

"This ability with the sword… it is certainly unique and no doubt it will require refining. There is rumor of a master instructor resident at Kurama Temple. Perhaps…"

Kyuzo was incensed. "Master Abbot. I beg you. Kurama is so near to Keishi and the main body of the Shogun's forces… you would be sending the boy to his death."

Sonkan shrugged. "A man's fate is a man's fate."

"But Master Abbot… what of the girls? They have such potential."

"An unfortunate cost. You must remember, Master Kyuzo; this is for the good of the whole monastery. We cannot have killings… it is sacrilege and defiles our harmony."

Kyuzo could see that Mifune agreed, and that it would be a waste of breath to protest further. "What about the guard? Tatsuo?"

Sonkan looked to Mifune who shrugged. "Our creed would normally require his immediate expulsion. However, we recognize that there are… mitigating circumstances. He should be confined to quarters until the boy departs."

Mifune chuckled. "He can take his harlot with him as well."

Sonkan softly rebuked him. "Come now Master Mifune. We are open with our bodies… and a man has needs. Nikko has been willing. But perhaps you are correct. Mistress Taka has mentioned that her apprentice has been… distracted by the man."

"Sensei Watanabe will not like this. He believes our order is allied to the Soma," Kyuzo said.

"Ah," replied Sonkan, "but this is not an expulsion. No. This is… an opportunity for the boy to hone his unique skills. Yes, an opportunity with those far better equipped than we are to deal with the child. If the boy succeeds, then he will say how wise our advice was. If the Shogun captures him… then we can say we delivered an adversary."

"Master Abbot!" Kyuzo was outraged. "That is not our way… such… such… treachery."

Sonkan laughed gently. "Ah Kyuzo my old friend. Ours is a time of war and politics. We must do everything we can to safeguard the future of our order. That is more important than a mere boy, no?"

"A *mere* boy?" Kyuzo spluttered. "What about the prophecy? The three stars…"

"What about the prophecy?" Mifune replied. "There is nothing to suggest that he has anything to do with it. No, the Master Abbot is quite correct."

Kyuzo could see he was defeated. "Very well then. How long?"

"Before they leave?" Sonkan asked. "It will take at least two months to get a messenger to Kurama and something similar for him to return with a formal acceptance of the boy. By then the snows will have come, but he could leave with the first melt. No more than six or seven months time."

*

Watanabe sat cross-legged in the bedroom chamber, and the three children bowed deeply. "Sit up. You too Tatsuo. And you Nikko."

"Sensei," Tatsuo began, "I take complete responsibility for what happened today…

"So you should," Watanabe barked, and then softened. "You did well. I apologize. The Council frustrates me. They debate things endlessly only to reach the wrong conclusion."

Nikko stifled a smile, but Watanabe saw it and glared at her. "Our position is precarious. The killing… within a monastery… it is sacrilege regardless of the justification or provocation," The Governor continued. "The Council Elders are seeking… an alternative place to study. When the first melt comes we will be invited to leave."

"Where will we go?" Masako asked a pitying note to her voice.

"I cannot be certain," The Governor replied. "There are tales of a master swordsman who instructs at Kurama Temple. The Council is seeking an invitation for Jion to be admitted."

"Kurama?" Masako exclaimed. "But that is the heart of the Shogun's political empire. Surely it is too dangerous?"

Gozen bowed and then said softly, "Sensei, if I may?" Watanabe nodded at her to continue. Now aged thirteen, the girl had become an exceptional strategist during her time at the monastery.

"Kurama presents a number of opportunities," Gozen began. "The Temple is only accessible by a single mountain path. Here we are vulnerable to attack from all sides. Additionally by staying so close to the Shogun's parliament… it may not occur to his forces to look there. We would in effect be hiding in plain sight. Finally, if there is a master swordsman there who would instruct our Lord, it might help to… rejuvenate his other abilities."

Jion nodded in agreement. Despite the trauma of the day, he felt a sense of inner calm. "Sensei, I believe that there is merit in this strategy. Since The Council Elders have forbidden the training of my abilities they have… withered. I can now barely hear into the next room, let alone the leagues that I used to."

Watanabe knew well enough that Jion practiced his abilities at night, but even he acknowledged their diminishment in recent months. "My Lord, I am glad that this strategy finds your favor," he said bowing, and then turned to Nikko. "The Council will extend their invitation to you as well."

"I had hoped as much. Perhaps I will be of more use to My Lord at Kurama than The Council has permitted me to be here," Nikko replied, and looked sideways at Tatsuo with a smile.

The one-armed swordsman smiled back but said nothing. His reply would come much later in the vermillion chamber.

"Yes. I hope so too," said Watanabe. The Governor knew that a man's needs should be satisfied, but he found that such long-term attachments were unnecessary complications for the bujin class. "This brings us on to our next matter. Jion, what happened today with the arrows?"

The boy shrugged. "Sensei, I am not sure. It was as before, but this time I saw the arrows... not just the mark of death. I knew that I could not move Tatsuo and Nikko in time..."

"Wait," Watanabe interrupted. "An arrow was destined for each of you?"

"Yes Sensei."

"Choisai and Ienao said they were only aiming for you."

"Yes Sensei. They lied. They meant to kill us all."

"Over a mere scuffle nearly a year ago?" Watanabe could not understand it.

Jion and Masako looked sideways at each other, but said nothing.

"Sensei," Gozen bowed again. "If I may? The scuffle last year was neither the first nor the last of the matter. Our Lord has long been singled out by the other novices. The instructors turned a blind eye to the matter because of their opinions of Jion's high birth and their fear of his abilities. After the disaster at Ise, many privately blamed him for the death of Master Otsuno."

Watanabe's eyebrows knitted together. "Jion? Is this true?"

The boy nodded. Tears welled up in his eyes and it took all his will to forbid their fall.

"But... Lord, why did you not tell me?"

Jion looked at him. How could he tell? How could he say how alone he felt? How much he missed his brother and father. That even in a group he was an outsider. That all he saw about him was darkness, death, and the only solace he ever had was with his Goddess.

"It is not the way of our class," he said finally, trying hard to prevent his voice from cracking.

In that moment Watanabe felt both immensely proud of the boy, and utterly remorseful for the journey he had been dragged on and what it had made him into. "As you say My Lord. Still, I wish to know more. The novices have... bullied you?"

"Not as such," Jion replied. "At first it was just hard to make friends and I was isolated. Then the whispers began. They are scared of my abilities. Some said I was a warlock, that there was a curse on me, and that I was responsible for the death of my father and Tanemochi. The instructors heard what the other novices said, but did nothing to quash the rumors. They felt that because of my noble birth I should not be here. Then in the corridors, when we were moving between classes, some of the boys would barge into me. They never bruised me and so I had nothing to show. Then I heard others talk…" the boy's voice tailed off.

"My Lord, please go on," Watanabe coaxed.

"Some of the novices said that I would fail, like all the Emperor's lieutenants, and that Gozen and Masako were destined to become nothing more than back door whores of the fifteenth rank… just like my mother. That was what the fight with Nobuo was about last year. I challenged him, but he laughed and would not face me…" again his voice tailed off.

"And today?" The Governor asked.

"I was with Tatsuo and Mistress Nikko. I had seen them going through some left-handed sword forms and I asked if I could train with them. Then Nobuo saw us. I knew that he had sworn revenge and was planning something. Sensei, I swear if I had known what he going to do I never would have fought with him…"

Watanabe held up his hand. "You did the right thing. Nobuo was utterly without honor. There is no shame upon you." The Governor turned to Nikko. "What was it you were practicing today?"

"They are nothing Sensei. Simply some old training scrolls," the woman replied.

"For left-handed swordsmen?" Watanabe asked.

Nikko shook her head. "Oh no Sensei. Tatsuo and I have… re-written them. We have taken the original documents and mirrored the poses, switching right for left."

"Was there anything in them that could have… stimulated our Lord's abilities?"

"I don't think so," Nikko replied. "But the documents were old… from when the bujin first worshipped Marishiten. Maybe…"

"Do you have the originals with you?"

"Yes Sensei." Nikko slid over the sheaves of parchment that were yellow and brittle with age.

Watanabe looked through them carefully, not seeing anything obviously out of place. "What are these?" he asked eventually. "The role of the sword?"

Nikko leaned forward to see where The Governor was pointing. "It is about how the bujin and the sword must be one… how the sword is to be an extension of his body."

"And this here?" Watanabe was indicating to one of the diagrams.

"That depicts the sword as an arm."

The Governor squinted at the crude drawing. "That does not look like an arm… maybe an octopus muscle or something like that."

*

November 1360 – Yugyo Monastery

The Hunter moved through the forest, the boughs creaking under the weight of snow. He was near. He could feel it, almost as if he could taste the scent of the child in the air.

It had taken more months than he could count to find this place, following whatever whispers he could. The talk of a one-armed swordsman who had survived the cruelest torture. A pirate that sailed under protest. The trees that moved with the whisper of a goddess rising.

He had been careful. He had lurked in the shadowy corners of taverns, never drinking from the full bowl in front of him, but listening to the idle gossip of peasants. He had secreted himself in the roof voids of the houses of headmen, village elders, and even local lords, always straining his ears for the smallest piece of information. Hiding in the long grass of the fields as merchants went back and forth, careless in their conversation.

He had zigzagged across three provinces, enduring two summers and a cruel winter, only to meet with dead ends, conflicting information, and children who were not those he sought. But he was patient. He was *very* patient.

As The Hunter stalked through the ice-covered floor of the forest, the outline of the monastery walls began to form, solidifying in the freezing haze. This was it. He could feel it in the ground like pulses of energy. If he had even one of the Eleven Armies he would have stormed the monastery there and then, but his orders had been explicit.

There is a greater plan in play. Locate the child and send for reinforcements.

*

December 1360 – Yugyo Monastery

It was the end of the day and Jion leaned his head back in the onsen, feeling the hot waters soothing away the ache of training. He and Masako were kept in isolation from the other novices and were guarded by Tatsuo, although the boy suspected it was also to keep his retainer away from Choisai and Ienao. Watanabe had been allowed limited privileges, together with Gozen, and it was the older girl's form that Jion now saw coming through the steam towards him.

She bowed her head saying, "May I join you?"

"Of course. Please," the boy heard himself reply. Watanabe had been *very* clear that he was to make more of an effort with his future wife.

Setting her robe to one side, she slipped into the bath and scooped milky water over her shoulders, rubbing them gently.

"How has your day been?" Jion asked.

"Very good thank you. And yours?" Gozen replied formally.

"Good thank you. Tatsuo has continued my sword training and Nikko has been showing your sister more spear techniques."

"My Lord is becoming quite accomplished with the sword. His reputation spreads throughout the monastery."

Jion bowed his head. "It is nothing. I would not have made such progress without such an excellent teacher."

"My Lord should not be so modest. Your expertise far exceeds your years."

"Thank you. I only hope one day to be worthy of restoring my father's name," Jion replied, watching the tendrils of steam slowly rising from the hot water, creating a shroud around Gozen.

She really is quite intoxicating, he thought. The first signs of manhood had presented themselves in the previous weeks, and although Watanabe thought that such signs were early in a ten-year old boy, he had nevertheless begun Jion's instruction in the ways of Men.

Gozen continued, pretending not to notice her Lord's attention to her petite breasts. "I bring a message from the Abbot."

The words broke through Jion's reverie and his eyes flicked up to her face. "Really? What is it?"

"The messenger from Kurama Temple has returned. My Lord has been accepted."

Jion tried not to betray his excitement and kept his voice even. "That is good news. Is it Sensei's intention for us to leave at the first melt?"

Gozen paused. "It is… if My Lord is well enough."

"What do you mean?"

"My Lord… you have been very pale these last few weeks. You do not eat properly and your sleep is disturbed. We are worried about you."

Jion knew that what the girl was saying was true. He had been unable to commune with his goddess for nearly two weeks and he constantly felt sick and sweaty despite the cold of the winter.

"It is nothing," he said. "Perhaps just a cold."

"I hope so My Lord, I hope so."

*

January 1361 – Yugyo Monastery

"Remember," Lady Altera whispered to her troops. "The child is to be brought to me. Everyone else dies."

The Hunter nodded and gestured to the entry points on the crude plan that he had drawn.

"Division One will take the south wall," he began. "There is no gate so the archers will provide cover whilst the spearmen use grapples. Division Two will take the west. There are stables just through the gate so fire those as soon as you get through and turn the horses loose. Division Three will come over the east wall. This is where the barracks are so you will go in first and bar the doors. Fire the roof and we'll trap all their Sohei warriors inside. Division Four will be mounted and will sweep in through the main gate. The novices' quarters will be on the left and the servants on the right. The adepts and masters are in the center. The child sleeps in this building over here," he jabbed a finger at a small rectangle to the left of the central building. "He has been separated from the rest and there are two other children, plus The Governor and the one-armed swordsman. Go, and may the love of our Mother carry you to victory."

*

Jion stretched, his limbs aching from the afternoon's training. Nikko's instruction with the sword had seen his skills begin to re-emerge but he had not been able to shake his cold all winter, and it was dragging him down.

Unfastening his belt, he allowed his robe to fall to the floor and he sank beneath the warmth of the onsen, feeling the waters relaxing the knots in his muscles. He had sprained his wrist the previous day when Masako had distracted him, and Nikko had seized the opportunity to teach him the importance of maintaining focus by disarming him. Now the soothing waters and heady incense began to soothe the dull ache in his joints, and he felt himself begin to drift.

Outside, he could hear the sounds of the dying day. The few novices and adepts that were still up were finishing their chores and hurrying to their rooms. The Masters had already retired; Mifune was already asleep, snoring like a fat hog; Kyuzo was in a light doze, troubled by the latest reports of the Yoshiakira's build up of forces in the west.

Only Sonkan was still awake and Jion flexed his mind, feeling the old abbot with his senses. He was reading some dispatches, but these were to do with the general administration of the monastery and Jion was uninterested. His newly revived skills had not yet strengthened enough to go beyond the walls of the monastery and instead he cast around the courtyard, hearing the cook preparing the vegetables for the following day; the maids discussing the latest rumors from Yokohama, about the Pirate Kagetaka's new found wealth and that he was now looking for a wife; the sound of the cats as they chased after the mice, past the dead guard dogs, into the granary...

Jion's eyes snapped open, now fully alert and awake.

... past the dead guard dogs...

*

Altera motioned to the archers and another volley of arrows flew silently through the night, this time dispatching the guards who walked along the high perimeter wall. They gurgled, wheezed, and then collapsed forward over the battlements, and down to the waiting arms of the hordes below, who silently dispatched them with a knife to their throat before casting their bodies into a snowdrift.

No sooner had the blood began to pool like a winter blossom than the grappling hooks were cast over and the spearmen began their ascent. As soon as they reached the top, Altera would send the mounted cavalry to the front gate, providing the diversion the rest of the divisions needed.

*

Even before he heard his young ward's patter of running feet or his shrill voice warning him, Watanabe smelled smoke.

Fire!

Abbot Sonkan ran the monastery too well for there to be any accidental outbreak. Fire meant death for a building in Oyashima, and more often than not, a whole village.

The Governor roused himself, quickly put on his robe, and woke the children.

"What is it?" asked Gozen blearily.

"Sshh. Follow me," Watanabe replied, grabbing his sword.

"Sensei?" Tatsuo was up now.

"To arms," Watanabe whispered back. "There's a fire. I think we're under…"

"Sensei! Sensei!" Jion burst through the door and Watanabe grabbed the boy putting his hand over his mouth.

"Be quiet. What do you sense?"

"The guard dogs are dead," said Jion, his voice barely above a murmur. "I think the wall guards have been killed too, but I'm not sure. And I smell fire."

Watanabe looked to Tatsuo. "It'll be the Shogun's Oni. We need to leave right now."

"Yes Sensei," the one-armed swordsman bowed and hurriedly began stuffing provisions and belongings into satchels. "Gozen. Masako. Help me."

The Governor looked back to Jion. "We will need to be fast. No looking back. Is the main gate clear?"

There was a loud crash of heavy wood against heavy stone, a scream, and the sound of horses stamping on the courtyard.

Jion looked mournful. "No," he whimpered. "They're here."

Nikko appeared at doorway. "Sensei. We're under…"

"We know," Watanabe replied. The sound of distant crackling told of fires that had already taken hold, and the banging of fists against wooden doors and shouts for release informed The Governor that no help would come from the Sohei barracks. "Can you get us out?"

"I will try. We might be able to circle around them as they sweep into the center," Nikko replied.

Gathering what belongings they could, they hurried out into the freezing night air. The scene that greeted them was one sent from Jigoku itself. Smoke rolled from the building roofs in thick billowing blankets that blotted out the stars and moon. Dark figures were running along the building tops, starting new fires and using their vantage point to issue commands to the ground troops. Somebody had escaped the initial assault and was now furiously ringing the large bronze bell, sounding the alarm. A hail of arrows flew through the air and the bell ringer was silenced.

Horses stamped and snorted and from the barred doors of the barracks came screams of agony as the burning thatched roof began to collapse in a shower of soot and sparks. A few adepts had begun a rearguard action, desperately trying to protect the masters' quarters and give them time to escape. The Shogun's black steeds charged the line and the adepts fell to the floor, clutching at limbs that were no longer there.

Although he could not see them, Watanabe could hear the shrieks of the monastery's own horses, bucking and kicking out against the stable doors as they smelled the advance of fire… and then a stampede as the bolts were released and the terrified creatures fled into the inky night. More cries now – human this time. That would be the maids. One ran past a black clad swordsman and headed for the main gate, only be to felled by an archer. The Governor knew that their attackers would spare no one.

Watanabe watched the main force sweep into the center of the courtyard and begin to fan out. All around was the sound of crackling fire and the screams of the dying. "Come on," he said grimly, indicating towards the main gate.

The group edged along the wall, using the shadows cast by the pools of fire to shield them themselves from view. As they neared the mighty pillars of the torii gate, they heard the unmistakable sound of metal on stone, marching towards them. Out of the swirling black smoke The Hunter emerged, eyes fixed on the small band of would be escapees.

Jion felt the icy grip of fear upon, slowing him down to stop as he beheld the demonic apparition before him.

Watanabe eyed The Hunter and drew his sword. "Tatsuo. Take the children and run."

"Sensei, I will not leave you…"

"It is your *duty*," The Governor barked back. "I will cover your retreat."

"As will I," Nikko said softly, drawing her own sword.

Watanabe looked sideways and grunted an acknowledgment. He knew that he was unlikely to win a contest with such a creature, but he did not intend to. He only had to buy enough time for Tatsuo and the children to escape. Once they were into the wilds of the country, they would be safe. The Shogun's Oni would not be able to track them across such a harsh environment, and with a little luck Lord Soma would quickly become lost to the searching eyes.

"Very well," Watanabe continued. "My Lord. It has been an honor to serve you and your family." The Governor looked to Nikko. "Ready?"

The librarian's assistant nodded.

"Attack!"

The two set off at full pelt towards the advancing Hunter, swords held high, and Tatsuo gathered the children and hurried along the wall. As they half stumbled in the freezing dark, the stench of burning flesh filled their throats, and Jion stopped to catch his breath. Turning, he watched his governor go to his fate, knowing that he should be by his side but powerless to do anything about it.

Watanabe was ahead, with Nikko just two steps behind, each screaming their battle cry, smoke swirling around them like a silk scarf woven from the night itself. From where the boy stood, gasping against the rough stone of the wall, the silhouette of The Hunter seemed to fill his view, towering above all else, and Jion felt paralyzed.

As Watanabe reached the figure his sword slashed through air, driving for the chink in the armor between the cuirass and neck guard. For a moment all three seemed frozen, and Jion's eyes watered in the smoke and he tried to hold his concentration to stop himself from being sick. Tatsuo turned to grab the boy, to bring him under the shield of the night.

Jion refused his retainer's imploring, but stood transfixed as he saw his sensei's strike bounce harmlessly off The Hunter. Following his own momentum, Watanabe span, his sword now coming upwards, aiming for the kill shot by driving from hip to shoulder. Nikko arrived at his side and thrust her own sword at The Hunter in an effort to take his balance.

The Hunter seemed to barely notice either of them, but looked through the dark to Jion, Tatsuo and the two girls. Without even acknowledging the defenders, he batted Nikko's thrust away with his forearm, and stamped down on Watanabe's sword, shattering the blade on the cold courtyard flagstones.

In a single move, The Hunter lunged forward, driving his own sword underneath Watanabe's chin and exploding through the back of his skull, permanently freezing the look of shock onto The Governor's face.

"No!" Jion screamed, not noticing how his voice echoed across the courtyard attracting the attention of the other Oni. Slipping past Tatsuo, he ran towards The Hunter who was now turning his attention to Nikko.

Without thinking, the boy drew his father's sword and the Ishin Blade hissed through the air. Time slowed. Particles of blood and smoke and snow hung suspended about the soon-to-be-destroyed monastery. The Hunter glanced up from the shattered form of Watanabe as the figure of a child emerged from the black coils of smoke that rolled through the night like waves of ill omen.

A Farravashi…

The Hunter felt the void at the center of his being scream out in satisfaction, knowing that it would soon devour what he had sought for so many years.

... and so ill trained...

The creature that walked like a man positioned himself to meet the child, taking a guard. The boy's sword was high above his head and he was already off balance. A peasant could have parried the stroke.

...and so much disharmony...

The Hunter smiled to himself, waited for Jion's strike and prepared his own counter. This victory would be glorious. And then he could go home.

The Ishin Blade began its swing, the boy screaming in fury and grief, already overstepping, his balance carrying too him far forward. The Hunter began to shift his weight, bringing his own sword up to defend, preparing the counter strike.

The two swords connected, sparks flying from each blade only to fall in to the night where they withered and died before hitting the ground. The Hunter could feel the weight of the child already beginning to spin to the right as he shifted his back foot in preparation.

And then The Hunter's sword shattered into a million luminous shards, briefly filling the night with the reflected radiance of a thousand fires that burned around him. The Ishin Blade continued its downward arc, hip to shoulder, the way all young bujin were taught. The sword seemed to have a life of its own, finding the needle thin gap between the cuirass and the arm-guards, cleaving through the too hot flesh and muscle, and then bone, like a peasant's sickle bringing down the harvest wheat.

Down, down, down. Through the chest. Puncturing both lungs. Past the heart. Slicing through what passed for the liver and then a kidney. And then finally through the hip joint, and back out into the cool of the night.

Time returned to normal.

Jion stood transfixed, as blue and purple light rushed skywards from the fallen creature, unable to comprehend what he had just done; unhearing of the echoes of the dying Hunter's scream; unfeeling of the fine spray of dark purple life essence that seemed to rain down from the creature. All he could do was look down at the thing that had walked as a man, which now lay in two in front of him and try to comprehend what he had just seen.

"Jion!" Nikko was getting to her feet. "We have to go. Now!"

Jion looked up at her, his face expressionless and covered in The Hunter's blood.

Tatsuo had given chase to the young lord and was only a few seconds behind, skidded to a halt, struggling to take in what he too had witnessed.

"My Lord," he said, Nikko's words galvanizing him into action. "Please."

Jion allowed himself to be half-carried, half-led away, and as the party slipped through the gates, the night swallowed them.

*

Ullar started forward, but felt Altera's hand on his arm, holding him back. The Hunter's scream was still reverberating around them, setting his teeth on edge. Altera's lieutenant had seen The Hunter dispatch Watanabe, floor the woman… and then smoke had rolled across his vision. But he could have sworn that he had seen a bright flash of blue and purple – an ominous sign for his kind.

As the bank of smoke had rolled away, Ullar had seen the body of The Hunter split in half and then slump to the floor, revealing a boy who did not seem to believe what he had just done.

Ullar could not believe it either. "Filthy little Farravashi…"

"Leave him!" Altera barked, stopping the bigger man in his tracks.

"My Lady?"

"I said leave him."

"I don't understand."

Altera shook her head. "What did we just see?"

"The Hunter… he's been sent back."

"It does not matter. He was already weak. We were lucky not to lose him when Ashikaga died. But I ask again; what did we see?"

Ullar looked confused and looked from his mistress to the body of The Hunter, and back to Altera again.

"Their weapons can't hurt us," Altera said. "It is a blessing of our Mother."

"But…"

"That was no sword forged by the hand of a mere man. That was Skylord metal."

Ullar smiled, realization dawning on him. "Follow the sword…"

"… find the source," Altera finished. "We've found what we came for in this star-cursed land."

CHAPTER SIX

May 1362 – Kurama Temple

Kwon sat in his chamber watching the scene in the courtyard below, but made no effort to join the throng. On a normal day, The Temple gates were locked and barred at sundown, and the residents would have begun their night-time rituals. But this was not a normal day.

Even before the bedraggled party had arrived, Kwon had sensed them. Many of the masters had, as the small group had gradually drawn nearer and nearer, hiding in small farmsteads, gathering what information they could, trying to determine if it was safe to carry on. Kwon did not have to look at them to know who they were. Whatever training these refugees had received at the Yugyo Monastery was insufficient – theirs were noisy minds.

Yugyo... the name was now synonymous with pride and terror. Everyone in the surrounding provinces, if not the whole country, knew the story; a boy with unique abilities had arrived, desperate for sanctuary and, instead of welcoming him, the monastery elders had restricted his training through fear until the child's tormentors had caught up with him. There were several versions of what happened next. Some said the boy slew the Oni's champion but was mortally wounded and cast his father's sword back into the sea at Yokohama, where a baby found it in on the beach only forty days later leading some to declare he was the reincarnation of the gifted boy.

More said that Amaterasu himself had witnessed the titanic struggle that fateful night and as reward for the boy's courage he raised him into the heavens. And there were others who whispered that the boy still lived, that he had escaped into the night only to be rescued by Ainu tribesman who took him back to their secret village to be their defender.

There had been other survivors from Yugyo. Not many, but a few. A cook of the third class. One of the maids. Two stable boys. A few novices. They had told their incredible tale and others had retold it and more had then retold that.

It did not matter to Kwon or any of the other masters. Almost as soon as the message had been received of the massacre at Yugyo, The High Council had been convened. The decision had been unanimous – the child was to be found, even if it was just his body, and brought to Kurama. If he were dead, then he would be given the funeral he deserved. However, if he were alive… he would be embraced as one Yamabushi to another.

The Council elders knew too well that these were dark times and they would soon be forced to declare their loyalty to Yoshiakira or face the consequences. Many smaller temples and shrines had dared to defy the Shogun and instead pledged allegiance to Emperor Go-Murakami. News of their swift and violent destruction had now become commonplace.

And so the elders of Kurama had sent out discrete search parties with a simple mission. *Find the boy.*

Kwon had been instrumental in this policy, and openly admitted that he believed the child to be linked with the appearance of the three stars some seven years previous.

Abbot Shimada had approached him after The Council meeting. "You knew?" he asked quietly. "You knew the boy was destined to come here?"

Kwon had looked away in embarrassment. "I… I… I suspected."

The old abbot smiled. "No. You believed. *Really* believed. That speech you gave in there… you have been preparing that for years. The other elders may not see it, Master Kwon, but I do. How did you know?"

Kwon did not look to his mentor. Learning the ways of The Temple had been difficult and it would have been impossible without Shimada. "You would not believe me," he muttered.

The abbot's reply was calm and soft. "My belief is not of relevance. Yours is."

The foreigner looked to his friend and smiled. "How I wish my people had your way with words… I wish they had but one tenth of the wisdom I have learned here."

"You seldom speak of them. Where are they?"

"Gone. A long time gone."

"They will be reborn. Or dwell within nirvana."

Kwon looked away, silently biting his own tongue. If only these people knew the truth behind their beliefs… but he was not here for that. He was here for the boy. "I hope so," he said. "After my people fell, I journeyed a great distance. I met many people, fought many battles, and learned many things. It was during this time that I felt the land change. The shadows…" his voice tailed off as he struggled for the words.

Shimada nodded. "I know of what you speak. It is something that I and only the most senior masters discuss. The shadows are becoming… it is as though they have weight. The night is becoming heavier. The darkness is deepening."

Kwon nodded. "But... whatever is happening is so slow and so insidious... You would not notice from one year to the next... Master Abbot, I digress. I apologize. During my travels, those who knew of such things spoke of a child... a rare child of noble blood, forged by the hand of Death, who would heal the land and drive back the darkness."

"Our land has many such stories, as does every other. What led you here?"

Kwon hesitated, unsure how much to say. "Many years ago there was a great war. It makes the conflicts of Oyashima look like a childish squabble. There were millions on the battlefield. Tens of millions. I fought under the banner of a woman... I never knew her real name, but we called her The Queen of Murkwood.

"She rescued me when I was a prisoner and I pledged myself to her. Her tribesmen... they claimed she was not one of them either, but had been found by them. I only spoke to her on a few occasions, but she claimed to be out of time and land. I did not understand and I confess that I still do not, but she showed me things... such things that I do not believe even though I have seen them with my own eyes. And she told me of the child. She described the land, the portents, and how, if I positioned myself, he would come to me."

"And you believe this woman? This Queen of Murkwood?"

"I do, Master Abbot."

"And what do you propose for the child?"

"Exactly as The Council has agreed: he should be nurtured and trained. Eventually he will outgrow The Temple and depart, but not before he has saved it. I hope to join him when he leaves and steer him towards The Queen."

"She lives still?"

Kwon nodded.

"You won that great battle?"

Kwon looked to the floor. "No. We were betrayed. The Queen - and what is left of our armies - are in hiding, waiting for the right time to strike again."

"It sounds like this Queen and our Emperor have much in common. But I am curious, Master Kwon. How does your Queen know so much about our land and this child?"

Kwon's gaze did not shift from the straw mats on the floor. "She told me that it has already happened."

For a moment Shimada said nothing, and then laughed loudly. "I like your Queen very much. A man's fate is a man's fate, no? Is she a Buddhist?"

Kwon looked up, smiled, and shook his head. "No, no; she is not."

"Maybe by another name. We shall see if she is right about the boy coming here."

And she was. As the throng at the gates broke apart, novices ran in all directions; some for the kitchens and some to prepare the onsen baths. Kwon got his first look at the boy and the rag-tag party that had traveled with him.

*

July 1362 – Anrakuji Temple, Mount Homan, Tsukushi Isle

Prince Chokei rode the dappled mare along the thin path that wound around the black slopes of Mount Homan, his personal bodyguard riding close alongside him. The morning was clear and warm, and from his vantage point the young prince could see the paddy fields below, the smell of water and sun drifting up to him. Although not yet twenty, Chokei was already an accomplished general in the army of his father, Emperor Go-Murakami.

Other than his lust for the battlefield, falconry was his only passion, and he loved to see his prize bird hovering in the air before silently diving for its prey. It gave him an incredible stillness of mind and, more importantly, provided an excellent means by which to arrange secret meetings in the woods.

Officially, his father was trying to broker a peace with the treacherous Northern Court and the puppet Emperor Kogon. Unofficially, Chokei had a mandate to harry the northern lines, cut off their supply routes, and bribe the provincial lords into supporting his father.

As the party rounded a bend in the mountain path, the track widened and there sat his three spymasters, each with their own retinue of guards. Quickly, Chokei dismounted, bowed to the three men, and knelt.

"My Lords," the Prince began, "please forgive my lateness. The Scourge of The Chrysanthemum Throne has spies everywhere, and it was necessary to come by a different route. What news do you bring?"

The eldest spymaster grunted, nodded to one of his retainers, and a young boy was brought forward. Dirty, emaciated, and wearing little more than rags, the teenager had new bruises about his face and arms, and Chokei knew he had put up a fight.

"Tell our Lord your name," the spymaster barked.

The youth dropped to his knees, pressing his forehead into the dirt. "My Lord Chokei, my name is Ienao… formally of the Yugyo Monastery."

Chokei looked to the spymaster, and said to the silver-haired man, "You found a survivor?"

The spymaster bowed. "As you instructed My Lord."

"Can he be trusted?"

"Yes My Lord."

Chokei turned back to Ienao. "Sit up. You survived the Yugyo Massacre?"

"Yes My Lord."

"What did you see?"

"It was the Oni My Lord. They were everywhere…"

"The Oni? You are sure?"

"Yes My Lord."

"The same Oni who defiled the Ise Shrine? Who corrupted my Aunt? Princess Sachiko?"

Ienao began to stammer in his nervousness, knowing that his life hung in the balance. "My Lord… I… I… I don't know. I was too young to go on that campaign."

Chokei looked to his chief spymaster who nodded but said nothing.

"What of this champion I hear about? The Hero of Yugyo who slew the great Oni warrior?" the prince continued, turning back to the boy.

Ienao felt himself begin to shake with rage. "My Lord should not believe what he hears…"

The spymaster slapped the boy hard on the ear, sending him tumbling into the dirt. "It is not for you to tell your liege lord what he should or should not believe."

Ienao, whimpering, righted himself and pressed his forehead back to the dirt in submission.

"What do you know of The Hero of Yugyo?" Chokei asked, not allowing the boy to sit up this time.

"He is a witch My Lord. A filthy witch. I saw it myself…"

"And what was it you saw?"

"He uses black magic My Lord. I saw him cut arrows from the sky… and he destroyed the Oni when the swords of everyone else simply bounced off them."

"Cut arrows from the sky? The power to destroy the Oni? You saw these things?"

"Yes My Lord."

"You swear it?"

"Yes My Lord. I swear. I saw it with my own eyes. He's a filthy witch. Him and all his whores."

Chokei nodded to his spymaster indicating that he was done with the boy. The spymaster grunted again and one of the guards grabbed Ienao by the scruff of the neck, pulled him onto a horse, and began the short ride back to the Anrakuji Temple.

The prince stood, indicating that the spymaster should join him, and walked to the edge of the mountain path, looking down on the lush valley below.

"Well old friend," Chokei began, "it's an interesting fairy story."

"I believe it is more than that, My Lord. Our sources corroborate the boy's account."

"Hmm… what do we know of this Hero of Yugyo?"

"Very little, My Lord. Our spies have picked through the ruins of the monastery and it has been completely destroyed. Including the archives. The boy's identity is a mystery."

"Did he survive the massacre?"

"Yes My Lord. We have an approximation of where he was heading, although he seems to travel by different names."

"Very wise. A warrior that can cut arrows from the sky and slay the Oni would be a powerful ally, especially if he could teach the same skills to our troops. Where do you believe him to be heading?"

"Deep into Yoshiakira's territory My Lord. Perhaps even to Keishi itself."

Chokei's brows furrowed. "A boy against the Northern Armies? He could not hope to storm parliament. He would be dead before the First Bridge. An assassination attempt?"

"That was my reading of it My Lord. Or maybe he is trying to hide in plain sight. Perhaps to recover his strength?"

"Yes," said Chokei. "Maybe. Either way, if he is fighting the Oni, then he is an enemy of Yoshiakira, which makes him at least sympathetic to our cause."

"Do you wish me to find him, My Lord?"

"Yes… but do not bring him here. Not yet. Observe him. Let us see if his reputation is deserved, and then if he is loyal to us we will recruit him. There is no sense bringing him to our side if he will cause more harm."

"Very wise, My Lord. What do you wish us to do with the informant?"

"Ienao? What do you recommend?"

"Although he was a novice at Yugyo, My Lord, he has lived as an eta for the last eighteen months. He has no worth."

The prince was silent in thought and then spoke. "Do not kill him yet. Clean him up, feed him, and crosscheck his information. Get as much from him as you can. Then teach him the ways of bushido. Make him a bujin warrior."

"My Lord? He is a filthy eta… an outcast…."

Chokei held his hand up. "Maybe, my friend. But it is clear that Ienao and The Hero of Yugyo have history. You saw the boy's rage. If the Hero cannot be brought to our cause, or is a risk to us in any way, we dress Ienao as a ronin and send him to dispatch the Hero for us. We lose nothing either way."

"Very wise My Lord."

*

September 1362 – Kurama Temple

"But it's not fair!" Masako fumed, her face reddening with fury.

"Sshh," Nikko chided and continued to comb through the young girl's long black hair. "You will wake the other novices."

Masako harrumphed loudly and sulked. It was dark outside and the sound of the crickets enjoying the last of the unusually mild autumn filled The Temple grounds.

"You should be pleased for your sister," Nikko continued. "To be invited to be Abbot Sonkan's personal novice is a great honor. You should bask in her reflected glory. Surely one day she will be appointed to The High Council and that can only aid our cause."

"But why not me?" Masako whined. "I'm every bit as good as her. She always gets everything."

Nikko smiled to herself. The young girl would begin her teenage years in only a few months time and the previous week had experienced her first bleeding.

"Your sister will be a great diplomat one day," Nikko continued. "She is already an accomplished negotiator and arbitrator. You have… other talents."

Masako felt a chill run through her and she stiffened. "What do you mean by that?" she asked.

Nikko leaned forward and whispered into her ear, "I know you walk with the Goddess. Jion too…"

Masako span around, grasping for the stiletto knife in the sleeve of her robe. Jion had warned her to keep their nightly prayers secret.

"It's alright," Nikko said softly, resting a cool hand on the girls arm. "I dwell on that hillside too."

"But…" Masako's eyes were wide with shock.

"Sshh. The Goddess is rising again. Soon Marishiten will walk with us all. But you must get word to Jion; he should not voice our faith. Not everyone here can be trusted."

*

October 1362 – Kurama Temple

The council sat hushed as the report was read out. The final words of the messenger echoed into silence and no one stirred or made a reply.

The atmosphere had become tense and heavy, and Abbot Shimada leaned forward to clear his throat. "Thank you," he said, dismissing the courier, and turned to his Head Librarian. "Master Nanshu?"

The old monk stood, his limbs visibly trembling through age. "Master Abbot, I am afraid that the report has been verified. Yoshino has fallen."

The room rippled with consternation and Shimada held up a hand to quieten his brethren. "Master Nanshu, what happened?"

"It would appear that the Emperor's forces took Keishi during the summer. However, in doing so, they over-extended themselves and Yoshiakira retook the city within twenty days. The evacuation seems to have been badly managed and the Shogun's army overtook the retreating forces and…"

His voice trailed off and every monk knew what would have happened. The Scourge of The Chrysanthemum Throne was as ruthless as his father and there would have been no survivors.

Nanshu continued. "Yoshino was left relatively unprotected and the Shogun continued his advance… I am sorry to report that the city was razed to the ground."

"What of the Emperor?" Kwon asked, ignoring the etiquette of directing all questions through the Master Abbot.

Nanshu looked to Shimada who nodded, forgiving the foreigner for his petty slights. "He escaped to the Tsukushi Isle… with the royal regalia. Yoshiakira cannot crown his puppet yet."

"What of our Order within the city?" Shimada asked.

Nanshu shook his head. "We have had no word from them. We must assume the worst."

"Master Kwon," Shimada said, turning to face his one-time apprentice. "I appreciate that the complexities of our land may be confusing for you. You should know that this loss gives the Shogun near complete control of Yamato Isle. He already holds five of the other islands. His total victory is near. Soon all monasteries and temples will be ordered to swear allegiance. Those that refuse…"

Kwon bowed deeply. "I shall redouble the boy's training Master Abbot. We shall live to see the darkness fall."

*

January 1363 – Kurama Temple

"No no no," Kwon exclaimed, berating his young student. "You *must* focus."

Jion picked up his *bokken* – the wooden sword he trained with - from the floor and brought it to a guard. "Yes Master, I will try harder." Despite the cold of the winter day, sweat was pouring off the boy.

Kwon put his bokken into his belt. The boy was determined to learn but his mind was too cluttered. "Let's take a break," he sighed.

Jion nodded, bowed, and moved to the edge of the mat where he took a noisy slurp from a bowl of water and toweled the sweat from his face.

"Jion," Kwon said quietly, sitting next to him. "I won't pretend to understand everything you have been through, but the way you cling on to the past… it is holding you back. You will never realize your full potential if you cannot let go."

"Yes Master, I apologize." The words were automatic and without sincerity.

"You know, Kurama has a story. Many years ago a master and his adept were walking in the mountains when they came to a swollen river. A beautiful peasant woman stood by the banks trying to cross, and the Master offered to carry her on his back. She accepted and all three crossed the river, and then went their separate ways. Many miles later, the adept could not contain his indignation.

'Master,' the adept said. 'It was not seemly for one as holy as you to carry one such as her.'

'Really?' the master replied. 'I put her down hours ago. Why do you still carry her?'"

Jion looked at Master Kwon blankly. "Are you saying that I should forget the past?"

"No Jion. By remembering the past, we learn. But don't hold on to it. It is like a boulder, weighing you down in the lake of your thoughts. Let it go and you will rise to the surface."

"I do not understand Master. How can I remember *and* let go?"

Kwon smiled. "If I could explain that one I would have been appointed to The Council many years ago. Let me put it this way; you have attachments, yes? And in some ways that is good – they ground you and give you a bearing. But we all grow, Jion, and you must recognize those attachments that you have outgrown and that are holding you back. You are so fixated on them that you let them shape your future. Your fate is your own and no-one else's. You can shape your own destiny."

"Master, you ask me to forget my father? My brother? Master Otsuno? Sensei Watanabe?"

"Like the adept in the story, you carry them on your back and your arms. Your movements are predictable and ponderous because you are weighed down. When you come into this dojo and bow to the kami, put them down. When you leave, and bow to the kami… it is your decision whether you pick up your burden again."

Jion looked silently at his master. "What if they are the source of my power? What if I direct my feelings for them outwards…?"

"Be careful Jion," Kwon interrupted. "Actions that stem from grief and fear are seldom good. They will open an abyss within you that cannot easily be filled."

"Yes Master. I understand."

*

April 1363 – Fujigatani Castle, Inzai Valley, Shimosa Province

As Lord Mutsu heard the words he had long dreaded, he felt his stomach tighten.

"Do you understand and obey your Liege Lord's instruction?" Lady Altera asked.

Mutsu bowed, his forehead touching the cool soft mat on the floor which gave temporary respite from the warmth of the spring afternoon. "I do My Lady."

"And do you swear to be bound by it?" Altera continued, still reading from the scroll in front of her that bore both the imperial seal and that of the Shogun.

"Yes My Lady. I shall see that the message is delivered immediately."

"Good," Altera said brusquely. "My presence is required by Lord Yoshiakira. I will depart immediately, but be assured that the Shogun expects his vassals to be absolutely trustworthy… especially those to whom he has already granted such favors."

"Yes My Lady."

Mutsu saw Altera out, and breathed a sigh of relief. "You can come out now."

A panel slid from the wall, and Lord Koichi stepped out from the secret compartment. The son of Lord Chikatane, Koichi strongly resembled his father not just in girth, but also in the heaviness of his brow and sallow complexion.

"How could you agree to such a thing?" Koichi hissed. "After everything my father has done for you? After everything we have built here?"

"What choice did I have?" Mutsu cried plaintively. "We are all the Shogun's vassals. His command is our deed."

Koichi shook his head. "But it is unthinkable. Did the witch leave the scroll?"

Mutsu nodded and handed it to Chikatane's son.

"At the command of His Imperial Highness Emperor Kogon, Lord Yoshiakira decrees that the sentence of death on the House of Soma is lifted," Koichi read aloud. "And that all survivors should present themselves to Utsunomiya Castle for strategic marriage for the peace and good order of the realm… This is outrageous."

"It bears the seals of the Emperor," Mutsu said, resignation heavy in his voice.

"I don't care if it bears the mark of Amaterasu himself!" spittle flew from Koichi's lips. "The Shogun wants to marry those cowardly dogs back into our family? It is unthinkable!"

"It is for the good of the land…"

"My eye! It is for the good of the Shogun and no-one else."

"Sshh…" the old strategist said, his eyes flashing. "You will be heard. You speak treason."

"Then let me declare treason," Koichi countered hotly. "I'll raise an army and march on Keishi itself."

"You would be slaughtered before you even got to the border."

"It would be a good death... an honorable death. Not this... this... affront to decency," Koichi finished, throwing the scroll onto the floor.

"Be calm. Just because we have been outmaneuvered does not mean we have lost the battle."

Koichi stopped and turned to look at Mutsu. "What do you mean?"

"The Shogun desires the boy... your cousin. We have all heard the stories of Yugyo. No doubt Lord Yoshiakira believes that Yoshimoto was involved."

"Soma was a foul leader. He would rut with a dog," Koichi charged. "My cousin's blood is like water... less than an eta."

"My Lord... the Shogun believes that Yoshimoto has value. Maybe even the Nawa girls too. He is reaching out to them, trying to bring them to his side."

"You speak in riddles, old man. What is the point?"

"The point is that the Shogun does not yet have them. This decree does many things. Firstly, it tests your loyalty. Secondly, it tells the dogs of the South that the boy has worth."

"So?"

"So we are in a time when the South sues for peace. If they find the boy first and bring him to their side, then they act dishonorably. Whichever few provincial lords still support them would rally to the Shogun's side rather than be associated with such underhand dealings."

"But that does not help us," Koichi retorted. "If Yoshimoto is found by the Shogun, he will be forced to marry into our family and will become Clan Leader again. I cannot permit such a thing."

Mutsu smiled. "Then perhaps we should ensure that the Southern Court find him first."

Koichi looked at his uncle, and finally shook his head. "No. You cannot guarantee that those dogs would not hand my cousin over to the Shogun as a bargaining chip in the peace process."

"You have an alternative suggestion?"

Chikatane's son turned and looked out the window, across the verdant canopy of the Inzai Valley, and marveled at how the land had recovered so quickly from that terrible day nine years ago. "Yes," he said eventually. "I do."

*

May 1363 – Kurama Temple

Kwon bowed in unison with his two colleagues who flanked him as they approached The High Council, who returned the courtesy.

"Masters Takamori, Hiroyasu, and Kwon," began Abbot Shimada. "It has been a year since young Jion presented himself at our gates and, as agreed, you three have been responsible for his tuition. What is your report after these initial twelve months?"

Takamori, the oldest and most senior of the three, stepped forward and bowed. "Master Abbot, Honorable Council members, brethren all. There now follows the report by the three tutors to the boy known as Jion on his first twelve months of training.

"The boy was initially difficult to manage. He had received insufficient training whilst at the Yugyo Monastery and the deaths of Master Otsuno and Sensei Watanabe caused him to act badly, albeit out of grief.

"However he has taken to his studies well. I have taught him military tactics and history. Master Hiroyasu has focused on his spiritual training. And Master Kwon has begun the boy's martial education.

"In respect of my classes, he is an adequate student. He is able to grasp concepts quickly enough, but he is easily distracted and is often inattentive and forgetful. However, considering his age, that the change is upon him, and his previous upbringing, I recommend that his classes are continued.

"In respect of the spiritual training, Master Hiroyasu reports good progress. The child is learning, albeit slowly, to let go of his feelings. The recommendation is for his classes to continue.

"Finally, Master Kwon reports that Jion has little or no aptitude for the bow or spear. However, the boy is turning into a first class swordsman and is becoming increasingly proficient in unarmed combat. It is Master Kwon's recommendation that the bow and spear be dropped from the boy's syllabus, but for all other training to continue."

Abbot Shimada leaned forward. "And what of the boy's... other abilities?"

Takamori shifted uneasily. "The boy does present... extraordinary traits, however he is reluctant to use them."

"Why is that?"

"By his own admission, and due in part to the lack of training at Yugyo, the boy has previously abused his talents. The effect on his physical self has been extreme and he likens it to putting a needle in a bruise."

"Is there any chance of recovery?" Sonkan asked.

"Yes, Master Abbot, but it will be slow. During our time of observation, we, his tutors, have noticed that his range of hearing has increased as has his speed and dexterity. We have also witnessed an ability to sense that goes far beyond our power; by focussing on an object, he can determine its history as if he were seeing through the eyes of a kami. However when he does so, the object seems to lift or raise itself, but Jion is unable to control this at the moment."

"That is very interesting Master Takamori. And what of the boy's loyalty?"

"There is no doubt that he is grateful to The Council and The Temple as a whole and we believe that he is unquestioningly loyal."

"I sense something else... what is it?"

"Forgive me Master Abbot. All of the boy's instructors feel... it is a symptom of his previous years. There is a certain hardness within the child that is born of fear and hate. To those that show him kindness he will love and protect without question. But to those who he believes have wronged him in the past... he clings to vengeance. His perspective is one of absolutes."

"Will he soften?"

"Master Abbot, I cannot say."

*

"I hear that your ward passed his annual review," Nikko said, countering the strike from Tatsuo.

"Yes," the one-armed swordsman replied, parrying and then lunging. "On the whole, The Council were pleased, but more will be expected of him next year."

Nikko knocked the wooden training sword downward and tapped Tatsuo on the wrist with her own. He instantly released the handle, letting it fall to the floor.

"Yield?" she asked.

"Only for you," he smiled, and turned to reach for a towel to wipe away the sweat that poured from his face.

"You know what you did there?"

Tatsuo nodded. "I should have closed the gap first. It was silly to over-extend like that. Even after all these years I still struggle to remember that what was on the right is now the left."

"It'll come in time."

"I hope so. How did The Council receive the report on Gozen and Masako?" Tatsuo asked.

"You didn't hear?"

Tatsuo frowned and shook his head, still wiping the sweat that continued to pour from him. "No. What happened?"

"Gozen no longer has to submit to an annual report. Because she trains with the Abbot, he assesses her privately."

Tatsuo began to stand, a look of indignation on his face. "Is there...?"

"Oh don't be silly. The Abbot knows well enough the commitment between Gozen and Jion. He will respect it."

"Hmmm... how did Masako take the news?"

"How do you think?"

"That bad, huh?"

"There were certainly a few tears."

Tatsuo shrugged. "It is a shame that there is not more love between those two. Sisters should not fight or be jealous. Still, teenage years are difficult. Perhaps they will grow out of it. How did your report go?"

"The Council was pleased with the progress I have made in their library, although there is still much to do. Master Nanshu is very ill indeed and they asked if I would be prepared to become the Head Librarian when he passes."

"What did you say?"

"Of course I said yes."

"Very good. It will be a great honor for you. I heard that Nanshu's tumor is becoming apparent. He is so old; it is a wonder how he hangs on."

"Yes," said Nikko, putting down her own towel and smiling. "Now, do you have something for me to hang on to?"

*

Jion stretched out on his bedroll, closed his eyes and let his mind drift out across The Temple, taking in the sounds of the closing evening. It was like a song that he knew off by heart but still wanted to hear anyway. The monks talking – satisfied with his progress but fearful that he could not let go of hate.

Kwon studying the scrolls in the library, deciding how advanced next year's syllabus should be. Gozen in Shimada's room, reciting the genealogy of The Chrysanthemum Throne. The grunts of Nikko and Tatsuo coming from the furthest dojo. Jion felt his groin twitch and begin to harden, and he allowed his second sight to drift the entire length of the great courtyard and seep under the door to observe the two naked bodies, contorted around each other in the agony of ecstasy. Sweat was flung high into the air as they rolled on the mats, Nikko finally pinning her lover underneath her and thrusting down heavily onto him, arching her back as she did so.

Jion began to move his hand to his groin when a knock at the door snapped him out of his reverie. Instantly he grabbed his sword, prepared for an attack.

"Who is it?" he called.

"It's me," the voice of Masako came. She sounded small and upset. "Can I come in?"

Jion slid the door open and invited the tear-stained girl in. "What's the matter? Why are you crying?" he asked, pretending not to already know that Gozen did not have to submit to annual reports, and that she did.

*

The night was cool and the moon hung low and fat as Tatsuo and Nikko walked down the courtyard, the cool breeze soothing their sticky bodies.

"What are you thinking?" she asked.

"Nothing. Everything. This place."

"What of it?"

"Just how... the harmony is better here than at Yugyo. How the children have adjusted so well. How we have been welcomed. Do you think we're safe here?"

"It depends how you define safe," Nikko said distractedly, looking through the window of one of the buildings.

"What do you mean?" Tatsuo asked stopping and following her gaze.

"Safe from the Shogun? Maybe for a while. Safe from each other..." her voice trailed off as she took in the scene in Jion's chamber.

Tatsuo looked through the window and saw the sleeping form of Jion and Masako wrapped around each other, lit by a pale moonbeam.

"Well that's gone and torn it," he muttered.

*

Jion was indignant. "I'm telling you. *Nothing happened.*" Tatsuo had ambushed him the next morning as soon as Masako had left.

"It does not matter," Tatsuo fumed. "It's that something *could* have happened. You are betrothed to her sister."

"So?"

"So? So? My Lord, please think about your actions. It is unseemly for you to court both sisters. You jeopardize the very future of your clan. You *must* marry Gozen."

"And I will do. It is my duty, I know that. But Masako was upset and I offered her comfort. That was all."

Tatsuo was exasperated. "My Lord, it is not your place to offer comfort to your fiancée's sister. Think how this will look."

"How does it look? Have you not told me how a Clan Lord may have a wife and a mistress and pillow with as many concubines as he wishes?"

"You pillowed her? She is now your concubine?"

"No, I told you... she is like a sister to me. But you said as Clan Lord..."

"You are not the Clan Lord. And a lady of the House Nawa is certainly no concubine. My Lord, please... if Gozen learns of this, she would be within her rights to break off the engagement."

"Then we will have to make sure she doesn't," Jion retorted hotly.

*

It was three days later and Abbot Shimada carefully picked up the rice with his chopsticks, ate it slowly, and then returned for some of the pickled vegetables. Nikko knelt in silence, head bowed. When the old monk had finished, he addressed her.

"I understand my favor of Gozen has caused some consternation," he said.

"Yes Master Abbot."

"The younger sister is upset by this?"

"Yes Master Abbot."

"Can she be made to see reason?"

"Yes Master Abbot, I believe so."

"Hmm… it is concerning that there is such a divide between sisters. Mistress Nikko, do you still stand by your previous recommendations?"

"Yes Master Abbot. Gozen is gifted and is best serving her apprenticeship under your expert tutelage. Masako's talents… they lie in a different direction and it is best that she remains under my guidance."

The abbot shrugged, brought the bowl of cha to his lips and slurped noisily. "Very well," he said eventually. "Now, you have heard about Master Nanshu?"

"Yes Master Abbot. So very sad. He was a great man and a great master. He will be missed."

"Indeed. His cremation will be tonight. We will install you as the Head Librarian tomorrow morning."

"Thank you Master Abbot," Nikko said, bowing low. "I hope I live up to your expectation."

*

July 1363 – Anrakuji Temple, Mount Homan, Tsukushi Isle

It was the hour of the horse, and the summer sun was approaching its peak. Prince Chokei stood next to his spymaster and both men watched the ceremony of promotion, where novices were moved up to the adept classes.

"It is truly remarkable what you have done with him," Chokei said, looking at the statuesque form of Ienao, waiting in line.

"Thank you, Your Highness."

"He was little more than a wild thing when you brought him to us, and now… well, as I said, remarkable. Will he be able to undertake his mission soon?"

"He needs a year or two yet, Your Highness," the Spymaster cautioned. "He understands theory very well, but putting it into practice… he is lacking in experience."

"I understand. Walk with me," Chokei replied and turned from the parade. "My father is concerned about reports of a buildup of the Shogun's forces in Yamato."

"Yes Your Highness. The Great Scourge was said to be furious when he took Yoshino and found that the Emperor was gone… and the royal regalia."

Chokei smirked. He had been the architect of his father's rescue, and the fact that his enemy had missed his target gave him no end of pleasure. "What do our spies say?"

"They say that Yoshiakira intends to invade Tsukushi, Your Highness."

Chokei snorted. "Impossible. The island is a natural fortress…" he caught the look on his Spymaster's face and stopped. "What is it?"

"There are rumors, Your Highness, that a number of merchants in the port have been… compromised."

Chokei rolled his eyes. *Merchants and their bribes!*

"We believe that we have identified them and we can arrest them…"

Chokei stopped and thought. "What is their plan?"

"Your Highness, we believe that they will smuggle weapons into a warehouse over the next year. Then they will charter a Tianxian Junker… except that the oarsmen will be the Shogun's men. They will establish a beach head and…"

"Yes yes yes," Chokei interrupted, understanding the plot. "This sounds like an opportunity."

"Your Highness?"

"Whichever one of your men that you plant in the merchants homes… have Ienao as his servant. That will give him the experience he needs."

"Yes, Your Highness."

*

August 1363 – Keishi, Yamashiro Province

Altera never felt more uneasy than when she was in one of the big cities, and, as the political center of the Northern Court, there were few cities bigger than Keishi. The whole plain seemed to be filled with houses and shops, and filthy merchants called out, while the sounds of blacksmiths and stonemasons threatened to drown them out.

Inwardly she smiled; glad that her latest shrine was having such an obvious effect. Outwardly she remained grim and resolute as she stalked through the streets, flanked by the imposing forms of Ullar and Birag.

"You're sure this is the way?" she snapped.

"Yes, My Lady," Ullar replied. "Our informant was exact."

Even though many of the peasants instantly recognized the small group as bujin and bowed deeply, Altera still felt the need to knock a few out of the way. She was frustrated at the slow progress in tracking down the survivors of Fujigatani and their Skylord metal.

Perhaps allowing The Hunter to be sacrificed was the wrong decision, she thought, and toyed with idea of bringing another through. She dismissed the notion; Yoshiakira had been quite explicit – no more magic. At least not until his lieutenants were more unified. The fragile alliance could break apart at any time, and an accusation of witchcraft so close to the Shogun could spark any number of treasonous plots.

"Here," said Ullar. "This is the one."

The smell of saltpeter and iron greeted Altera like a slap in the face, almost overwhelming her. The interior of the shop was dimly lit and she could only just discern shapes in the dark by the dull glow of the forge at the back.

"Yes?" a thick voice said and a dark form stood.

"Are you Masamune? The blade smith?"

The man laughed, wiping his brow as he did so. "You are about twenty years too late. I'm Muramasa. I was a student of Masamune. What can I help you with?"

"Is this your work?" Altera produced a small cloth from her robe.

Muramasa took the cloth, feeling the weight of the object inside, and unwrapped it. "It's too dark in here," he said. "Let's go outside."

Altera followed him out onto the street, but nodded to Ullar and Birag to remain inside, and hoped they had they brains to search quietly.

"They won't find much," Muramasa said, not looking up but turning the small dagger over in his hands.

Altera ignored the statement. "So, is it one of yours?"

"I wish it were. The craftsmanship is exquisite. But no, it is not one of mine. Where did you get it?"

"A peasant."

Muramasa laughed heartily. "Not likely. Come on, tell me. I'd like to know who my competition is."

"I told you… a peasant. But he said he found it in the body of a monster in a cave. The Tengu King."

"There is no such thing," the blacksmith said, still chuckling. "Sojobo is just a story to frighten children."

"Maybe, but I was told that this is your work." Altera did not want to tell the story of her search for the source of the Skylord metal; how they had learned the legend of the Ishin Blade, before tracking the story of its origins to a peasant village in the north. Nor did she wish to tell of the things that she had to do to the same peasants to get them to talk, or how long she had searched for someone knowledgeable in the way of metalwork.

Muramasa shrugged. "It's similar to some of my pieces. I could show you why it's *not* one of mine, but we'd be here all day, and you don't look like the sort of Lady who has much patience."

"Do you know who could have forged this?"

"My first guess would be one of Masamune's other students. There were eleven, including myself."

"Do you know where they are?"

"Several are dead already. Some of have gone to Tianxia… the money is better over there. Kanemitsu lives on the northern coast. I'm not sure if he is still alive."

"What about the metal?" Altera asked.

"Ah … you noticed that. Interesting, isn't it?"

"You tell me."

Muramasa turned the knife over in his hands again, looking at it carefully. "It feels heavier than it should be, but when it moves it takes very little effort... like it has a life of its own. And..." the blacksmith brought the knife to his nose, "it smells wrong."

Altera was growing bored of the conversation. "Smells wrong? What do you mean?"

"Here," Muramasa offered the knife back. "It smells like the land after a storm. Like lightning has struck it."

Altera brought the blade up to her nose and realized the blacksmith was right. "Do you know what ore has been used?"

Muramasa shook his head. "Nothing local. There have been rumors of a secret Ainu settlement along the Sea of Oyashima, not far from where Kanemitsu used to live. They have some dark practices. It might be that knife has one of their blessings on it. You never know these days. There are witches and demons everywhere."

Altera looked up from the knife in her hand. "Maybe it is just a matter of perspective," she said sweetly. "You could see those that seek to break you as demons. Or you could see them as angels, trying to set you free and guide you to Nirvana."

Muramasa grunted an acknowledgement but said nothing more, sensing that he was being led into a trap.

Altera returned to looking at the blade in her hand. "If you had the patronage, could you find the miners who smelted the ore, and make one like this?"

"Sure," Muramasa nodded. "It may take a few attempts to get the detail exactly right, but it should not be too difficult."

"Good," Altera replied. "Don't leave town. The Shogun might have a job for you."

*

November 1363 – Kurama Temple

Master Hiroyasu closed his eyes and asked his body to ignore the harsh wind that was blowing through The Temple grounds, finding its way through every gap in the doors and windows. Autumn was nearing its end and winter was about to fall upon the land like a ravenous dog.

"Focus," Hiroyasu said softly, sitting cross-legged on the straw mat. "Focus on the point deep inside you. Down... deeper..."

He could hear Jion's breathing slowing. The boy continued to show improvement in his meditation and where his mind had once been in turmoil, like the surface of a sea in a storm, today it was like a mountain lake on a summer's day.

"Good," Hiroyasu continued. "Let yourself go. Feel the weight of your body dissolve. Become nothing. Without the need for anything. There is no hunger. No fear. No cold. No warmth. You are the Void..."

The smell of ammonia rolled into his nostrils, causing his eyes to water, and the old monk felt his ears pop.

Coughing and spluttering, Hiroyasu opened his eyes to find the source of the stench, and then wider in shock at the empty space on the mat where Jion had been.

*

Jion felt a soft warm hand slip into his.

"Yoshi," the voice was that of a woman, soft and lilting like the nightingale song he heard when he was a child. "Yoshimoto. Wake up little Yoshi."

Jion opened his eyes, taking in the gentle face of the woman before. Instantly he dropped to the ground, bowing low and pressing his forehead into the dirt. He knew this place, although it had been weeks since he had been here. The hill. The tree. And he knew who the woman was.

"Goddess…" he whispered, "I am not worthy…"

"Sit up little Yoshi."

Jion sat up but kept his eyes to the ground out of reverence.

"Let me look at you Yoshi… lift your head young one."

Jion looked up, admiring the naked woman before him. Her skin was pale, luminescent, like virgin snow and flawless as though made of the finest Tianxian silk. Her dark hair cascading down her shoulders like a waterfall at night.

"Finally, you have come to me Yoshi," Marishiten said. "I have waited so long for you."

Jion frowned. "I do not understand My Goddess. I have been with you many times."

Marishiten tilted her head and smiled sadly. "No. Before, you looked through an open window. Now you have stepped through the door. I have such things to show you, Little Yoshi… such gifts."

Jion bowed deeply again. "I am not worthy, My Goddess."

"Oh Little Yoshi. Your fate is more than that of your clan or your land. If you serve with duty and honor, you will be rewarded with your heart's desire."

"If it is your will, My Goddess, I will obey."

"Good. That is very good Little Yoshi. Now remember your lessons. The usefulness of a cup is its emptiness. It must be drained before it can be filled. You must be like the cup Little Yoshi. You must empty yourself before I can fill you."

*

Kwon stood and watched the Abbot Shimada as the older man knelt in the garden, examining the stones.

"Your thoughts betray you, Master Kwon," Shimada said eventually. "Even after all these years, yours remains one of the noisiest minds."

"I have been... disturbed Master Abbot."

"Yes. Come, sit next to me. I want to show you something."

Kwon took a few short steps to the Abbot's side, and knelt next to him.

"Please, look at this stone. Examine it closely," Shimada said.

Kwon looked the lichen-covered boulder over, and nodded to the Abbot.

"Now... watch." The two sat in silence, observing the stone. Minutes passed. Then half an hour. And then an hour.

Kwon shifted. "Master Abbot? I regret that I do not understand. What are we doing?"

Shimada smiled. "What I always do when my harmony is disturbed. I watch rocks grow."

Kwon groaned inwardly. He had never taken to what he considered to be the more obscure practices of The Temple. Outwardly, he grunted but said nothing.

"Now," Shimada said. "I take it that the source of *your* disharmony is the boy."

"Yes Master Abbot."

"And his disappearance from Master Hiroyasu's class."

"Yes Master Abbot."

"But he came back?"

"Yes Master Abbot. Three days later. No-one can explain it."

"What does the boy say?"

"Nothing. He claims not to remember where he went or how. But I am not sure I believe him."

"Why not?" Shimada asked, still examining the stone in front of him.

"Master Abbot... not long ago we spoke of my Queen, and her knowledge of the boy."

"Yes, I remember. What of it?"

"Master Abbot, she wrote down her knowledge for me. It is one of the few things I carry with me. Her account predicts that the child will develop these powers."

"I apologize for my lack of understanding Master Kwon, but if your Queen prophecised this event, then what is the cause of your disharmony?"

"Master Abbot, the child has developed this ability *early*. Far earlier than my Queen's account suggests."

"How early?" Shimada stopped looking at the stone and turned to Kwon, his interest piqued by this new development.

"Nearly sixty years Master Abbot. I am concerned that Jion does not have the maturity to use this ability wisely."

"I see. Could it be that your Queen did not prophecise correctly?"

"Yes Master Abbot, that much is evident. But it is more than that," Kwon replied.

"How so?"

"It means that Jion is unlikely to grow into the warrior he is supposed to. Something that is not supposed to be here is affecting him. I fear that he may become a threat to us all."

*

August 1364 – Kurama Temple

Jion knelt, his long slim legs folding smoothly underneath him, and he addressed the shrine where he had just lit an incense stick. Despite the intense heat of the summer day, the evening promised to be cloudless and cool, and he could feel the warmth from the glowing embers of the sun on his neck.

"May I join you?"

He did not have to open his eyes to know that it was Gozen. He had sensed her approach from the moment she had left her chamber. His gifts of sense and hearing were almost fully restored, though he did not openly admit it. However, his ability to manipulate his environment had not returned in any meaningful way and this frustrated him.

"Of course," Jion replied. "It would be an honor to have you with me to mark this day."

Gozen knelt beside him and lit her own incense stick. "It is hard to believe that nine years have passed since that day in Fujigatani. We have lost so many. Sensei Watanabe. Master Otsuno. Gasan. All those we knew at Yugyo…" her voice tailed off.

"Their deaths were honorable," Jion said through a clenched jaw. He knew the conversation that was coming.

"If you say so," Gozen replied meekly, seeing her fiancé's body tense. "I had hoped that our course would not cost us so much."

"We will pay the cost," Jion answered grimly. "However high it might be. It is our fate."

Gozen did not reply immediately, but considered the thin plume of smoke that came from her stick; the intensity at the source but how it quickly dissipated on the evening breeze.

"What if it was not?" she said eventually.

Jion frowned. "What do you mean?"

Now aged seventeen, Gozen was being introduced to the higher lessons of spiritual thinking by Abbot Shimada, and although she was not permitted to teach Jion until he was of age, she remained keen to pass on her insights.

"What if fate is not fate unless we make it?" she asked.

"I do not understand," Jion replied, not softening his tone. "A man's fate is a man's fate."

"That may be so, but consider this; Lord Chikatane betrayed your father and killed him. As is your right, you claim vengeance against him. But will his son then claim vengeance against you? Will our children claim against him? Are our families locked into this cycle forever? Can it be that all we can expect from life is revenge and death?"

"What else is there? To die an honorable death... it is the way of our people... the way of the bujin. If we do not follow this path then we are not bujin. Then what are we? We are nothing. Truly, we would be less than a merchant. Less than the eta even. To follow our path is to *be*."

Gozen's reply was soft. "But what if we could *be* something else? Something not wedded to death?"

Jion shook his head. "Death is honorable. We must live and die with honor. Without that... what is the point? You say that we could *be* something else as though we have a choice. Could we *be* a tree or a cloud? No, because a tree is a tree and cloud is a cloud. That is what they were born to be. It is the same with us. We are born to be us... unless you do not want to be *us*?"

Gozen paled. "Not at all. Were we a tree or a cloud I would still be betrothed to you and would go to that willingly, as I do now."

Jion said nothing, but sensed the conflict within the older girl.

*

March 1365 – Kurama Temple

Jion lurched awake, a scream caught in his throat, sweat glistening on his sinewy limbs by the moonlight.

"Sshh... it's alright," a voice whispered softly. Cool arms wrapped around him, instantly calming his pounding heart. "Here, take some water."

Through the dark, a cold bowl was pushed into his trembling hands, and Jion gulped the water down.

"Thank you Masako," he said. "I do not know what I would do if you were not here."

"You would be fine," the girl said, smiling coyly in the dark. "The mightiest of warriors always are."

"Maybe. But all the same, thank you."

"You do not need to thank me. Thank the Goddess. It is She who watches over us... you especially."

Jion nodded and gulped at the water again.

"You do remember what you were dreaming?" Masako asked.

Even though it was dark, Jion shook his head. "No... not really. Just half images."

"Tell me."

"There was a woman crying. And there was a city like none in Oyashima. It was all black towers, reaching to the sky. The clouds were dark and seemed to boil as if there was something in them. I think Master Otsuno was there...

we were watching a fight… a battle. It was big. And there were strange horses that sound more like dogs. But the sea rose up and swept everyone away. Then I was bleeding from my mouth and I was pulling my teeth out. They were rotten. Whoever it was who was with me… Master Otsuno or Sensei Watanabe… said that it did not matter who won the battle, my teeth would still fall out. Then there was something else, and I was falling and flying at the same time… then I woke up."

"Oh Jion," Masako said sympathetically. "That is the fifth time this month. This may be another power emerging. You should speak to one of the masters."

"Maybe. But who?"

"What about Master Kwon? He likes you very much and takes a great interest in your well being."

"No. Even though he is the best fencing instructor, he is still a foreigner. He does not really understand our ways."

Masako thought for a moment, and eyed the approaching dawn. She would have to go back to her own chamber soon, before anyone saw them together. "What about Mistress Nikko?" she said. "Maybe there is something in the library that could explain the dreams?"

"Yes," Jion replied. "Yes, that is a good idea. I will speak to her after training."

*

July 1365 – Kurama Temple

Tatsuo inspected the parchments that Jion had prepared and then looked up to the kneeling form of his lord.

The one-armed retainer nodded. "My Lord… these are very good," he said putting the scrolls down.

It was the hour of the monkey and the summer sun streamed in through the windows, lighting the whole room with a glow that warmed the soul as well as the body.

"Thank you Tatsuo," Jion replied. "But it was only through your guidance that I was able to come to a solution."

Tatsuo bowed his head respectfully. He had been charged with teaching the young man advanced military tactics and, after a year of training, Jion had begun to offer insights and strategies beyond anything he could draw up.

He is excelling, Tatsuo thought and then frowned as he saw Jion try to suppress a smile. *He is reading me.*

"If I may offer some advice, My Lord," Tatsuo said, picking up a brush and pointing to one of the scrolls. "In this scenario here, you may wish to think about moving your archers further up the hill. This may allow for a third volley before you commit your cavalry."

Jion nodded. "I see... but would a third volley not catch some of the infantry over here."

"Maybe My Lord... but they are expendable."

Jion looked up, the sunlight playing in his hair. "Are *all* my troops expendable Tatsuo?"

"Yes My Lord. It is their duty to die for you."

"What about you? Is that your duty too?"

"If that is my fate, I go to it willingly, My Lord. I can think of no finer death than in your service."

Jion paled a little and when he spoke his voice was distant. "I hope not Tatsuo."

"My Lord?"

"You are very important to me... to all of us. I remember what you did for me at Yugyo. The way you would sit with me and play games when I was still a child... your actions when Nobuo threatened me. The way you got me to safety during the attack. Your sacrifice at Ise..."

"My Lord honors me," Tatsuo said, bowing his head to avoid Jion seeing his flush of pride.

"I mean it... I would not be here if it was not for you. I wonder if, in another life, we might be brothers."

Tatsuo looked up. "Oh no My Lord. My position is to serve. I should always be by your side."

"I hope you are, Tatsuo, I hope you are."

*

September 1365 – Kurama Temple

"If you hesitate, you are lost," Nikko said, tapping Jion's wrist gently.

Autumn sunlight streamed into the library where Jion, Gozen and Masako were taking a calligraphy lesson with the librarian.

"Do not hold the brush and wait," Nikko continued. "Pick it up... and flow. All as one movement... do you see?"

Jion nodded. "But... sometimes I am taught to wait... to consider."

Nikko looked to Masako's work. "Very good," and took the parchment from the girl. "See here Jion... the flow of the brush and the ink. To wait and consider... that is for lesser students. You... all of you... have such potential. But you must act on it. Feel the flow of life about you... join it. Let it embrace you.

"You sense the brush. And you know what must be done. The purpose of the brush is to paint. So paint. If the brush lies idle then it does not fulfill its purpose. And so it has no meaning. However, if you pick it up, it reaches its potential. There is no hesitancy. It only paints... or it does not."

Jion considered this, remembering how he had hesitated that fateful night at Yugyo. "Mistress Nikko... should I be like the brush?"

The librarian smiled. "Why do say that?"

"Because it is better to act and realize my purpose than not to."

Nikko's smile broadened. "What do you think, Jion?"

*

December 1365 – Anrakuji Temple, Mount Homan, Tsukushi Isle

Against the driving sleet, Ienao stood in the cobbled street of the port town, unfazed by the winter wind that whipped around him. He held out his long and short sword out on either side, letting the thick film of ichor run off the deadly blades and onto the floor where they froze into dark pools.

The Spymaster stepped out of the small shop and nodded. "You have done well Ienao."

The boy's voice was flat and monotone. "Thank you Master."

"His Highness approaches," the Spymaster said, hearing the familiar approach of horses. "Remember your manners,"

Prince Chokei pulled his mount up in front of his Spymaster, surrounded by his usual retinue. Both the man and Ienao knelt and bowed their heads.

"It is done?" the Prince asked.

"Yes, Your Highness," the Spymaster replied, not looking up. "The traitors have been dealt with. All of Tsukushi is back under your control."

"Very good," Chokei said, trying to control the horse that had begun to step sideways. "I understand that we have you to thank for this," he continued, looking to Ienao.

"It was only my duty, Your Highness," the teenager said, following his master's example and not looking up.

"Nevertheless, The Chrysanthemum Throne is grateful for your efforts. I will see you that you are rewarded."

"Thank you, Your Highness, but that is not necessary."

"Your dedication to your duty is a credit to yourself and your master," Chokei said leaning forward. "I think we have a mission for you. A search for an old friend of yours…"

*

June 1366 – Kurama Temple

"Good," Kwon said, parrying a sword strike. "Excellent. Now be careful of your…" He knocked Jion's bokken to the ground and brought his own under the teenager's spotty chin.

"Remember. Keep your focus," the foreigner finished.

Jion bowed. "Thank you for your instruction, Master. May I?" he said looking to the fallen sword.

"You may. Nevertheless, I must say, that was very good. You have been studying very hard. I am impressed. You are learning to let go of your attachments. Remember; when you are in battle, *be* the battle."

"Thank you Master. I am only what you make me."

Kwon took a towel, wiped the sweat from his face, and offered another to his apprentice. "Master Hiroyasu tells me you are making great progress with your little disappearing trick… that you are able to control it more?"

Jion looked to the floor uncomfortably, unwilling to say that it was only at night that he would step through the doorway to visit the Goddess.

"Don't be bashful Jion. You should be proud of your progress. The Council is even talking about letting you out in to the field. An assignment will surely be granted to you."

Jion looked up excitedly. "Really Master?"

Kwon smiled, knowing how frustrated the boy felt, having been confined to The Temple ground for all these years. "Be calm. Not just yet. But maybe in time. Even if it does come to pass, do not expect grand missions. You will need to train with a master for several years before you are allowed out on your own, and even then it will be minor assignments – gathering evidence regarding a dispute. Maybe standing guard over a traveling dignitary whilst he rests in one of the nearby villages."

"But Master… I am ready now. I know I am. I will serve whatever apprenticeship The Council demands, but let me prove myself."

"In good time Jion. You must learn patience. And you must learn to protect your right side when you are feinting," Kwon smiled.

"But Master, if I could just have one opportunity…"

Kwon rolled his eyes, regretting that he had said anything. "Jion, please. You are not ready yet. In time you will be. But that time is not now. You still have much to learn."

Jion stood for a moment, his jaw clenched in frustration before slowly relaxing. "Master, may I demonstrate something for your approval?"

Kwon knew better than to agree. He had seen the boy perform many tricks with a blade over the years. Each was impressive enough in its own way, but ultimately lent nothing to the art of swordsmanship. The instructor let his kindly nature get the better of him. "Go on then."

"Please Master… raise your sword as if to attack," Jion did likewise, bringing his sword up ready to fight. "Now cut at me, right shoulder to left hip."

Kwon brought his bokken to bear as instructed, unsure what to expect. Jion parried the shot easily.

"No Master. Really through me."

Kwon narrowed his eyes and struck again, harder this time. Again Jion parried the blow, the sound of wood on wood echoing through the training hall.

"No Master. Really through me. Strike me down."

Kwon stood back. "No Jion. I have no wish to harm you."

"Please Master. I promise that you won't. Please. I just want to show you this."

"Very well. Attend." Kwon leapt forward slashing at Jion… and then at thin air.

Kwon felt the end of a wooden sword pointing gently into his neck and heard the familiar sound of his student's breathing. Kwon held his sword out, and dropped it noisily on to the mat before turning around.

"How did you do that?" Kwon asked darkly, turning to face his Jion.

The teenager was beaming broadly. "It takes great effort. Great concentration. I cannot do it often. Maybe once or twice in a fight and then not for many hours after. Sometimes it takes a day or two for me to recover," the boy said, lowering his sword and bowing to his instructor.

Kwon picked his own sword up. "But how? How did you learn that?"

"Mistress Nikko suggested it to me."

"Mistress Nikko?" Kwon asked, incredulous.

"Yes. She has observed my training with Master Hiroyasu and my lessons with you… she suggested it."

"What was it that she suggested Jion?" Kwon had a tightening feeling in his stomach. This new skill was not mentioned at all in the Queen's book.

"That if I could meditate while in combat I could disappear and reappear around my enemies," the boy replied, slurping water noisily from a bowl on the side of the hall.

"I see. Jion, please listen to me. I want you to be very careful around Mistress Nikko."

"Careful, Master?" Jion looked confused.

"Yes."

"Mistress Nikko has been nothing but a friend to me Master. She saved me at Yugyo and has looked out for me here. What should I be careful of?"

"I don't know. She knows the politics of The Council too well for a mere librarian and now she is instructing my student… in such things that she should not be. Is she everything that she says she is, Jion?"

"Yes Master. She is."

*

July 1366 – Utsunomiya Castle, Shimotsuke Province

Lady Altera smiled thinly and crumpled the newly delivered scroll in her hands before tossing it on the brazier where it smoked and then briefly burst into flames before falling into black ash.

Clever little boy… in plain sight all this time.

"My Lady?" Ullar asked.

"An… old friend has re-established contact. We have the child's location."

"Very good My Lady. Shall I assemble the battalion?"

Altera paused, weighing up her options. "No," she said eventually.

"My Lady? Won't the Shogun be angry…?"

"Let him be," Altera said dismissively. "He's nearly outlived his usefulness anyway. All this talk of peace... it's disgusting. No, we will get the child a different way. A way that advances *our* cause. What was the name of that girl… you know the one? Always wears the red and black robes."

Ullar shook his head in confusion. "My Lady?"

"Yes… oh what is her name? Lord Mutsu's favorite."

The large man smiled knowingly. "Masuda, My Lady?"

"Yes, that is her name. Send her to me. I have an errand for her."

*

September 1366 – Kurama Temple

Night had fallen across the mountain pass that led to Kurama Temple and not even the thin sliver of light from the waning moon could pierce the full dark. Had Kwon not been completely absorbed rereading his Queen's book, desperately trying to make sense of Jion's advancing abilities, he would have heard those leaves that had already succumbed to autumn shifting a little too consistently.

Had Abbot Shimada not been so deep in conversation with Master Takamori he would have noticed that the normal chatter of night-time animals had dwindled to silence, and had Tatsuo not had so much shochu to dull the pain of once again being rejected for an external assignment, he too might have noticed a darker shadow moving between the trees, approaching the barred gates of The Temple.

Jion lay alone in his bedchamber, listening to the unfamiliar song of The Temple.

Something is wrong, he thought standing and pulling his robe on.

From across the courtyard his keen sense heard Masako shifting. *Jion…*

Hers was the only mind that he could talk to directly, although they never admitted it to anyone.

I can sense… something is coming, she thought.

I know, Jion replied. *Stay inside. I'll take a look.*

No. I'm coming with you. He heard her door slide open.

Stay where you are. It's too dangerous.

She hesitated, and then Jion heard her pull on her robe and slide her recently presented swords into her sash. *What is it you always say? A man's fate is a man's fate? Well mine is by your side.*

Jion sighed. *Fine, but be careful.* He slid his own door open and stepped out into the darkness.

For all intents and purposes it was as any other night. The guards walked along the wall. The silhouettes of the trees swayed gently. Some of the dogs grumbled to each other. Two novices were sharing a bedroll. One of the Masters was considering whether to ask permission to marry his adept.

There was nothing out of the ordinary, except a feeling of...
Jion!
What is it? What have you got?
There is something coming up the river. I can hear it.

Jion squinted, but the glow from the lanterns that lined the wall was ruining his night vision. Clutching the Ishin Blade, he bent his knees and jumped upwards, catching one of the protruding beams of the building, and hauled himself up one-handed before padding on to the thatched roof.

Go up, he thought, and a moment later saw the outline of Masako coming up to the roof on the building opposite his. Although he did not like sharing his Goddess with anyone, he was glad that She had blessed Masako in the same way She had blessed him.

Can you see it?
No, he replied, crouching low and preparing to jump to the next building.
Wait! There are two of them. No... three. One is coming through the trees. The other along ...
The wall, he finished. *I've got them.*
What do we do? Sound the alarm... Stars! Jion, the one in the trees just killed two of the wall guards. He's coming over... hiding the bodies.
How? An archer?
I don't know. He threw something. It was smaller than a dagger but I couldn't see. Oh Jion, what do we do?

The boy thought for a second, and then acted. *Stay where you are. I'll take the one coming up in the river, but cause a noise so as to draw the other two. You come behind them. That'll show The Council how accomplished we are.*

Masako hesitated, clearly thinking that superior numbers would defeat whatever threat they faced, and then changed her mind, following Jion's lead.

The boy crouched and then leapt to the next building, and then to the next, repeating until he reached the western wall where the river ran noisily. The recent rains had caused the river to swell and the water foamed white across the bigger boulders. From his vantage point, Jion could see the silhouette advancing along the bank, padding softly on the damp earth.

Can you see him?
Yes, Jion replied. *I... I... think they are the Nokizaru.*
Are you sure? I thought they were only a myth.
I don't know. He's not wearing any armor... he's all in black, and wearing a hood... a mask over his mouth as well. And his sword is on his back, not through his belt.
Jion! I don't like this. We should sound the alarm.
No. Just follow my lead. He felt Masako hesitate, torn between her allegiance to The Temple and to him.

The dark figure had reached the wall and Jion watched him throw a cloth-covered grapple up to the guard tower. It barely made a sound as it dug into the stone, and the boy crawled along to where the would-be assassin would climb over the battlement. From here he could see the outline of the other two; the first moving along the opposite wall, extinguishing the lanterns, while the second had slipped poison to the dogs and was waiting on the signal from his comrades. And Masako, laying flat against the roof of her building, watching the scene unfold.

Jion heard the soft padding of clothed feet slowly coming up the wall and readied himself. The figure slid silently over the battlements, signaled to the other two and was about to jump down to the courtyard below when Jion struck.

In a single fluid movement, the Ishin Blade left its sheath, hissed through the night air, and sliced through the assailant's neck. Jion's battle cry reverberated across the courtyard and for a moment everyone paused, turning their attention to the far corner of the courtyard.

The body fell to the floor, gushing dark blood, and Jion jumped down next to it, scanning the night for the other two assassins.

Masako! Where are they?

One is advancing on you. He's on the opposite side of the second building... I can't see the second one.

Jion could hear the sounds of people gathering themselves, approaching their windows to see the source of the disturbance.

Jion! He's coming around. He's on your left! Stars! Watch out...

Jion turned on the balls of his feet and saw the silhouette coming out of the darkness. Without hesitation he ran at the intruder, his sword coming up. The assassin had drawn his own blade and the sound of metal against metal reverberated through the night.

Parrying and countering, Jion drove the Nokizaru back into the shades, feinted to the left and drove the Ishin Blade up under the man's armpit, through the lung, and out through the side of his neck.

The assassin collapsed to the ground soundlessly.

Masako! Where is the third one?

I... I... I don't know. I can't see him. He split off from the other one... Oh stars! Jion! He's heading for the Abbot's chamber.

Jion felt a chill enter him that was more than the night air. Silently he jumped up, landing on the roof of the thatched building next to him, and squinted into the darkness.

The third assassin had not followed his comrade as planned but had slipped past Masako and was now running towards the Abbot's building. Lanterns were appearing at windows as more residents realized that something was wrong, and someone called for guards. Jion knew that he would never catch the Nokizaru before he reached his target. Closing his eyes, Jion mustered all his strength and sent his mind into the night.

Master! Master Kwon...

Kwon was already moving towards the door, his sword in his belt, when he heard the voice of his protégée like a whisper on a breeze.

The Abbot… protect the Abbot…

Kwon knew that questions could wait until later and set off at a sprint. As he raced out into the courtyard, the fencing master saw a black figure jump for the Abbot's first floor veranda and pull himself up. Without hesitation Kwon raced into the building, screaming at the still dozing servants to raise themselves, and dashed up the stairs, hearing the splintering of wood.

Abbot Shimada was at his door, his own sword in his hand, looking stunned and disheveled.

"He came right past me… he's after the girl."

Kwon could see the door to Gozen's chamber had been ripped off and without stopping he bounded into the girl's room. Gozen was pinned to her bed mat by the steely arm of the black clad assassin; the raised other hand clutched a dagger.

Kwon threw his sword at the attacker and continued running, determined to tackle the assailant. His sword connected with the assassin's arm, drawing blood and staying the descent of the dagger. The Nokizaru turned and looked up in shock as the full weight of Kwon collided with him.

The two tumbled, locked together in a deluge of fists and kicks, and rolled across the floor. Kwon pinned his adversary's back to the floor, mounted him across his waist, and brought his elbow smashing down into the assailant's throat. The assassin tried to parry, failed and sent a fist up under Kwon's chin. Before it connected the fencing master grabbed the wrist, twisted until he felt the shoulder and the elbow lock, and then raised himself a little before he spun out, feeling the joints crunch, break and then separate.

To his surprise the assailant did not scream despite one arm hanging useless by his side, but barreled into Kwon; sending them both through the thin screen wall and into the next room.

The foreigner brought his forearm under the assassin's chin, felt the windpipe, brought his fist to his shoulder and savagely yanked upwards.

The crunch of the spinal column disconnecting reverberated loudly, and the body of the last Nokizaru went limp. Kwon let the body fall and wiped the blood from his mouth. Drawing his short sword the fencing master hacked at the lifeless body to be sure that the attacker was not feigning death and when he was satisfied, he stepped back out on to the landing.

Abbot Shimada was holding a sobbing Gozen and Jion was just coming up the stairs.

*

"What were you thinking?" Kwon railed. "Tell me. Explain to me exactly what was going through your mind."

THE SHACKLES OF A NAME

Jion knelt in the center of The Council chamber, his head cast down in shame. "Master, I apologize," he mumbled. "I have no excuse."

"You're damn right you don't," Kwon's eyes blazed. "Your arrogance very nearly cost your fiancée her life."

Jion bowed in supplication, his forehead touching the mat, but he made no reply.

"As soon as you knew The Temple was under attack you should have sounded the alarm. It was not bad enough that you chose to take the assassins on yourself, but you also dragged Masako along as well? You're a fool." Kwon whirled around, and stalked back to the dais where The Council Elders sat in stony silence.

Abbot Shimada held a hand up to the fencing master. "Peace, Master Kwon. Whilst our young apprentice has made many mistakes tonight, there is much that we have learnt."

Kwon bowed his head to the Abbot. "Master Abbot, I apologize for disturbing the harmony of The Temple. I was… frustrated by tonight's events. I am sorry."

"Frustrated? No Master Kwon, you were scared," Shimada replied. "We all were. We so nearly lost a great hope this evening, but maybe it is good that our enemy reveals himself, no?"

Kwon's brows knitted together. "Master Abbot?"

Shimada motioned for one of the maids to come over and the servant girl approached the stage, holding a cushion of deep red velvet on which a silver dagger lay.

"This is the weapon that was used to attack Gozen. You are the expert on blades Master Kwon. What can you tell us?"

Kwon leaned forward inspecting the dagger and then turned to Shimada. "May I?"

The Abbot nodded and Kwon picked the blade up, feeling its curious weight in his hands. Perfectly balanced, the cutting edges showed a fine serration and Kwon knew that this was a weapon not just designed to kill, but to do so obviously and with the maximum amount of gore.

"Master Abbot," Kwon began still examining the dagger. "The blade is new, only recently forged, but it follows a much older design… or tries to. It has been adapted in places. It is an effective killing tool, but this is not a traditional assassin's instrument. As the dagger is removed from its victim, it would wrench out all the surrounding muscles, tearing them from the bone. The Nokizaru are known for their stealth and secrecy. Many kills committed by them often seem to be natural causes."

"That is the opinion of The Council as well, Master Kwon. Either the assassins were not really Nokizaru agents, or their attack style has changed… perhaps at the behest of whoever employed them," Shimada replied. "The

Council would be interested in your views of the symbol on the hilt, Master Kwon."

Kwon looked at the curious symbol at the base of the hilt; two concentric circles linked by nine zigzagging lines. His eyes widened in surprise.

"Master Kwon?"

"Master Abbot… I don't know what to say… I… I… this symbol… it is the sign that my Queen fights under."

The Council Elders began whispering to each other, discussing this latest development and what it could mean. Could the foreigner still be trusted? Where did his loyalty really lie? Shimada held a hand up to silence them.

"Master Kwon, that is certainly… interesting. However, a number of the Elders have seen this before."

"Master Abbot, I don't understand."

Shimada turned his attention to Jion. "Boy, you may stand. Please, draw your father's sword and present the hilt to Master Kwon."

Jion obeyed the instruction, and Kwon looked to the hilt of the Ishin Blade, seeing the same symbol repeated on there.

"I don't understand," Kwon said. "That should not be possible."

"And yet it is, Master Kwon," Shimada said. "Boy, you may put your sword away. Master Kwon, the Ishin Blade is one of the oldest and finest swords in our land, tracing its history back to Amaterasu himself…"

Kwon tried not to snort in derision. If these monks knew the true story of Amaterasu they would not hold him in such reverence.

"… and there is concern that someone may be attempting to use that lineage to their own ends," the Abbot finished.

"Yoshiakira?" Kwon said, appalled. "Surely he would not dare. The lineage of Amaterasu *is* Oyashima… it would be like striking at the heart of The Chrysanthemum Throne."

"It is not *like*, Master Kwon. It *is*. The line of Amaterasu *is* The Chrysanthemum Throne. If Yoshiakira's forces seek to carry this symbol on their weapons, then they claim that the will of Amaterasu is with them."

"But…," Kwon felt his mind reaching, trying to understand the enormity of the Abbot's words. "But… that is heresy, surely?"

Shimada shook his head. "Only if he loses. If he wins, then he will claim that the Divine was on his side all along. And the more the people see, the more they will believe… almost until it does not matter what is true or not anymore."

"Master Abbot, this sacrilege must be prevented," Kwon said.

"The Council agrees, Master Kwon. You are to be dispatched to find both the smith and the mine that are responsible for that… that abomination, and shut them both down. Permanently."

*

The Council had dispersed and Kwon sat with Shimada in the empty hall.

"Master Kwon, your mind is troubled."

Kwon looked up, and inwardly braced for his admonishment. "Yes Master Abbot."

"The assassination was prevented. Despite his failings, young Jion is becoming quite the warrior. To dispatch one of the Nokizaru is impressive. To dispatch two... that is noteworthy indeed. Why are you so fearful?"

Kwon shifted, thinking how best to phrase his response. "For many reasons, Master Abbot... I have relied on the word of my Queen for so long... and perhaps overly so... but there is no mention in her accounts of any attack like this... and the symbols too. I am confused Master Abbot."

Shimada shrugged. "Things are the way they are, no matter who tells us that they are otherwise."

"Yes Master Abbot... but it is as though history is diverging. Ever since the boy arrived, more and more things are not as they were foretold."

"Ah, you mean the prophecy Master Kwon?"

"Yes... and other accounts. I can no longer see the future that was promised."

Shimada smiled. The foreigner still had much to learn. "Then it is simple Master Kwon. Believe in another."

Kwon knew that he should have laughed at the Abbot's little joke but instead he remained grim-faced. "I wish I could Master Abbot. In truth I am not sure that I should even go on this assignment. There is still danger. The Nokizaru will no doubt try again. And the boy..."

Shimada held up a hand. "Despite his arrogance, Jion is becoming a man. Yes, he is flawed, but on the whole he acquitted himself tonight. You have completed many assignments for us in the past, and your skills with the sword make you the best candidate for this one."

"Thank you Master Abbot. However, what of Gozen and Masako? Surely they remain at risk?"

"Maybe. Maybe not. But The Council has resolved to give Jion his first assignment. He will be personal guard to the two ladies in your absence."

Kwon frowned. "Master Abbot... given the relationship between three of them... it is complicated. I mean no disrespect, but is this wise?"

"Jion will not be unsupervised. Master Takamori and Master Hiroyasu will watch over him. And it will give him the opportunity he so badly craves."

"Yes Master Abbot... but his pride... his ego. He knows nothing of humility."

"So it is with all nobility Master Kwon. But he will learn, in time."

The sword-master nodded. "I hope so Master Abbot. I should go to the library and see what I can find out about the ore that this is made of, and then I will depart."

"Very good Master Kwon, but before you go you should be aware that this will not be an easy assignment. Yoshiakira was enraged when Jion did not respond to his proclamation of a pardon. That is no doubt why he sent the assassins."

"But Master Abbot, why target Gozen?"

"Perhaps he knows of the betrothal. By removing her, the Shogun may hope for someone he approves of to be selected as Jion's wife."

Kwon considered the point. "Then the Shogun must know of Jion's abilities. He would have known the Nokizaru would have little chance of capturing Jion so he targets those around him."

"Yes Master Kwon, that is what I am trying to tell you. If Yoshiakira really did send the assassins, then *you* can expect to meet many more before you complete this assignment. Travel with care my friend."

*

The pale light of dawn began to creep across the mountain pass, driving back the dark of the night. On a high ridge that only ever knew a covering of frost, two figures stood watching Kurama Temple.

"We failed," Lord Mutsu said, shivering more from fear than from the cold. "The Shogun will have our heads."

Lady Altera smiled thinly. "Lord Yoshiakira never planned for your master to succeed. It was simply another test of loyalty."

"Then I am dead?"

Altera suppressed a chuckle. "Did you order the Nokizaru? Or your master?"

"Of course it was Lord Koichi… but those men were not the Nokizaru. They were our…"

Altera silenced him with a look. "I personally armed and equipped those men. For all intents and purposes, they were the Nokizaru."

Mutsu's eyes widened. "You meant for them to fail?"

Altera turned to look back at The Temple, the wind whipping through her dark hair. "Lose the battle to win the war," she said absently.

"My Lady, I do not understand," Mutsu whined. "You know where the child is. Why do you not strike?"

Altera's eyes flashed with anger. "Why? You foolish little man, you dare question me? What do you know of the child? What do you know of the great plan? You are so small minded. You think it is enough to kill and that it is all over. You understand nothing," she spat. "It is not enough to kill a man. You have to kill the *idea* of man. If I destroy the child then others will take up his name and cause. No, it is far better for the child to destroy himself… to disgrace himself in front of all those who so blindly followed him. Then history will do the rest. Come along. We do not have much time."

"Where are we going?"

"*I* am required by our Shogun. *You* will take my orders to the blacksmith, Muramasa."

"Yes My Lady. And what are your orders?"

"He is to increase production of the weapons that Lord Yoshiakira ordered. Our time draws near."

*

The sun streamed through the window offering faint warmth to all those who were studying in the library. The news of the failed attack, Jion's abilities, and Kwon's assignment had become common knowledge, and now novices and adepts alike scoured the shelves for sources of knowledge that could lead them to such a dangerous and exciting life.

Nikko turned the Nokizaru dagger over in her hand, examining it closely.

"What do you think Mistress Nikko?" Kwon asked, desperately trying to hide his dislike of the woman. "Do your texts speak of such a metal? It has confounded me."

Nikko knew that was a lie but did not react. "The metal… I cannot truly say. It is very similar to Jion's sword – the boy was kind enough to let me examine it several years ago – but it is not an exact match. The design on the other hand…"

"Yes?"

Nikko placed the dagger back on the cushion, stood, and crossed to one of the shelves. Retrieving a thin scroll she returned, knelt, and rolled the document out.

"Can you see here and here," she said pointing to the almost invisible watermark within the blade. "This is strongly reminiscent of Masamune."

"The sword smith?"

"Did you know him?" Nikko said, looking up.

"No," Kwon replied. "Only by reputation. He was said to be the finest smith Oyashima ever knew."

"A reputation well deserved."

"But I thought he was dead."

"He is," Nikko said and went back to examining the dagger. "This blade mimics aspects of his style, but it is far too new."

"A forgery?"

"No. More likely a student of his. Can you see the way the guard twists around, and the darkness at the bottom of the blade?"

Kwon leaned in, taking a better look. "Yes, I see. Is that important?"

"Maybe. It's quite unique."

"How many students are there of Masamune?" Kwon asked.

"He had many students. Of course most are either dead or have moved to Tianxia… they get more money and better living conditions over there."

"Hmm, always the money" Kwon muttered under his breath, and then spoke up again. "Are there any still in Oyashima?"

"Maybe. It is difficult to say…"

"How do you mean?"

"The most well known was Muramasa. He was active up until a year or two ago… and then he vanished. Some said that Yoshiakira recruited him whilst others said he had been assassinated. What is known is that his blades continue to come on to the market."

"Then he is alive," Kwon replied. "Where can I find him?"

Nikko held up a hand. "Patience Master Kwon. Just because his blades are for sale does not mean he is still alive. If he was killed, then it might be that someone simply took his stock of completed blades…"

Her words drifted into silence and Kwon looked up from the dagger. "What? What is it?"

Nikko sighed. "The name of Muramasa… it is used as an *Onryo*. Do you know this word?"

Kwon shook his head. "No Mistress Nikko. There are still parts of your language that I have not yet learned. I apologize for my ignorance."

The librarian smiled. "An *Onryo*… it is someone who is dead and has come back."

"A ghost?"

"No… more than a ghost. The Onryo… they are spirits driven mad for revenge who come back to haunt the land. Do you understand?"

Kwon nodded. "Yes I do. Thank you. So legend is that the spirit… I apologize… the Onryo of Muramasa still makes swords?"

"Oh more than that Master Kwon. They say that the blades forged by Muramasa since his death are infected with his madness… that if drawn the blade must kill or it will drive itself into the wielder."

Kwon sat back on his calves considering the points made and how to find Muramasa, or whatever it was that was producing his blades. "Tracing the Nokizaru will be impossible," he said eventually. "The best strategy would be to find where the blades are sold and see if they can remember who purchased it."

"A very wise strategy Master Kwon," Nikko said, bowing her head in respect.

"Do we know who deals in these blades?"

"All merchants seek to deal in them because they are valuable. Nevertheless, the greatest concentration is north of here, across the mountains, towards the Northern Coast. But it is many months travel."

"Then I had better get packing. Thank you Mistress Nikko. Where will I find the Library's maps?"

*

"No!" Masako said, addressing her sister fiercely. "We should not be hiding. We are of the Clan Nawa. We are bujin, not some timid peasants."

Gozen flushed with embarrassment at her younger sister's uncontrolled outburst. She turned to Jion and spoke softly. "I apologize for Masako. We will obey The Council's orders and we place our lives in your hands."

Masako turned to her friend. "Jion, surely you can see this is madness. Our enemies know where we are. If we wait here they will just come for us again."

Jion sighed. "I understand... really, I do. But The Council's orders are clear. In many ways this is good. They have seen my abilities and have charged me to guard you both... this is my first assignment. And besides, we don't know who we are fighting. It could be Mutsu or Chikatane or even Yoshiakira himself. Master Kwon will find out who hired the Nokizaru and then we will know where to strike..."

"I don't believe you!" Masako spat. "You are The Hero of Yugyo. Three nights ago you were out there," she pointed to the courtyard, "fighting for our lives. And now you want to sit back like some... some... frightened eta!"

"That is enough," Gozen snapped. "You will address our Lord with respect."

Jion flushed at the insult but held up his hand. "I have spoken with Master Abbot at length. What I did was wrong. I was more concerned with proving myself than the welfare of The Temple. My arrogance... it nearly cost us very dearly..." he looked meaningfully to Gozen who blushed and tried to hide a smile.

"My Lord has grown," Gozen murmured.

"This is true," Masako said. "But not all see it."

"It is true," Jion replied addressing them both. "Sometimes my Masters do frustrate me. But this is part of the training process. To learn patience. To know when to strike and not to run into battle mindlessly."

"It is the unpredictability of your powers that gives The Council cause for concern," Gozen said. "The Elders have a way of seeing the flaws we wish to keep hidden. When the time comes, you must be able to be relied on."

"Well, I don't think it is fair," Masako pouted. "I've seen you train with Master Kwon. He is overly critical; he never listens and does not understand – how could he? He is some filthy foreigner. I think he is jealous of our Lord."

Gozen stood, her frustration showing. "I will not sit here and listen to your childish ramblings. You need to learn some manners, little sister." The door slid closed behind her with a bang.

Jion winced at Masako's outburst. This was becoming too much, even for him. "Please. Let go of your pride. Our time will come. A man's fate is a man's fate, is it not?"

"And when will *our* time come?" Masako hissed, looking at Jion meaningfully.

"When Master Kwon says that I am ready."

"And when will that be? A year? Two? Five? And all that time you are still betrothed to my sister. When you are made a Master you will be able to make your own fate… for both of us. But until then we are bound by these fools."

Jion leaned forward, stroking Masako's lily white hand. "It will be soon. I promise." He began to lean forward for a kiss and Masako recoiled.

Her eyes blazed. "Remember your father. Remember your brother. And remember *me*. That is where your duty lies. That is what you *promised*."

Masako stood and left the room without bowing.

*

"Come in Master Kwon," Abbot Shimada said, acknowledging the knock at the door.

The door slid open and Kwon bowed before coming in. "Thank you for seeing me at such short notice Master Abbot."

"I understand that you have a lead and will soon be departing."

"Yes Master Abbot. That is what I am here to talk to you about."

"Very good. Then what is it that I can help you with?" the old monk said kindly.

"Master Abbot, with the death of the Nokizaru assassins we have thought it best to trace who hired them by following the blades."

Shimada's brows furrowed. "Is that wise Master Kwon? Those blades may have been held within the assassins' families for many years?"

"Master Abbot, they are believed to have been recently forged. Certainly within the last year or two. If I can find the merchant who sold them then…"

"You can discover who bought them, and from there who ordered the Nokizaru. Very clever Master Kwon, very clever indeed. But I do not understand how I can help."

Kwon unrolled a scroll showing a map of the northern extent of Oyashima, from The Temple to the coast. He pointed to an area on the other side of the mountains. "This is where the greatest concentration of blades similar to those used in the attack is being sold from. Eleven merchants in total."

Shimada peered down his nose at the map. "Yes. I see."

"Master Abbot, how long have you been at The Temple?"

Shimada looked up, surprised by the question. "Since I was a child. Seventy years or so."

"And you came to be Abbot the usual way? Apprentice, novice, then adept and Master?"

"Yes. But I don't…"

"Please Master Abbot. Forgive me. I just ask for your forbearance for a few moments."

Shimada nodded, intrigued by this new line of questioning.

"When you were a Master did you undertake assignments?"

"Yes, of course. It is expected of every Master."

"And what were these assignments?"

"Much the same as we do now. Intelligence gathering. Some relief work. A little education here and there."

"So you journeyed beyond The Temple?"

"Yes."

"Far?"

Shimada smiled. "Master Kwon, in my time I have been from one end of Oyashima to the other. I am the only living Master who has been to all eight isles. Yes, I traveled far."

"Then you know this area?" Kwon pointed back to the map.

"Yes. Very well."

"Master Abbot, do you notice anything wrong with this map?"

Shimada looked at the map again. "Master Kwon, you will have to forgive an old man his memory, but…"

"Master Abbot, do you recall a highly reclusive Ainu Tribe in this area," Kwon jabbed at the map again, not far from the circle of eleven merchants, "who worked a mine?"

Shimada sat back and thought. "Yes. I think I do. I only met them once or twice. But it was many years ago."

"Master Abbot, neither that mine or the Ainu tribe appear on the map."

"Could it be a copying error? Perhaps an adept missed it? It would not be the first time…"

"Master Abbot, I have been through every map in the library that covers this area. The tribe is simply not referenced at all."

"That is strange. Have you spoken to Mistress Nikko?"

"No. But I asked Master Takamori to."

"I see," Shimada said, knowing full well there was an unnamed tension between the Librarian and the foreigner. "And what did Master Takamori report?"

"He reported that Mistress Nikko told him that the tribe was a myth… that it did not exist."

Shimada considered the possibility. "She may be right. The Ainu are widely persecuted and their greatest concentration is in the Northern Isles. Perhaps they moved?"

"Master Abbot, I have traveled across these mountains more times than I can count. I *know* they are there."

"Then what are you saying Master Kwon?"

"Master Abbot, I am saying that somebody is tampering with library records. And it is not an amateur either. Whoever it is… they are being *very* thorough."

"Do you know who is responsible?"

Kwon shook his head. "I have suspicions but no proof."

"Mistress Nikko?"

Kwon said nothing and then nodded.

"You two have never got along have you?"

"No Master Abbot. I apologize if this has disturbed the harmony of The Temple."

Shimada paused, considering his next words with care. "Master Kwon, is it possible that the source of your friction with Mistress Nikko, and indeed with other members of this temple over the years, is that you have not been entirely honest with us?"

Kwon felt the color drain from his face and when he spoke his voice was weak. "Master Abbot?"

"Come now Master Kwon, there is no need to be embarrassed. I have suspected for some time, but it was only after the attack on Gozen that I really knew."

Kwon looked directly at the Shimada but said nothing.

"Master Kwon, foreigners have come to our land before. Not many, but a few. But their ways were so different, their manners so base, that they did not last long. You are an exception in that regard, and you are to be commended."

"Thank you Master Abbot."

"You're welcome. However, that was my first clue. A foreigner who displayed patience… The Council told me it was unheard of. 'They are all barbarians. Savages. Cast him out.' But I kept my promise to you Master Kwon, and you studied our ways, becoming one of us. And that marked you out – you are a man who is not restricted by time. Then there was the assault on Sojobo. Few would dare take on the Tengu King. Moreover, no one had ever survived the encounter. Except you. And when you returned… do you remember how badly hurt you were Master Kwon?"

"Yes Master Abbot."

"Your wounds were… grievous to say the least. I will freely admit that I did not expect you to survive. And yet here you are. And not even a scar on you."

Kwon looked up sharply.

"Oh don't be embarrassed Master Kwon. I had one of the maids at the onsen report to me. No, there is not a blemish on you. Then the night of the attack. After you had dispatched the Nokizaru, you did not see me standing in the adjoining room, looking through the broken screen. Why should you? The lanterns had all been extinguished, and your fight had taken under a minute. But I saw you Master Kwon. I saw you pull the assassin's dagger out from under your ribs and step out on to the landing as though you were uninjured."

Kwon looked down at the mats, saying nothing.

"You know Master Kwon, if foreigners have come to Oyashima, you should not be surprised that a few of our people have journeyed to your lands. Of course the reports are never favorable. Is it true that most of you never bathe except once a year? And you eat meat all the time?"

Kwon nodded, but said nothing.

"Incredible. And yet you take at least one bath a day here. Truly your assimilation is remarkable Master Kwon. Still, I digress. Those of us who have returned from your lands bring tales that would make the Buddha weep. Tales of a king who turned everything to gold. Another, of a god who betrayed his brother and condemned him to Jigoku. One particularly dark story is of a race of men who struck a deal with the Mother of All Oni. In return for their service their skin would know no thinning…"

"… their limbs no weakening, and their eyes no dimming," Kwon finished, his voice low and filled with humiliation and shame.

"Ah. I see you know the story Master Kwon."

The foreigner nodded, still looking at the mats. "Who else knows?"

"The story? Oh very few, Master Kwon. Documents regarding foreign lands are only for the wisest masters. Do not worry my friend. Now, I believe you have merchants to investigate and I have a library to be scrutinised. Off you go."

Kwon stood, surprised that he was being let off this easily. "Thank you Master Abbot. I will not fail you."

"I know you won't Master Kwon. I look forward to your report when you return. And perhaps you could finish that story for me too. I'd be intrigued to hear how it ended."

*

"You understand your assignment?" Kwon asked.

"Yes Master," Jion said bowing formally, the echo of his master's chastisement from the previous week still ringing in his ears.

Kwon's tone softened. "Jion… I am sorry that I was so hard on you. I lost my temper and that is unforgivable. I should have known better and I apologize."

Jion was caught off guard and stammered "Master… the fault was mine. It is I who should apologize."

"You have already done so, to me and to The Council. It is my turn. Even though I am a master, I know that I am not perfect. I should have tried to comprehend your actions. I now understand why you did what you did… this temple must be stifling for one such as you. Nevertheless, there is a plan here… a prophecy that must come to pass. You are destined to become a great light."

"Thank you Master," Jion bowed.

"You are welcome. It is the truth. Now, you understand that I will be away for a while?"

"Yes Master. I wish I was coming with you."

"Yes, I'm sure that you do. Nevertheless, this is a particularly dangerous assignment. For whatever reason, your enemies want Gozen dead. You will stay here and guard over her and Masako. Is that clear?"

"Yes Master. Do you have any idea why they should target Gozen? I always believed that I was their enemy."

"It is perplexing and I have no definitive answers. My best guess is that Yoshiakira has got wind of your betrothal. He has been trying to lure you out since Yugyo, and whilst you are proving difficult to kill perhaps the death of a softer target would have spurred you into a rage and a direct assault on the Shogun."

"A trap?"

"I cannot say for certain, but most likely, yes."

Jion considered this, and then nodded. "It might have worked too. If Gozen had been killed… I don't know what I would have done. She is very precious to me Master Kwon."

"I know you are fond of both girls. You have all been through so much. But be weary of attachments Jion. You are only a few weeks away from your sixteenth birthday and you will be formally recognized as a man. You will be a child no longer, and that means making hard decisions. Attachments… they have a habit of confusing even the simplest of issues. Your marriage to Gozen will be one of political necessity, do not forget that."

"I know Master. Thank you."

"Good. Now I understand from Master Takamori that you have drawn up a security schedule for the girls?"

"Yes Master. Would you like to see it?"

"No, that is quite alright. Master Takamori was quite impressed and that is enough for me. You are growing up Jion. We are all very proud of you."

"Thank you Master."

"Now, I will be gone many months. Possibly a year or so. I want you to remember your assignment at *all* times. Keep the girls safe. Is that clear?"

"Yes Master."

"Good. Don't let yourself become distracted. Focus on your studies and your training too. And don't do anything without having consulted The Council first. I want nothing but good reports when I return."

"Yes Master. I will not disappoint you."

*

Kwon was packing the last of his equipment into a rough cloth rucksack when there was a knock at the door. He had recognized the sound of the approaching footsteps from the end of the corridor.

"Come in Master Takamori."

The door slid open and Takamori bowed. "It always unnerves me the way that you do that Master Kwon," said the older man.

Kwon smiled and shrugged. "Just luck. It was you or Master Hiroyasu."

Takamori looked at his friend hard. "You know there is no such thing as luck."

Kwon knelt and offered cha which Takamori accepted. "Maybe. Maybe not."

"You have spoken with the boy?" Takamori asked, sipping from a small china bowl.

"I have. He seemed compliant enough. Although I must confess that I am still worried. He can be volatile."

The older master nodded and put the china bowl down. "We'll keep a good eye on him Master Kwon. If anything, it is the younger sister I would be worried about."

"I know very little of her. How so?"

"The maids say she has quite a temper and often goads Jion into rash mistakes. She is usually to be found around trouble."

"A pity that she is not more like Gozen."

"I think that is the problem. Masako does not believe that she can match her sister and so does not even try. Gozen has very unique talents. I have debated with her many times and she is both eloquent and erudite. More than once she has nearly convinced me that white is black."

Kwon chuckled and nodded. "She is exceptional. Master Abbot was wise to select her for special training."

Takamori frowned. "I thought you knew. Master Abbot did not select her. She was recommended by Mistress Nikko."

Kwon felt his insides tighten and tried to remain composed. "No, I did not know that."

"Yes. Mistress Nikko began teaching both of the girls but quickly recognized Gozen's skills and referred her to Master Abbot."

Kwon paused considering this new information. "Does Mistress Nikko still teach Masako?"

"I think so. I am not involved with training women and so I cannot say for certain. Is there something wrong?"

Kwon looked up from the mat. "I'm not sure. I am due to depart tomorrow morning, and if I had the time I would look into this. Something does not feel quite right. Master Takamori, could you mention this to Master Abbot for me?"

"Of course my friend. Is there anything in particular I should tell him?"

"Yes. Please ask him the name of the novice who most recently redrew the maps."

*

Mistress Nikko was extinguishing the lanterns in the library, letting the winter darkness flood in. It had been a long day, recategorising and refilling countless manuscripts and scrolls, and dust streaked her heavy robe was. She was looking forward to a relaxing onsen and massage when the library door slid open.

"Jion," she said politely. "I was just closing. Is there anything I can help you with?"

The lanky youth bowed and the librarian caught the faint whiff of male mustiness. "Mistress Nikko, I apologize for the hour. May I have a few moments of your time?"

"Of course. Come and sit," she replied, gesturing to the mats. "Would you like some cha?"

"Yes please. Thank you."

Nikko bowed her head as she offered the bowl and Jion returned the cha, bowing lower to acknowledge her superior rank.

"What is it that you wish to talk about, Jion?"

"It is Masako."

"Ah," Nikko said smiling knowingly. "What about her?"

"I… I… ask you, as her teacher, to speak with her."

"Oh? And why is that?"

"Mistress Nikko… I care very much for Masako… and Gozen too…"

The librarian said nothing, but looked knowingly over the lip of her bowl as she sipped her cha. The girl had often confided in her and she had been expecting this conversation.

"… but Masako," Jion continued, "she is impatient… she gives way to her feelings too often. It is causing friction with Gozen. And with me. And as their protector, the situation is becoming increasingly difficult."

"I see," Nikko said, putting her bowl down, and moved closer to Jion so that no one would hear their whispers. "Don't you think it is *your* feelings that are the problem here?"

Jion swallowed hard. Underneath the smell of sweat and dust, Mistress Nikko smelt of sweet water and jasmine, and Jion tried not to notice that her robe was slightly undone revealing just the barest outline of a perfectly pert breast.

He cast his eyes down to the floor. "Mistress?" he said weakly.

"Jion. I *know*. Masako and I," she leaned closer, whispering into his ear, "are very, *very*, close."

Her nose gently caressed his lobe, and Jion willed the swelling in his crotch to subside.

Nikko chuckled and pulled away. "The truth is, Jion, that these feelings are natural. The most natural thing in the world. One day you will realize that our Goddess inspires them; allowing us to perform her orders. If we had no feelings where would we be? We would be like stones, never moving and covered in moss."

Jion frowned, his brow knotting together. "These feelings are… good?"

"Of course. So are Masako's. She desires you. You desire her. The Goddess approves of the union of two such devotees. What could be wrong with that?"

"But what about Gozen?"

"What about her?"

"I am betrothed to her."

"So?" Nikko asked. "Is it not the custom of this land that a lord may pillow with whom he wishes?"

"Yes… but why do I feel guilty?" Jion asked his voice tinged with anguish.

"You should learn to let go of that. It will only hold you back. Your marriage to Gozen is necessary for your clan. Your… relationship with Masako is necessary for *you*. Do you understand?"

Jion shook his head. "But I *am* my clan…"

"Jion… your feelings are the source of your power. They enable you to act. Remember the elders at Yugyo. Fear is the root of inaction, and that is death. When you give in to your feelings, you will become the most powerful lord in the land. You will be invincible. But, as long as you try to restrain yourself, you will never realize your destiny."

"And what about Masako?"

"Her frustration is born out of yours. Take what you need from Gozen. Give Masako what she wants. You will see that it will balance out. You will have harmony."

Jion nodded accepting the wisdom of the argument but still wished that Master Kwon had not left the previous day. He wished to consult the mentor that was becoming his friend. "Then there should be no restraint?"

"None at all," Nikko smiled.

*

February 1367 – Mount Ibuki

Despite the early melt on the plains below, winter held the mountain ranges in its icy grip as the snow clung to the volcanic slopes and the wind shrieked like an Onryo around the peaks. Master Kwon huddled in a shallow cave, desperately trying to protect his small fire from the gale outside.

"This is not right," he muttered, thumbing through a thin collection of map scrolls. "The peaks… they're in the wrong order… this route…"

Frustrated, he threw them to the floor and then quickly picked them up again, regretting his actions. Deep inside he knew the maps were useless.

They looked genuine enough, but the gradients were all wrong and the paths that should have led to the valleys had taken him up impossible climbs to the most dangerous of peaks.

Noticing that the darkness of his skin around his fingertips had deepened to a purple-black, Kwon looked out into the driving blizzard, accepting for the first time that he was lost.

*

April 1367 – Kurama Temple

Jion sat on his mare, feeling the warmth of the sun on his neck, as he watched Masako on the grassy plateau, picking through the rice paddy. Since his conversation with Mistress Nikko, he had felt more at peace and now divided his time equally between each of the two sisters and his training. The new security regime appeared to work well and whenever he was not on duty The Temple guards shadowed the girls.

Masako stood and waved to Jion who waved back.

"Come and help me," she called happily.

Jion smiled back and shook his head. "That's work for a farmer."

Masako put her hands on her hips and puffed out her chest in mock outrage. "You once dreamt of such a life. Now look at me, I am one with the land."

Jion laughed. "You are one with the mud."

Masako pretended to be insulted and cried out, before bending down to scoop up a handful of earth and throwing it at Jion. He ducked it easily, dismounted, and scooped up some of the wet earth with his gloved hand and threw it, laughing as he did so.

Masako scooped up two more handfuls and ran at him, smearing his cuirass. He grabbed at her playfully and the two of them tumbled into the long grass where they lay panting. Silence fell naturally between them and they both looked up to the thin wisps of cloud that scudded across the spring sky.

"What are you thinking?" said Masako, turning over and propping herself up on her elbow.

Jion shook his head. "Nothing. Just how happy I am."

"I know," Masako smiled. "Me too."

"I can tell. I am glad that Master Takamori has allowed me to replace Master Kwon's lesson with Mistress Nikko's."

"Yes. It makes me happy that we can train together, like we used to. Do you remember?"

Jion nodded. "That feels like a life-time ago, almost as if it happened to someone else."

"Maybe it did. We are not the children that we were."

Jion grunted an agreement but made no other reply.

"Mistress Nikko said that your abilities are increasing… that you are spending more time with Our Goddess."

Jion turned from the sky to look at Masako. "Yes. Does it bother you that She favors me?"

"No," Masako said smiling. "Not at all. I am so proud that she has chosen you. It can only mean that we will soon have our revenge on Yoshiakira and his dogs."

"Yes. I hope so."

"You are not sure?"

"It is what Our Goddess wants. Justice. That is why she is training me."

"Truly She is of our class. She understands the ways of the bujin because she is the warrior spirit itself. If we let go of honor and justice then what are we?"

Jion turned back to the sky. "We would be nothing. Not even eta. We would be empty, devoid of any reason to be."

Masako followed his example, rolled onto her back and gazed into the heavens. "I cannot imagine what it would be like not have a purpose."

*

Without knocking Jion slid the door open, his face a mask of anger and frustration. Gozen looked up from her calligraphy, the quill still poised in her delicate hand.

"Who ordered those guards outside your building?" he raged. "I demand to know."

"Good evening Jion," Gozen said gently, putting the quill down. "Would you like some cha?"

"Don't play with me," Jion hissed. "Answer my question."

Gozen looked to his sword hand, noticing that his grip on the Ishin Blade was getting tighter. "I did," she said politely, and poured the tea into a plain bowl.

"*You* are not in charge of your security. *I* am," Jion barked.

Gozen sipped delicately from the bowl. "Forgive me Jion, but I understood that your watch began fifteen minutes ago. Have I misunderstood the roster?"

Jion blanched. "I… I was only a few minutes late. I was held up on the road."

Gozen picked her quill back up. "You have been held up quite a lot recently," she said pointedly. "I simply… took precautions. We cannot be too careful, don't you agree?"

"I… I… Your protection is *my* responsibility."

Gozen sighed. It was obvious that she would be unable to continue her calligraphy with this disharmony. "Jion, the guards were stationed in accordance with *your* schedule. All the points of entry were covered and there was a spotter on the opposite roof, together with two archers."

Jion's eyes narrowed. "What do you know of military tactics?"

Gozen suppressed a laugh. "What do you think I learn from the Master Abbot? It is more than diplomacy and philosophy." She stood and approached him. "I have been taught a great many things Jion. You should make use of my knowledge."

Jion's jaw clenched tight. "In matters of security *I* am in charge. You *will* obey."

"Even if it leaves me exposed to another assassin?"

Jion did not flinch from the answer. "Yes."

*

May 1367 – Kurama Temple

"My Lord, please," Tatsuo implored.

"What would you have me do?" Jion barked back. "Masako can follow orders. Why can't Gozen?"

The unusually humid spring day had caused moods to sour and tempers to fray. Masako was diligently following Jion's security protocols whilst her older sister remained obstinate and instated her own. The disharmony this was causing around The Temple was becoming a source of gossip for the younger adepts, and even the masters were beginning to comment.

Tatsuo sighed. "My Lord… the matter is delicate. Each lady requires a certain… approach. What works for one will not necessarily work for the other."

"Well it should," Jion retorted hotly, knowing better than to be angry at his retainer.

Tatsuo saw an opening in the argument and smiled. "If only that were so, My Lord. If the same words worked in the same way on every woman… the whole of Oyashima would be a much more peaceful place."

Jion could not help himself, and laughed. "They are curious creatures, are they not?"

"They are My Lord, they are. It is hard enough getting them to do what *they* want, much less what *you* want. I very much doubt that they understand themselves, much less each other. And when they do, the rules are suddenly changed."

The teenager laughed again. "Oh Tatsuo, what am I to do?"

"My Lord, if I may…"

Jion nodded, indicating that his retainer should continue.

"Both women love you… in their own unique way. They do not know it, but they compete for your attentions. You may scold Gozen, but do you know that she still wears that wooden pendant you gave her when you were on the road to Choshi?"

Jion frowned. "I had completely forgotten about that. She still has it?"

Tatsuo nodded. "She does My Lord. When the ladies act out… it is because of jealousy. Both want your attention."

"I cannot be in two places Tatsuo… at least not yet," he smiled, remembering the scrolls Nikko had shown him that hinted at the abilities Master Otsuno had wielded.

"No My Lord, but you can be *two people*."

"I don't understand," Jion replied.

"My Lord, consider the personalities of the sisters. They are very different. If you wish harmony to return you must strive to balance each one," the one-armed swordsman advised.

Jion considered the point. "What do you suggest?"

"Masako… she is passion, a being of action. When you are with her you can run and shoot and train. Gozen… she is more reflective. She spends her days with scrolls and debating philosophies. When you are with her, speak of the Buddha or Confucius. Each will feel that you are matching them… giving them balance. Do you understand?"

Jion smiled broadly and clapped his retainer on the shoulder in a rare display of affection. "I do Tatsuo, thank you. Truly you are the most worthy friend I have ever had. I don't know what I would do without you."

*

June 1367 – Nonoichi Village, Ishikawa Province

Kwon hobbled into the coastal village of Nonoichi, leaning heavily on his staff as he did so. The unusually hot summer had done much to restore his health since the brutal winter, but he had yet to regain full use of his frost bitten feet. The medicine man at the town of Tsuruga had been adamant that he would lose at least one leg if not both but despite this conviction, and several months of recuperation, Kwon had proved him wrong. His journey had continued northwards, following the trail of rumors and whispers, searching for the merchants who dealt in the new Muramasa blades, and any snippets of the Ainu tribe that mined the eldritch metal ore.

Nonoichi was an unremarkable village, similar to other small fishing hamlets that lined the northern coast of Oyashima. Thatched roofs lined the sea front, and the tiled buildings that were set further back denoted a healthy mix of merchants and bujin warriors.

As he had come through the town gates, he had made a note to check in on the local temple. Like the rest of the village, it was small and circumspect, but Kwon was relieved that the resident monks did not belong to the Shogun's Pure Land Sect, nor had any of the new shrines that he had heard so much about been built. The countryside was alive with gossip of what these new installations brought; some claimed great power and wealth; others said that to worship at them only invited death and madness. However, Kwon had yet to see one for himself and knew, from bitter experience, not to believe peasant's tales.

As he walked through the main street, he saw the large merchant's shop that he was looking for. He held little hope that this would provide any real answers, much the same as the previous nine he had visited, but it was another step along the path.

Standing in the porchway entrance, Kwon rapped loudly.

"Good after... Master," a man said, walking out from the deep shadows and noticing Kwon's robe and shaved head. "This is a rare honor."

"I am looking for the Merchant Imai," Kwon said, leaning heavily on his staff. "Is this his shop?"

"It is and I am," Imai replied. "Please come in. Cha?"

"Yes, thank you," Kwon said stepping forward and, finding an area of matting illuminated by the sun, he sat down slowly.

"Have you come far Master?" Imai asked, returning with two bowls of tea.

"Yes. From Kurama Temple."

Imai's eyes widened. "Oh, you are here to inspect your order?"

Kwon knew better than to react. "Yes," he replied. "Our order."

"Well you are a little early. The majority of the swords are being assembled now, but a one or two of the blades still need tempering, Master…?"

"Kwon. Master Kwon. Forgive my manners," the monk replied bowing his head, trying to keep up the pretense that he knew the subject of the conversation. "I have been sent here to speak to the mine workers, and also while I am here to check on the progress of our order."

Imai shook his head. "The mine is not far from here. It is on the other side of Mount Garyu – maybe a week's travel or so by foot. But the workers are Ainu… filthy creatures. Less than eta. Why would one as holy as yourself want to go there?"

Kwon thought quickly. "We received a report of an outbreak of disease. I am here to assist… to ensure that our order will be met."

"Ah I see," Imai nodded. "But I would advise against it Master Kwon. Those Ainu… they are beasts. I sent a courier up there to offer their headman provisions for the winter. Do you know they did? They sent me back his head. They are savages with no manners. Unless they have invited you personally, they will attack you on sight. The only person they speak to is Muramasa."

Kwon kept the surprise out of his voice. "The smith?"

"Yes. He seems to be the only one who can manage them."

"Perhaps I could speak to him then."

Imai shifted uncomfortably. "He does not see many people."

"He's a recluse?"

Imai nodded. "There are only a few merchants that he sees, and one or two lords. He says that visitors disturb his harmony, and he needs stillness of mind to perfect his blades."

"I understand completely," Kwon replied. "Focus is very important. Nevertheless, we have received a report. Perhaps you could petition Muramasa on my behalf. Explain the situation to him."

"I will certainly try, Master Kwon. Would you like to see the swords that have been produced so far?" Imai said, trying to change the subject.

"Certainly."

The two men stood and Imai led the way to the back of the shop. Half a dozen swords were laid out on the bench, waiting for their sharkskin scabbards to be fitted, and the rays of the sun through the window picked out the exquisite detail on each blade.

"May I?" Kwon asked. Imai nodded and the monk picked one up, feeling the weight and examining the blade. "Impressive," he said.

"They are made exactly to Mistress Kiku's specifications. It took such a long time to find a smith who would be worthy of the work and of course the ore was so difficult to come by. I hope that Mistress Kiku will be pleased with them."

Kwon recognized the name. Whilst many monks came and went from Kurama, few ever renounced the order. In the entire history of The Temple, there had only been eleven, and Mistress Kiku had been the last. Known as The Lost Eleven, there was a private gallery of their portraits reserved for the newly initiated master who would have to contemplate the history of each and offer a view as to why they had taken such drastic action.

Kiku had left not long before he had joined, and although he had never met her, the ripples of her actions had continued for many years, giving him a sense of the person she had been. It was no secret that The Lost Eleven were all women and the loss of each one continued to be mourned by The Temple. Their reasons for departure varied, and over time their stories had become embellished as the events that surrounded them turned to myth, so that no-one could be really sure what had happened.

"Ah… Mistress Kiku passed away a few years ago," Kwon said. Technically it was not a lie. When a master left the order they renounced their title, and as such could be considered to no longer exist. "Master Abbot Shimada has taken over the order personally."

"Oh, it is a very great honor for me to serve a Master Abbot personally," Imai responded, bowing his head in humility.

"How many more blades are there to come?" Kwon asked nonchalantly.

"There are to be fourteen in total. Would you like to see the specifications?"

"Oh I'm only a healer," Kwon lied. "They would not mean much to me… but I would certainly be interested."

Imai bowed low again and retreated to the other side of the shop where he opened a drawer in a wooden chest, retrieved a set of scrolls, and then returned to Kwon.

The monk looked at the designs carefully, nodding and making the appropriate grunts of approval as he compared them to the finished product. He allowed his eye to drift to the bottom of the order, noting the signature, and the date.

Eleven years ago, he thought. *Around the time of the Fujigatani Massacre.*

The seal was that of the Master Abbot and Kwon handed the scrolls back before returning to the swords.

"They certainly are things of beauty," Kwon commented.

"I am glad that you like them," Imai replied. "It took such a long time to find the right smith and the right ore. Of course, they are very popular now."

"Really?"

"Oh yes," Imai puffed his chest out in pride. "Muramasa and his swords are much sought after."

"Who else is ordering his blades?" Kwon asked innocently.

Imai's countenance darkened but the merchant kept smiling. "I'm sorry Master Kwon but I cannot say. You understand, there has to be a certain… confidentiality between the buyer and seller."

"Of course," Kwon replied. "It was rude of me to ask. Please forgive me."

Imai bowed his head, accepting the apology.

"How soon will you be able to see Muramasa and petition him?" Kwon asked, turning from the swords.

"The smith is a two day ride from here. I will leave tonight. Let me know which tavern you will be staying at and I will find you."

*

Kurama Temple

"Do you believe the reports?" Masako asked. "Is the Shogun really beginning his march on the Emperor?"

Jion nodded, not looking at the young woman that Masako had become, but out across the mountain lake. "It seems that the peace negotiations have broken down. Soon the whole country will be at war again."

The two sat in silence on the stony shoreline of the mountain lake, Masako's head resting on Jion's shoulder, her long dark hair falling almost to the ground.

"I'm afraid," she said eventually.

"Don't be. I'll protect you."

"Do you promise?" she asked softly.

Jion turned his head to look at her. "I promise. I will never let anything happen to you."

Masako nuzzled into him. "I'd follow you anywhere," she said. "Battle. Jigoku. Anywhere."

"I know," he replied. "Mistress Nikko says that your spearwork is amongst the best she has ever seen. Will you take the grading?"

"Yes, if only so I can join you in the fight. I cannot think of a better way to die than by your side."

Jion chuckled. "I will never let you die. You are too important to me."

Masako sat up and looked at him. "Am I? Really?"

He frowned. "Of course you are. You must know that."

Masako cast her eyes down. "Sometimes I don't know…" her words tailed off.

Jion took hold of her shoulders. "Hey, what is this about?"

Masako looked up at him, teary-eyed. "I heard the maids talking. The preparations have begun for your wedding."

Jion smiled. "That is more than eighteen months away. Anything can happen."

"Do you intend to go through with it?"

"It is my duty as Clan Lord…"

"And what about me? What about us?" Masako's voice was rising in pain and her face contorted. "What are we going to do? I cannot bear to be apart from you…" Tears began to cascade down her face.

Jion embraced her. "Don't worry. I will think of something," he whispered into her ear.

"You're sixteen now… seventeen in only a few months time," she said pulling away from him. "You're a man already. Call the engagement off… delay the wedding… anything. Just don't put me through this. Please, Jion. I beg you. It's killing me to know that you're with her."

"Sshh," he moved closer to her. "It's alright," he said, trying to kiss her on the lips.

She pulled away again. "Alright? Alright?" she said incredulously. "What is alright? The country is on the brink of war. We all have a death sentence on us. And the man I love is going to marry my sister. And you… you try to seduce me when I am *like this!*" She stood and turned before turning back in frustration.

Jion rose to his knees. "I am sorry. I meant no disrespect."

He reached out for her hand and took it gently in his, pulling her to him as they both turned to look over the lake, each wishing they possessed the harmony of its still surface.

*

Nonoichi Village, Ishikawa Province

Kwon stood by the window of his bedchamber in the tavern, watching night overtake the village. The last of the fishermens' boats were coming in, the stalls were being packed away, and lanterns were being lit. From downstairs, the smell of raw fish and vinegar reached up to him, his stomach growling in acknowledgment, but he did not think about ordering food. Instead, he continued to stand as he had done for the previous three hours, watching the street. Watching for Imai.

Finally, at the hour of the pig with the moon already risen and fat, Kwon saw the distinct form of the merchant leave the shop, mount a horse, and trot towards the village bounds.

So he really is going to see Muramasa, the monk thought, surprised that Imai was keeping his word. He had learned a long time ago never to trust a merchant and, now that Imai had left, Kwon intended to return to his shop and discover who else was ordering Muramasa's swords.

Reaching for his staff, Kwon hobbled to the door. The tavern's onsen had temporarily relieved his aches but now they were slowly creeping back into him like storm clouds building on the horizon.

At least they are not as bad as they were, he thought, remembering how he almost been invalided and the relief he felt when he realized he could move his toes. Full movement was returning and whilst he was sure his wounds would completely heal in time, he did not like the idea of continuing an assignment when he was not at his peak.

Still, I've had worse. Remember what The Cannon Master did to you? he said to himself as he stepped out on to the street. The glow of lanterns punctured the full dark like an arrow wound, and by their light Kwon could see the outline forms of a few villagers walking back from one house to another. Some were clearly intoxicated whilst others were steady, and the monk decided that it would be best to enter the shop from the rear. Villages like this were small enough that everyone knew everyone else's business. Imai would have made it known that he was leaving for a few days and no doubt a few friends would be keeping an occasional eye on the shop.

Moving to the back road, Kwon was grateful that there were fewer lanterns and it was much darker than the main street. Whilst he seldom admitted it, he preferred the deep shadows, feeling at home in them. They reminded him of his motherland so many thousands of miles away and the monk felt a pang of homesickness that he not felt in decades.

Home… nothing like this place. Wilder. Savage. For a moment Kwon wondered what any of the locals would make of his land. Would they still see their kami in his mountains and lakes? Would they recognize the feudal barons as clan lords? How would they react to the near constant star-damned rain that passed for what his countrymen called summer? Kwon half smiled to himself and then put the thought from his mind. There was work to be done.

Keeping to the walls where the shadows were darkest, Kwon approached the back of Imai's shop. The back door was locked and the monk silently slipped out a thin dagger and pressed it into the gap between the frame and the wall, feeling for the clasp arm. Sliding the dagger upwards he felt the catch unhook and he stepped silently in.

It was darker in the shop than he had anticipated and, after sliding the door shut, he waited several minutes for his eyes to adjust to the total gloom. He had considered bringing a small lantern with him but, if anyone saw it from the street, the local guard would be alerted.

Feeling his way through the shop Kwon quickly found the table with the swords and, beside them, the drawers with the scrolls of future orders. As he eased the top drawer open, he heard a sigh from behind, and a lamp spluttered into life, dispelling the darkness.

"You see," said Imai. "This is why I don't like foreigners. They are never honorable and skulk in the shadows like petty thieves."

Kwon turned, smiling weakly, and noted the two guards that flanked the merchant. They all had their hands on their swords and the monk knew that he should have sensed them from the street. There could be little doubt that Imai had sent a decoy on his horse.

"And how was Muramasa?" Kwon said brightly. "Or did you not keep *your* word." He was goading the merchant and he knew it.

Imai spat on the floor, disgusted by the monk's behavior. "You… you are not even an eta. You are filthy and without honor."

Kwon shrugged. "Maybe. But I really need to know who else is ordering Muramasa's swords."

The merchant smiled, his skin taking on a waxy hue by the glow of the lantern. "You have no idea what you are dealing with. You are but a pawn in an infinitely larger game. Take him!" Imai nodded to the two guards.

Kwon took a step back as the two larger men drew their swords and advanced on him. With an almost imperceptible movement, the sword-master drew his own weapon and quickly stepped forward, using the half-gloom to his advantage, and slashed twice in quick succession.

The guards dropped to the floor without even a moan.

Kwon looked down at them and then back to Imai. "Now that is why you should not like foreigners. We're really, *really* good with death." He advanced on the quivering merchant, his sword still drawn, and shook his head. "I wouldn't if I were you," he said, noticing Imai's hand was still on his sword hilt. "Now, where is Muramasa and who is ordering his swords?"

It was Imai's turn to shake his head. "If you kill me you'll never find out."

Kwon lifted his sword up so that the tip touched the merchant's throat. "Would you bet on it? Would you bet… your life?"

Imai's features darkened and his eyes became like coals. "The Goddess damn you Celus of The Tuatha! The Mother will reclaim you and all your stinking kind," he rasped.

Kwon was stunned at the revelation and, before he could react, Imai had drawn his short sword and plunged it deep into his own belly. Dark fluid bubbled around the merchant's lips, spilling down his chin, and he toppled forward with a noisy wheeze.

"Well that's not good," Kwon muttered to himself as he sheathed his sword and looked around to make sure there was no one else in the shop.

He knew his mind should be alive with questions, but there was an assignment to complete. Kicking at Imai's body to make sure he really was dead, Kwon turned to the chest of drawers and began pulling scrolls out.

It was clear that Imai had sold Mistress Kiku's designs to the Shogun years ago, but the returning orders had small modifications, which included Amaterasu's symbol that featured on the Ishin Blade. The monk felt a certain disconcertion that the orders for Muramasa's swords did not appear to be for money or indeed anything of value, but rather just for time spent in the company of an unnamed woman in the far north.

However, what disturbed Kwon the most was that the orders did not bear the seal of Lord Yoshiakira, but that of a lieutenant he did not recognize. The monk felt himself tense, knowing it would belong to the Oni Witch he had heard so much about.

"Riah…" he muttered to himself, flicking through the scrolls. "Always star-blasted Riah." The final parchment made him stop and he examined the document closely. The script of Oyashima had mystified him for years and it was only in the months before Jion had arrived that he had made a concerted effort to learn. Whilst far from fluent he had the basics, and rolled the scroll up and put it into his robe.

Turning to the back door, he looked down at the body of Imai. "Thanks for the map. Give my regards to Mother."

*

Kurama Temple
Jion sat cross-legged on the bank of the mountain lake, his eyes closed and deep in mediation. The past few days had been good. His relationship with Gozen had thawed and she now appeared to accept his orders more readily, although he still resented the way the older girl talked down to him.

Masako was more understanding of her role and Jion suspected that he had Mistress Nikko to thank for that. And his training was going well. *Very* well. Although he had not told anyone yet, he could feel the full range of his abilities returning. They were not as strong as they had been, but he knew that would come in time. For now he was just glad to have them back.

Jion smiled inwardly, feeling a measure of rare peace. His time was coming. He could feel it.

"There you are," came the lilt of Masako's voice. "I couldn't sense you anywhere."

Jion opened his eyes and smiled broadly, seeing his lover approach and marveled at her first bloom of womanhood. He had felt her presence from over a mile away but said nothing.

"Your mind was completely still," she continued sitting down next to him. "Master Hiroyasu said that he was impressed by your progress."

Jion felt himself flush a little with pride. His reputation was beginning to spread through the expansive temple grounds, and yesterday a young novice had asked to have the honor to train with him. Respect meant followers, and followers now meant an army tomorrow. "I think it is more than Master Hiroyasu's teaching," he said.

"Our Goddess?"

Jion nodded. "At least in part. But I think there is something else... I'm not sure how to describe it. It is like the land has a song that only I can hear."

Masako frowned. "How do you mean? Do the kami talk to you?"

Jion shook his head and looked out across the still surface of the lake. "No. There are no kami. There is just one voice, but it sings a different song for every part of the land."

"You should tell Mistress Nikko. It doesn't sound right."

"Maybe. What about you? How has your morning been?"

Masako shrugged and looked down at the grass.

"Did you and Gozen have another fight?"

"She started it. She is just so... so... oh you know how she is."

Jion chuckled. "I know how *sisters* are."

"Oh it's more than that," Masako pouted. "She is so judgmental. She believes everything the Master Abbot teaches without question and cannot accept there might be another way."

Jion turned from the lake to look at Masako. "What was the argument about?"

"She wanted me to talk to you... to ask you to rethink your vengeance on your Chikatane and Mutsu."

"Ah. That again. Interesting that she asked you to talk to me."

"Do you think she knows?"

Jion shook his head. "No. We've been careful. Everyone just thinks we're close friends. Like brother and sister. What do you think of Gozen's view?"

"You know what I think. We are what we are and we must do what we must do. It is our fate, no?"

Jion considered the point and said nothing.

Masako frowned. "What is it? Are you having doubts?"

Jion shrugged. "No. I don't know. So much has happened. I'm not the child I was. There are bigger things going on... so much more at stake. There is the Emperor to support. The Oni to vanquish. Our devotion to Our Goddess. What if we could fight fate? What if we really could choose our path and who we could become?"

Masako listened to him closely and when she spoke her voice was soft and low. "I think that you can do whatever you want. There are so many paths that you could choose… all laid out before you. All you have to do is decide. As long as I can walk them with you, I don't care."

As she reached out to touch his hand he looked up and deep into her eyes.

"It's funny," he said. "When we were children, I hated expanses of water. Even the sight of a lake or ocean would make me feel sick. But now… it calms the turmoil inside of me. I think that is you. I wish you were the sea and I was the river running into you."

"I love you," Masako whispered. "I think I would die without you."

"And what if The Council sends me on an assignment? What if I am away for months or years like Master Kwon?"

"I would follow you. I would defy their orders to be by your side."

"And if fate decrees that I must die?"

"Then I would lie down next to your body and wait for death to take me too."

Jion half smiled. "No. You should live - carry my memory and name with you."

"I don't think I could. Life would not be worth living," she murmured and laid her head against his neck.

"And what if I chose a path that split us?" Jion said, watching the play of light on the water.

"Why do you talk of such things on a day as beautiful as this?"

"Because we make choices every minute of every day. And they are building. You can feel it too, I know you can. It won't be long now."

"I know. But I don't want to admit it. At least not right now."

"That does not hold fate at bay. Death is always with us, biding its time."

"You sound like Master Hiroyasu. Always so gloomy."

"No… just contemplative. There is so much that is out of balance… so much to consider."

"I know. But promise me one thing."

"What is that?"

"I know that something is coming. Something big. You were right, I can feel it. If our destinies do part us, don't marry *her*."

Jion looked down at Masako. "Gozen?"

She nodded. "She is not right for you."

"I know. But she has the diplomatic skills to bring others to our cause. She is right for the clan."

"No. She isn't. And if you marry her, it means that everything we're doing now… everything we have been doing… we're living a lie. I can't do that."

Jion sighed. "Sometimes I wonder if I could wish away all these feelings. The hate. The fear. The guilt. It would make things so much simpler and I could see which path I should take."

"Do you wish you had never kissed me that night?"

Jion chuckled. "I thought it was you who kissed me."

"No," Masako replied giggling. "I'm certain it was you who kissed me first."

"You are constantly on my mind," he said, suddenly serious. "I know that I should be torn between The Council and Chikatane and Gozen and you… but I'm not. It's only you."

"Jion," she said softly into his ear and wrapping her arms around his neck.

"Yes my love?"

"Sshh," and she pulled him down on top of her, loosening her robe as she did so.

*

It was the hour of the rooster, and the summer sun was still high enough to warm Jion's room. His fencing lessons with Mistress Nikko had been good, but she was not Master Kwon. After a late lunch, Jion had allowed himself a long soak in the onsen before his evening class with Master Hiroyasu.

He was fastening his robe when he heard a knock at his door. He had heard the familiar approach of Gozen from across the courtyard but was a little surprised that he had not sensed her companion until they had arrived at the door. Abbot Shimada seldom bothered with him, instead entrusting his care and education to the other masters.

"Master Abbot, Gozen," Jion said, sliding the door open and bowing. "This is a rare honor. Please come in. May I pour you some cha?"

"Thank you," Shimada replied. "That would be acceptable."

"Yes, thank you," Gozen said returning the bow. "I will have some too."

Jion returned to the center of his room and began assembling the tea bowls and pot. "You both look serious," he said. "What has happened?"

The Abbot and his apprentice knelt on the opposite side of the tea tray and it was Shimada who spoke. "Do you know?"

Jion looked up from the bowl he had been pouring the tea into. "Do I know what, Master Abbot?" he said, offering the bowl to the abbot, who accepted it and in turn offered it to Gozen who made a play of refusing such an honor before accepting.

"Do you know… about today's events?"

Jion looked to Gozen and then back to Shimada. Of course he knew. There was nothing within The Temple that now escaped his ever heightening senses. "You refer to Master Hogen?"

The abbot nodded.

"Yes Master Abbot. I know about Master Hogen."

"How?"

"Master Abbot? I apologize but I do not…"

"How?" Shimada replied, frustration edging into his voice. It had been a terrible morning and a long afternoon and he was in no mood for this youth's coyness. "How do you know? Who told you? Or did you sense it?"

Master Hogen's horse had thrown him earlier that morning. His injuries were not serious but a monk was supposed to be at one with his mount. It had been over a century since any monk had been unseated and this latest incident had caused great consternation throughout The Temple.

"I sensed it," Jion finally admitted, not seeing the point of any further pretense.

"I see. And did you sense The Council meeting this afternoon?"

Jion knew that this was dangerous ground. It had been more than a regular Council meeting. It had been an emergency summit where each Master and his or her adept had admitted that their abilities were weakening; that whatever darkness was coming was now accelerating, clouding their vision and senses.

"Yes Master Abbot. I did sense the meeting this afternoon. Please forgive me," Jion said bowing low.

Shimada nodded slowly. "I see. Jion, how many birds are there in the cherry tree halfway down the mountain pass… the one next to the guard tower."

"Three Master Abbot," Jion replied instantly. "An early nightingale and two ravens."

The abbot stopped nodding. "Jion, less than two years ago every master in this temple could have sensed those birds… some could have even sensed two or three villages over. However, today none of us can. Not even me. Our powers are dwindling… whatever link with land we have is fading, and fading fast. This is true for all of us. All except you. How is that possible, Jion?"

"I do not know, Master Abbot," Jion replied handing Shimada a bowl of tea. "Truly, my abilities are strengthening… but I confess that their source is a mystery to me."

"Yes, and to all of us too," the abbot replied, accepting the bowl and bringing it to his lips. "If matters continue on their present course, it will not be long before you are the most powerful monk here…"

I already am, and you know it, Jion thought

"… should we fear you?" Shimada finished.

"No Master Abbot," Jion replied immediately. "I am pledged to The Temple… to you and all the masters. It is my sword duty to uphold our laws and protect all of you."

The abbot looked at the boy hard. "And do you reaffirm that promise here and now?"

"I do Master Abbot," Jion said, bowing deeply. "I swear on the spirit of my father and brother."

"Good enough," Shimada muttered. "Gozen tells me that your talents are quite something to behold."

Jion reddened. "No Master Abbot. They are really nothing…"

"Jion, stop," Shimada commanded. "The situation is serious. All over Oyashima the Shogun's forces are being put into a heightened state of readiness. Our spies report that the Oni Witch is getting ready to march, although we do not know her target. You are The Hero of Yugyo… your reputation has spread more than you can possibly imagine. The Shogun was outraged that you refused his invitation to surrender. That he sent those assassins proves he knows where you are and he will reason that if you are not with him, then you are against him, and he knows of your loyalty to the Emperor. If he means to strike at The Chrysanthemum Throne then he will seek your destruction as well, and that means your enemies will come here. Jion, with our dwindling abilities, we may not be able to repel them. So please understand that this is not the time for modesty or reserve. So I ask again, are your powers truly something to behold?"

Jion looked to Gozen, simultaneously loving and hating her for revealing the extent of his talents. "Yes Master Abbot. They are."

Shimada visibly relaxed, glad that Jion was now being open and honest with him. "Thank you Jion. This is important to me and the whole temple. Talk to me about your abilities."

Jion shrugged, unsure where to begin. "I have a certain… forewarning of death. Things turn black and white and slow down allowing me to move out of the way. I have had that since just before I was six."

"When your village was attacked?"

"Yes Master Abbot. I also possess great dexterity and speed."

"This is what allows you to cut arrows from the sky?"

"Yes Master Abbot."

"And is this skill increasing? Are you better able to track your targets?"

"Yes Master Abbot. Before I could manage to defend against three or four arrows, but with Mistress Nikko's tuition that is now up to ten… maybe more."

"Good. What else?"

"Uh… well my gift of sense you know about…"

Shimada held up a hand. "Not the full extent. How far can you sense? With what clarity?"

"After Yugyo it was not far… maybe a hundred meters. However, today it is four or five miles with perfect clarity. I can go further but I start to lose some of the detail. It gets worse the further I go. The range is improved if I am shoeless… if my feet are in direct contact with the land."

"I see," Shimada replied, looking both concerned and impressed, as he weighed up whether the teenager was really a blessing or a curse. "What about this business of disappearing I have heard about?"

Jion felt himself tense, remembering Nikko's words to be careful to whom he revealed the existence of the Goddess. "If I concentrate very, *very* hard, I can see myself in another place… and then I am there. But the experience drains me and it might be several days before I can do it again."

Shimada frowned. "How far can you go?" he asked. "Miles?"

"Oh no Master Abbot. Meters. It is useful in a fight if I am cornered."

"Yes, I am sure that it is. What else?"

Jion thought for a moment. "I can talk without moving my lips. But only to those that I am close to," he said, looking meaningfully at Gozen and smiling, remembering the secret conversation they had shared not so long ago. *Perhaps I can have both sisters*, he thought. *Perhaps I won't have to choose.*

"Over what distance?" the abbot asked.

"I'm not sure Master Abbot."

"Further than you can sense?"

"Yes Master Abbot."

Shimada considered this. "You can… what do you call it?"

"Think-speak Master Abbot."

"Yes, a good phrase. You can think-speak to Gozen and Masako. Who else?"

Jion decided not to say that he had recently begun to talk with Nikko this way but instead replied "I once was able to communicate with Master Kwon. It was the night of the Nokizaru attack."

"Can you speak to him now?"

"I don't know Master Abbot."

"Hmmm… well, try later. If you succeed then tell him about Master Hogen and the meeting this afternoon. After that report to me, even if you are not successful."

"Yes Master Abbot."

"Good. Now what about these elemental abilities?"

Jion frowned. "I'm not sure what you mean Master Abbot."

"Your ability to… dissolve your consciousness into the water or the air."

"Oh Master Abbot, I have not been able to do that for many years. Not since Yugyo…"

"I understand," Shimada replied. "But I am led to believe that you when you did… you were able to see through time. Is that right?"

Jion nodded. "Yes Master Abbot… sort of. I can see the echo of life, and work backwards to certain sources."

"Backwards *and* forwards?" The abbot leaned in, his curiosity now fully aroused.

Jion shook his head. "I never tried forwards Master Abbot… not since Port Choshi. Only backwards. I… I… abused my abilities whilst at sea and they were…" his voice tailed off in shame.

Shimada had heard the story of the miracle typhoon, and leaned back. "I want you to resume your training in this area. I will instruct Master Hiroyasu to make it so, assisted by Mistress Nikko – her knowledge of all things esoteric is impressive. I want you to begin small, Jion. Don't overstretch yourself. But you must understand; if the Shogun sends his demons to attack us, you may be our only defense."

*

August 1367 – Kurama Temple

The scream pierced the night, echoing around the sleepy stone buildings, and shattering the serenity of the hour of the tiger. Even as Gozen scrambled to put her robe on she knew it was Jion; she would recognize that cry anywhere.

It came again, reverberating around The Temple grounds, and as Gozen stepped out into the night she saw others hurrying towards Jion's chambers.

As she arrived, she turned, seeing Masako just a few steps behind her.

"What is it?" the younger girl asked. "What is happening? Is Jion alright?"

Gozen tried to keep the panic from her voice. "I don't know…"

Master Takamori appeared in the doorway. "All of you go back to your rooms," he ordered and then saw Gozen. "Not you. You come with me," he said turning back into Jion's bedroom chamber.

Gozen stepped forward but Masako grabbed her arm. "You have your orders little sister," Gozen said.

"Please…" Masako begged. "Please… ask Master Takamori's permission."

"No. You heard him. I'll come and see you as soon as I can. I swear." She shrugged out of Masako's grip and turned to join Master Takamori.

The two of them walked down the short corridor and Gozen heard Takamori muttering. "This is becoming too frequent…"

They arrived at the door to Jion's bedchamber, ripped and hanging from its frame. The scene inside was as it had been the three previous nights. What little furniture there was had been smashed through the screen walls, the mats ripped up, and in the corner was the huddled form of Jion, quietly sobbing.

Takamori looked to her and pointed to Jion. "Go and do your thing. But I want to know what happened this time."

Gozen bowed and quickly crossed to Jion, noting the light smell of ammonia and the dark stain on the bedroll. Kneeling next to him, she gently touched his hand, reassuring him that he was now safe.

"Sshh… Jion… it's me. It's Gozen."

A tear stained and swollen face looked up at her, the bottom lip trembling in anger and grief. "Gozen… help me. Please."

She could see he was shaking like a peasant's house in an earthquake and she reached out for him, putting a reassuring arm around his shoulders and pulling his weakened form into her chest.

"It's alright," she said softly. "I've got you."

"No…" he whimpered. "No, you haven't. You don't…" his voice cracked and fresh tears began to fall.

"Sshh," she said gently rocking him. "Sshh. You're safe."

"No," the voice in the dark said. "None of us are."

*

It was the hour of the dragon, and dawn's early light had washed through The Temple grounds, warming the stones and breathing fresh life into the surroundings.

Abbot Shimada sat with the other masters in a semi-circle around the kneeling forms of Jion and Gozen. The atmosphere was heavy and still, each master knowing The Temple's need for the boy but secretly fearing him too.

Shimada spoke first. "Jion, do not be ashamed. This is a safe place. We will protect you…"

The youth bowed, his head touching the mat.

"… and watch over you," the abbot continued. "What can you tell us about last night? Or indeed about the previous nights?"

Jion cleared his throat and when he spoke his voice was low and gravelly, betraying the damage done to his throat by his screaming. "At your command Master Abbot, Master Hiroyasu and I have tried to reactivate my skills… my sight through time. I am not deserving of such a great instructor and my progress over the last week has been slow.

"I am able to see backwards now… maybe one or two days depending on the object and my familiarity with it. My future sight… I am ashamed to report that it only extends maybe ten or twenty seconds. But when I am asleep… it is hard to describe Master Abbot. Time does not feel like a straight line. It is not continuum of causality. I apologize… I do not have the words to explain. But imagine that instead of the past affecting the future, the future could also affect the past… as though all points of existence were connected."

Shimada looked to Hiroyasu, wondering if the old Master had showed the teenager the most secret of their teachings. Hiroyasu glanced at the abbot, sensing the question, and shook his head slowly.

"And when you are asleep, you see the future young Jion?" Shimada asked.

"See it? No Master Abbot… it is more like I *feel* it."

"And these dreams… these are the source of your nightly disturbances?"

"Yes Master Abbot, although I can only remember half images."

"What can you tell us about them?"

"I... I don't know Master Abbot. There is a village in the mountains. I have never seen it before, yet it is familiar to me. The people are not like us... thick set and hairy... hair all over and they carry Yoshiakira's banner. I believe that they are Ainu... but they are corrupted somehow. As if their very souls have become twisted and deformed. Then something happens... everything shifts, as though I have traveled without walking, and I am in the center of the village where I see Gozen and Masako. They are being hacked to pieces by the villagers, and I can see the Shogun drinking their blood and he is growing fatter like a tick or a leech. Then... then we are both on a mountain. I try to run at him but suddenly there is a fire, and all the mountains are burning. Below... in the valley, I can see the Ainu village is on fire too... but now it is Fujigatani and all the bodies on the ground are the masters and adepts from The Temple..." his voice trailed off.

Silence returned to the hall as the masters considered what they had been told.

"Mistress Gozen," Shimada finally said. "You and Jion have developed a bond... you have become closer in recent weeks. This... mind-talking. Do you get any sense of these dreams?"

"Yes Master Abbot," Gozen said, bowing as she did so.

"And what is your interpretation?"

"Master Abbot, I believe that when Jion is relaxed he can see further in time than when he is awake and concentrating. However, as to the nature or meaning of the dreams... I regret that I can only offer speculation, but I do sense great danger."

Shimada turned to his Head Librarian. "Mistress Nikko, do our texts have anything to say on such matters."

"In part Master Abbot," Nikko replied. "In Jion's dream it seems that the villagers are providing power to the Shogun by sacrificing Mistresses Gozen and Masako. If it is the future that Jion sees, then it is only one possible timeline. Some of our most ancient writings speak of such gifts but they say that to see the future is to change it."

Hiroyasu shook his head. "I am sorry Mistress Nikko, but do our teachings also not say that a man's fate is a man's fate? This must be inevitable."

Nikko bowed her head respectfully. "It does Master Hiroyasu, but it says nothing of *choosing* a fate. It may be that our end is already written but it is our decision which path we walk to get there."

Some of the other masters muttered amongst themselves as they considered the philosophical point.

Shimada raised his hand for silence. "Jion, what do *you* think?"

The teenager flushed with the honor. Few adepts were ever asked their opinion and certainly no one under that rank. "M... M... Master Abbot," he stuttered. "I do not know. All I can say is that it felt real. It was as though I was awake. For my own part… I feel that there is great danger. Not to myself, but to others," he looked meaningfully at Gozen, "and to The Temple. Master Abbot… I would like to ask permission to find this village… to assess the danger."

Shimada raised his eyebrows in surprise and looked to Takamori before turning back to Jion. "Do your instructors consider that you are ready for such an assignment?"

Takamori and Hiroyasu exchanged glances, although neither man looked to Nikko. "It is our feeling," Takamori began, "that although Jion's training will not be completed until Master Kwon returns to us, he is capable of such an assignment. His skills have grown considerably in the last few months. However given the precarious state of our abilities, and that Jion would be the most effective defense against any attack… we would recommend that his request is denied."

Nikko coughed loudly. "Master Abbot, I am not sure that I can agree. The Shogun targets Jion… the boy is what brings the danger to us. By allowing him to undertake this assignment you will draw the danger away and give The Temple more time to discover the cause of your ailing abilities."

Takamori harrumphed loudly, irked that the woman had spoken against him. "You would send the boy out there?" he snorted. "Against the Shogun's army? You would sacrifice him for The Temple? And what would happen if Yoshiakira returns to us once he is through with him?"

Nikko shook her head and kept her voice soft and respectful, infuriating Takamori further. "Master Takamori, you said that the boy is capable… that his talents have grown and strengthened. We do not send him out to confront Yoshiakira's hordes, but rather to divert them away…"

"But in his vision he fails… everyone is dead," Takamori interrupted.

Nikko shrugged, allowing the older man's rudeness to go unnoticed. "His vision begins with the death of Mistress Gozen and Masako… they should not accompany him. The path changes…"

"But fate does not Mistress Nikko, you said it yourself. The destination is set. Only the path must be chosen," Takamori retorted, now openly irritated by the woman.

Shimada looked hard at the two bickering instructors and both fell silent. The Abbot turned to Jion. "There is much to consider, young Jion. What was once certain is now clouded. Allow The Council three days to reach a decision."

*

It was the hour of the rat, and darkness had swept across the mountains like a black cloak falling over the land. Silently, Jion put the saddle on the mare and tightened the straps. She was a good horse – one of his favorites –

and he carefully swung his supply sack up and onto her back so as not to startle her.

A sound from the rear of the stable building caused him to stiffen and then he sighed loudly.

"I know you're there," he said. In truth, he had known for more than a half hour, but had hoped that Masako and Tatsuo would change their minds.

The two figures stepped out of the deep shadows and into the light of the half moon.

"We're coming with you," Masako said.

Jion did not look at her but carried on preparing the horse. "Are you now?"

"Yes. We are. And you cannot stop us," Masako said defiantly.

Jion turned to look at her, both knowing that was not true. "And what about you?" he said, turning to Tatsuo.

"I am Soma first and servant to Kurama second. My place will always be by your side," Tatsuo replied.

"You know that we will get into trouble for this," Jion said turning back to the mare.

"Yes," Masako and Tatsuo whispered in unison.

"We may get expelled."

"Maybe," Masako replied. "But as Mistress Nikko said, we should embrace our fate, not hide from it."

"You listened to my conversation with Mistress Nikko?" Jion already knew the answer to that.

Remember Jion, the librarian had said. *To hesitate is to be lost. Pick up the brush. Fulfill your purpose... focus your feelings into actions.*

He had allowed himself to be overheard, reasoning that Masako's abilities were not far from his own skills, and he could use the help. Tatsuo was an unexpected passenger on this journey but blind loyalty never hurt a general.

Masako and Tatsuo looked at each other guiltily but said nothing.

"You know that we might be gone a while?" Jion asked sensing their discomfort. "And I'm not completely sure where it is I am going."

Masako stepped forward and whispered to him. "Trust in the Goddess. She will guide us."

"I certainly hope so. Have you got your kit with you?" Jion replied.

Both grunted an acknowledgement.

"Good. You'd better saddle up then."

*

September 1367

The wet summer was giving way to a cool autumn and the green leaves of the forest were tinged with yellow.

From the position of the sun, Jion guessed it about the hour of the horse and had ordered a break for lunch. Tatsuo was feeding the horses and Masako was stirring a small pot of steaming vegetables that had been purchased in the village they had stayed in the night before.

Jion sat cross-legged on the damp mossy ground, his eyes closed as he practiced the mental exercises Mistress Nikko had given him before he left. Even from this great distance, he could still sense the echoes of outrage from The Temple masters. That he had left before The Council had reached their decision was a source of great disharmony.

Nevertheless, Mistress Nikko had been right. Sitting around talking about action while their fate crept up on them was no way for a Clan Lord to live. The bujin always met their fate head on and Jion was determined to do the same.

He allowed his mind to relax, and sent his inner self out into the trees, following the trail on the small stream, along its reedy banks, past the lonely farmsteads…

Master Kwon… where are you? We need you… Master Kwon…

He had repeated this exercise, amongst the many others, every day since leaving Kurama three weeks ago, and had never had a reply.

*

Kwon knew he was lost. Imai's map was in code and although he had a rough idea where to find Muramasa, the foreigner felt that he had been walking in circles for weeks.

The few people he had met had been less than helpful, shaking their heads and telling him that all those who sought the smith invited madness and death. Kwon sat on a rock that had been warmed by the noonday sun, looking up at the dark mountains that made up the North Coast of Oyashima. Muramasa was here somewhere, as was the lost tribe who mined the ore… but he was damned if he could find them.

The wind picked up unexpectedly, gusting around him in the way lovers fold themselves over each other after too much time apart.

Master Kwon…

Kwon stopped chewing and tilted his head, unsure of what he had just heard.

Master Kwon…

The monk concentrated hard. *Jion?*

Master Kwon! The voice, surprised and excited, came through stronger. *Where are you?*

Somewhere between Nonoichi and Mount Yake. Are you well?

Yes. We have left Kurama… I know the source of Yoshiakira's power…

Left Kurama? Jion, what happened?

It is only temporary Master Kwon. There is a village of Ainu... I have dreamed of them. They are a threat.

Kwon frowned. It was too much of coincidence to believe that the Ainu the boy was seeking would be different from his. *Where are you?*

Somewhere north-north-east of Chukyo.

Kwon looked at his map. Jion was on the other side of the mountain range to him. The most direct route between them was up and over the active summit of Mount Yake. Without knowing the boy's exact location Kwon guessed they were a two week journey from each other - three at the most. He put his map down and looked up the clouds gathering overhead.

Jion, I think the Ainu are mining the ore for Yoshiakira. I am searching for the smith. When you find them, do not engage. I will be with you as soon as I can.

*

Sakakura Village

"I am not sure we should have come here," Jion said uneasily, looking around the small village, and then up the imposing slopes of the Yake mountain range.

Tatsuo stepped forward, holding the bridle of his horse. "What is it?"

"I don't know. I cannot sense anything beyond the mountains... it is as though they absorb everything. My mind can gain no purchase."

"Do you want to move on?"

Jion looked at the setting sun and guessed it was the hour of the rooster. Turning, he looked back at the slumped form of Masako over the pommel of the saddle. She was exhausted. Jion knew that Tatsuo was used to this sort of travel but Masako... she had grown comfortable at Kurama. Where he had frequently spent nights in the mountain forests, she had enjoyed the comfort of a bedroll, and was certainly not used to the rigors of the itinerant life.

Jion turned back to Tatsuo. "No. We'll stay here tonight, but we'll leave at first light."

*

"I'm sorry," the Innkeeper said. "But we have no spare rooms. None at all."

Tatsuo shook his head in disbelief. "Nothing?"

"I'm sorry," the Innkeeper repeated, bowing. "It's the trouble up north. I've never seen so many refugees."

"What trouble?" Jion asked, sensing the man was telling the truth and the inn was full.

"I'm not sure. The stories seem to change. Some say that a pack of wild animals is attacking the outposts and carrying people off into the night. Others say the Oni walk the land, corrupting everything and driving the people out. The Headman asked the local Lord to send a scouting party up to the mountain… they never returned. The people that come through here… they are mad with grief. We had the garrison doubled last week, and tripled as of last night. These are dark times to be traveling."

"Where can we find your Headman?" Jion asked, keen to get some answers.

"I will go and fetch him for you."

*

"It is as you have heard," Ohari, the headman of Sakakura, said, bowing deeply to the bujin and the novice monk. "Something is driving the people from the villages at the foot of the mountain."

"Do you know what it is?" Jion asked, sipping his cha slowly. Night had fallen and he was uncomfortable with the idea of camping outside.

"Not for certain, no. But our Lord is very worried. There are many soldiers here to protect us. Even so, many people are fearful and leaving."

Tatsuo leaned forward. "The innkeeper said that a scouting party had gone north?"

"Yes," Ohari replied. "That was three weeks ago. They never returned."

Jion turned to the bleary-eyed Masako. "What do you think?"

The young woman thought for a moment and then bowed to Ohari. "The refugees who have come through in the last few weeks… did they report seeing the scouting party?"

"No," Ohari replied, returning the bow. "It is as if the mountain has swallowed them."

Jion pondered their predicament. "What about before the troubles? Was there anything unusual?"

Ohari paused, struggling to recall. "Unusual? I do not think so… We are a small village… out of the way, you understand? We are far removed from the clan wars and the struggle for The Chrysanthemum Throne… There were some of the Shogun's troops who came through here about a month ago… maybe six weeks."

Jion felt his stomach tighten and made an effort to relax. "Is that normal?"

"Yes and no. We sometimes have a regiment come through… maybe once a year. Perhaps once every two years. But they are usually going either east or west…"

"And this time?" Jion interrupted.

"They were heading north. They claimed to be on a training exercise, but we have never known the Shogun's forces to train in the mountains. They usually keep to the valleys and the flats, leaving the slopes to the Yamabushi."

Jion frowned, sensing there was more to this story. "Who was their commander?" he asked.

Ohari shook his, trying to recall. "Please… one moment. It will be in our ledger." The headman crossed the room and opened a wooden chest that was crammed with scrolls – the records of the village. They would list every birth and death, every movement of the people, crop yields, taxes, marriages… and every visitor.

"Here it is," Ohari said. "Yes. Forgive me, it was not a regiment, but rather a small unit of eleven. Yes…" he ran his finger down the lines of text. "The commander…. Lord Mutsu."

Jion felt his hand clench on the hilt of his sword and the familiar chill of his rage filled his veins. "You are sure?" he said with a clenched jaw.

"Yes," Ohari replied. "There is no mistake."

Jion looked to Masako and then to Tatsuo. Each stared back at him, their faces a mask of grim resolve, but neither said anything.

"Headman Ohari," Jion said, returning to their host. "We believe that it is Lord Mutsu who will be the cause of the trouble."

"Really?" Ohari replied. "You are sure?"

"There can be little doubt. He is well known… for dabbling in the black arts," Jion lied. "We will hunt him down for you."

"Thank you. But I regret that this village is poor. We cannot reward you."

Jion shook his head. "No reward is necessary. But perhaps we could impose on your house for a bed tonight."

*

Jion had lain awake for hours, his mind churning. Mutsu was so close and had so much to pay for. The faces of his brother, Master Otsuno, and Sensei Watanabe floated in front of him as he willed himself to sleep, to rest for the exertions that tomorrow would bring.

It was the hour of the rat, and fully dark, when he had drifted off, exhaustion finally overtaking him. This place made him feel uncomfortable and he was already craving the return of the full extent of his abilities. Had he possessed them, he would have sensed the arrows that whistled silently through the air.

The gate guards fell heavily to the ground and the dogs ran barking to their stricken masters. A face appeared at the barrack doors to investigate the disturbance and, having seen his dead comrades, disappeared again to sound the alarm.

The bell rang frantically as a second hail of arrows came from the north, and another from the east. Black-clad figures overran the low village wall and swept through the buildings with swords drawn, setting fire to the thatched roofs.

Jion felt himself wrenched from the oily depths of sleep by Masako's screams. Shadows were all about him and he could hear Tatsuo shouting as he was dragged through the broken screen wall. In an instant, the Ishin Blade was in his hands and hissed through the air, cutting down one assailant and then another.

He made to follow Tatsuo when Masako screamed again. "Jion!"

A shadowy figure stood over her with a drawn sword and Jion willed himself to shift as he had done in training with Master Kwon, crossing the large room in the blink of an eye, parrying the death blow meant for Masako, and driving his sword first downward, slicing the assailants knee, and then back up through his chin. The back of his skull exploded in a shower of blood and bone.

"Are you hurt?" he panted.

Masako shook her head. "They got Tatsuo…" she whimpered.

Jion turned and leapt through the broken screen, out into the cold night air. Several buildings were well alight and he could see the men of the garrison fighting a valiant rearguard action. They were losing.

As Jion crossed the small village square, a horn sounded in the distance and the attackers instantly broke off, heading back through the gate and towards Mount Yake.

*

It was the hour of the rabbit and Jion knew that he should eat some breakfast, but he was not hungry. Masako sat next to him on the steps of Ohari's veranda, her head resting on his shoulder and her eyes red-rimmed from crying. Smoke hung in the air, as did the smell of charred flesh and wood.

"I can only apologize," Ohari was saying. "It was my duty to see that you were protected, and I failed. Please allow me to commit seppuku."

Jion shook his head, still feeling numb. "It is not necessary. No one could have prevented what happened. There were too many of them."

Ohari bowed but said nothing.

Jion looked around. Already the assembly of the cremation pyres had begun, and the local priest was giving funerary rites to a long line of bodies on the ground.

"How bad is it?" Jion asked, turning back to Ohari.

"Very bad. Nearly a dozen villagers. More are missing. Perhaps two dozen soldiers were killed… I am not entirely sure. If you had stayed in the tavern last night you would be dead – it was burned to the ground."

"How many of them did we get?"

"Not as many as they got of ours."

"Can I see one?" Jion asked.

The headman nodded and Jion stood, following Ohari as Masako trailed after them.

Ohari poked at a body on the ground. It was large, rounded, and the skin was sallow and yellowing. It was lightly clothed and Jion could see large clumps of dark hair through the loose shirt.

As he bent to roll the body over, he said to Ohari, "Do you recognize him?"

"No," the headman replied. "Not as such. He is Ainu."

"There is a tribe around here?"

Ohari shook his head, uncomfortable with Jion's examination of the body. "I am not sure. There is always rumor and myth. I think our records document the last trade with them…" he broke off as he cast his mind back. "Maybe twelve or thirteen years ago. They used to come down regularly from the mountain to barter. And then they just stopped. We thought that maybe disease got them. Or perhaps they had moved on…"

Jion, having completed his examination, stood. "Please," he said, bowing formally, "can you check the date you last traded with them?"

Ohari returned the bow and hurried back to his home.

"What is it?" Masako asked.

"These are the Ainu from my dreams."

"How can you be sure?"

Jion knelt down and lifted the man's eyelids back, revealing sclera so black it was like coal. Masako gasped, her hand moving to her throat in shock.

"Oh Jion," she whimpered. "It's coming true. Master Takamori was right. A man's fate *is* a man's fate."

"No," Jion replied sternly and then softened. "In my dream you *and* Gozen were their captives. She is not here. Remember what Mistress Nikko said; to look at the future is to change it. That's why you're going to stay here."

"Where are you going?" Masako asked, dreading the answer.

"I'm going after Tatsuo. He might still be alive."

Before Masako could protest Ohari returned brandishing a scroll. "I have the records here."

"When did you last trade with the Ainu?" Jion asked.

"May of fifty-six."

The young warrior turned to his love. "Three months before my father was betrayed and Fujigatani was razed. I'm telling you Masako, these events are connected. I know they are." He turned back Ohari. "Do you know where their settlement is?"

*

The Northern Slopes of Mount Yake

Master Kwon trudged up the narrow mountain path, sending a small avalanche of pebbles down the blasted slope. Far below him, the valley floor was still a vivid green despite the onset of autumn, but up here was only black volcanic rock, an occasional patch of snow, and the stench of sulfur as though the bowels of Jigoku itself had opened up.

He had seen the cave opening from three peaks away. It was as if Amaterasu himself had punched a hole in the mountainside. The range was riddled with caves and Kwon had lost count of how many he had searched. Some had quickly narrowed to a dead end whilst others had led into a maze of tunnels and high vaults full of infinitely complex crystal structures and ear pounding waterfalls. But all had been empty of human life.

As Kwon continued to toil, the wind gusted around him as it had for the whole week, telling him that the weather was beginning to change and he should not consider dwelling on the high slopes much longer.

The sword-master stopped and strained his ears. The wind had brought something else with it. The moment seemed to last hours as though time was being stretched… and there it was again.

Tink… tink…. tink…

Kwon felt his whole being lift. He knew that sound. Metal on metal. A smith. He hurried forward with renewed purpose, the wind falling calm so as not to impede his progress.

It was the hour of the monkey when Kwon reached the cave mouth and the sun was already beginning to set behind the far peaks. Darkness came early in the mountains and Kwon found himself secretly wishing that he could stay in the cave and rest. The past few nights had brought terrible screams that had kept the foreigner awake, but the range was so vast that it was impossible to tell where they came from.

Taking a deep breath, he entered the cave.

*

Jion looked about himself and then back at the map that Ohari had given him. Despite the lengthening shadows, he recognized this place. The way the three slopes from the surrounding snow-covered peaks met at this plateau… the formation of rock that looked strangely like a tower… even the way the stars were coming out… This was the place of his dreams.

But there was nothing here. No village. No shogun. No fire.

There may have been once, many years ago, Jion thought, looking at the rotted wooden staves that might have been part of a raised platform, or maybe a support for a wall. *But not now… not for a very long time.*

He crouched on his haunches, looking at the floor of the plateau for some sign… tracks or a footprint. Even the detritus of discarded rations or a recently extinguished fire. There was nothing.

Frustration welled up inside. Frustration at the loss of Tatsuo. Frustration at The Council's dithering. And frustration that in this bleak landscape he could sense so little. He kicked out at a loose rock and watched it tumble before slowly coming to a halt, its echo fading quickly away like the memory of the dead.

Jion caught himself, aware that he was the source of his own disharmony, and he made a conscious effort to breathe and relax. The Goddess would not have guided him to this place without reason. He began his search again, carefully picking through what little rubble there was, following what appeared to have been the main path into the settlement, and trying to build an image in his mind of what the village would have looked like.

Nothing presented itself, and he turned back to his horse, patting the mare on the rump and then giving her a scratch behind the ears.

"What do you think?" he asked her, bringing a handful of seeds from his pocket for the horse to eat. "Have I brought us out here for nothing?"

The horse shook her head, refusing the seeds, instead whinnying softly in the way that Jion had come to recognize as a request for water. He looked about and saw a thin rivulet coming down one of the slopes. It was not a stream as such, but probably the melt from some snow that had fallen too close to the active summit of Mount Yake.

The mare lapped at it gratefully and Jion leaned against the slope, closing his tired eyes as he did so. He would be seventeen in a few weeks, but it was times like these, when he was cold and hungry, aching from the exertions of the day, that he felt so much older, as though he had lived a lifetime each and every day since leaving Fujigatani.

Without warning, the mare startled, cried out, and backed away from the slope, stamping her feet as she did so.

"Whoa. Whoa," Jion whispered into her ear, grabbing at the reins, and trying to calm her.

She whinnied again and took several more steps back.

"What is it?" Jion asked the mare.

Deep eyes met his and the teenager could see his horse was scared.

Turning back to the slope, he touched the water, bringing it to his nose and then his lips. There was a tang to it that he did not recognize, but it did not taste bad.

And then he heard it, like a faraway prayer.

Da da Danu ha...

Surprised, he too took a step backwards and the words faded away.

Jion looked at his horse. "Did you hear that as well?"

The horse made no reply, but stood dutifully.

Jion approached the slope again and this time put his ear against the black rock. The chant came again.

Da da Danu ha...

"They didn't leave," Jion muttered to himself. "They went underground." He stretched his arms out; trying to find some purchase on the rock, desperately hoping that there was some secret lever or handle that would reveal a hidden doorway. There was none.

Jogging, he retraced his steps to the outcrops of old timber, picking through them, trying to find some sign or symbol that would betray the Ainu's secret. It was getting too dark to see properly and again the knot of frustration began to tighten in his stomach.

It was from the glow of the final embers of the dying day that Jion saw what at first glance looked like a mat of moldering rushes in a corner of the plateau. Jet black against the mountain rock, they were perfectly camouflaged until the sun struck them at just the right angle, revealing their location with a thin film of glinting oil.

Jion knew instantly. *This is it*.

The rushes covered a large wooden panel, and his sinewy arms strained under the weight as he heaved it up.

He tossed the panel to one side, and looked down a shallow ramp that was at least three horses wide and seemed to fade into inky blackness. Jion turned back to his mare.

"Stay there. I will return for you."

Drawing the Ishin Blade, he entered the darkness.

*

Kwon made his way forward cautiously. The darkness of the cave had given way to an iridescent glow of reds and yellows that played on the walls and the ceilings like the ghostly insects of the night that he knew so long ago. There was enough light to see where he was going but not enough for the foreigner to make out the details of the obviously man-made tunnel that he now found himself walking down.

The sound of the smith's hammer falling onto metal was clearer now and continued to drag him on, like a ship on the tide. The smell of sulfur had become nearly overwhelming, and Kwon had torn one of his sleeves off to make a temporary mask over his mouth. His eyes continued to water but he forced himself not to cough, lest he give his position away to whatever secret eyes may be watching for him.

The tunnel had bent and twisted many times and Kwon could no longer be certain in which direction he was heading, only that the floor was now angling downward, dragging him into the bowels of the mountain. Presently the tunnel curved sharply and the sword-master found himself standing in a high-vaulted chamber.

Stalactites hung from the ceiling like giant black icicles and, in the far corner, a pool of lava bubbled ominously, casting a sickly yellow glow into the darkness. Not far from the fresh magma, a solitary figure stood over an immense anvil, hammering rhythmically on a sliver of metal before turning it over and repeating the process. From his vantage point, Kwon could see that all manner of blades lined the walls. Their cruel dark edges glittered in the glow of the molten rock, and he knew that there were enough weapons here to outfit the Shogun's army many times over.

The smith straightened and turned, the same dark eyes that Kwon had seen in Imai scanning the hall.

"Ah," the powerfully built figure said loudly. "I've been expecting you."

Kwon stepped out of the shadows. "Who are you?"

"Oh you know who I am. How long is it that you have been looking for me? A year? More?"

"Muramasa?" Kwon asked, aware of the echo of his own voice.

The smith bowed deeply, the streaks of sweat and dirt on his bare arms and torso showing clearly by the light of the pool. "The very same."

"Do you know who I am?" Kwon asked as he edged forward, taking in the colossal scale of the underground hall.

"Oh you have many names don't you?" Muramasa smiled. "Some are older than this mountain and can only be spoken by the wind on a cruel winters' night. What do you go by these days?"

"Your lackey knew. Why don't you?" Kwon was measuring the distance between himself and the smith, judging the optimum kill range.

"There are so many things you do not understand. You never communed…"

"Understand?" Kwon spat. "What is there to understand? The things your kind made my people do? What they made Greine do to his own flesh and blood?"

Muramasa shrugged. "It is all part of the plan. You will see."

"I don't *want* to be part of the plan. Why can't you leave these people alone?" Kwon's voice was rising.

The smith laughed. "It was never about what you *wanted*. It's about what you *need*."

"You're not like the others are you?" Kwon said, walking around Muramasa and looking into the darkness beyond to ensure that no assassin lay hidden.

"The people of this land… they *see* the essential nature of The Mother… They *embrace* it."

Kwon frowned, lowering his sword. "I don't know what lies you have been told… but you are self-aware, aren't you? You're not under the thrall…"

Muramasa shook his head sadly. "Even after all these years, you still do not grasp the enormity of existence. We *belong* to Her. We *are* Her."

"That's not true. Her power is stolen and She will make slaves of us all."

"And isn't that beautiful?" the smith asked. "She removes all doubt, all fear and anxiety and all we have to do is follow Her word."

Kwon could see that this line of conversation was getting him nowhere and he changed tack. "Who are these for?" he asked, nodding to the weapons that lined the wall.

"You already know the answer to that."

Kwon frowned. There were too many for the Shogun. Then realization hit him like the smith's hammer. His eyes widened. "The Raven Men are coming through, aren't they?"

It was Muramasa's turn to frown. "Raven…?"

"The Oni. Here, they call them the Oni. It's an invasion, isn't it?"

"It is a homecoming."

"When? Tell me! When?" Kwon roared, feeling the advantage slipping from him.

Muramasa shook his head. "You're too late. In time, you will come to see things our way. You will understand."

Kwon paused, desperately trying to think. "You said that you were expecting me."

"As you expected many things in this land."

The sword-master paused. "You know of the book?"

"There are many books."

"Don't play games with me Muramasa. You know about The Queen's Diary?"

Muramasa nodded. "Yes. We all do."

Kwon paused. "If you knew what was happening all along then why…?" his voice tailed off. The diary had not been accurate. He had said it himself. Events had become out of sequence, disjointed and lacking the certainty of what been foretold.

"Why observe time when you could mold it?" the smith was laughing and shaking his head. "We never understood that about you. Why would you wait for what was already foretold to happen? Why did you not seize the opportunities when you had the chance?"

"I don't understand," Kwon said backing away, his mind reeling. "This has happened before. It *must* happen again."

"According to whose rules? Yours?"

"But… but… but then you'll change *everything*." Kwon stopped and made a deliberate attempt to calm the panic within him. "If I am here, then you know what must happen to you."

"I do," Muramasa replied. "I welcome my fate. I will finally be with our Mother."

It was Kwon's turn to chuckle. "You know, I looked upon Her face once… your so-called Goddess. I think you're in for a shock."

"It does not matter. What matters is that *you* are *here*."

Kwon brought his sword up to the smith's throat. "Why?"

As the man laughed his muscular chest moved up and down like a barrel at sea. "Don't you ever look at the series of events that brought you to this place? The escape from Murkwood? Your discovery of the Prophecy Child? The interruption half-way through his education because of a dagger you thought you recognized? How little you understand. Even after the eternity that you have wandered you still do not perceive the endless chain of causality."

Kwon looked at him blankly, not understanding what it was that Muramasa was saying.

"Because if you are here," the mad smith continued, "then who is protecting the child?"

Kwon felt his blood turn to ice. The attempt on Gozen's life... the tampering with the maps... the encounter with Imai.... It had all been a ploy to separate him from...

"Jion!"

With a single movement, Kwon removed the mad smith's head and ran from the chamber.

*

Jion had followed the ramp down into a darkness far blacker than any night. Ahead of him came the sound of mine workings and, against the glow of torches, he could see the silhouettes of the Ainu from his dreams as they swung crude picks, digging for the ore for Muramasa's swords. The hairy beasts that had once been men seemed oblivious to his presence, and Jion was able to pass by them unchallenged.

At the third level, the tunnel abruptly changed from the rough-hewn walls of the upper levels to being completely smooth as though some monstrous maggot had burrowed its way through the mountain. The tunnel began to splinter and fork, leading into a myriad of caverns and chambers that were not lit by conventional torches but by a soft blue glow that seemed to come from the walls themselves, making the high-vaulted halls appear cold despite the heat pumped out from the violent heart of the mountain.

There were no Ainu down here and, the further Jion made his way into the depths of the Yake's core, the more he fancied that the walls were inscribed with some ancient text that he could not understand. In a moment of curiosity he reached out, touching a wall and realized they were not made of rock at all but some kind of metal.

The main passage abruptly ended and Jion found himself looking down on what appeared to be a vast room. The floor was the same as the walls, and seemed to have been worked from a single block. The ceiling arched high above him and he could barely make out its full extent in the gloom. The air was dry here, almost musty, and Jion could feel his eyes prickle from the lack of moisture. The blue glow from the walls was more intense than in the tunnel, and the teenager was able to clearly see three figures standing close together.

"My Lord, I understand. But this," Ullar said, gesturing to the colossal door in front of them "is a very complicated mechanism. It requires a very precise… imprint to activate it."

"Imprint?" the shorter man snapped. "What is this imprint you speak of? How many more subjects must we go through to get this door open?"

Ullar shrugged. "As many as it takes."

The lord turned away in frustration and began to walk towards the stairs that led to the gallery where Jion crouched. The boy felt his breath catch in his throat and his sword arm began to tremble with barely contained rage. There was no mistaking Lord Mutsu.

Beside Ullar and his companion lay a dozen bodies, each wrapped in white sheeting with just their heads exposed. Jion could not see whether Tatsuo was amongst them.

Birag shrugged and said to his comrade, "I don't know why he is so worked up. If we can't get through this door, we'll just break through from above."

Ullar shook his head. "This is your first time working with Skylord metal, isn't it? Those savages may be able to scrape and scratch… perhaps even take a layer off to be forged into Altera's swords… but break through? No. The Home Skin really knew what they were doing when they built this place."

Mutsu just caught the Oni's softly spoken words as he walked up the final steps. *Fools!* He thought. *More than anyone, they should know the risk that the Home…*

A figure stepped out of the darkness, interrupting his internal monologue, bringing a sword to his throat.

"Well well well," Mutsu said. "What do we have here?"

"You know me," the boy whispered. "Look at me Mutsu. Don't you remember me? No? What about my father?"

Mutsu looked at the youth hard and then smiled. The child was almost the exact image of his father. "It's young Yoshimoto, isn't it? You've been quite the pest these last few…"

Jion did not allow the treacherous strategist to continue. With a single stroke he took Mutsu's head from its body and watched both fall to the floor with a wet thump.

"The time of words is long since past, traitor," he murmured.

The Hero of Yugyo knew he should feel something. A sense of justice served. Revenge sated. Closure.

Instead, he felt nothing. His world remained unchanged and deep down he felt a twinge of disappointment that this death was just another to add to his personal tally.

Ullar and Birag looked up from their conversation, expecting to see Mutsu returning. Instead, a figure swathed in the dark robes of the priesthood descended the wide staircase, flicking the blood from his drawn blade.

"That's him," Ullar murmured.

"The Hero of Yugyo?" Birag replied drawing his own sword.

"Uh-huh. Can you take him?"

"Not a chance. But I'll keep him busy long enough for you to get word to Altera."

Ullar grunted an acknowledgement and began jogging to the opposite wall where an identical staircase led to another gallery.

Jion pointed his sword as he walked towards Birag. "Return my friend, and I will let you walk out of here."

Birag shrugged. "You can have what's left of him," he said nonchalantly and then ran at Jion, drawing his own sword.

The boy deflected the clumsy attack with ease, parrying the blade and stepping to one side, forcing Birag through the space where he had just been and exposing his back. Jion drove his sword backwards and felt it nick Birag's side.

The commander turned to face Jion, holding the wound that was now gushing hot life essence onto the floor with a sickening splatter. "You have learned much…"

Jion did not let him finish. Spinning, he cut diagonally from Birag's shoulder to his opposite hip and watched the body parts slide to the floor.

"Too much talk," he muttered to himself and crossed to where the wrapped bodies lay before the closed door.

Even before he reached Tatsuo, Jion knew that his retainer was dead. Each body seemed to have been drained and now wore a deathly white pallor that was only a fraction darker than the shroud they were wrapped in.

When he found his old friend, Jion touched his exposed skin, desperately praying for there still to be some warmth. There was none. The face of Tatsuo no longer looked like that of the man that had played with Jion so many years ago. It was cold and empty, the lips having taken on a blue tinge, the spirit having long departed.

Jion felt his lower lip beginning to tremble and a watery feeling of cold grief rose up within him. They had come so far together. Tatsuo had sacrificed everything for him. The memory of Tatsuo cutting the bully Nobuo down swam in front of him. His kind and gentle words whispered in his ear. Even the chastisements had been filled with love and devotion.

How was he going to tell Mistress Nikko?

Jion felt his mind begin to fog with anguish and guilt that he had not been able to protect Tatsuo when his protector had needed him most.

"It should have been me," he said quietly, holding Tatsuo's body. "They should have taken me."

Deep within Jion, the splinter of sorrow became a crack, and the crack became a chasm. Rage howled from the abyss, surging like the ocean in a typhoon. The stone in his heart that had been dormant for so long once again began to smoke and then flared brightly into life like the very soul of Jigoku.

Jion stood up, feeling this new power flow through him and walked purposefully for the stairs, determined to hunt down every last soul in this forsaken place. His words came softly, as though he was speaking an unbreakable vow to a loved one.

"You're all going to die."

*

Kurama Temple

Abbot Shimada looked up sharply and the heads of Master Takamori and Master Hiroyasu snapped around, each sensing the same disturbance. The Council Hall was empty except for three men who had been discussing the latest efforts to find and retrieve Jion and his missing comrades.

The Abbot frowned as if he were unable to identify the source of his distraction. "Did any of you… feel that?"

Hiroyasu nodded. "Yes Master Abbot."

"It was as if I was dizzy for a moment," Takamori said. "The whole floor seemed to slant as if we were at sea… but now… What was it?"

"A great turmoil in the heart of the land," Shimada said quietly, looking around at the long shadows about them. "I fear that one darkness has given way to a greater one."

*

Sakakura Village

It was the hour of the horse, and the noonday sun had burned off the autumn mist that had enveloped the small village that morning. Masako knelt on Ohari's veranda as she had done for the previous nine days, scanning the main road into the mountains for any sign of Jion. A lump was in her throat that promised never to dissolve.

The headman and the other villagers had been good to her, bringing cha and a few steamed vegetables that she had nibbled on and then discarded. She had no appetite. Every evening she had sent her soul to her Goddess, praying for Jion's safe return. But the Great Tree had remained just that, and Marishiten had not appeared to her.

All around the rebuilding works continued, although she barely noticed, and more than once she had fallen asleep on the porch in the evening and had awoken in the morning to find that one of Ohari's servants had carried her to her bedroll during the night.

And still she waited.

She had read poems of great loves that had been lost, to war or to earthquakes or to the inequities of fate. She remembered how the authors had spoken of the constant yearning, of the abyss that had opened inside only to be filled with a mountainous glacier that never melted. Masako had never imagined that she would feel that way, that she would spend days pining and praying for news. Any news.

With the mountains hindering her mind-talk abilities, she knew that all she could do was wait. And wait. And wait.

For the briefest of moments, Masako thought that she heard the far away rumble of distant thunder, and scanned the clear cerulean sky for any sign of a coming storm. The sound came again, closer now, and she realized that it was not thunder at all but the approach of a galloping horse.

Ohari rushed out on to the veranda. "Is it another attack?"

"I don't know," Masako whispered, shaking her head.

The headman barked an order to one of the militia who ran to the village and began to sound the alarm. Soldiers poured out of the rebuilt barracks and ran to the northern gate, bows and spears at the ready. The villagers who had milled around the small square ran in the opposite direction, gathering small children and preparing to flee into the forest.

The sound of hooves came closer, and as the mare crossed the distant rise, Masako saw that it was a lone rider.

"Jion!" she screamed to the soldiers who were already drawing their bows back. "It's Jion!"

The captain looked first to the girl, then to Ohari, who nodded, and the captain ordered the archers to stand down.

Masako ran to the gate, pushing past the soldiers who were moving back to the garrison. She could now see Jion clearly, and felt hot tears well up in her eyes and then cascade down her pale cheeks, as relief swept through her like a tidal wave engulfing a fishing port. All reason and sense left her and Masako began to cry hysterically for her love.

The mare and its mount rushed past her, slowing and then wheeling about outside Ohari's house. Jion dismounted and for the first time Masako noticed the dried blood that clung to him like a second skin.

"Jion!" she called as she ran to him.

He turned to face Masako but did not embrace her, his face an expressionless mask.

"Jion?" Masako asked quietly, cautiously approaching the boy she knew so well. "Are you hurt?"

"No."

"But... you are covered..."

"It is not mine." He turned from her, reaching up to the white shrouded body that lay across his saddle.

"Oh Jion. Is it...?" her voice tailed off as she realized the awful truth.

He grunted an acknowledgement and carried the still form towards village's small shrine.

Ohari called down to him from the veranda. "Praise the Buddha that you have returned. What happened?"

Jion turned so that the headman could plainly see what he was carrying. "Prepare a pyre immediately," he said, without emotion.

*

Night had fallen, and all that remained of Tatsuo's cremation were a few fading embers and a thin wisp of smoke that hung in the air like a courtesan's scarf. Masako knelt next to Jion who continued to stare ahead. The villagers had faded away with the priest who had conducted the funeral, wary that the young man who had returned from the mountain was not the same as the one who had gone to rescue his faithful retainer.

They sat for several hours, neither one saying anything, letting the cold of the evening settle over them.

"He was proud to serve you," Masako eventually said.

Jion made no reply and continued to look at the few remaining cinders. Masako had no sense that he had even heard her.

I missed you, she mind-talked. *Are you even going to speak to me?*

Something stirred, like a shadow on a cliff and, when it came, his voice was like a faint echo within a cave, whispering in her mind. *He didn't need to die. I should have saved him.*

You didn't kill him. It was those… those beasts. It was not your fault.

I should have got there sooner. I should have sensed Mutsu was behind…

Masako's head snapped around to look at Jion. "Mutsu was there?" she said incredulously.

Jion still did not look at her, but nodded.

"Did you…?" her voice tailed off.

"Yes." His voice sounded hoarse as though he had been crying for days, although Masako had seen no tears.

"Then there is just Chikatane…"

"No," he croaked. "They *all* must die. Every last one of them."

Masako frowned. "All? Who do you mean?"

"All of them. The Emperor-Pretender. The Shogun. The Oni. Every lord who allied himself to that dog. Every vassal who carried a message. Every farmer who paid a tax… all of them. Oyashima needs to be cleansed."

Masako said nothing, struggling to understand the enormity of Jion's vow.

"I should have saved him," Jion continued. "I failed him. I won't fail you. Or Gozen. I'll protect you all," he finished, finally turning to look at her.

"Jion," Masako said laying a soothing hand on his. "What happened up there?"

"I killed them," he replied. "I killed them all. Hundreds of them. Maybe thousands. I can't be sure. But don't you see? I let my enemies live and Tatsuo died. Just like Master Otsuno and Sensei Watanabe…"

"You were only a child then. You could not..."

"Yes. Yes I could. I always could. I just did not try hard enough. Don't you understand? I've *always* had the power inside of me. I realize that now. I just needed to use it. I... I can hold back death itself. You and me... we can be together. Forever."

"Jion... you're scaring me."

He put his hand on top of hers and she felt how cold he was. "There is nothing to fear. I know now... all of my trainers.... my instructors... they have been holding me back. They wanted me to practice *their* way. They were jealous of my abilities. I understand it all... everything. If I had lived up to my true potential no one need ever have died. Not my father. Not Tanemochi. It is as Mistress Nikko said; my feelings are the source of my power. They give rise to action. To sit in a dusty old hall trying to let go of them... that is the way of inaction. That is why so many have died. It is my fault. Do you understand now? It is my fault because I did nothing."

"Jion... that's not..."

"Yes it is," he interrupted her again. "That is the truth . I must accept it. But now I know... I can do something about it. We need to return to Kurama. I need to save Gozen from those priests. And once we have left that place I promise that no-one will ever threaten us again."

*

Altera knelt in her tent at the base of Mount Yake. The noises of the forest echoed around her, but it was not these she was listening so intently for. She had heard Ullar arrive and begin his approach, already knowing what he was going to tell her. The entrance to the tent parted and the loyal commander stepped in.

"My Lady..." he began.

Altera opened her eyes and smiled. When she spoke, her voice was soft and happy as if she had just awoken from a pleasant dream. "Thank you. I already know of Birag's sacrifice. You have the Farravashi's location?"

"Yes My Lady, but I don't..."

"Don't try to understand. Order the men to mount up and pursue him openly... but be sure to allow him to maintain no more than a few days lead. The end game begins."

*

December 1367 – Kurama Temple

The expected snows had not materialized and Jion and Masako's race back to Kurama had been largely unimpeded. Master Kwon's returning route had merged with theirs at Nonoichi, as Jion had predicted, and the three of them had sped through the cold sleeting rain of the countryside. Behind them marched the Shogun's army, driving them ever onwards like a boat towards some hidden reef.

Yet it was not the pursuing army that unsettled the sword-master, but his protégée's silence.

The Temple Council had been hastily convened for a closed session and the masters sat listening to the accounts that each gave.

Abbot Shimada looked to Kwon. "So the mad smith is dead?"

"Yes Master Abbot."

"Can his work ever be resurrected?"

"Unlikely Master Abbot. I cast all his tools into the lava pool before I left, together with the weapons he had already forged." Kwon lied. He had not had time to destroy all Muramasa's creations, but instead sealed the entrance to the cave. Such distractions were not necessary at the moment.

"I had a courier bring the swords that were in Imai's shop here," the foreigner continued. "I trust they arrived safely?"

"They did, Master Kwon, thank you. They have been entrusted to the care of Mistress Nikko who is making a study of them. And what about you?" Shimada said turning to the impassive form of Jion. "What of the Ainu in your dreams?"

Jion's voice was a monotone. "They were mining the ore for Muramasa. I begged them to stop… I pleaded with each and every one of them. They would not listen and they attacked me. I regret that I was forced to kill them."

"All of them?"

Jion nodded. "Yes."

Shimada noticed the other masters shifting uncomfortably. Killing was not against their creed but there was something about the young man before them that gave them all cause for great concern.

"And what do you dream of now?" the abbot continued.

Jion did not reply immediately as if considering the question. "I do not dream," he eventually said.

"Nothing at all?"

"Nothing at all."

Shimada looked to the other masters. Whilst their abilities had continued to diminish, they were still able to sense some people when they were this close. Yet the young man gave away nothing. The Council may as well have been trying to read a block of granite for all that they could discern of Jion's thoughts and emotions.

"And what do you have to say about your disobedience towards this Council?" the Abbot asked.

Jion remained impassive. "It was necessary. Action was required. The threat of Muramasa arming the Shogun with swords that told of divine endorsement has been removed. The true Emperor remains on The Chrysanthemum Throne and Gozen and Masako are safe."

"And what of the loss of Tatsuo? You not feel responsible for that?"

"No. He was a retainer of the Soma Clan. It was his duty to fight and die for our cause. He went to his end willingly, and when the Clan Wars are over he will be amongst the most honored of the bujin."

Shimada suppressed a sense of pride. The young man had learned what was necessary to be a true leader; that sacrifices were necessary no matter how painful. However, The Council could not ignore the matter of disobedience.

"Regardless of the victory you perceive," the abbot began, "the laws of this temple must be…"

Jion turned his head as if listening to a distant voice and then looked to Masako, ignoring what Shimada was saying. "Get your sister. Now."

The young woman looked startled by the command and turned to The Council, looking for approval.

"Jion?" Shimada said. "What is it?"

"The Oni… they are three days from here. There are…"

Shimada looked shocked and turned to Kwon. "Is this true?"

The sword-master nodded. "We had hoped that we had lost them… but they were pursuing us from…"

There was a loud knock on the large wooden door of The Council Hall. The assembled masters muttered to themselves. This was a closed session and only the direst of emergencies could permit such an interruption.

The inner guard approached, knelt and bowed before The Council. "Master Abbot. Please forgive my rudeness. The Tyler reports that Mistress Nikko begs an audience… to report a most urgent matter."

"Admit her, inner guard," Shimada replied, unsettled by the news of the approaching army.

The door was quickly unbarred and Mistress Nikko entered and, like the inner guard before her, knelt, and then bowed to the floor.

"Sit up Mistress Nikko," Shimada said. "What do you have to report?"

"Master Abbot. The Captain of the Gate has reported a sighting of troops in the forest. Our scouts tell of a forward base being set up at the bottom of the pass."

"Do we know who they are?" the abbot asked.

"Master Abbot. The soldiers bear the Shogun's insignia."

CHAPTER SEVEN

December 1367 – Kurama Temple

"You must not leave," Mistress Nikko said. "Now is not the time."

Jion shifted his sword as he wiped the gore from his robe. "There are advance guards throughout the forest already. The Shogun means to take The Temple. I must get Gozen and Masako away."

"And what about the rest of us?" Kwon asked, rinsing the blood from his hands. For the last two nights he and Jion had undertaken raids on Yoshiakira's forces; ambushing scouting parties and intercepting messengers. Despite Jion's assertions, the Oni remained elusive and the sword-master suspected that they were hanging back, ready to act as an elite guard when the final assault began.

"What *about* the rest of you?" Jion answered coldly.

"Do we not merit your protection?" Kwon replied, stung by the young man's callous response.

"I cannot protect all of you," Jion said. "It is better that I save those I can before the fighting begins."

"Jion," Kwon said passionately. "You have a duty to this temple."

"My *duty* is to the Emperor," the young man replied. "I am sworn to restore the Soma Clan and unite the Clan Lords against the Scourge of The Chrysanthemum Throne."

"Jion," Nikko said softly. "There is much here that would benefit the Emperor… much that could be of use. The guards here are well trained… the library offers many military…"

"There is not enough time," Jion interrupted. "Yoshiakira will attack within three days. There are not enough of us to repel them."

Kwon listened to the arguments. He could see the young man's reason but there was still so much he had to learn – not just from him but from the other masters too. If Kurama fell then Jion's training would never be complete. "What about a preemptive strike?" he asked. "We take our elite and attack their main camp… give them a bloody nose. Master Abbot has already sent messengers over the mountains seeking reinforcements. We could buy them some time."

Jion tilted his head in the way that Kwon had come to recognize as the young man sending his sense out into the world. "They have been intercepted," he said eventually. "All of them. There is no help coming."

*

Ullar knelt on the frozen ground before Lady Altera and presented the message to his mistress.

"When did it arrive?" she asked, surveying the troops that trained about her.

The camp was a hive of activity as more soldiers poured in from the surrounding areas, ready for the final assault. Every Clan Lord prayed to the Buddha that it would be his men that would capture The Hero of Yugyo, and present him to the Shogun for some mark of his favor.

"Less than an hour ago, My Lady. It had to be verified," replied Ullar.

"And what does it say?"

"My Lady, the message reads 'Not yet'."

*

The door to Jion's bedchamber slid open and Gozen stepped in and bowed.

"It is good to see you," Jion said smiling. "I was worried that you would be angry with me for leaving."

"I was," Gozen said. "But I understand. You did what you thought was right… what the Emperor needed you to do."

"And what do you think?"

"You are My Lord and my husband-to-be. Whatever you do I think is right."

"That is a very diplomatic answer."

"That is the way I have been trained," Gozen replied.

For a moment the two sat in silence and the sound of novices and adepts rushing around outside drifted into the quiet room. The defense preparations were being accelerated. Guard towers were being raised, walls strengthened, and full battle drills carried out almost every hour regardless of whether it was day or night.

"How will it be?" Gozen said quietly. "When the end comes?"

"I do not know for certain," Jion replied. "Every member of The Temple… they are *so* determined to repel the Shogun… *so* sure they can win. Their conviction is inspiring but…"

"But?"

Jion shook his head. "It is not just that we are outnumbered three to one… there are Oni out there too. I know that I can kill one or two but… there must be hundreds of them now. The Oni Witch has been calling more through…"

Gozen's voice was low. "Will we die here?"

"I cannot be sure. They want me. They believe that I can be turned to Yoshiakira's cause, to fight against the Emperor… as for the rest of The Temple… you and Masako… they don't need you. We should have left as soon as I sensed them."

"Even if we could leave, where would we go? Surely you will always be hunted?"

Jion's reply was barely a whisper. "I don't know. I don't know who can be trusted."

"You can trust me," she said reaching for his hand and touching it gently.

"Thank you," he smiled. "I know."

"Is it true what you told The Council, that you have not dreamt since you killed Mutsu?"

Jion looked at Gozen, judging whether to tell her the truth. "No," he said eventually.

Her eyes widened as the realized that her fiancé had lied to The Council. "You *are* still dreaming?"

"Yes. But the dream has changed."

"What do you dream now?"

"You and I are back in Fujigatani. You look… amazing. Radiant… as if you are glowing. We find Chikatane… but then there is shouting and things become confused. I think that there is someone else there too… maybe more than a single ally…"

"What happens?"

"I don't know. It ends in a jumble of images and noise."

"What does Master Kwon say?"

Jion looked at her meaningfully. "I haven't told him."

"But… he's your most trusted instructor… you rode for how many weeks with him?"

"He is the same as the others. They fear me and are jealous of my abilities. I sense it in all of them."

"No Jion. That cannot be true. They gave us sanctuary… looked after us all these years… they only want what's best for you."

"I don't believe that. They have always known what I am. You have seen them… how they are around me. How they try to mold me… shape me into being something that they find acceptable. It is like Mistress Nikko said…"

"You have spoken to her?"

Jion nodded. "When I first returned."

"Why do you trust her over the other masters?"

Jion shrugged. "She has been with us since Yugyo. She saw what really happened there. Everyone else… they talk about it, but they don't really *know*. They don't appreciate what we went through. Mistress Nikko… she has always taught me to be myself… that I am an instrument of action. She understands what I am."

Gozen spoke softly again. "I understand what you are."

"I know you do," he replied, squeezing her hand back in a sign of mutual affection. "I don't know what I would do without you or Masako. I think I would go mad if you were both not with me."

"Jion," she said, moving closer into him. "If we are to die here, I… I want to have known you. At least once…" she whispered, bringing her lips to his.

*

It was the hour of the rooster, but already winter had cast the shawl of night over the land. The walls of The Temple were lined with guards, and torches burned brightly, casting long shadows into the forest. Jion slipped silently out of his room, leaving the sleeping form of Gozen behind him, and began to make his way across the courtyard towards the library.

"You're playing with fire," Kwon said, stepping out of the gloom.

Jion stopped and turned to face his instructor. Of all the masters at Kurama, the sword-master had developed the quietest mind in recent months, and although Jion knew that he was there, he believed that the foreigner was asleep.

"Maybe. Maybe not," the young man replied noncommittally.

"You missed The Council meeting this afternoon," Kwon continued. "The debrief from last night and…"

Jion smiled and shook his head. "We lost two scout parties but took seven of theirs. Forces continue to build at the bottom of the pass but the climb up to The Temple is too narrow for them all to come through so when they attack we'll hold them in a bottle neck and strike from the sides in a pincer movement. I heard everything thank you Master Kwon."

It was Kwon's turn to smile. "Be careful of the faith you put in your abilities Jion. If you rely on them too much they will be your undoing. Will you partner with me again for tonight's assignment?"

"I will."

"Thank you. Now, what are you going to do about Gozen?"

"What is there to be done?"

"Jion, do not be so foolish as to think that you are the first man to believe that he can have everything. I saw how Masako looked at you when we rode from Nonoichi. I also saw how you looked at her."

"You're imagining things," Jion turned and made to walk away.

Kwon stepped in front of him, blocking his path. "I very much doubt that. Jion, remember what I taught you. The more you become attached to things… the more you try to own them, the more they own you."

"Thank you. I remember the lesson well." Jion tried to side-step past him, but the sword-master anticipated the young man and moved with him.

"Jion, listen to me," he said, grabbing the boys arm. "Death is a natural part of life. If you hold on to your attachments too hard you will break them and then forever blame yourself. You must let go. Accept fate."

The young man looked down at the sword-master's hand, feeling the fingers that held him and knowing how easily he could cast them off. "There is no fate but the one I make," he replied, shrugging out of Kwon's grasp and walking past his instructor.

"Jion, please," Kwon called after him. "We need you now more than ever."

Jion carried on walking.

*

"Do you trust me?" the head librarian asked.

"Yes Mistress Nikko," Jion replied. The two sat in the darkened library that was empty except for them, the usual students having gone to man the walls.

"You sense that all is not as it should be? That events are moving too quickly?"

"Yes, Mistress Nikko. I do not trust The Council either. Two of our scouting parties were killed last night because of their folly. There was no need for them have been on the western ridge without proper support."

"Yes… you are quite right," Nikko replied. "Their powers have weakened so much that they are blind to the consequences of their own actions."

"They teach that the enlightened let go of attachments but they cling stubbornly to their old beliefs. We are trapped here because of them," Jion said.

"You know your destiny, Jion. You *must* accept your father's mantle. You must become the next Lord Soma."

"Yes," he replied. "I know."

"Good. Trust in the Goddess. She will guide your way."

*

"Well?" Abbot Shimada asked.

Kwon bowed low before the abbot and the few Council elders who were not on duty with the guards. "Master Abbot, as you commanded, I have consulted my Queen's chronicle. It is quite clear. The boy will save The Temple. He *is* the child of the prophecy."

"Prophecies can be interpreted in many ways," the abbot replied. "How sure are you, Master Kwon?"

"Very sure, Master Abbot."

Shimada nodded but remained unsure. "Tell us again Master Kwon, what was it the mad smith said about Jion?"

"He seemed to suggest that... that time was malleable... that Jion would not live the life we believed he would."

"Is that possible, Master Kwon?"

"Anything is possible, Master Abbot... we cannot deny that, since Yugyo, the Shogun has sought to acquire Jion rather than kill him... and we all know the influence that the Oni Witch exerts over Yoshiakira... but what she wants with him, who can say."

The Abbot breathed deeply. "Master Kwon, whatever their intent may be, this temple is now committed to battle. Three more scouting parties have failed to report back in the last hour and there are now open skirmishes in the forest."

"I understand, Master Abbot."

"I hope you do, Master Kwon, because we are losing out there. I am withdrawing you from your scouting assignment tonight. I want you to go through your Queen's chronicle line-by-line and report to this Council how Jion is going to save us."

*

Jion stood in the courtyard, watching The Council Elders leaving the main hall.

"Come out Masako," he said, not turning around.

The young lady stepped out from the shadows. "You always know where I am, don't you?" she said smiling.

"Always," he said, smiling back.

"You're going scouting tonight?"

"Yes. It is The Council's order. I must find some weakness in Yoshiakira's strategy."

"I know..." she replied, looking down at the flagstones. "... but I worry. I wish you weren't going."

"I'll be fine," he laughed. "Master Kwon will be with me..."

"Actually," a voice said behind Jion, "Master Kwon has been given another assignment. I will be your companion tonight."

Jion turned to see Master Takamori, and bowed.

"Jion," he said nodding his head. "Masako," he bowed more deeply to the young lady, and then looked back to his charge. "The Council commands us to follow the line of the river down to the pass, report what forces have built-up since last night and, if possible, interrupt their lines."

Jion bowed his head. *At last*, he mind-talked to Masako. *Action.*

Please Jion... be careful.

*

The moon was but a sliver of silver in the clear night sky, and Lady Altera watched the swelling ranks of her army as they prepared their weapons and armor.

"You are sure?" she said.

"Very sure, My Lady," Ullar replied.

"Show me the message," she demanded, holding out her hand.

Ullar put the fragment of parchment into her palm and stepped back, bowing his head respectfully as he did so.

Lady Altera looked down at the single word inscribef upon it. *Now!*

"Do it," she whispered.

Ullar turned. "Captains!" he bellowed. "All captains to report immediately! Weapon masters to your stations!"

The camp erupted as senior officers ran forward to receive their orders and began relaying them down the lines. Companies of soldiers formed up, messengers relayed deployment instructions, and bows and spears were handed out as horses whinnied and stamped impatiently.

Altera looked about her as her war machine swung smoothly into a combat formation like some well-oiled siege engine, and she knew that her victory would be glorious.

*

Master Takamori and Jion stepped quietly through the mountain forest, following the line of the river but never stepping out onto its bank where they would be seen easily.

They had already come upon one of Yoshiakira's scouting parties and had killed the three men quickly and quietly. Jion was throwing his inner-self repeatedly into the trees but there were so many troops in the woods that he was finding it difficult to keep track of them all.

Takamori knelt beside a thick cedar and pointed to an outcrop. Jion nodded and sent his sense along the stony floor and over the top of the rocks.

"Clear," he whispered, and the two men stepped gingerly forward. Keeping low to the ground, they ran for the cover of the shadows.

"What have you got?" Takamori asked as they leaned against the large stones, catching their breath.

"There are two units about a mile east. No more than two or three soldiers in each. I think they're searching for a tunnel in case there is a secret escape route from The Temple," Jion replied.

"They'll be lucky. That place was built to keep everyone in," the older man chuckled. "What else?"

"There's a build up along the western ridge again. But the path is too narrow for a bujin in full armor. They've already lost eleven men to slips and falls…"

"Shame…" Takamori said sarcastically.

"There were some horsemen coming up the main path but I cannot sense them now. I think they turned back," Jion continued. "There are plenty of men in the trees… none near us… I don't think they are heavily armed. Just a sword and one or two have short bows. They're watching us as much as we're watching them."

"How many of them are out there… in total?"

Jion sent his sense up into the night sky, feeling for the telltale signs of the noisy minds. "A few hundred in the forest. Maybe a thousand. There are more in the pass."

Takamori nodded grimly. "That's nearly double what they sent out last night. It's getting too dangerous to be out here. We'd better go back."

"But what about our assignment?" Jion asked, once again frustrated by the lack of direct action. "We are to interrupt their lines."

"*If possible*, Jion," Takamori hissed. "You must not look on everything as being so black and white. We could not undertake that part of our assignment without substantial risk…"

"Then you would not die for Kurama? You would not die for what you claim to love?" Jion challenged.

"You know that it is not that simple," Takamori said softly, trying to calm the young man down. "What good would we be if we were dead? Come on. We've got a report to file."

"No," Jion said obstinately, standing up. "We were given an assignment. It is our duty to complete it."

"It is your *duty* to obey me," Takamori snapped. "Now sit back down before you're seen."

"No," Jion replied, taking a step backward. "You are a coward. Always running and hiding and debating things until it is too late…"

"Jion!" Takamori barked. "This is not the time to discuss such things. Follow me."

"I *will* complete our mission," Jion retorted and made to move off in the direction of the main path.

"Jion!" Takamori stood, enraged at the young man's disobedience.

Jion looked back at the old monk and at that moment the world turned black and white. He stood watching the death cloud chattering behind Takamori but made no move to save his instructor. The man was a coward. He knew that now. All of The Temple masters were cowards, skulking in the dark like rats. Endlessly talking matters over. Fleeing at the first sign of danger.

As the world regained color Jion carried on walking and he heard the sound of two arrows thumping into Takamori's back, sending his instructor to the ground. He sent his sense up into the trees and realized that there were more spies than he had first thought. Jion knew he could cut some of their arrows down but not all of them.

With a heavy heart, he turned north and began jogging back to The Temple.

*

The candle in Master Kwon's room spluttered as another wintry blast rattled the screen wall. Instinctively the sword-master shielded it with his hand and turned the page of the Queen's chronicle, desperately searching for answers.

For the first time he appreciated how vague the descriptions were. The boy would do this and that, but the detail was lacking. The account did not give exact dates or reference wider events from which Kwon could put the boy's actions into context.

What was clear was that it was the Oni Witch who was influencing Yoshiakira, and she in turn seemed to have some deeper insight into Jion's character as though she was being fed information…

Kwon paused, realizing the conclusion his reasoning was bringing him to.

A traitor?

With renewed fervor, he began to rescan the pages. There was no mention of Jion going to Mount Yake, so that was new. The order in which his abilities manifested was wrong. The Nokizaru attack was early. Sensei Watanabe should not have died when he did. The reason for leaving Yugyo was different…

Kwon began to make a note of all the names the chronicle listed. Shimada and Sonkan were there. Takamori, Hiroyasu, Otsuno… all the principal players were mentioned. Gozen, Masako, even his name.

The sword-master felt himself tense as realization broke over him like a wave, threatening to drag him into the depths of madness.

I know who is not supposed to be here…

*

Jion leaned against the outer wall of Kurama Temple, breathing hard as the cold of the night pressed upon him. He had run the last two miles up the steep slopes of the mountain, dispatching what enemies he chanced upon, and could now feel sweat beading on his back in spite of the winter chill.

A face appeared at the top of the wall and an array of loaded bows pointed down at him. "Who goes there?" a voice commanded.

"It's me… Jion," the young man panted. "Sound the alarm… they are not far behind… an hour at most."

Jion had sensed the advancing cavalry; a vast body of men and weapons flanked by more infantry and archers. And behind them the darkness that was the Oni spurred them on. For the last mile, his jog had turned into a sprint as he had sensed the horde of death surging forward up the pass while all about him the forest filled with ever increasing numbers of scouts who called and whistled back down the line, bringing the enemy forward.

The gate swung open a fraction, allowing Jion to dart inside The Temple grounds. Already the bell was sounding and novices and adepts mixed with the guards that poured out from the barracks. Commands echoed around the courtyard as the vast body of soldiers was coordinated to a multitude of positions, and the warriors prepared for the coming onslaught, desperately trying to shrug off the sleep that they had been enjoying. Master Kwon appeared in a doorway but did not join his comrades.

"Jion," he barked at the still panting young man.

The Hero of Yugyo looked up, still trying to catch his breath, and instantly knew something was wrong. Kwon's unlined face was grim and hardened like granite, and now the master was crossing the courtyard towards him.

"I know that we've had our differences over the years," Kwon began, "but everything I have ever done is because I have loved you like my own son… because I believe in you. Do you understand me?"

Jion shook his head, not looking the man in the eye. "Not really."

"Jion… I am going to ask you something. And I need you to tell me the truth… Has Mistress Nikko ever asked you to keep a secret? From me or from anyone?"

Jion paused a fraction too long and Kwon guessed the answer.

"I knew it!" the sword-master said, stamping his foot in frustration. "Jion… you need to come with me. Right now."

"But…" the young man looked around as the soldiers began to form up into their respective companies. "What about…?"

"They do not matter. What matters is you. *You* Jion. *You* are our hope!"

"Against the tyrants?" he muttered. "I know."

Kwon whirled around, grabbing the young man by his robes and forcing him back up against the wall. "Where did you hear that?" he hissed and then, realizing what he was doing, let go. "Come with me. You need to hear something."

*

The Bandit King, Nagamasa, stood at the lookout point, watching the procession of torchlight make its way up the mountain pass towards Kurama Temple, and sighed loudly. It had taken so many years to coax these events together, and he was proud of the small part he had played.

"My Lord?" Tamazaki asked, grateful for the furs that held the worst of the cold at bay.

"You know what this means, don't you?" Nagamasa said, pretending to be grumpy.

"No My Lord."

"It means that once again, I am going to have to help the Emperor… and you know how I hate doing that."

"What is your wish My Lord?" Tamazaki asked, silently praying that he was not going to be ordered into the maelstrom to rescue the boy. The years since he had assisted Gasan and Tatsuo had not been kind, and his face was now weathered from travel and scarred from a dose of small pox.

All the time he had sought, on his Lord's orders, to maintain balance between the Shogun and the Emperor… to keep the two sides evenly matched. War was profitable, but if The Hero of Yugyo fell to the Shogun… well that would mean a lot more work for him, and he was getting old and tired. He knew what he wanted and for a moment he drifted off, thinking about the courtesan he had rescued three years ago from some ransacked village or other, and how grateful she had been. Yes, too much war and not enough pillowing.

"Did you hear me?" Nagamasa said, turning to his lieutenant.

Tamazaki flushed. "I… My Lord, I apologize."

Nagamasa rolled his eyes. In his youth he would have taken the man's head for such insolence, but in his advancing years he had learned that permitting such a slight often endeared him to his now expanding City of Thieves. If someone knew that they should have been killed, they tended to be very grateful for being alive.

"I said that Prince Chokei has a scouting party at Himeyama Castle. You'd better go and fetch them. The Buddha knows how long he has been searching for the boy."

"But… My Lord, Himeyama is at least a day's ride from here. They'll never get here in time," Tamazaki protested.

Nagamasa stifled his frustration. "They don't have to get in here in time to save The Temple… just in time to lead the boy to safety."

"But…"

Nagamasa looked hard at his lieutenant, his eyes now blazing. "I said go."

*

The doors to the library burst open and the dark robed figure of Kwon strode forward, sword already drawn. Jion followed with a look of confusion.

Mistress Nikko sat on a cushion, flanked by Gozen and Masako who were leaning forward, examining a scroll that told of deep meditation, trying to ignore the clamor of war outside.

"It's you, isn't it?" Kwon accused, pointing his sword at Nikko. "All this time it was you. I should cut you down where you are."

Gozen and Masako's eyes widened and they scuttled quickly backwards to one of the shelves.

Nikko stood, every inch the demure and disciplined master. "You come to accuse me, Master Kwon?" she said, spreading her hands in a sign of innocence.

"I do... I accuse you. What are you? Oni?"

Jion paled and turned to the librarian. "Mistress Nikko? What is he saying? Is it true?"

Nikko smiled softly and looked at Kwon. "That word has no meaning here and neither do you, foreigner," she replied, spitting the last word out as if it were a bitter fruit.

Kwon approached Nikko cautiously. "Jion... this is not a woman. She looks like one but, like all the devils, it is just a mask."

"I... I... I don't understand," Jion began, torn between his two instructors.

Kwon reached into his robe and tossed a dark leather bound book to Jion. "Where I come from," he began, "my Queen knew you. She knew you very well and she chronicled your life... it's all there, in that book. Except the life you live now... it's not the one you were *supposed* to live. Something has taken your fate Jion... it has twisted it. We're all in that book... me, Gozen, Masako, the Abbot... everyone. Everyone except *her*..." he jabbed at Nikko who did not flinch.

"She... She is not supposed to be here," Kwon continued. "She never existed... and whatever she has been telling you... it's all lies. Everything about her is a lie. Everything!"

Jion was thumbing through the tome in his hand but could make no sense of the strange script. He looked up at Nikko and asked, "Is it true?"

"What is truth?" Nikko asked. "You know that the world is what you make it. We saw you... we saw your potential, and I was sent to guide you..."

"Then you *are* Oni?" Jion cried, feeling betrayal and rage rush up from the abyss within him, and drew the Ishin Blade, letting the book fall noisily to the floor.

"Oni is a term... like bujin. You have known warriors who have supported you, and those who have betrayed you. The word is no measure of character or indication of allegiance. It tells you nothing of purpose or capability. Think Jion... think of everything I have done for you. How I nursed your talents... how I encouraged you to save Gozen and Masako from the Ainu..."

"What about the Goddess?" Jion asked, his voice beginning to crack as tears prickled in his eyes.

Kwon's head snapped around to look at his young ward. "The what?"

Tears were now cascading down Jion's cheek. "Marishiten... she helped me pray to the great Mother..."

Kwon looked back to Nikko his face contorted in rage. "Is that what She is calling Herself now? The last time it took the bujin three hundred years to drive Her from their hearts… it will not take the same again."

The sword-master advanced on the librarian, but to his surprise, she reached into the folds of her robe and drew her own sword. "She already walks with the children," she said, and then turned to Jion. "Think for yourself. Think what I have shown you while these fools just sit and talk."

"Don't listen to her Jion," Kwon barked, advancing on the librarian. He jabbed with his sword, but she parried it easily.

"If my words were so blasphemous you would know them as such. But all the things I have taught… that I have yet to teach you. Think of the power Jion. *Think*. Think of your brother and father… think of your revenge."

"No. That is not the way," Kwon replied. "You must let go of the past or it will consume you. Do not believe her lies!"

Again the swords clashed and the library filled with the sound of steel on steel as the rest of The Temple ran to their positions along the wall, unaware of the battle that raged within their own grounds.

*

Nagamasa was coming down the narrow mountain path when a figure stepped out from the deep shadows. Although it had been many years since he had seen Lady Altera he recognized her immediately.

"My Lady," he said bowing deeply.

"Nagamasa," she replied curtly. "How goes the day?"

"Fair. You?"

"As you can see, we will have The Temple."

Nagamasa turned to look at the slope that led up to Kurama. The front line was minutes away. "And the child?" he asked.

"Arrangements have been made."

"Rumors are that a foreigner is there too."

"Sadly true. But he has played the game poorly."

Nagamasa chuckled. "They always do. You have new orders for me?"

"Just make sure the child is delivered to the Emperor. Then make a few strikes on some of Yoshiakira's outer villages. It'll keep the war going."

"Very good, My Lady. However it is said that both the Emperor and the Shogun have revived their peace talks."

"Unfortunately so."

"Have enough of our shrines been built to have made this venture worthwhile?"

"Not yet."

"It would be a shame if peace came too soon. The people of this land only pray when they are faced with strife. Do you have… a contingency?"

Altera smiled. "Don't worry my Bandit King. The people will have their war and our Mother will have Her prayers."

*

Shimada stood in the guard tower looking down on the line of advancing torchlight that was the Shogun's army. Despite all his years of training he still felt the barest tremble of fear that Yoshiakira had dared to invade holy ground. Just like his father, the man was capable of anything.

The abbot turned to Hiroyasu. "You're sure about this?"

The old master bowed his head. "Yes Master Abbot. It is the last thing they will expect."

"It is the last thing *I'd* expect," Shimada muttered and turned to the captain. "Very well. Make it so."

The captain lit a torch and signaled to his opposite numbers in the other guard towers along the wall. More torches were lit in response and orders were barked down the lines. In the courtyard three divisions of infantry prepared themselves.

The captain turned back to Shimada. "We are ready, Master Abbot."

The old monk nodded grimly. "Make it so."

The captain shouted a command and the thick wooden gate of The Temple began to swing slowly open. Behind the lines of infantry, archers drew their bows back and released a volley into the woods followed by a second. As soon as the arrows were away, the infantry charged forward, streaming down the mountain slopes, using the higher ground to their advantage.

*

Ullar listened to the clash of blades from further up the pass, and frowned. He had not anticipated that The Temple would send its soldiers out to meet the Shogun's forces, and this would mean committing his cavalry earlier than he had expected.

Still, it was not as if they could win. Ullar brought his horn to his lips and sounded the cavalry to charge Kurama's spearmen.

*

Again Kwon's sword sliced down, hissing through the air. Nikko parried but this time the foreigner sidestepped, bringing himself inside her guard, and shoulder-charged the librarian. She saw it just in time and began to spin out the way but the foreigner caught her, sending her off balance. Kwon kicked out at her rear leg, and Nikko sprawled to the floor.

"Jion!" she implored. "Think of all I that have taught you… all that I have yet to teach you."

"Don't listen to her," Kwon replied. "She is Oni. All they know is lies."

"Jion!" Nikko begged, looking to the young man. "I helped you save the girls… you know that there is more danger ahead… you have dreamed it. I know you have. You need me…"

Jion stood still, confusion and indecision etched on his face as Kwon struck down at the prone form of Nikko, who only just blocked the killing strike.

"Stop," the young man said. "Master Kwon… this is madness. You are both senior instructors here…"

"Don't listen to her Jion," Kwon replied, his eyes bulging in rage as he pressed down on his sword and forcing Nikko's down to her throat. "Her kind needs to be exterminated."

"No… that's not what you taught me. You have always taught me to forgive. If what you say is true then forgive *her*… I still need her."

Kwon looked to his ward, instantly feeling the conflict between his teachings and his actions. Nikko saw the distraction and snapped her leg out in double sidekick, first connecting with Kwon's groin and as he doubled, his shin. The sword-master sprawled to the floor and Nikko rolled away, picked herself up and brought her sword to a guard.

Kwon lay choking, trying to catch his breath as the too familiar ache radiated from his crotch upwards through his abdomen to settle as nausea in his stomach. Jion stepped in between the dueling instructors.

"Tell me the truth," he said to Nikko.

She smiled and spoke softly. "You know better than that. There are no truths. There are only perspectives."

"Then tell me yours," Jion demanded. "What do you know of this Queen of Murkwood? What is your role in my fate?"

"His so-called Queen?" Nikko nodded towards the rising form of Kwon. "She gathered all the traitors together… to battle a true lord of the land. You know about that sort of betrayal, don't you? She claims the power of prophecy to manipulate the weak minded…"

"But what about his book?" Jion challenged. "Master Kwon says it tells of a different path that I walk…"

"Have you read it?" Nikko retorted. "Can anyone read it? It is nothing but a mass of indecipherable gibberish. And even if it wasn't… would you believe something just because it is written down?"

"Lies," Kwon gasped, still sagging from the pain in his belly. "You cannot believe her."

"Use your mind Jion," Nikko said. "Look at the evidence. I have shown you how to use your powers… how to save the ones you love. What has this fool ever done? Tell you to wait and consider matters whilst everyone you care about is taken from you."

"That's not true," Kwon staggered, bringing his sword up and sidestepping Jion. "I have taught him to cut through the noise of his own mind… to become aware of all things. He will know the truth."

Kwon swung his sword lazily at Nikko who parried it easily and sent the foreigner spinning into a shelf laden with old scrolls.

"Jion," Nikko implored. "You *must* help me. Kwon… he is deranged… blinded by lies and half-truths. I have so much still to teach you. Only I can help you save your love…"

"No!" Kwon shouted and made a desperate charge for the librarian.

*

The Shogun's cavalry leapt over the first line of spearmen and charged towards the main gate that lay open before them like some submissive concubine. Kurama's archers let another volley go, cutting the black clad horsemen down, but some made it through. The horses wheeled in the courtyard, stamping and snorting as their riders fought to bring them under control, and then charged the line of bowmen. The archers scattered and then reassembled, letting another volley go as more horsemen came through the gate.

In the forest, companies of infantry clashed and the cries of the dying echoed through the trees. The Kurama line surged forward, pressing the enemy back, only to be repulsed as the Shogun's men were reinforced from behind.

Although the monk's tactics had surprised Ullar at first, from his vantage point he could see that his troops had regained the initiative and were pushing the infantry back on to The Temple walls where they would be pinned and then slaughtered. He sounded his horn again and watched as runners brought flaming braziers up to the thousands of archers, who lit their arrows and took aim at The Temple.

*

Shimada frowned as the twinkling of flames filtered through the woods, and then his eyes widened in realization.

"Everyone down!" the abbot shouted as the sound of whistling arrows filled the air.

What little starlight shone down was briefly obscured as thousands of arrows filled the air like a black swarm, and rained death along the walls. The Temple's own runners began to fill buckets from the river, hastily trying to extinguish the pockets of fire before they spread.

The sound of galloping hooves told of another advance of Yoshiakira's cavalry, and a moment later more horses poured through the gate, forcing Kurama's spearmen into a desperate rearguard action as they became pinned against their own forward-facing comrades.

More flames were lit and shouts echoed through the forest, warning of another hail of arrows. Some of the previous volley had taken, and thick smoke began to roll across the scene as thatch kindled and then burst into flames.

"There is more incoming," Shimada muttered and ducked as the arrows sliced through the air and brief screams filled their immediate surroundings before quickly dwindling to a gurgle and then nothing.

The abbot turned and saw Hiroyasu slumped against the guard tower wall, a black arrow cruelly protruding from his side. The old monk looked at the abbot, smiled weakly, and pulled the arrow from his body, allowing himself to bleed out and pass quickly away.

Shimada shook his head and tried to ignore the swell of grief inside him. "We're losing, captain," he said to the soldier beside him.

"Yes Master Abbot," the captain replied.

Beyond the main gate, he could see the Shogun's forces pushing his men back. Their lines were in disarray as more cavalry charged, and the horses that had already made it through were harrying their archers, not allowing them to fire any clean shots. What infantry were not already committed were held in a bottleneck between the woods and the path, and the volley of arrows that was raining down on them was now picking these off too. All around were the bodies of his men, and the captain knew that the day would not be theirs.

"Do you have any suggestions?" Shimada asked.

The captain saw the twinkling fires in the distance and instinctively knew that another shower of arrows was imminent. "Down!" he said, pulling the abbot to the floor.

*

"Jion!" Kwon barked, as he parried another shot. "Listen. Think!"

Nikko slashed at him again. "That is all you do. Think."

Kwon parried her blade downwards, tried to charge her again but missed, and the gap between the two combatants opened again.

"Jion. Your father's sword. She has seen it, but never touched it. Am I right?" Kwon did not need to look at his apprentice for an answer. "The symbol on it... the two concentric circles linked by the nine lines... it is one of the few things that kills the Oni. You know this. It's how you killed the demon at Yugyo.

"Gozen wears it too. The amulet you gave her. But Masako... she has always been vulnerable. You had your sword, Gozen her pendant... but Masako had nothing. She..." Kwon jabbed at Nikko, "saw this. It was her who split the girls up. She sent Gozen to Shimada's side because she knew she could never corrupt her whilst she wore that amulet."

"No," Masako whined from the library shelf. "It's not true."

"It *is*," Kwon said. "Think where all the jealousy has come from. She has played you. She has played us all. All the division... the arguments... all the words Masako spoke to you… those were *her* words. She has been turning you from your true path all these years."

"Your true path?" Nikko laughed, jabbing back at Kwon. "To sit and discuss while the world burns? Kwon sees shadows where there are none and yet does nothing about the darkness at our door. Everything he has said is a lie. Jion… who else but I could have made you what you are today? Who else could have helped you save the women you love?"

The teenager felt his mind fog with confusion. Mistress Nikko had not denied her part but, without her, he would have never known Marishiten. And what of Master Kwon? There was more to this foreigner than …

The familiar shades of black and white returned, and Jion felt the wheels of time slow and then stop. Arrow shafts lined the library's wooden floor, having punctured through the roof above and their cruelly serrated heads still burned, threatening to set light to the whole building.

But that was not the young man's concern right now.

In front of him, his two instructors stood a few meters apart, swords held aggressively as their respective swings hung frozen in mid air. He recognized the dark cloud that chattered like insects, hanging over both Kwon and Nikko, and knew what it meant.

There was no time to save both of them, and even if he could he was not sure that he wanted to. The onslaught of accusations was tearing him apart. He wanted to believe in each of them but knew that he could not follow both the teachings that were laid out before him.

One was the way of forgiveness and calculated reaction. The other was that of passion and deed.

Both had brought him this far and yet Jion could not escape the feeling that he was not the warrior that he was meant to be… that somehow his destiny eluded him still.

As the seconds began to run out Jion exhaled and let go of his attachments.

*

Ullar watched the first wave of his infantry being cut down, forcing the temple's defensive line to break. Before they could reform, his cavalry had cleared the fallen bodies, advanced into the courtyard, and had begun to harry the troops within.

Too late, the temple guards had wheeled to face the threat from behind only to be cut down as the archers concealed in the trees rained death on to their exposed backs. Spearmen picked off what was left, and Ullar was bringing the horn to his lips to signal another volley from his archers when Altera appeared from the darkness behind him and laid a hand on his shoulder.

"The boy has chosen. You may raze whatever is left to the ground."

CHAPTER EIGHT

March 1368 – Anrakuji Temple, Mount Homan, Tsukushi Isle

It was the hour of the monkey, and the spring breeze cooled Jion's hot body as he performed another one-handed handstand. Slowly, he began to press himself up and down, pushing his already aching muscles to their limit. Using his sense of the ever present flow of life about him he corrected his balance without toppling, his long sinewy arm working hard as sweat flowed freely from him.

"Good," Masako said as she balanced on one leg and slowly turned, extending her other leg high above her head in a perfectly executed sidekick. "Now do it with no-arms."

Jion gritted his teeth and smiled. With great concentration, he withdrew the arm supporting him and hung motionless in the air, a few inches from The Temple flagstones. Closing his eyes, he willed his body to remain in place, suspended for Masako to see.

She tried not to be impressed, but could not help herself. They had been working on his abilities since their arrival a month ago, as Jion rededicated himself to his mission. This was the first time that the young man had truly succeeded in his mastering his physical self.

The distant sound of approaching footsteps caused Masako to turn her head, and Jion lowered himself to the ground slowly, swinging his legs over his head so that he was upright.

"It's Gozen," he said, having sensed the conversation in Chokei's private room. "The Prince wishes to see us. He is going to make us an offer."

Masako grunted an acknowledgement, lowered her extended leg, and pulled on her robe. "Have we got time for an onsen? I could really use one."

Jion shook his head, putting his own clothes on. "No."

"What's the offer?" she asked.

Jion smiled. "You'll see."

The familiar form of Gozen walked up the steps to one of the many training courtyards that made up The Temple complex. Where Kurama had been a small town, The Temple of Anrakuji was like a bustling city, filled with tens of thousands of priests and politicians, and acted as the de facto Imperial Court following the fall of Yoshino. Gozen's diplomatic skills had come into their own in this environment as she lobbied and petitioned both Clan Lords and Imperial Ministers to support Jion's cause and grant him an army to strike a deadly blow to the Shogun's war machine. The proposal to attack Fujigatani and sever the supply lines provided by the northern lords had met with a mixed response, with some seeing the benefit whilst others believed there to be more important targets.

"Master Jion," Gozen said, bowing her head and acknowledging the rank the startled Temple Council had conferred on the young man when they had witnessed his powers. "Sister," she continued, bowing perfunctorily to a sour-faced Masako. It was no secret that their flight from Kurama had done nothing to heal the rift between the two girls, despite the elder's hopes. "Prince Chokei demands your presence."

"Does he?" Jion said smiling, still ill at ease with the intense formality of the Imperial Court.

"Yes Master Jion. He does," Gozen said coolly.

"Well then, it won't do to keep him waiting. After you, My Lady," he replied, indicating that his fiancé should lead the way.

Despite his jovial demeanor, Jion was nervous. He knew that Chokei would make him an offer that would allow him his revenge on Chikatane, but the cost would be high.

As he trotted down the steps, he marveled at The Temple about him. Despite the impressive buildings, he found his attention drawn to the svelte figure of Gozen in front of him, and he struggled to remember the girl that she had been. It was a testament to them all how far they had all come in the few months since The Fall of Kurama.

They had fled eastwards along one of the lesser used paths. With all of the Shogun's forces focused on a frontal attack, they had faced no serious challenge. Nevertheless, the lack of provisions had been worrying, and more than once Jion had become convinced that they would all die of exposure on the mountain slopes.

However, The Hero of Yugyo knew it was not through luck that Prince Chokei had found and rescued them. The man had been searching for him for years, but Jion was shocked that the Prince had done so with the aid of Ienao, who had confirmed his identity.

The bully who had so tormented him at Yugyo had grown into a strong bujin, albeit one that wore a perpetual scowl around Jion, and he sensed that he would have to address the unfinished business between the two of them at some point. For now, Jion was glad that there was someone independent of his group to vouch for him.

From the slopes, and the pall of death that hung over the forest as Kurama burned, Jion's party had traveled to the port city of Naniwa. The whole province had been in uproar at the attack - and the loss of so many lives - that it was necessary for the band of survivors to travel as refugees, lest they be recognized, or worse arrested and handed over to the Shogun. Ships had been impossible to come by as merchants charged extortionate rates for safe passage out of the region, and it was only when Jion had sent word to his old pirate friend Captain Kagetaka that they had been able to charter a vessel to Tsukushi Isle. The corsair had been less than happy that his passengers were of the imperial line – such cargo tended to bring unwanted attention – but Chokei sufficiently compensated the pirate, and Kagetaka's mood had lightened a little.

Even now, The Sophia lay anchored in one of the island's secluded bays, the entire crew now on the imperial payroll, waiting for the Prince and Jion to reach an accord. The sailors did not mind being paid to do nothing but sit in a tavern and compete for the attention of the local ladies, but Kagetaka was unused to being on land for so long, and more than once he had mentioned to Jion how he longed to be back at sea. For his part, Jion found himself repeating his master's words, urging the captain to be patient and to wait for events to reveal themselves when the time was right.

It was during these moments that Jion wondered if he had saved the wrong instructor.

*

"Master Jion," Prince Chokei said warmly to the kneeling figure who had pressed his head to the mat, "please, sit up."

Jion raised himself but kept his eyes on the floor directly in front of him, as was the custom. "Thank you Your Highness. I am not worthy to be in your presence."

Chokei smiled thinly. "Your worth has yet to be determined. Your companions have made a strong case on your behalf and your skills have impressed The Temple Council. I am minded to petition The Emperor, my father, on your behalf. However, as is our tradition, he will expect something in return."

"I understand Your Highness."

"Not yet, you don't," Chokei replied. "Your skills with the sword are most noteworthy, especially given your age. Your instructor has said that you believe that you can destroy Lord Chikatane and retake Fujigatani with the aid of only fourteen men. Is that correct?"

"Yes, Your Highness… if I am permitted to train them myself."

"I see. Then the bargain is this: if you are successful, on your return you will instruct the whole of The Emperor's army in these... skills. The fourteen men will become your most trusted lieutenants and they too will teach as you train another intake and so on. Additionally, on your return, you will marry the Lady Gozen and unite the clans of Soma and Nawa against the Shogun. Is this agreeable?"

"Yes, Your Highness."

"Then swear it."

Jion looked up from the mat, his face one of grim resolve. "I swear it."

*

It was the hour of the pig, and night had fallen across Tsukushi. On a stony beach, not far from Anrakuji Temple, a single figure stood looking out across the small sea that separated the island from Yamato. The spring tide was high and, despite the choppy waters, a little boat made its way towards the lonely silhouette. Presently the boat ran on to the shore and the waiting figure stepped forward to greet her mistress.

"Lady Altera," Nikko said, kneeling low and addressing the figure on the rickety craft. "It has been many years."

"It has Nikko," Altera replied, stepping off the boat and onto the deserted beach. "You may stand."

"Thank you, My Lady. I was relieved that you have been receiving my messages. Truly, I did not know if they would reach you. The people of this land are such savages..."

"I could not have taken Kurama without you," Altera responded warmly, hugging Nikko in the way a mother would hug a child. "And I am sorry that you have had to spend so long amongst these barbarians. What is it? Twenty years now?"

"Nearer thirty, My Lady."

"Stars, has it really been that long? The Great Mother thanks you for your service and so do I."

"No thanks are necessary My Lady. I was only doing my duty to The Goddess. Did you find Kwon?"

Altera shook her head. "No. We razed The Temple... burned everything and everybody. But, when we sifted through the rubble, his was the only body unaccounted for. What happened in the library?"

"The Farravashi... he has some sort of precognition. He can tell when those he feels an emotional attachment to are in mortal danger. Jion told me he sensed that arrows were about to strike at me and the foreigner and he had to choose... he chose me."

"You have done well with that one. Does he know that Kwon is probably still alive?"

"My Lady, he does not. I thought it for the best to let Jion believe his former master to be dead."

"Good. That was the right decision. Our spies reported that a foreigner booked passage to Tianxia from one of the northern ports. Kwon has fled Oyashima and I doubt very much that he will ever come back. He must know that he has nothing to return for."

"Then this land is ours?"

"Not yet," Altera replied. "The Shogun has offered the Emperor a peace deal; an alternating court. When a southern emperor abdicates, a northern emperor is crowned and then a southern… You see the problem."

Nikko's eyes widened with shock. "But… that would unite the whole of Oyashima. We don't have nearly enough shrines in place…"

"That is why The Great Mother has need of your services again."

"What would She have me do?" Nikko asked.

"The Emperor, Go-Murakami… what is he like?"

"I've never met him," Nikko replied truthfully. "Few ever do. I had Jion sense him out… he said that Go-Murakami was an old man who had grown tired of fighting."

"Hmmm…" Altera said, considering the point. "Yoshiakira is much the same. He claims to have seen too much blood…"

Nikko chuckled. "They have no idea what too much blood looks like."

Altera smiled with her kinsman. "Indeed. What about the Emperor's son? Chokei?"

"Much like his father was in his youth. Angry. Headstrong. He believes in the absolute unquestioning power of The Chrysanthemum Throne."

Altera smiled again. "Just like Yoshiakira's son, Yoshimitsu. What is the Emperor's health like?"

"I am led to believe that it is good. Would you like me to change that?"

Altera shifted her weight as she thought. "Yes. But wait until the summer. If something happens to him so soon after your arrival it will seem suspicious. Fortunately, the Shogun's health has never been good…"

"I understand, My Lady."

"Good," Altera said, getting back into the small boat. "And what of the Prophecy Child?"

"Masako is ours," Nikko replied. "She will lead the Farravashi wherever we tell her and she will fulfill her destiny."

*

The air around Jion was warm, and he felt relaxed as he watched the giant tree become the familiar form of the Goddess Marishiten. Masako stood by his side, scowling.

"You were with my sister again," she muttered.

"It is the command of the Emperor," he replied softly as they both knelt before their deity. "I must go along with his wishes… at least until we return from Fujigatani. Then we will see if the contract cannot be renegotiated."

"And if it can't?" the young woman said sourly.

"We will be together. I promise you," Jion replied.

Marishiten stood before Jion and Masako, her long hair stirring gently in the breeze and her skin as luminescent and perfect as ever.

"My children," She began, her voice velvety and reassuring. "You have done so well… been so loyal to me and my servants. Yet there is great danger ahead for you both. There are many who do not hear My call… many lands that do not know the marriage of Earth and Sky. You have come so far but there is farther to go. Accept this blessing as one of many…"

Marishiten reached out to the kneeling figures and placed her pale white hands gently on to their heads.

"Let those who speak my name with all reverence and humility know that I am the truth of the light. Yoshimoto… Minami," she continued, speaking their secret names. "Your skin shall know no thinning, your limbs no weakening, and your eyes no dimming. In my name, so mote it be."

CHAPTER NINE

August 1368 - Fujigatani Village, Inzai Valley, Shimosa Province

It was the hour of the ox and Jion crawled on his belly along the grassy border where the Tega Marshes met the outskirts of Fujigatani. The night sky was cloudy and there was a light rain in the air. The village was in total darkness save for the few torches in the market square.

Jion felt his heart pounding. It had been twelve years since he had fled this place. Twelve years of pain and loss and an aching for revenge. And now he was here. The land of his father was now that of his enemy.

The village had been rebuilt after the attack and everything looked the same but slightly different. The castle had an additional floor and some of the buildings were not orientated the way they had been. The main road seemed narrower and the barracks were much larger than they had been all those years ago. There were more soldiers too.

Jion sent his inner-self out, feeling the weak minds of the guards that patrolled the streets. Judging by the number of them, Chikatane was expecting an attack... but not like this.

Jion had trained his fourteen lieutenants personally under the auspices of Mistress Nikko. He was not surprised that Gozen and Masako had insisted on joining them, although it still was a source of contention that Prince Chokei had forced Jion also to accept Ienao. The man harbored a deep grudge against The Hero of Yugyo, and Jion knew that he reported directly to the Prince. It did not matter. His time was at hand, and when he was back in Anrakuji... well, then they would see.

From the other side of a village came a deer call and Jion sensed that Masako and her team had taken out three of the guards with garrotes. They would begin moving north and then fire the barracks, driving the fleeing soldiers into Gozen's team. The alarm would sound soon after, causing the peasants to flee and the castle to come to full alert. The guards would rush out, and Masako's team would flank them, allowing Jion to come around the back and enter the castle. Each of the women commanded three others. Ienao was waiting at the village bounds with five more, ready to mop up any who slipped past. They intended to be in and out in less than fifteen minutes.

At least that was the plan.

*

Utsunomiya Castle, Shimotsuke Province

Despite the late hour, Lord Yoshiakira considered the scroll in front of him. It was one of many that covered his small lacquered desk and, although he found such matters of state to be too dry for his sensibilities, he gave it his full attention. Normally he would have left the day-to-day administration to his ministers but, with a truce so close, Yoshiakira needed to make sure that all of his Pacts of Allegiance were as they should be.

Part of the Shogun longed for the days of riding his steed into war, but he had seen too many fine men fall… too many good friends had died in the ten years since he had assumed power.

This war could not continue indefinitely.

The Emperor's resources too closely matched his, and he realized that a war of attrition that only ended in the destruction of both sides was no war at all. It was a slaughterhouse.

The door to his chamber opened and his Hatamoto announced Lady Altera, before withdrawing. Yoshiakira was not worried. There were plenty of guards secreted in hidden alcoves and his lieutenant knew it too.

"Lady Altera," he said with a weary smile. "How good to see you. Please, sit up."

Altera raised herself. "Thank you for agreeing to see me, My Lord."

"I understand that you bring news from the South… from Lord Chikatane?"

"From his son My Lord, Lord Koichi."

"Ah yes… I think I met him once. Too much like his father, I seem to recall. All plots and machinations. What does he have to say?"

"Only that he wishes to move his family to Utsunomiya that he may better serve you."

Yoshiakira sat back. Over the years, he had diverted significant resources to keeping Chikatane and his son in check. Fujigatani was strategically important as it acted as a gateway to the both the north and the west, and the Shogun had received more reports than he cared to remember about Chikatane's aspirations to subvert his rule and claim the Shogunate for himself.

Koichi must know, Yoshiakira reasoned, that if he based himself in Utsunomiya then he would be under constant watch. This meant that he was effectively giving up any challenge to become Shogun. And why would he do such a thing? Fear. Maybe The Hero of Yugyo was still out there, swearing bloody revenge against all those who betrayed his father. What was more of a worry was the way complaints against Lady Altera had ceased in the last few months. He had become accustomed to being constantly petitioned for her removal, but of late she appeared to have made more of an effort to ingratiate herself, and she now appeared to even have a few public supporters.

"Lady Altera," Yoshiakira began, "Thank Lord Koichi for his offer but sadly it must be rejected. With peace looming… the castle and its grounds are too full of diplomats and advisers. Separately, you may like to mention that just because men are dressed as the Nokizaru does not make them so." As he finished he turned his attention to the scroll in his hand, indicating that the meeting was over.

Altera bowed her head, smiling inwardly. Yoshiakira had been furious when she had told him of Koichi's failed attempt to assassinate the Soma child, and now that disclosure was reaping the dividends that she had hoped for.

"Very good, My Lord. If I may…"

Yoshiakira looked up sharply, unaccustomed to a conversation continuing when he had so clearly signaled that it was over.

"Lord Koichi would like to present you with this bottle of vintage sake as a mark of his loyalty and respect," Altera continued as if she had not seen the Shogun's displeasure, and handed over a meticulously wrapped bottle.

Yoshiakira accepted the bottle with suspicion. "Has it been tested?"

"Of course My Lord," Altera said as a maid appeared with two bowls and hot water to warm the sake. "I tested it myself. Lord Koichi says, 'To peace'," she continued, pouring from the bottle and offering the Shogun a bowl.

Yoshiakira accepted with a sense of reservation. "Please Lady Altera, after you. I insist."

Altera sipped at her sake looking over her bowl to the Shogun who had likewise begun to drink from his, and said. "To peace, My Lord."

"To peace, My Lady."

*

Fujigatani Village

The barracks were well alight, and acrid smoke poured into the stygian night sky as the soldiers, still thick with sleep, ran out into Jion's waiting team. The Farravashi and his men cut their enemy down without mercy.

"What kept you?" he snapped as Gozen arrived at his side.

"There was another patrol further out. Masako began too early and they tried to flee. We had to chase them down," the young woman panted.

Jion looked at her critically and then softened. She had been sick for the entire month that it had taken to sail from Tsukushi and although she had claimed it was simply the motion of the sea, Jion knew better. She was pregnant. From what he could sense, maybe four or five weeks. He knew that she was completely unaware and had decided to let her tell him when she was completely sure.

Like his first night with Masako, or the death of Mutsu, Jion knew he should feel something other than the cold emptiness that had set up permanent residence inside him. He wanted to be happy. He knew he should be overjoyed. Instead all he felt was a sense that this was happening to someone else and all that he had to hold on to was his mission.

"Fine," he finally said. "We're going to take the castle and find that traitor Chikatane. Are you coming?"

Gozen grinned, wiping the soot and blood from her face as she did so. "You try and stop me."

*

Lord Koichi looked down at the pools of fire that were beginning to spread through his estate. The flames leapt from the burning barracks, cinders drifting high into the night sky and then gently falling back down to earth before landing on the thatch of some peasant's roof.

"Where is Lady Altera?" the son of Lord Chikatane snarled. "She should be here."

Ullar's tone was relaxed. "My Lord, she continues to petition the Shogun to allow your family shelter…"

"The Shogun be damned! That boy… that whelp… he is here *now!* He'll kill us all."

Ullar shrugged. "A man's fate is a man's fate, My Lord, and…"

"I don't want to hear it," Koichi barked back. "What I want to hear is what *you* are going to do about this… this… invasion. This is *my* home, not his. Do you hear me?"

"I understand, My Lord," Ullar said smoothly. "We have something *very* special planned for this one."

*

Anrakuji Temple, Mount Homan, Tsukushi Isle

Emperor Go-Murakami listened attentively as Mistress Nikko gently strummed the biwa, singing a song of a god betrayed by his closest vassals and the epic battles that followed. Her voice was soft and lilting, reminding the Emperor of his second wife, Shoshi. She had been a rare sort, the most exquisite of hostesses, but vigorous in the bedroom. It had taken him many years to get over her passing.

"This… nun?" he whispered, leaning over to his son.

"Priest or monk, Your Majesty," Prince Chokei corrected. "This particular order does not differentiate between the genders."

The Emperor nodded. "I am sure the Buddha would be gladdened by that. However, this… monk. She has always been within orders?"

"Yes, Your Majesty, ever since she was a teenager. Maybe eighteen or nineteen."

"And before?"

"She is reticent to discuss it. From what our spies have gleaned from general conversation, several monasteries admitted her but succumbed to bandit attacks. Yugyo appears to have been just another step on her path. Prior to that… she has made mention of rice fields, so most likely a farmer's daughter."

"A pity," the Emperor replied, looking back at the young woman. "It would never do for one such as I to pillow with a peasant. Are you *sure* that is her history?"

Chokei smiled at his father. They had played this game many times over the years. "I shall see that her lineage is… amended Your Majesty."

"Thank you my son," the Emperor said, returning the smile. "I would like to hear her playing in a more… private surrounding. Please ask her to retire to my bedchamber. Some cha too perhaps? I'd be intrigued to see her tea ceremony."

Nikko raised her eyes a fraction from her instrument. Despite the two men's determination to keep their conversation between themselves, her keen hearing had allowed her to hear every word.

She felt the weight of the vial Altera had given her so many months ago nestled into her robe, and smiled.

*

Fujigatani Village

The village inhabitants were streaming out of their homes, making for the gates at the end of the valley. Masako nodded to her team and made to give chase.

"No," Jion commanded, ignoring the surge of rabble and eyeing the domineering form of the castle. "Ienao and his team will see to them."

Gozen frowned. "They are only peasants. We have no quarrel with them."

Jion turned to stare at her, his face lit by the flickering shadows of the ever expanding fires. "They serve Chikatane. They are the enemy," he said coldly.

"A peasant does not choose his Lord," Gozen countered. "They are innocents."

"No-one is innocent," muttered Jion, turning back to look again at the castle.

From far behind them they heard more screams, signaling that Ienao and his men had begun their work.

Gozen wore an expression of disgust. "That was not necessary," she said.

"It was completely necessary," countered Masako. "Those loyal to the Shogun are like knotweed. You can burn it all back, but if you miss one tuber it will always return, and stronger than before."

"This is not their war," replied her sister. "Peasants are not weeds."

Jion remained impassive. "You're right. They are less than that," he said and began moving towards the castle.

Masako and her team of three - Shinmai, Miyamoto, and Tan – made to move forward but Gozen held her ground.

"Jion, you cannot be serious," she said.

The young man turned from the glow of the spreading inferno. "They serve my enemy."

"Some of them served your father too."

"Then, more than the others, they deserve to die. Where is their fidelity? Where is their honor? They are less than the eta. This is their judgment." Without looking back Jion set off and Masako followed with her team.

For a moment, Gozen hesitated and looked to her men – Higuchi, Yui, and Tsustumi.

"He is our Master," shrugged Higuchi.

Gozen shook her head as her inner feelings conflicted and rose to the surface. "Do you think he is right?"

Higuchi responded automatically. "Yes. Look where he had led us. We are about to strike at the enemy's heart. When we return, thousands more will receive our training. The Emperor will be victorious. All we need to do is prove ourselves worthy. We must keep faith with our Master."

"I hope you're right," Gozen said and began to follow the path where Jion led.

Their approach to the castle was unhindered and only the sound of distant cries and burning wood broke through the silence of night.

Jion sent his sense out before him, feeling for enemies who might be hiding from his sight. There was none. He sent it out again, further forward this time and felt the nest of frightened minds that feigned unflinching resolve. He would make them flinch.

"They're in the donjon," he said to the women and their surrounding men.

"How many?" asked Masako, as they stepped through the castle gate and into the courtyard.

"A few hundred. Nothing we can't handle," Jion said smiling, feeling the minds of his comrades as they prayed that he was right.

Reaching into his robe, Jion pulled out a compact ball-like package and lit the small protruding fuse with a flint. Mistress Nikko had designed these, claiming to have traded the knowledge with the resident Tianxian ambassador at Go-Murakami's court, and had refined them so that several could be carried.

Jion hurled the lit ball through the donjon gate, using his inner-self to send it further than would be expected. There was a distant explosion followed immediately by screams and smoke began to pour out of the gate.

Masako looked at him questioningly.

Jion shrugged. "She added pottery fragments and nails. Here they come…"

Men were pouring out of the doorway. The first few were bloodied, disorientated, and crying as they desperately tried to douse their flaming hair. Behind them came the main body of soldiers, all bearing Chikatane's insignia.

The spearmen rushed forward first, jabbing at Jion and his squad, trying to force them back to allow the archers room to break through the smoking doorway and have space to fire. The Emperor's men countered, ducking and parrying with their swords, and then moved inside their guard, slicing at the vulnerable joints where the armor met, sending their enemies to the ground in a spray of vital life essence.

The team seemed to move as one, as though they were a troupe of graceful dancers. Parry, parry, turn, slice. Another wave of soldiers fell to the floor, missing arms and heads as if they were nothing but broken toys.

The courtyard flagstones began to darken as pools of blood merged, forming a thick viscous coating over the stones. Still Jion and his men held their ground, not challenging for access into the castle but rather drawing out the scum that served his treacherous uncle.

Their blades sang through the air, deflecting spear heads and arrow shafts, sweeping low and then back up, under the chin strap, and out through the head.

The bodies were piling up around the door and Jion ordered his team back a few paces to allow the castle defenders the space to get out rather than remaining bottled up within the keep.

The battle raged on. Masako parried, feinted, and spun at the last minute, whipping her leg out and sending her assailant to the floor. Another spear came at her and, with the flat of her sword, she deflected it downwards into the exposed belly of the stunned soldier and then slid back up the shaft, taking the head of the second.

Gozen struck down, taking a sword arm. Her style was more reserved than her younger sister's but no less effective. Bringing two spearmen on, she deflected the shaft of the first towards the eyes of the second, slipped under the poles, and whirled, slitting the bellies of both men simultaneously.

Jion could feel his men about him as he twisted one spearman around and then sent him headlong into his comrades, letting them impale each other. Each worked in unison with the rest of the team. They had trained so hard together that even without the gifts of Marishiten, they would still have been a formidable fighting team. Some would even call their dance of death, with its constant flurry of blades, so exquisite as to be beautiful.

Behind him, Jion felt something drop down from the castle walls... and then another and another and... No mortal man could survive that jump. Which meant...

"Oni!" Tan cried out. "I've got Oni!"

The group backed away from the doorway as more dark figures landed in the courtyard. Too late, they realized the main gate had been closed behind them.

That was quiet... Jion thought

"I've got four over here," Masako called out, as they began to form a circle that was retreating in on itself.

"Three on me," Higuchi called out, backing away from the advancing figures.

"I've got five," Gozen said, trying to keep a note of terror out of her voice.

Jion sent his sense out and felt the Oni warriors try to deflect it. There were at least twenty of them, and probably more. The mind of each one was calm and flat, allowing him no grip or hold.

"Well well well," Ullar said, stepping forward. "The Hero of Yugyo no less. We have waited such a long time for you, haven't we Lord Koichi?"

Jion's cousin lurked in the shadows, still unsure that victory would really be his.

"I am sorry to have kept you waiting," Jion said jovially. "But you can appreciate how long these things take to plan."

Ullar laughed and shook his head. "You Soma and your plans. It didn't work out too well for your father, did it?"

The smiled faded from Jion's face and his jaw clenched.

"There it is," Ullar said. "The warriors face. So, this is what you've grown into. Impressive, I suppose."

Jion gave an almost imperceptible nod to Higuchi who drew his short sword and ran the nearest oni through.

The dark robed creature looked down at the blade sticking down out of him, and chopped downwards, snapping the sword in two. Turning to Higuchi, the oni warrior punched out with an open palm, sending the young man sprawling back into the contracting circle that was Jion and his team.

Ullar sighed. "Still so much to learn, eh boy? I would have thought you would have at least realized that we are not like you. We are not... part of the herd."

"You are not shepherds either," Jion retorted.

Ullar brayed loudly and the laugh rippled amongst the rest of the oni. "No... we are not. Think of us more as... butchers."

Jion felt his team collectively tense and sent out his mind-talk to all of them. *Relax... concentrate... focus. We are not dead yet.*

He hoped he sounded more confident than he felt.

"You know," Ullar continued, "you have done well to come this far… to have become what you have. Not many would have survived the first year, and certainly not Yugyo. We could use someone with your skills. You would be rewarded. You all would," he gestured to the entire team with a sweep of his hand. "Anything you wanted. Power. Riches. Women."

"I'd rather die," Jion spat.

Ullar shrugged, never believing that the offer would be accepted. "That can be arranged."

The courtyard filled with the creaking sound of Oni bows being drawn back, and Jion braced himself.

*

Utsunomiya Castle

Lady Altera walked slowly down the winding corridors of the castle, Yoshiakira's Hatamoto in step with her.

"It is a terrible thing," Masijiro said, his voice strained. "Just like his father… a tumor in almost exactly the same place."

"Indeed it is," Altera replied.

"Only thirty-seven. His father had a better run than he…" the Hatamoto's voice wavered.

"It might have been the stress of office," Altera offered. "He insisted on doing so much himself… the way he held the Bakufu together and having to deal with the Southern Court's treachery… it must have been too much for him."

They arrived at a highly polished cedar wood door and, in the glow of torchlight, Masijiro knocked loudly. The room inside would have already been prepared by the attendants to the Shogun's son, Yoshimitsu, who would be up and dressed despite the hour.

The door opened and the two were admitted to enter. Altera and Masijiro stepped through, immediately knelt, and pressed their heads to the mat.

After a moment a small voice at the end of the room spoke. "Sit up."

They sat up in unison but kept their eyes to the floor out of respect.

"You bring news of my father?"

"Yes My Lord," Masijiro replied.

"What is it?"

"My Lord, I regret to inform you that Lord Yoshiakira, our Shogun, has passed away this evening."

There was a silence from the end of the room, as though all possible sounds had been smothered by a blanket of grief.

When it came, the voice was smaller than before. "How?"

Masijiro cleared his throat. "My Lord… it appears there was an undiagnosed tumor… similar to that of your grand-father."

Again there was a silence, and when the voice spoke the grief was obvious. "What... happens...now?"

Masijiro looked to Altera who pressed her head to the mat again and sat back up, this time looking directly at the ten-year-old boy who rested on an elegant cushion on the wooden dais.

"My Lord," she began. "The Clan Lords have sworn allegiance to your family. You will be Shogun... when you come of age."

"When I am twenty-one?" The child seemed incredulous that he would have to wait more than double his own lifetime before he could assume power. "Impossible...!"

"I understand My Lord," Altera replied smoothly. "The Clan Lords felt it prudent that you finish your education... get some experience of government..."

"But who will rule the country?" Yoshimitsu interrupted. "Who will defend Oyashima?"

"The Clan Lords have appointed a regent in your stead My Lord," Altera said soothingly. "The Regent will sit by you at all times and, once you have assumed your rightful position, will continue to advise you as long as you wish."

The child seemed mollified. "Who has been named as Regent?"

Altera tried not to smile. "My Lord, it is me."

*

Fujigatani Village

The world turned black and white and Jion knew it was time. The years of hardship... the months of training sixteen hours a day... the cost he had paid. Jion closed his eyes and focused.

Next to him, Masako did the same. And Gozen. Higuchi, Tan... all concentrated as they had been taught.

As the cruelly barbed arrows left their bows, streaking towards their targets, Ullar's brow furrowed.

This isn't right, he thought. *This is too...*

And then The Hero of Yugyo disappeared, along with his whole squad.

Even before Ullar could widen his eyes in shock, he knew why Altera had entrusted this mission to him. This was not a test of him. It was a test of the whelp. The boy was no mere Farravashi, he was...

In the blink of an eye, Jion and his team reappeared behind the Oni, long swords drawn and began hacking at their enemy.

The bodies of the black devils erupted into a volcanic orgy of blue and purple light that streamed skywards, just like The Hunter all those years before.

"Skylord metal!" Ullar screamed, parrying a shot from Miyamoto. "They *all* have Skylord metal!"

But it was too late. Ullar realized that he had been fooled and, as he watched his men fall before the unstoppable onslaught of whirling blades, he knew that this was the death his mistress had wanted for him. It would be a good one.

The Oni dropped to the ground, their corpses blackening and withering as the light streamed from their bodies like a celestial river. Still Jion's team battled on, forcing the remaining Oni back. Another fell, this time to Masako's blade.

Less than half a dozen left. Ullar felt an unusual tightening in his belly and chest and realized he was panicking for the first time in his long life.

Four.

Ullar saw Tan wheel and then slice, decapitating his opponent.

Three.

From his left, the Oni Commander saw Gozen and Shinmai double up on a…

Two.

Ullar desperately parried another shot, frantically searching for an escape route. Yui felled another.

One.

Silence came abruptly and Ullar knew he had lost. Jion's soldiers encircled him and the quivering form of Koichi. The Hero of Yugyo stepped forward, flicking his sword to cast off the sheen of death that coated the blade.

Ullar chuckled. "It was the merchant, wasn't it? Your master took his swords, didn't he? That's where you got them. Ah… it doesn't matter. What is it your kind says? A man's fate is a man's fate? Maybe it is time to go home."

Jion nodded as he walked toward the Oni devil. "The death you sought to spread has come for you."

Ullar tilted his head quizzically. "Be sure to remember that Hero of Yugyo."

Jion did not stop moving forward but brought his sword up and in a single movement slashed from Ullar's shoulder to hip. The two pieces of the Oni Commander fell to floor with a slop and a splatter. From within the expired shell, tendrils of light gathered together like some mystical twine before shooting into the night sky, leaving behind only a blackened husk.

The Hero of Yugyo turned his attention to Lord Koichi and advanced. Jion did not remember his cousin, although he knew of his existence from what Gozen had told him of his family tree over the years.

"Get up," Jion barked.

The older man shook his head. "So you can kill me too?"

"Maybe. Maybe not. Get up."

Koichi shook his head and Jion grabbed him by the topknot of hair and hauled him to his feet, squealing.

Jion pressed his face into his cousin's, and when he spoke his voice came as a hiss. "Where is your father?"

Koichi turned his head, trying to avoid the spittle that flew from Jion's lips. "He's not here…"

Jion brought his knee up into the man's stomach and held him up to stop him from crumpling to the floor. "That's not what I asked," he whispered again as he slammed him against the wall. "Where is Chikatane?"

Koichi looked up the mountain slopes towards the peak. "There," he said. "Yoshimoto, I swear… I was only a child when my father switched sides. Even if I could have argued I…"

The Ishin Blade was so sharp that Koichi did not notice at first that Jion had slid it into his stomach. He looked down at the source of radiating warmth with a look of confusion, trying to understand why he was not feeling any pain.

"You lived your father's treachery," Jion murmured, his eyes ablaze with the molten anger that poured from his heart. "Every day you lived an inheritance that was not yours. You reveled in it. You're as guilty as the rest of them."

Jion took a step back and savagely pulled the sword across, splitting his cousin's belly wide open. Lord Koichi gurgled as his legs gave way beneath him and fell to floor where he lay like a broken doll.

The Hero of Yugyo turned from the fallen figure, disgusted with his cousin that he should have allowed himself to have been captured and then going willingly to such a dishonorable death. This was not the way of the bujin.

Gozen and Masako were as grim faced as Jion, and he sensed the resolve of his squad to move on to their final target.

"No," he said aloud, sensing their question. Looking to Gozen and Masako he said, "You two are with me. The rest of you fall back and support Ienao."

Secretly he was proud of all them. They had practiced so hard and so long, each learning and sharing all aspects of the Goddess's training until they had become this unstoppable fighting unit.

Fourteen disciples Marishiten had said to him. *Fourteen to unite the land and bring order.*

Today was the start of the journey and as much as he wanted to congratulate each of them on their faith and perseverance, he knew that now was not the time. Celebrations could wait until The Great Traitor of The Soma Clan lay dead and they were all safely back on Tsukushi Isle.

Masako nodded to her unit, silently relaying the orders by mind-talk and reminding them of where their duty lay, regardless of what trinkets the enemy might offer.

Jion could feel Gozen's reservation as she similarly dismissed her men. Chikatane was supposed to have been in the castle, not in the mountains.

The Hero of Yugyo mentally shrugged. A man's fate was a man's fate, and Chikatane's was on its way.

*

Mount Akiro

It was the hour of the dragon and the sun had risen, casting the mountains in an early autumnal light. The three of them had walked for hours up the long-abandoned mountain path and Jion found himself disgusted that his uncle would so willing let nature reclaim what hundreds of men had spent months clearing and building.

Presently, the trees gave way to small shrubs and these too petered out to scrub and then to volcanic rock. At this height, they could see distant clouds building on the horizon. Whilst the typhoon season continued to plague the coast this time of year, it was unusual for one to come this far inland.

Unusual… but not unheard of, Masako mind-talked, sensing Jion's concern for his pirate allies back on The Sophia.

He smiled thinly but said nothing, choosing to press on.

A few hundred meters ahead was the mouth to the cave that he had heard so much about as a child. He had never been to visit Master Otsuno in his home, but his brother had told him so many stories of the great monk that for a moment the memory of those happy uncomplicated times lifted him.

But now his brother was gone. So too Master Otsuno. Gasan. Watanabe. Tatsuo. Kwon… and too many others. The roll-call of the dead never left him, but played in an endless loop in his mind, stoking the fires of anger and guilt.

Jion stopped for a moment to look down at the Inzai Valley below. Thick smoke hung in the air over what had been Fujigatani. He had secretly ordered Ienao to raze the whole village and it looked like his one-time tormentor was obeying his instructions. The village was too far to the east to be held, and rather than letting the Shogun rebuild his base, a policy of scorched earth was best.

He found it hard to believe that it had been more than a decade since he had left… since he had fled. It felt like a lifetime ago… no, more than that. The memories of his village felt like they belonged to someone else and Jion found himself torn between feeling love for his father's land, and despising his people who had so willingly accepted Chikatane's rule.

As they approached the cave entrance, Jion renewed his vow to end that reign.

"Ah, it is you…" an old man said, looking up from the fire that boiled water for his cha. "I thought I smelled smoke."

Jion frowned and sensed confusion in the two women. This was not what they had been expecting. Lord Chikatane was supposed to be cowering in a cave, perhaps with a squad of elite bodyguards. He was supposed to be dressed in all his finery… he was supposed to offer Jion anything.

Instead, the wrinkled old man before them was bald – shaved in the way of the Buddhist monks – and there were no guards and no finery, only a few pots and pans and drab robe.

"Chikatane?" Jion growled, feeling his anger growing.

"Yes Yoshimoto. It is I," the monk said, standing and trying to control the shaking of his liver spotted hands. "You have come for your revenge. Here I am."

"You betrayed my father… your own brother…" Jion snarled, drawing his sword.

"I did."

"Why?"

Chikatane shrugged and leaned heavily on his wooden staff, gasping for air as he did so. "Why else? Power. Greed. He was my elder brother. He had it all… the estate, the title, the adulation of his people. I was just some lowly noble. Ashikaga offered me everything I had ever dreamed of. All I had to do was to betray my best friend… my brother."

"You admit your crimes," Jion stepped forward, raising his sword above his head… and felt Gozen's hand on him, soothing him… telling him to let the old man speak.

"I do."

"Then… what is the meaning of this?" Jion said looking about the sparse cave. "Why are you not enjoying the spoils of your treachery in the castle?"

Chikatane sighed and looked out to the clouds that had begun to gather over the valley. "Because… because I have come to regret my actions."

"What do you mean?" Jion snapped, wary of some trick.

"Is it true what they say about you?" the old man asked, turning to face his nephew. "The talents…"

Jion nodded and kept his sword raised.

"Were you at Ise?"

"Not as such… no."

"I was," Chikatane turned back to the darkening vista before him. "I had seen war. I *enjoyed* war. But what Ashikaga brought… the deal with the Oni… that was not war. There was no glory. No honor. It has all been so… so… senseless. And for what? To decide who sits in a chair."

"The Chrysanthemum Throne is the preserve of the Divine Son alone," Jion retorted hotly, feeling himself flush.

"It is still just a chair," Chikatane said absently, looking out the dark clouds that now gathered over the village. For a moment he fancied there was something within the storm head… something dark and muscular. "Ise was not a battle. It was not a part of the war. It was one set of pawns butchering another... for lords they could not see and did not know. When I returned from Ise, the food was like dry bamboo leaves in my mouth, and the shochu tasted like filth. I even found the courtesans to be hard and unyielding. I realized what I had done... do you see?"

Jion shook his head.

"I shared everything with your father. *Everything*. The victories. The losses. The battles... *everything*. And I had given all of that up for things that simply had no meaning. And so I renounced it all and came here to meditate whilst I waited for you. I knew you would return. I had heard the stories, and I knew you would come back... to avenge Tadashige and Tanemochi. I am ready."

Jion raised the Ishin Blade high above his head. "Then it is time..."

"Jion!" Gozen snapped causing him to flinch and lower his sword a fraction. "You cannot go through with this..."

Confusion rippled across Jion's face. What was she saying?

"Look at him," she pointed to the old man. "He is a monk. He has lived with the crushing guilt of his actions for the last ten years... Don't you understand?"

Jion's brow knotted together.

"This..." Gozen spread her arms about them, indicating to the bare cave walls. "*This* is your revenge. Every day the memory of his actions causes him pain. You cannot kill him. He is a defenseless old man."

"No," Masako said stepping forward. "He is no such thing. He is a wily old devil. Jion, he betrayed your father, stole your inheritance and is responsible for the death of Sensei Watanabe and countless others. *This* is the way of our people... of the bujin. You must kill him."

"You're wrong," Gozen said shaking her head at her sister. "Look at what our way has cost. All those who died at Yugyo... Kurama... look at the village down there. Jion please... that was our home... and now all the people who lived there are..."

"They deserved it," Masako spat. "By serving...*him*," she sneered in the direction of Chikatane, "they were complicit in his treachery."

"They are peasants," Gozen cried, not believing that her fiancé could really do this. "This is not their war."

"This is *everyone's* war," Masako countered.

"Jion," Gozen took hold of her lover's shoulders. "Please... don't do this. Let's just leave. We've done everything we set out to do... let's just go home... back to Tsukushi."

Jion felt himself torn. He was not prepared for this. Chikatane was supposed to have been a monster that would have laughed at his brother's death and told his nephew how much he had enjoyed it. He was not meant to be contrite. He was supposed to be surrounded by undefeatable guardians who were to push Jion's training to its limits. He was not meant to be unarmed and looking forward to his death.

His mind fogged and he heard the voices of Kwon and Nikko, alternately telling him to let go of his past and to give into his emotions… to use them as a weapon. Still Gozen and Masako argued and their words sounded like battle horns blaring in his ears until he could no longer bear the pressure that had built in his head, threatening to…

"Stop!" he shouted, silencing the two women. Jion turned to Chikatane. "You," he said pointing with his sword. "You… you *made* me. Do you understand? I wanted to be a farmer… did you know that? I wanted to study crop rotations and rice yields… but you stole that from me. You *made* me into this… and now you try to deny me my purpose."

Chikatane shook his head and spoke softly. "I deny you nothing Yoshimoto, and I am guilty of everything you say… and much much more. I could tell you that I am sorry, but that would not mean anything…"

"Jion please," Gozen interrupted. "You have a choice. You can let yourself be what he has made you. Or you can choose what you want to become… you can *choose* to be better."

"No," Masako said flatly. "This is our path. This is his fate. It cannot be denied. If you don't do it I will."

Jion looked first to Gozen and then to her younger sister, feeling the struggle within both of them… and within himself.

"Jion… *please…*" Gozen's voice came as a strained whisper. "If you do this, you'll become a monster… worse than him… worse than the Shogun. *Please…* I do not want to lose you… stay with me."

Masako's voice was gravelly, and filled with vengeance. "You must become what you must become. Strike him down and the Emperor will recognize you as the mightiest warrior in all Oyashima. If I were your fiancée, *I* would never tell you what you should or should not be."

Gozen's head whipped round to face her sister. Of course she had known about her sister and Jion… she had always known. But a man's dalliance was his prerogative… as long he was discrete. Now that her sister openly taunted her with their affair Gozen felt her control begin to slip and hot tears welled in her eyes. "Jion… come back to me… I beg you," she whispered.

The part of Jion that was still Soma felt a pang of sympathy for the young woman. But the stone that was his heart only burned with the words of Mistress Nikko and he felt that Gozen's begging was nothing more than a means to illicit a sense of guilt from him.

He shook his head and Gozen saw the twisted fiend her lover had become. With a sob she turned and staggered out of the cave, holding on to the mountain walls for support.

Jion wheeled, facing Chikatane, and felt the rage course through him. Anger at Gozen for her ultimatum, anger at himself for being swayed from his true path… and angry beyond measure with his uncle.

As his fury poured forth in to the fatal sword strike, Chikatane smiled and whispered to himself.

"A man's fate is a man's fate."

EPILOGUE

October 1368 - Anrakuji Temple, Mount Homan, Tsukushi Isle
It was the hour of the goat and the sun had just passed its meridian. The typhoon season had been bad that year, and had exacted a heavy toll on the harbors of the warring factions. In the bay below, the sound of rebuilding works echoed around the high cliffs, driving the birds from the trees.

The smell of sea salt mixed with that of incense sticks and the unusual warmth of the autumn sun, and - as Mistress Nikko had promised - it was a beautiful day. The skies were clear of cloud and even the dark waters of the sea seemed calmed by the pending union of the two young people high on the cliff plateau.

Emperor Chokei nodded at Jion to step forward and The Hero of Yugyo obeyed immediately. His wedding robe was a deep red and his dark hair was pulled up into the traditional topknot of the bujin class, preventing it from being disturbed by the breeze.

With a sideways glance, first at the newly installed shrine where Nikko stood, and then to his beautiful bride, Jion knelt before Emperor Chokei and pressed his head into the grass.

"You may sit up," Chokei said in his now familiar monotone voice. The smiles on the happy couple's faces were infectious and it was all that the new Emperor could do to maintain the composure that his office demanded.

Mistress Nikko had already performed her part, and it was now the duty of the Emperor to solemnize the proceedings.

"Repeat after me," he began. "I, Soma Yoshimoto…"

Jion looked to Masako in her bridal robe and his smiled widened. He had learned so much since his return from Fujigatani; what it meant to be a leader; to be a lover; a faithful servant of Marishiten. The ways of his childhood were firmly behind him.

"No," he said quietly. "It is like Master Otsuno once told me; time to throw off the shackles of a name.

"I, Jion…"

Three stars turn,
The child will come,
To we faithful who do not sleep,
Our raptures burn,
With prayers begun,
So shall darkness fall from the deep.

AUTHOR'S NOTE

The story that you have just read is one of fiction. However, like all of my tales, it has a core of truth.

It may surprise you to learn that Jion really existed. Or the academics believe he did, but the details of his life become vague very quickly, perhaps due to more than one person taking the name.

This story is set in feudal Japan and, where possible, I have tried to use the place names of the time and reference key events that shaped the political map. The fourteenth century was a time of great upheaval in the Land of The Rising Sun, and, whilst the causes of civil war can be traced to the failed Mongol invasions of the previous century, matters would come to a head when The Emperor Go-Daigo tried to seize power from the government in the 1320's. This failed and he was exiled to the prison island of Oki where, in 1333, he was set free in a daring raid by Ashikaga Takauji. However, by 1336, Ashikaga had not been rewarded in the ways he had expected and so he led a rebellion against The Chrysanthemum Throne, sparking nearly sixty years of bloody conflict.

Into this maelstrom of politics and battle, Soma Yoshimoto was born. He was most noted for founding a sword-based martial art known as Nen-Ryu which is famed for its masters' abilities in cutting arrows from the air in mid-flight. Whilst the school dates its founding to 1368, with the teaching of fourteen disciples, it is traditional that Japanese schools cite the birth date of their founder as the establishment of the style. However, one of the traits that has made Soma Yoshimoto so noteworthy is that he was one of the first warriors to codify all his teachings and it is possible that, unlike many of the schools that followed, Nen-Ryu really was formally established in that year

In addition to traditional martial skills, Jion also taught spiritual discipline to his fourteen acolytes by way of worship to the goddess of war, Marishiten, who, it is said, rewarded him with deep insights and teachings. At the time, the marrying of faith and knighthood was almost unheard of, but the lessons of duty and courage proved popular and the idea would spread over the next hundred years.

What little is known of Yoshimoto's life is that his father was assassinated when he was five, probably by the henchmen of his uncle who had defected to the Ashikaga Shogunate, and he was forced to flee with his wet nurse, taking the Buddhist name Nenami Jion. Temple documents show him receiving training at Yugyo and then at Kurama before joining Prince Chokei on the southern isle of Kyushu, at The Temple of Anrakuji.

The records are unclear whether Yoshimoto ever exacted revenge on his uncle. It would appear that Lord Chikatane did abdicate in favor of his son in 1358 and took holy orders before dying of unspecified causes in 1368.

The story, as told in these pages, never happened. The purists will note that I have plucked characters from time and space, as well as alternately merging some and splitting others, to marry them into situations that simply did not occur. This is not intended to be a historical novel but simply a tale I feel I needed to tell.

My discovery of the Jion story came in early 2003, although I had been on the road to it for many years before. From a young age, I engaged in martial arts. Judo was followed by Karate, before I found a deep love of Kickboxing. In 1996, I went to Middlesex University to read Criminology and whilst there I joined a Ju-Jitsu school which fundamentally changed everything I thought I knew about martial arts. The school was Hontai Yoshin Ryu and was a traditional art that focused on deep stances and deeper self-reflection.

After leaving university, I moved to Borehamwood, North London, and it was there that I joined a modern Ju-Jitsu school run by Soke Pell. Named Ishin-Ryu, it acknowledges the philosophies of the earliest schools, and Jion's in particular, without claiming lineage.

The outline of Jion's story was taught to all new white belts and I felt myself captivated by the tale of a man whose legacy still echoed more than seven hundred years after he had lived. Jion himself was perhaps not as deeply involved with the war between The Two Courts as I have made out, and in reality he was at best a tertiary character.

Yet there is something about this man that haunts our world today. There is a form within some Karate schools named Jion, supposedly after our hero. A school that taught obscure chain and sickle techniques in the seventeenth century, before being subsumed by other more practical styles, would claim lineage some three hundred years after Jion's death. Today, his introduction and worship of Marishiten to the warrior class in the fourteenth century is the stuff of doctoral theses and numerous articles and discussions, and the school that he founded still exists in the small village of Maniwa in Japan.

In conclusion, man and legend have become so entwined that they are no longer distinguishable and, if I am honest, I would not wish to separate them. I hope that you do not either.

Martin Adil-Smith

ACKNOWLEDGEMENTS

So many people have had an input into this story, from editing to recommending sources, that it will be difficult to thank all of you.

Firstly to my wife and daughters, Jennifer, Jasmine, and Samira, who have put up with seeing considerably less of me than they deserve, and my keeping of the most unsocial of hours. I love you all more than words can ever say.

To my most trusted instructor, Soke Kevin Pell of Ishin Ryu Ju-Jitsu, who has stood by, inspired, and supported me ever since the first day I met him. A true father to us all.

To Graham and Judith McMillan-Cox for all of their hard work and support.

To Jonathan Weiss and his wife Anna without whom the book would simply not have been finished.

Sincerely, thank you all.

Martin

Printed in Great Britain
by Amazon